The Best
AMERICAN
SHORT
STORIES
1990

Selected from
U.S. and Canadian Magazines
by RICHARD FORD
with SHANNON RAVENEL

With an Introduction by Richard Ford

HOUGHTON MIFFLIN COMPANY
BOSTON · 1990

Shannon Ravenel is grateful to LARRY COOPER, *longtime manuscript editor for this series, for his years of unerring professional enthusiasm. She is also grateful to* JENNIFER TABIN *and* JOHANNA WOOD, *both of whom provided able assistance and valuable consultation on the 1990 volume.*

ISSN 0067-6233
ISBN 0-395-51596-3
ISBN 0-395-51617-X (PBK.)

Printed in the United States of America

HAD 10 9 8 7 6 5 4 3 2

FOR EUDORA WELTY

Contents

Publisher's Note

THE *Best American Short Stories* series was started in 1915 under the editorship of Edward J. O'Brien. Its title reflects the optimism of a time when people assumed that an objective "best" could be identified, even in fields not measured in physical terms.

Martha Foley took over as editor of the series in 1942. With her husband, Whit Burnett, she had edited *Story* magazine since 1931, and in later years she taught creative writing at Columbia School of Journalism. When Miss Foley died in 1977, at the age of eighty, she was at work on what would have been her thirty-seventh volume of *The Best American Short Stories*.

Beginning with the 1978 edition, Houghton Mifflin introduced a new editorial arrangement for the anthology. Inviting a different writer or critic to edit each new annual volume would provide a variety of viewpoints to enliven the series and broaden its scope. *Best American Short Stories* has thus become a series of informed but differing opinions that gains credibility from its very diversity.

Also beginning with the 1978 volume, the guest editors have worked with the series editor, Shannon Ravenel, who during each calendar year reads as many qualifying short stories as she can get hold of, makes a preliminary selection of 120 stories for the guest editor's consideration, and compiles the "100 Other Distinguished Stories," a listing that has always been an important feature of these volumes.

In the thirteen years that have passed since then, there has been growing interest in the short story, and the form itself has grown. The range of approaches and techniques and stances it attracts is ever broader. And so is its audience. In response to this anthology's increasingly enthusiastic readership, the 1987 volume introduced a new feature. Each of the authors of the twenty stories selected by the guest editor is invited to describe briefly how his or her story came to be written. The contributors have accepted what is clearly a challenging assignment, and their short essays appear at the back of the volume in the "Contributors' Notes" section.

The stories chosen for this year's anthology were originally published in magazines issued between January 1989 and January 1990. The qualifications for selection are: (1) original publication in nationally distributed American or Canadian periodicals; (2) publication in English by writers who are American or Canadian; and (3) publication *as* short stories (novel excerpts are not knowingly considered by the editors). A list of the magazines consulted by Ms. Ravenel appears at the back of this volume.

This is the last volume for which Shannon Ravenel will serve as series editor. For future volumes, the series editor will be Katrina Kenison (% Houghton Mifflin Company, 2 Park Street, Boston, Massachusetts 02108). Other publications wishing to make sure that their contributors are considered for the series should include Ms. Kenison on their subscription list.

Introduction

HAVING SPENT the last year and a quarter at the task of reading for this collection, I've begun to feel like the Professor Irwin Corey of the short story — the world's greatest living authority over a discipline which does not exactly exist, a professorship of nothing, tenured in the university without walls.

It's not surprising that I should feel this way, since I've believed for a long time that the short story, like the novel and unlike, say, the villanelle or the sestina, does not usefully exist in abstract form, hung out there in eternal, intelligent space *qua* short story. But rather that short stories, like lyrics, are invented new each time they're tried, becoming attached to the name-made-form only as a convenience for would-be students and syllabus makers and people who do what I'm doing now.

Still, when I began this enterprise I had a lot of "ideas" stored up concerning the short story, ideas which like the concept of the short story itself have now somewhat faded in importance, leaving me in nothing more than a spirit of complaint, out of which I would love to tell you what my year's been like as a way of comforting myself for spending it so extravagantly. I had it in mind to settle some hash, to set straight varieties of wrong-headedness, to burst a few bubbles, step right in the middle of embarrassing gibberish like minimalism and postmodernism; steal marches against retro-regionalism, pooh-pooh the fictitious short story renaissance and the purported watering down of the story writers' gene pool by insidious writing programs. Like Keats, I suppose, I felt I had a few axioms. And using them I meant to strike blows which would free writers everywhere — globally, as it were — to write what they damn well pleased, the best they could, and to like me for letting them.

I don't know what got into me. I don't know who I thought I was addressing or kidding or, unlike Keats, who I thought I was, although it's always a very good idea for people writing introductory essays to ask themselves these crucial questions.

In any case, I've decided to dial back quite a lot on my early feeling of mission and to say in this short space only the few things I've come to acknowledge in a year in which I read two hundred and fifty short stories in the hope of finding these twenty excellent ones to make a decent book.

A warming chestnut snugged into the heart of many introductions of this very sort protests that a virtual cornucopia of wonderful stories — far too many for one slender volume — made final choices nearly impossible. This was not precisely my experience in 1989. There were perhaps five more very good stories than the twenty I kept to the end of my considerings. And these I did not enjoy having to appraise in seemingly relative, pseudo-competitive terms. I would have preferred giving each story a chance at its own absolute excellence, a habit which served me well through most of my reading. But in the end I had to make a choice and that is what I did. It was in my job description. I did my best.

But there was something to learn from this great sea of stories, something more than the inevitable: that such choosings are at least gratuitous, possibly arbitrary, and that writers like me do their best judging in the context of their own work, not others'. So much of the reading for this volume was of stories I didn't want to reprint, stories that didn't seem good enough, that my strongest feeling of contact is and has been with that group of stories and their writers. Unarguably, writing short stories — a minor contribution to the saga of mankind — is something most people can't do very well. I don't know why. Maybe it's harder than it looks, and wonderful stories *do* seem like little miracles. Over the years, people have been gracious enough to point out that I've written some unexcellent stories myself, and if that's true I hope to God I never write another one. But I know that it's all right if I can't and others sometimes don't. No one should care — least of all me — if a hundred writing programs graduate a thousand people every year, all of whom can write a semicompetent but rarely interesting version of what they mean to be a short story; or if oldsters write them by the carload; or if in California story writing is thought of as a branch of psychotherapy or crisis intervention. That's fine. We're not talking about global warming or toxic waste here. It's a victimless crime if the "less gifted" thrive and have fun. Art's that way — free. And you couldn't stop people anyway, just as you can't stop scores of magazines large and small, famous and obscure, from publishing all that not-so-good writing, then turning their editors loose upon the world to sit on panels and brag about how good it all is. You won't get any hand-wringing or defenses of the form out of me. The form's most persuasive defenders, insofar as it needs any, are printed in this book. Good work is sufficient encouragement to those of us who write stories, and a pleasure to the remaining few who don't write them but merely like to read.

Form, though, persists as a bothersome if finally treatable obsession in conversations about writing short stories. Disputes over form, slurring naturally enough into more self-devoted disputes about content and execution (the three being inseparable from birth), are the source of all the magical/minimal/classical/traditional/neorealist quacking which has become the feed-call for so many suppressed intellectual appetites, as well as the subject of many, many, many tiresome essays and special issues and symposiums in countless magazines and universities — all best forgotten. I've even heard, to my amazement, some otherwise good story writers using these discreditable terms, uncharmingly trying to steal a few points for their own work, and always to their discredit. The bylaws of *The Best American Short Stories*, in one of their finest moments, state on the subject of form that for a story to be considered it must have as its intention to be free-standing. But that's about all. And at the risk of becoming that most pernicious of intellectual pretenders and subversives — the man without rules — I am, at heart, in agreement with my employer here.

Away from the shifting requirements of the writing I do myself, I don't really have much of a definition of the short story form and don't feel I need one. "Short" still seems somehow inevitable, though I'm pretty lenient about that. You can find plenty of primers and handbooks to tell you what a short story is and isn't, but in these months of reading I never once dismissed a piece of writing as not being properly a short story when it claimed it was one — the reverse of that being a casuistry practiced in graduate workshops, wherein tedious and litigious lesser lights unbravely meet the challenge of often glittering work they do not understand. (I'm sure I did it myself, once.)

On the other hand, I have been inclined to dismiss stories which were not interesting — no matter that they conformed to the strictest formal restraints, had their mimetic ducks in swank rows, offered a peripety, a denouement, and closed down tighter than banks at their earned endings. To me it's a relief to observe how many disparate pieces of writing can be persuasively called a short story, how formally underdefined it still is in the minds and hands of writers. And even if the excellent stories in this book do not represent formal variety as gaily as they might've twenty or so years ago, when Cheever and Ann Beattie and Updike and Joyce Carol Oates and Ray Carver were publishing toe to toe with Ron Sukenick and Donald Barthelme, Barry Hannah and George Chambers — the days of the "anti-story" and the early Fiction Collective and *Fiction* magazine, and when I guess the short story was dead and didn't know it — my rules are the same as then: liberal to a fault, and submissive to any consciousness of form that inspires invention and discovery. Almost thirty years ago, Frank O'Connor wrote that "there are dozens and dozens of ways of expressing verisimilitude." And if he and I wouldn't have concurred precisely on what verisimilitude was, I'm sure we could've agreed that abstractable standards of form will not very reliably predict or often inspire a first-rate short story, and that a good story is not good because it conforms to or rejects doggishly some pre-existing conceit. What we want from stories, of course, is to have eternal passion revealed in that heart where before all seemed known and discovered. But to write that, you're always going to be out there on your own, needless to say — out, as Browning wrote, on the dangerous edge of things.

*

What's interesting, of course, is what's interesting — if only for seeming less subservient to prescription and rule. Recently, on a flight back to New Orleans, a man seated next to me began to take notice of the fact that I was reading. I was reading, not surprisingly, from a stack of short stories, my digits jammed in my ears for semiquiet, my brows beetled, concentrating as fiercely as ever it's possible to concentrate while jammed into something like a big airborne aluminum storm drain filled, in this case, with Mardi Gras revelers. (Such is the cultural context of the American short story.) After several minutes of intermittent fixity upon me, during which my seat mate tried and finally succeeded in getting my attention loosed from my pleasure, he and I began a brief dialogue in which I tried to explain that I was reading short stories, and that I had already read many, many of them but still had more to go, and that there was this book to be published . . . on in that vein we talked. Biff was his name, like the chummy old Alan Hale, Jr., character on TV, whom he in some ways resembled.

When Biff had digested all my info, he looked at me somewhat gravely. He was a large, rough-skinned man in his sixties, who'd sold jewelry items to the trade, and had sold them for forty years all over America, but who had done enough reading that reading mattered to him. "But wait, now, Dick," he said to me (though there wasn't a chance I could go anywhere). "You're reading all these short stories . . ." He eyed my stack. "But what're your criteria here? You know what I'm talking about? What's good and what's not good? That's always been a pretty damn subjective area to me." He nodded.

And, well. Yes, of course. That's true.

I began immediately then, as we commenced our long descent toward Lake Pontchartrain and the city that care forgot, to enunciate my criteria for him — the ones I felt were good ones and that I believed I was using: nothing so narrow as to violate my instincts, yet nothing so wide as to make me seem vulgarly indiscriminate — the thing no one wants to be. Certainly he was serious enough that a good, crackling, stand-up answer was needed. "Well, Biff, since you asked, I'm looking for stories that will be axes for the frozen sea within us." That would've done the trick. Or, "I'm hunting for stories that'll add to the stock of

available reality, Biff. Or at least something to supply the satis-
factions of belief in their measure and their style." Either of these
would've done fine and been as true as true can be.

But the fact is I didn't say those things. I maundered something about good stories being "different," that the idea of a
"story" was somewhat arbitrary, that you couldn't predict what
would make a story good, and that the precise vocabulary of
one's standards often lay buried beneath impulse and taste
(though, of course, I'd always been envious of people who could
flash theirs like a police badge). It wasn't very good, what I said.
My criteria seemed to stay pretty damn subjective, not to mention fuzzy about first principles. And soon this polite, interested
man began admiring the approaching city out my window — at
first just a stitch on the horizon, but rising by seconds more and
more clearly into focus. We did not talk much after that, and in
a bit we did not talk at all.

People think of standards — criteria — as being clear rules
against which random experience is measured, thereby helping
randomness to seem less vexing and oppressive — like a foul line
in baseball, or the manual of arms, or the rules of admiralty.
And in general I don't believe the idea of standards is bad as
long as they stay as supple as the experience to be measured. It
certainly seems reasonable that I be able to address coherently
the question of what's an excellent short story and what's a less
than excellent one, and more, that I believe in what I think is
good, and that I believe *something* is good, and that I can lay it
down in terms a nonwriter, a "layman," can appreciate. Indeed,
even to recognize a laity with a corresponding set-apart priesthood of writer-readers is at least dubious and threatens to make
little princes of obscurity of us ostensibly in the know.

Literary critics, in the palmy days before deconstruction, used
to circle relentlessly the very issue of what's good, using a variety
of august terminologies — all meant, I suppose and in part, to
keep their own little voids filled. What's a classic? What has gusto?
Magnitude? What's sublime? What will last? — issues now largely
lumped into the care of book reviewers, with few others knowing quite how to be interested. A couple of years ago a dean at
Northwestern University wrote to me soliciting my opinion (free
of charge, naturally) about the creative work of a young col-

league, a novelist I didn't know but whose work I liked. What the dean wanted to hear from me was: Would this young man's work be read by later generations? Like Hemingway, I suppose he meant. Or Molière, maybe. Or Chaucer. In any case, this seemed to be the going rate and standard for tenure at Northwestern and apparently how good was measured. (Melville would never have been kept on there.)

Most writers I know and whose work I admire *want* to write something that later generations will read and be redeemed by, want, as my friend Barry Hannah says, to shoot for the stars in all that they write. But we all know there are no promises about that. No formulas. Adherence to the old? Adherence to the new? It's impossible to know if work will last, and slightly fatuous even to wonder, since we won't last ourselves, and literature may not either, though we all hope it does. In any case, our best expectation for literature might be closer at hand and our standards proportioned more to our immediate benefit. I wrote to the dean and told him that while I certainly liked the writing in question, what I would do if I had his job would be to forget about permanence and later generations (as I have done in choosing these stories), and just read the work, figure out if it was good according to what he thought good was, then live with the consequences. Most writers wouldn't want it any other way.

Taking my own advice then, and bearing in mind the importance of all this choosing and criteria-application to the fate of world harmony and the future of the two Germanies, I have sought to exercise few rules and to adopt as wide a notion as possible of what's interesting, in the conviction that one needn't like, or look for, only one thing in short stories, or fault one story for lacking the precise virtues of another. Good stories perform what wonders they do using wise standards all their own, discovered often in the private vicissitudes of being written. Some will essay to provide that ax for the frozen sea within us and do so gracefully. Others will have nothing but to reflect the connection between bliss and bale and be less than suave about it. Some will simply want to amuse us in a good cause.

If possible, I prefer to reduce my own stature as a tiny despot of culture; first, by borrowing on Keats's belief that axioms of philosophy — and, by extension, standards governing short stories — aren't worth much until they are proved on our pulses; second, by respecting Benjamin's mild assurance that excellent stories contain openly or covertly something we can use in life; and finally and simply by respecting my own everyday desire to be told something, straight out, that I didn't know, but that is important.

Don't get me wrong. I have *my* rules, for *my* stories. And with them I am as despotic as I please. I want to write only characters which have the incalculability of life; stories with Wordsworthian purpose and powerful feelings. For me there are many fewer ways than twelve to express verisimilitude — one, maybe one and a half. Max. My economies are drastic. I want endings (not stoppings) that close like supernovas and leave you gasping. But, hey. That's just me and *my* work. What kind of guy would I be, what kind of judge, if I insisted everybody do that? How much more difficult for Flannery O'Connor or Raymond Carver or Donald Barthelme if only one standard ruled our days?

Early last winter an editor from a large metropolitan newspaper called me to ask if I would write a book review about a volume of short stories soon to be published in America. The writer was a writer whose stories I'd admired, and I wanted to read this new book, wanted to like everything about it. But in the course of our conversation I said that if I read the book and didn't like it I wouldn't write about it at all, since I had no wish to complain about my colleague's work in public.

"Maybe I'd be all wrong," I said. "I'd hate to drive readers away from a good book I was wrong about."

"But don't you want to uphold high literary standards?" she said to me.

"Sure," I said. "But not at somebody's else's expense. Anyway, I write stories myself. I have a way to hold up standards if I'm able at all."

"Yes. Well," this person answered in a peckish voice, discernible from miles and miles away, "aren't you lucky?"

"Yes, I suppose I am," I said. "Though it's odd. That's not exactly how I feel."

But you can see what I'm getting at. Writing short stories and choosing twenty good ones are different businesses. Right brain, left brain, maybe. Who knows? I only know I've made no effort to "stamp" this volume as my own. I've meant not to set the world straight about the contemporary short story, or show people what they ought to be reading — only what they might like. The selector or his method isn't the star here. It's not my collection, it's the writers'. And although a skeptical reader might say these stories are bluntly predictable given their blunt chooser, their chooser has done his best not only to find stories he can stand up for, but also to put himself out of business with his choices. Beyond that, how hard can you argue that you're not dogmatic?

So, finally, we get to the back of the garage, the nuts and bolts.

There are not a lot of wonderful short stories published in America year to year, and partly in view of that rarity I have sought to publish here only the best I could find, with no attempt to distribute evenly the number of men to women, the number of small magazines to large ones; no attempt to include some percentage of gays or Chicanos or African Americans or Jews. I have not tried to encourage younger writers nor discourage southerners, West Coast writers, dyslexics, New Agers, Christians or Viet vets. I did not read these manuscripts "blind," as some of my predecessors have, but I trust myself to honor the basic primacy of the work to its author.

I have included six stories from *The New Yorker,* and I admit that this proportionately large number makes me a bit uncomfortable. But the fact is *The New Yorker* publishes more than fifty stories a year, and the numbers are there (as they say someplace outside the literary world), and so are the good stories. The same goes for my decision to publish two stories by Alice Munro and Richard Bausch. I'd have felt more balanced by seeming more balanced, but I simply couldn't believe I was publishing the best stories I found if I ignored these.

There were not many funny stories in my two hundred and fifty, and I regret that and hope I wasn't driven by large numbers to confuse soberness with seriousness, as Edmund Wilson was said never to have done. I would hate more than I'd hate a faulty judgment to be a man who was thought of as hard to tickle.

The only story I regret not including in this volume is one by William Trevor, called "In Love with Ariadne," published in

Harper's Magazine. There seems, though, to be no easy way I can pass off Mr. Trevor, who is Irish and lives in England, as a qualified American. I would say, however, and for what it's worth that the limits of choice for *The Best American Short Stories* ought never be so restrictive that the tail begins wagging the dog and good stories fall out of consideration for administrative reasons. Myself, I don't care a fiddle that Mr. Trevor is Irish. His story was written in English — one of the languages spoken in America — published in America, read by Americans and goodness knows savored by us. We Americans export a great deal of literature and import relatively little. It may be the only favorable trade imbalance we have left, and certainly it is one that serves to keep us in the cool dark of ignorance. But somewhere along the line the distinction of what is American literature and what is Irish or English or Polish or Hungarian or something else ought to come to mean less to us — though never nothing, I suppose — without devaluing our patriotism or breaking our rules. It is at least true that we ought not observe less welcoming standards in our literary freedoms than we do in our mercantile ones.

And that's that. I'm not going to say any more about these stories, or invent some dim scheme that allows me to string together all their titles with an obscure word of praise built on. I might say the wrong thing, say something that would make you not want to read the very story I liked best. In any case, I'd rather not represent an excellent short story — a little miracle — with something less than itself.

And with that said, I've reached the feeling which must only regularly come to authors of introductions of anthologies — a class of humans best represented by Professor Corey, the genial academic gentleman I began with — a feeling of having filled a much-needed void using the entirety of my passions and faculties. I fondly remember the professor, when asked if he favored Brownian movement over the second movement of Beethoven's Fifth Symphony, was heard to remark — and this after only a moment's consideration, far less time than it's taken you to read this essay, and God knows, for me to write it: "Why yes!" he said, smiling grandly. "Yes, yes, yes, indeed. I couldn't agree more." No fool he.

RICHARD FORD

The Best
AMERICAN
SHORT
STORIES
1990

EDWARD ALLEN

River of Toys

FROM SOUTHWEST REVIEW

I LOVE to walk with my eyes closed. At night, coming back to my apartment from work, there are almost no cars on the road, and I can walk and walk until I hear a car coming up behind me, or until I see through my closed eyelids the light of one coming toward me, and I open my eyes and find myself walking in the middle of Highland Avenue.

I love to walk in the middle of the night, past the dark Laundromats, past Kentucky Fried Chicken standing dim in its all-night utility lights. With the road empty, the students gone, most of the faculty on vacation, it's so quiet that I can hear the trickle of water where Highland Avenue crosses Fairfax Creek.

I like to close my eyes and think about where I used to live, in Ramapo Bungalow Colony in Spring Valley, New York, about the water in Pascack Brook, which flows past the bungalows, how in its three miles, from where it springs out of a patch of wet ground behind the Hillcrest Shopping Center, to the place behind the United Parcel Service distribution center where it joins Ramapo Creek to become the headwaters of the Hackensack River, it touches on everything that a neighborhood needs to become the kind of home that remains a home even after you've left it for something better, even in the long remainder of one's life that one gets stranded for perfectly good reasons away from it.

Pascack Brook begins in a patch of wet ground in the woods behind the Grand Union. It runs through some fenced-off land and into a long pipe that takes it under Wollman Street; but there is a mistake in Hagstrom's Suburban Street Atlas of Rockland County, which shows the brook crossing Hempstead Road on the wrong side of Williams Avenue. The galvanized pipe where the brook passes under Hempstead Road is actually just to the north of the house where I took piano lessons for a few months when I was a kid.

It rambles through the front yard of the Hillcrest Retirement Home, into a pond bordered in summer by weeds as tall as a man, runs downhill between the sloped back yards of the newer subdivision houses, whose older children have been warned not to let the younger ones drown in it. I can't remember what the place looks like where it crosses Route 45. All I can remember is a mountain of dirt that I'm sure isn't there anymore.

It runs along the edge of a field where somebody has a horse, the grass nibbled down to an even green fuzz, and there is a white horseshed, and a two-car garage with a wrought iron outline of a horse and buggy on the clapboard triangle formed between the top of the garage doors and the low peak of the roof. And then underground again, coming out in somebody's back yard so steep they can't run a mower over it, then down to a flat section where it loops through another subdivision where back yards slope down to it, yards full of toys in bright yellows and blues, wingless airplanes, trucks without wheels.

I have listened to the voices of children playing late into the night on nights when I had to go to bed early for the first day of a new job. I have heard the land ring with fireworks. I have memorized the placement of rocks in the brook beside my bungalow so that I could balance in the dark, have gone weeks of perambulating twilight reverie without once getting a soaker. I have thrown slivers of cheese product into the water, have tossed shreds of Steak-Umm sandwich meat to the school of chubs who thrashed and splashed around after it, have balanced between two rocks, nearing the end of my unemployment benefits, and heard the voices of children.

There are signs tacked to trees advertising lawn mowing services, there are posters with the names of candidates for county judge on pointed pieces of lath hammered into people's lawns. There are skeletons of dead animals, there was a girl next door to me with a German shepherd, and once there was a terrible hyperactive kid visiting his father in one of the other bungalows, and the kid wouldn't leave the dog alone. My neighbors and I were sitting on the porch, and all of a sudden we hear this piercing scream and the kid comes tearing around the corner of the other building with the dog two feet behind him and snapping at the small of his back, like a Bugs Bunny cartoon, the kid's belly seeming to arch out in front of him like a track runner swelling to break the ribbon first, his head bent back, his face a howling, huge-mouthed mask of terror.

A neighborhood is whatever anyone wants to remember about it, a place where the ground is warm under a man's feet, and the mud cool, and the smell of tar sprinkled over gravel, the lights of the Firemen's Carnival filtering over the trees on the other side of the high-tension wires. There are teenage girls who drive around in their mothers' Oldsmobiles, wearing heavy eye make-up and blouses with elastic at the neck pulled over one bare shoulder, but I'm exaggerating. There was one girl. I wanted to marry her. I wanted to tell her, in complete seriousness, "We couldn't be more wrong for each other; we have nothing in common but the leaves and the heat and the line of a crooked smile and the air like an umbrella of moisture and stars you can't see, domed above my dreams of a relationship that I say will work because we both know it never could; and so by the same implacable gravity that draws the small water in its bends and meanderings through subdivisions where the roots of trees haven't yet grown out of their burlap coverings and the kids play tag into the night from yard to yard, by that same law we shall be married, in the month of May."

I like to close my eyes and keep walking, see how far I can walk without opening them. You can feel the night. The night is a thing. It's harmless. It has a shape. It hangs over everything I hope to get back to, over my going home from work, over the food I choose to eat, over the books I tell myself I should be reading. The night is something completely without seriousness. Stars dance in the sky, whether you can see them or not, even on nights so thick with moisture that people who smoke cigarettes can't light matches.

On Pascack Road, I've seen one of those black barrel-shaped things on the top of a telephone pole explode with a shower of blue sparks. Once when there was an electrical fire at the Orange and Rockland switching station, I saw bands of light moving through low clouds the way the light moves through a worn-out fluorescent bulb. I don't know if it was just a reflection of the light from the fire or if the live wires on the ground were interacting electrically with the atmosphere. I called the power company, but they didn't know what I was talking about.

When the water in Pascack Brook was low, which it usually was, I used to walk every night in the dark, from rock to rock, with the soft light and the music from WPLJ, the "Stairway to Heaven" flagship station, coming out of my neighbors' rear window, around which the climbing thorns had grown so thick that the tendrils were starting to work their way through the holes in the screen. Whenever there was a heavy rain, you could hear the rocks moving under water with a muffled, blocky sound, and when the water went down, the layout of the stream would be completely changed, with different rocks to stand on, different crossings to remember, providing a rare example of geological history observable within our own lifetime.

I wonder what that girl's name was, so beautiful and cheap in her mother's car. I'll never know. People without names are special. They shift around when you think about them. She looked a little bit like a girl named Karen whom I used to be friends with, whose father was my mother's podiatrist, and whose house Pascack Brook runs past on its way to the bungalows and the Hackensack River. I want to tell her that I'm sorry about all my Rabelaisian remarks around the kitchen table, playing Sorry in the old farmhouse in Blauvelt that summer when nine of us shared the rent. I was like a dog chasing cars, who wouldn't know what to do if he caught one.

There is a wonderful temporary nature to the kind of poverty I find myself in this summer. Days are simple; I'm either working or not working. I've written out a budget, and I stick to it, more or less, except on days when the tips from the night before have been better than usual. In the daytime I follow the railroad tracks to work, past the elementary school and the Coors distributor and the Bloomington Elks Club and the municipal swimming pool and the Little League fields, and it's so ludicrously hot that I have to time myself to get there early enough so that

I can hang around in the bathroom waiting for the sweat to dry, and I always have to remember to bring my deodorant in my little blue nylon knapsack, along with my black pants and my black shoes and my white shirt and my bow tie. In the day, walking, I think about distance, how over a day of riding in a car you can see how the land changes, how it opens up toward the west and there is a kind of looseness in the wind with nothing to steer it or slow it down. At night, going home, my thoughts move east, back to the water whose meanderings I trace with my eyes closed.

I love to think about my car, and do arithmetic about it, and think how soon I can get it back from where it sits in the back yard of a garage in Russell, Kansas, where the engine blew up in June on my way out west to make a million dollars at a summer job that I had convinced myself I would be able to find in the salmon fishing business. The garage made me leave a two-hundred-dollar deposit with them to hold the car there against the time I send them the money to rebuild the engine. This left me just enough to fly back here, where I managed to get my job back at the Oak Room, from which I had taken a summer leave of absence. Although it's the off season, they are glad to have me back, because now there's somebody to look after things while my boss drives back and forth from University Hospital, where his mother is dying of cancer. So I watch the bar and answer the telephone. At least half the people who come into the bar are just asking for directions, for which I no longer have to look at the map or ask one of the other customers, which means, I suppose, that I really live here now and that the layout of the town has become the same as the layout of how I picture it to myself. A town has a face, composed of all the other faces, of brick buildings with round turrets on the corners and a great frowning brow over the French doors, and all the eyes going by in cars, kids making funny faces out the back windows of station wagons, people with expensive sunglasses, the painted eyes of girls in their mothers' cars, a party of luminous faces around the fluted glass candle dish that shines in the center of each table at the bar as I pad back and forth in my black shoes on the rubber mat in the orange light.

I am saving up my money, working as many nights as they ask me to, and doing elaborate mathematical calculations: about how much I'll have in the bank three weeks from now, about whether the night is five-eighths finished or closer to three-quarters, about how much money I will have saved by the time I've lived here long enough to be an official in-state resident and I can enroll in the university at a lower tuition, which is what I came out here for in the first place. Right now I have a crush on one of the waitresses, whose face catches the light in the soft way that the kind of light they put in cocktail lounges was designed to do, one of that class of army daughters from so many different places at once that she seems to have sprung, fully formed, from a generalized, nonregional landscape; and no matter how far away from this place I get, I will remember these days, because she is beautiful. Her boyfriend lounges in the bar every night, waiting for her to get off work, and filtering Heineken through his black mustache, as if extracting krill. He is so "laid back" that once, when I asked him how his glass bric-a-brac business was going, he couldn't work up the energy to tell me. I have discovered a rule by which the personality of the future husband varies in inverse proportion to the attractiveness of the future wife. In the meantime I answer the telephone, waiting at each ring for the inevitable news, at which time we will hang black bunting, which they have already shown me where it is, over the front door and close for a few days.

Going home, I love the smells of the night, the murky green pollen of the weeds that grow at the places where Fairfax Creek runs under Highland Avenue, the barely perceptible undertone of dead animals, the sweet lampblack of exhaust from cars that aren't running right, the carbon dust that hangs over the street long after most of the traffic has gone home. Sometimes cars go by with gasoline splashing out from underneath their license plates. I remember one night in the pouring rain when Pascack Brook had somehow become filled with gasoline, and the smell was so strong that my neighbors sitting on the porch were afraid to light their cigarettes. We called the police. When they came I walked out into the rain to speak to them. The smell had already started to go away. The two cops and I stood on the inclined slab of concrete beneath the floodlight at the edge of Bungalow C and watched the brown water speed past in the bright light, full of leaves and branches. They said to call back if the smell got strong again, and then they left, and since I was wet already I just stood there watching how the water would sluice past over a stationary wave in front of where I was standing, listening to the rocks clunking together on the bottom.

It's strange to think about how much I used to hate the police. I would sneer at the cars as they drove past. But I had a friend who spat on an old security guard's shoes at a B. B. King concert, because he was afraid to spit at a real policeman, and I decided that I had better find something else to hate. Now I hate people who drive around in cars with chunks rusted out of them. I'm not talking about poor people. I'm talking about people with tennis rackets.

When I lived in the bungalow colony I used to call the police all the time. At two o'clock in the morning a school bus was roaring around the neighborhood, barreling up and down the silent streets. It seemed very suspicious, so I called the police. A dog was trapped in the woods on the other side of the power lines, with his leash snagged in the crook of a tree. I was afraid to get too close to him, so I called the police. A red-bearded derelict was walking back and forth all day along Pascack Road; a very large dead gray tiger cat was lying by the road, his belly bloated, stinking up the whole neighborhood. For some reason the sanitation department was not listed in the phone book, so I called the police. I would have buried it myself; I had nothing else to do, but it's not my job. There are people who get paid for picking up dead animals.

I suppose you could call it a river, despite its small volume of water, because it follows the dentings of the land, and the title-abstract companies recognize it as a border between properties that go back for generations, and it's really just a random choice about which stream you designate as the headwaters of whatever more important river it joins up with farther downstream. It's always in the same place, and it's always there in the morning, except for the one summer when it dried up completely for a few weeks. A school of chubs, trapped in a pool that my neighbor Dominick had built by piling rocks into a dam, swam for a day with their mouths at the surface of the oxygenless water, and the next day they were all dead.

In the patch of woods where it begins, where kids from Cameo

Gardens have cleared an oval track where they ride round and round on their bicycles, jumping roots and rocks, it springs from a little puddle, forming a trickle of water no larger than what a garden hose would give forth if you were trying to fill a dog's dish without splashing. There in the woods, bright with cans and bottles and license plates not old enough to be worth collecting, there leads a path from the bicycle track to the edge of the parking lot, where you're not supposed to work on your car but everybody does anyway, and there is a sort of window in the foliage, and there is a black pit in the dirt where people from Cameo Gardens dump the used oil from their cars. I suppose you could say that the water is born dirty, like a child born with its mother's virus. On the other side of the patch of woods from the Cameo Gardens parking lot is the rear of the Grand Union, with its leading dock, and a large turning-around space for trailer trucks, and one of those enormous hydraulic dumpsters that people get killed in once in a while. One door south from Grand Union is the back door of Hillcrest Liquors, outside of which, on Mondays and Thursdays, are piled dozens of empty boxes that people who are moving come by in their cars and take.

Across the brook from the bungalow I used to live in, there stands a cement cone four feet high, connected to some sort of waste conduit that runs parallel to the brook, a rounded shape that rises from the weeds like a tiny volcano, or an African anthill, with a round iron lid cast in a crosshatched pattern like a mint wafer. In summer there comes from that conduit some nights a thick odor in the air, full of methane and phosphorus, something old and rich and round-edged, steaming out from underground.

I have found so many toys washed downstream in Pascack Brook that I always had something to play with in the days when I was collecting unemployment insurance. I found plastic sand trowels and water-powered rockets. Once in the winter I found a yellow water pistol, very serious looking, half embedded in ice; and all that afternoon in the snowless cold with plumes of smoke blowing from the bungalow chimneys and the high-tension wires buzzing, I walked up and down the river of ice, water pistol in hand, upstream to where a low bridge crosses it, and downstream to where dogs began to bark at me. I called myself the Ice Patrol.

I found so many toys in Pascack Brook that the kids who lived upstream from me must have been thought fools by their parents. I have found toy cars, toy helicopters, submarines, an army truck full of drowned soldiers, one with his head knocked off. I have found balls: volleyballs, Spaul-deens, waterlogged softballs, Wiffle balls, a hollow ball for dogs with bells inside it, a blue and black and white ball that if I spun it on the floor looked like the planet Jupiter, and another that looked almost exactly like the *Voyager* photos of Jupiter's moon Ganymede. I have found armless dolls drowned against the gridwork of abandoned Waldbaum's shopping carts. For some reason, people always throw shopping carts into the water, and they roll downstream with every big rain, ending up wedged between boulders, like ruined lobster traps, twisted, covered with algae, bits of chrome shining through the rust, their caster wheels pointing up in the air and snagged at the hubs with tufts of dried grass.

I have bounced tennis balls with the nap worn off them against the walls of my bungalow and wondered how far upstream they originated, if they have passed, rolling in the dark water, beneath the windows of the house where my friend Karen used to live. Now she's in Colorado, married to some guy I've never met, whose personality I can only assume fulfills the usual algebraic requirement of inverse proportionality. But then of course Colorado is so beautiful that it doesn't matter; you can be the most boring person in the world and nobody will notice. I apologize for all the jokes about your breasts, there at the Sorry table, but even if you were still around, that would be all over now; my doctor says I have to give up half my sex life, and I have to choose which half: thinking about it or talking about it. All I know is that loving you has made me a better person — look! Peter had a picture of you naked, that summer at the farmhouse, standing in a field, your back to his Nikon. I used to turn the picture around and hold it to the light to see the front.

I was sorry to hear that your father died. I would have sent a card, but those cards are strange, and it's strange to think that the person who died hadn't even gotten sick yet when the card was written.

He was a nice man, a bit silly. He did wonders for my mother's feet. I wish my father could have done as much to help him manage his psoriasis. "Manage" is a key word here, of course,

and that's the beauty of dermatology: patients rarely get well
and they rarely die. His nickname for you was Pussycat, which
he had the unfortunate habit of shortening to just Pussy, and he
could not be made to understand, or you could not bring yourself to discuss with him, the vulgar meaning of that word; hence
your embarrassment that day in the Goodyear Service Center
when the car was ready and your father called to you from the
service desk into the waiting room: "Pussy! We're going home
now. Pussy!" and all the way up and down the six bays of the
service area, the mechanics were laughing so hard that the
wrenches fell out of their hands and clanged on the floor.

Oh, the water, the dirty water. I'd like to walk in it and let the
water run all over me, as it ran over that little kid, according to
my neighbors who had been in the bungalow colony for five years
when I moved in, the kid from the federal housing project up
on the hill who drowned in the brook and his body washed under the wooden bridge leading from Pascack Road to Eden Acres
and rotted there for weeks until the skull floated free and some
kids found it. I would like to spend a whole day waxing nostalgic
for that water, and maybe even squeeze out a tear, because it
would feel good, and I have read in *Psychology Today* on the plane
back from Kansas that tears contain a kind of protein that the
body is trying to get rid of. And when my body has gotten rid of
enough of that protein, that means that I will be good at whatever I do, and I shall have my master's degree, and I shall be
able to fly back for a weekend without having to worry about all
the things I've let myself get behind on to get there. I shall buy
long wading boots for sloshing upstream on the slippery green
rocks. I shall rent a mid-sized car at the airport. I shall start at
the ocean and follow the water upstream by whatever roads run
closest to it, from the Verrazano-Narrows Bridge, where you can
look east from the roadway into the open sea, then north along
the edge of Staten Island, overlooking the supertankers riding
at anchor in the Upper Bay, then to Bayonne, along Newark
Bay, through Jersey City, and up the mighty Hackensack, all the
way to Hackensack, upstream through Westwood and Hillsdale,
to Woodcliff Lake, beside my favorite restaurant, the Golden
Musket, where in the middle of the day fierce geese with bulbous
red knots on the bridge of their bills honk and hiss at the drivers

from the food service companies, to Pearl River, to Nanuet; and there, where the Hackensack River begins, at the confluence of Pascack Brook and Ramapo Creek, overlooked by the windowless blond brick of the UPS building, so new that no grass grows on the dirt sloping down from it, at that confluence, where any toys that have rolled this far downstream will sink to the bottom and never come up, there stands a flat rock, and upon that rock I say I shall stand and look downstream to all the places I have never been, shall build my dynasty of one that goes back as far as I want to say it goes back; I bid you welcome, lovely ladies, kind gentlemen. The name of my house is Falling Water.

RICHARD BAUSCH

The Fireman's Wife

FROM THE ATLANTIC MONTHLY

JANE'S HUSBAND, Martin, works for the fire department. He's
on four days, off three; on three, off four. It's the kind of shift
work that allows plenty of time for sustained recreation, and
during the off times Martin likes to do a lot of socializing with
his two shift mates, Wally Harmon and Teddy Lynch. The three
of them are like brothers: they bicker and squabble and compete
in a friendly way about everything, including their common hobby,
which is the making and flying of model airplanes. Martin is
fanatical about it — spends way too much money on the two planes
he owns, which are on the work table in the garage, and which
seem to require as much maintenance as the real article. Among
the arguments between Jane and her husband — about money,
lack of time alone together, and housework — there have been
some about the model planes, but Jane can't say or do much
without sounding like a poor sport: Wally's wife, Milly, loves
watching the boys, as she calls them, fly their planes, and Teddy
Lynch's ex-wife, before they were divorced, had loved the model
planes too. In a way, Jane is the outsider here: the Harmons
have known Martin most of his life, and Teddy Lynch was once
point guard, to Martin's power forward, on their high school
basketball team. Jane is relatively new, having come to Illinois
from Virginia only two years ago, when Martin brought her back
with him from his reserves training there.

This evening, a hot September twilight, they're sitting on lawn
chairs in the dim light of the coals in Martin's portable grill, talking about games. Martin and Teddy want to play Risk, though

they're already arguing about the rules. Teddy says that a European version of the game contains a wrinkle that makes it more interesting, and Martin is arguing that the game itself was derived from some French game.

"Well, go get it," Teddy says, "and I'll show you. I'll bet it's in the instructions."

"Don't get that out now," Jane says to Martin.

"It's too long," Wally Harmon says.

"What if we play cards," Martin says.

"Martin doesn't want to lose his bet," Teddy says.

"We don't have any bets, Teddy."

"O.K., so let's bet."

"Let's play cards," Martin says. "Wally's right. Risk takes too long."

"I feel like conquering the world," Teddy says.

"Oh, Teddy," Milly Harmon says, "please shut up."

She's expecting. She sits with her legs out, holding her belly as though it were unattached, separate from her. The child will be her first, and she's excited and happy; she glows, as if she knows everyone's admiring her.

Jane thinks Milly is spreading it on a little thick at times: lately all she wants to talk about is her body and what it's doing.

"I had a dream last night," Milly says now. "I dreamed that I was pregnant. Big as a house. And I woke up and I was. What I want to know is, was that a nightmare?"

"How did you feel in the dream?" Teddy asks her.

"I said. Big as a house."

"Right, but was it bad or good?"

"How would you feel if you were big as a house?"

"Well, that would depend on what the situation was."

"The situation is you're big as a house."

"Yeah, but what if somebody was chasing me? I'd want to be big, right?"

"Oh, Teddy, please shut up."

"I had a dream," Wally says. "A bad dream. I dreamed I died. I mean, you know, I was dead — and what was weird was that I was also the one who had to call Milly to tell her about it."

"Oh, God," Milly says. "Don't talk about this."

"It was weird. I got killed out at sea or something. Drowned,

I guess. I remember I was standing on the deck of this ship talking to somebody about how it went down. And then I was calling Milly to tell her. And the thing is, I talked like a stranger would — you know, 'I'm sorry to inform you that your husband went down at sea.' It was weird."

"How did you feel when you woke up?" Martin says.

"I was scared. I didn't know who I was for a couple of seconds."

"Look," Milly says, "I don't want to talk about dreams."

"Let's talk about good dreams," Jane says. "I had a good dream. I was fishing with my father out at a creek — some creek that felt like a real place. Like if I ever really did go fishing with my father, this is where we would have fished when I was small."

"What?" Martin says, after a pause, and everyone laughs.

"Well," Jane says, feeling the blood rise in her face and neck, "I never — my father died when I was just a baby."

"I dreamed I got shot once," Teddy says. "Guy shot me with a forty-five automatic as I was running downstairs. I fell, and hit bottom, too. I could feel the cold concrete on the side of my face before I woke up."

Milly Harmon sits forward a little and says to Wally, "Honey, why did you have to tell me you had a dream like that? Now *I'm* going to dream about it, I just know it."

"I think we all ought to call it a night," Jane says. "You've all got to get up at six o'clock."

"What're you talking about?" Martin says. "We're going to play cards, aren't we?"

"I thought we were going to play Risk," Teddy says.

"All right," Martin says, getting out of his chair. "Risk it is."

Milly groans, and Jane gets up and follows Martin into the house. "Honey," she says. "Not Risk. Come on. We'd need four hours at least."

He says over his shoulder, "So, then we need four hours."

"Martin, I'm tired."

He's leaning up into the hall closet, where the games are stacked. He brings the Risk game down and turns, holding it in both hands like a tray. "Look, where do you get off, telling everybody to go home the way you did?"

She stands there staring at him.

"These people are our friends, Jane."

"I just said I thought we ought to call it a night."

"Well, *don't* say — all right? It's embarrassing." He goes around her and back out to the patio. The screen door slaps twice in the jamb. She waits a moment and then moves through the house to the bedroom. She brushes her hair, thinks about getting out of her clothes. Martin's uniforms are lying across the foot of the bed. She picks them up, walks into the living room with them, and drapes them over the back of the easy chair.

"Jane," Martin calls from the patio. "Are you playing or not?"

"Come on, Jane," Milly says. "Don't leave me alone out here."

"What color armies do you want?" Martin asks.

She goes to the patio door and looks out at them. Martin has lighted the tiki lamps; everyone's sitting at the picnic table, in the moving firelight.

"Come on," Martin says, barely concealing his irritation. She can hear it, and she wants to react to it — wants to let him know that she is hurt. But they're all waiting for her, so she steps out and takes her place at the table. She chooses green for her armies, and she plays the game to lose, attacking in all directions until her forces are so badly depleted that when Wally begins to make his own move she's the first to lose all her armies. This takes more than an hour. When she's out of the game, she sits for a while, cheering Teddy on against Martin, who is clearly going to win; finally she excuses herself and goes back into the house. The glow from the tiki lamps makes weird patterns on the kitchen wall. She pours herself a glass of water and drinks it down; then she pours more, and swallows some aspirin. Teddy sees this as he comes in for more beer, and he grasps her by the elbow and asks if she wants something a little better than aspirin for a headache.

"Like what?" she says, smiling at him. She's decided a smile is what one offers under such circumstances; one laughs things off, pretends not to notice the glazed look in the other person's eyes.

Teddy is staring at her, not quite smiling. Finally he puts his hands on her shoulders and says, "What's the matter, lady?"

"Nothing," she says. "I have a headache. I took some aspirin."

"I've got some stuff," he says. "It makes America beautiful. Want some?"

She says, "Teddy."

"No problem," he says. He holds both hands up and backs away from her. Then he turns and is gone. She hears him begin to tease Martin about the French rules of the game. Martin is winning. He wants Wally Harmon to keep playing and Wally wants to quit. Milly and Teddy are talking about flying the model airplanes. They know about an air show in Danville on Saturday. They all keep playing and talking, and for a long time Jane watches them from the screen door. She smokes half a pack of cigarettes, and she paces a little. She drinks three glasses of orange juice, and finally she walks into the bedroom and lies down with her face in her hands. Her forehead feels hot. She's thinking about the next four days, when Martin will be gone and she can have the house to herself. She hasn't been married even two years and she feels crowded; she's depressed and tired every day. She never has enough time to herself. And yet when she's alone, she feels weak and afraid. Now she hears someone in the hallway and she sits up, smoothes her hair back from her face. Milly Harmon comes in, with her hands cradling her belly.

"Ah," Milly says. "A bed." She sits down next to Jane and then leans back on her hands. "I'm beat," she says.

"I have a headache," Jane says.

Milly nods. Her expression seems to indicate how unimportant she finds this, as if Jane had told her she'd already got over a cold or something. "They're in the garage now," she says.

"Who?"

"Teddy, Wally, Martin. Martin conquered the world."

"What're they doing?" Jane asks. "It's almost midnight."

"Everybody's going to be miserable in the morning," Milly says. Jane is quiet.

"Oh," Milly says, looking down at herself. "He kicked. Want to feel it?"

She takes Jane's hand and puts it on her belly. Jane feels movement under her fingers, something very slight, like one heartbeat.

"Wow," she says. She pulls her hand away.

"Listen," Milly says. "I know we can all be overbearing sometimes. Martin doesn't realize yet some of his responsibilities. Wally was the same way."

"I just have this headache," Jane says. She doesn't want to talk about it, doesn't want to get into it. Even when she talks to her mother on the phone and her mother asks how things are, she says it's all fine. She has nothing she wants to confide.

"You feel trapped, don't you," Milly says.

Jane looks at her.

"Don't you?"

"No."

"O.K. — you just have a headache."

"I do," Jane says.

Milly sits forward a little, folds her hands over the roundness of her belly. "This baby's jumping all over the place."

Jane is silent.

"Do you believe my husband and that awful dream? I wish he hadn't told us about it — now I know I'm going to dream something like it. You know pregnant women and dreams. I begin to shake just thinking of it."

"Try not to think of it," Jane says.

Milly waits a moment and then clears her throat and says, "You know, for a while there after Wally and I were married, I thought maybe I'd made a mistake. I remember realizing that I didn't like the way he laughed. I mean, let's face it, Wally laughs like a hyena. And somehow that took on all kinds of importance — you know, I had to absolutely like everything about him or I couldn't like anything. Have you ever noticed the way he laughs?"

Jane has never really thought about it. But she says nothing now. She simply nods.

"But, you know," Milly goes on, "all I had to do was wait. Just — you know, wait for love to come around and surprise me again."

"Milly, I have a headache. I mean, what do you think is wrong, anyway?"

"O.K.," Milly says, rising.

Then Jane wonders whether the other woman has been put up to this conversation. "Hey," she says, "did Martin say something to you?"

"What would Martin say?"

"I don't know. I mean I really don't know, Milly. Jesus Christ, can't a person have a simple headache?"

"O.K.," Milly says. "O.K."

"I like the way everybody talks around me here, you know it?"

"Nobody's talking around you —"

"I think it's wonderful how close you all are."

"All right," Milly says, standing there with her hands folded under the bulge of her belly. "You just look so unhappy these days."

"Look," Jane says. "I have a headache, all right? I'm going to go to bed. I mean, the only way I can get rid of it is to lie down in the dark and be very quiet — O.K.?"

"Sure, honey," Milly says.

"So — good night, then."

"Right," Milly says. "Good night." She steps toward Jane and kisses her on the cheek. "I'll tell Martin to call it a night. I know Wally'll be miserable tomorrow."

"It's because they can take turns sleeping on shift," Jane says.

"I'll tell them," Milly says, going down the hall.

Jane steps out of her jeans, pulls her blouse over her head, and crawls under the sheets, which are cool and fresh and crisp. She turns the light off and closes her eyes. She can't believe how bad it is. She hears them all saying good night, and she hears Martin shutting the doors and turning off the lights. In the dark she waits for him to get to her. She's very still, lying on her back with her hands at her sides. He goes into the bathroom at the end of the hall. She hears him cough, clear his throat. He's cleaning his teeth. Then he comes to the entrance of the bedroom and stands in the light from the hall.

"I know you're awake," he says.

She doesn't answer.

"Jane," he says.

She says, "What?"

"Are you mad at me?"

"No."

"Then what's wrong?"

"I have a headache."

"You always have a headache."

"I'm not going to argue now, Martin. So you can say what you want."

He moves toward her, is standing by the bed. He's looming above her in the dark. "Teddy had some dope."

She says, "I know. He offered me some."

"I'm flying," Martin says.

She says nothing.

"Let's make love."

"Martin," she says. Her heart is beating fast. He moves a little, staggers taking off his shirt. He's so big and quick and powerful; nothing fazes him. When he's like this, the feeling she has is that he might do anything. "Martin," she says.

"All right," he says. "I won't. O.K.? You don't have to worry your little self about it."

"Look," she says.

But he's already heading out into the hall.

"Martin," she says.

He's in the living room. He turns the television on loud. A rerun of *Kojak*. She hears Theo calling someone sweetheart. "Sweetheart," Martin says. When she goes to him, she finds that he's opened a beer and is sitting on the couch with his legs out. The beer is balanced on his stomach.

"Martin," she says. "You have to start your shift in less than five hours."

He holds the beer up. "Baby," he says.

In the morning he's sheepish. Obviously in pain. He sits at the kitchen table with his hands up to his head, while she makes coffee and hard-boiled eggs. She has to go to work too, at a car dealership in town. All day she sits behind a window with a circular hole in the glass, where people line up to pay for whatever the dealer sells or provides, including mechanical work, parts, license plates, used cars, rental cars, and, of course, new cars. Her day is long and exhausting, and she's already feeling as though she worked all night. The booth she has to sit in is right off the service-bay area, and the smell of exhaust and grease is everywhere. Everything seems coated with a film of grime. She's standing at her sink, looking out at the sun coming up past the trees beyond her street, and without thinking about it she puts the water on and washes her hands. The idea of the car dealership is like something clinging to her skin.

"Jesus," Martin says. He can't eat much.

She's drying her hands on a paper towel.

"Listen," he says. "I'm sorry, O.K.?"

"Sorry?" she says.

"Don't press it, all right? You know what I mean."

"O.K.," she says, and when he gets up and comes over to put his arms around her, she feels his difference from her. She kisses him. They stand there.

"Four days," he says.

When Teddy and Wally pull up in Wally's new pickup, she stands in the kitchen door and waves at them. Martin walks down the driveway, carrying his tote bag of uniforms and books to read. He turns around and blows her a kiss. This one is like so many other mornings. They drive off. She goes back into the bedroom and makes the bed, and puts his dirty uniforms in the wash. She showers and chooses something to wear. It's quiet. She puts the radio on and then decides she'd rather have the silence. After she's dressed, she stands at the back door and looks out at the street. Children are walking to school, in little groups of friends. She thinks about the four days ahead. What she needs is to get into the routine and stop thinking so much. She knows that problems in a marriage are worked out over time.

Before she leaves for work, she goes out into the garage, to look for signs of Teddy's dope. She doesn't want someone stumbling on incriminating evidence. On the work table along the back wall are Martin's model planes. She walks over and stands staring at them. She stands very still, as if waiting for something to move. But nothing moves.

At work her friend Eveline smokes one cigarette after another, apologizing before each one. During Martin's shifts Jane spends a lot of time with Eveline, who is twenty-nine and single and wants very much to be married. The problem is she can't find anyone. Last year, when Jane was first working at the dealership, she got Eveline a date with Teddy Lynch. Teddy took Eveline to Lum's for hot dogs and beer, and they had fun at first. But then Eveline got drunk and passed out — put her head down on her arms and went to sleep like a child asked to take a nap in school. Teddy put her in a cab for home and then called Martin to laugh about the whole thing. Eveline was so humiliated by the experience that she goes out of her way to avoid Teddy — doesn't want anything to do with him or with any of Martin's friends, or with Martin, for that matter. She will come over to the house only when she knows Martin is away at work. And when Martin calls the dealership and she answers the phone, she's very stiff and formal. She hands the phone to Jane as though it were a piece of hot metal.

Today things aren't very busy, and they work a crossword together, making sure to keep it out of sight of the salesmen, who occasionally wander in to waste time with them. Eveline plays her radio and hums along with some of the songs. It's a long, slow day, and when Martin calls, Jane feels herself growing anxious — something is moving in the pit of her stomach.

"Are you still mad at me?" he says.

She says, "No."

"Say you love me."

"I love you," she says.

"Everybody's asleep here," he says. "I wish you were with me."

She says, "Yeah."

"I do," he says.

"O.K."

"You don't believe me?"

"I said *O.K.*"

"Is it busy today?" he asks.

"Not too," Jane says.

"You're bored, then."

"A little," she says.

"How's the headache?"

"Just the edge of one."

"I'm sorry," he says.

"It's not your fault."

"Sometimes I feel like it is."

"How's *your* head?" she says.

"Terrible."

"Poor boy."

"I wish something would happen around here," he says. "A lot of guys snoring."

"Martin," she says, "I've got to go."

"O.K."

"You want me to stop by tonight?" she asks.

"If you want to."

"Maybe I will."

"You don't have to."

She thinks about him where he is: she imagines him, comfortable, sitting on a couch in front of a television. Sometimes, when nothing's going on, he watches all the soaps. He was hooked on *General Hospital* for a while. That he's her husband seems strange, and she thinks of the nights she's lain in his arms, whispering his name over and over, putting her hands in his hair and rocking with him in the dark. She tells him she loves him, and hangs the phone up. Eveline makes a gesture of frustration and envy.

"Nuts," Eveline says. "Nuts to you and your lovey-dovey stuff."

Jane is sitting in a bath of cold inner light, trying to think of her husband as someone she recognizes.

"Let's do something tonight," Eveline says. "Maybe I'll get lucky."

"I'm not going with you if you're going to be giving strange men the eye," Jane says. She hasn't quite heard herself. She is surprised when Eveline reacts.

"How dare you say a nasty thing like that. I don't know if I want to go out with someone who doesn't think any more of me than *that*."

"I'm sorry," Jane says, patting the other woman's wrist. "I didn't mean anything by it, really. I was just teasing."

"Well, don't tease that way. It hurts my feelings."

"I'm sorry," Jane says again. "Please — really." She feels near crying.

"Well, O.K.," Eveline says. "Don't get upset. I'm half teasing myself."

Jane sniffles, wipes her eyes with the back of one hand.

"What's wrong, anyway?" Eveline says.

"Nothing," Jane says. "I hurt your feelings."

That evening they ride in Eveline's car over to Shakey's for a pizza, and then stroll down to the end of the block, to the new mini-mall on Lincoln Avenue. The night is breezy and warm. A storm is building over the town square. They window-shop for a while, and finally they stop at a new corner café, to sit in a booth by the windows, drinking beer. Across the street one of the movies has ended, and people are filing out, or waiting around. A few of them head this way.

"They don't look like they enjoyed the movie very much," Eveline says.

"Maybe they did, and they're just depressed to be back in the real world."

"Look, what is it?" Eveline asks suddenly.

Jane returns her gaze.

"What's wrong?"

"Nothing."

"Something's wrong," Eveline says.

Two boys from the high school come past, and one of them winks at Jane. She remembers how it was in high school — the games of flirtation and pursuit, of ignoring some people and noticing others. That seemed like such an unbearable time, and it's already years ago. She watches Eveline light yet another cigarette, and feels very much older than her memory of herself. She sees the person she is now, with Martin, somewhere years away, happy, with children, and with different worries. It's a vivid daydream. She sits there fabricating it, feeling it for what it is, and feeling, too, that nothing will change: the Martin she sees in the daydream is nothing like the man she lives with. She thinks of Milly Harmon, pregnant and talking about waiting to be surprised by love.

"I think I'd like to have a baby," she says. She hadn't known she would say it.

Eveline says, "Yuck," blowing smoke.

"Yuck," Jane says. "That's great. Great response, Evie."

They're quiet awhile. Beyond the square the clouds break up into tatters, and lightning strikes out. They hear thunder, and the smell of rain is in the air. The trees in the little park across from the theater move in the wind, and leaves blow out of them.

"Wouldn't you like to have a family?" Jane says.

"Sure."

"Well, the last time I checked, that meant having babies."

"Yuck," Eveline says again.

"Oh, all right — you just mean because of the pain and all."

"I mean yuck."

"Well, what does 'yuck' mean, O.K.?"

"What *is* the matter with you?" Eveline says. "What difference does it make?"

"I'm trying to have a normal conversation," Jane says, "and I'm getting these weird one-word answers, that's all. I mean what's 'yuck,' anyway? What's it mean?"

"Let's say it means I don't want to talk about having babies."

"I wasn't talking about you."

Each is now a little annoyed with the other. Jane has noticed that whenever she talks about anything that might border on plans for the future, the other woman becomes irritatingly sardonic and close-mouthed. Eveline sits there smoking her cigarette and watching the storm come. From beyond the square they hear sirens, which seem to multiply. The whole city seems to be mobilizing. Jane thinks of Martin out there where all those alarms are converging. How odd to know where your husband is by a sound everyone hears. She remembers lying awake nights, early in the marriage, hearing sirens and worrying about what might happen. And now, through a slanting sheet of rain, as though something in these thoughts has produced her, Milly Harmon comes, holding an open magazine above her head. She sees Jane and Eveline in the window and waves at them. "Oh, God," Eveline says. "Isn't that Milly Harmon?"

Milly comes into the café and stands for a moment, shaking water from herself. Her hair is wet, as are her shoulders. She pulls the hair behind her ears and wipes her forehead with the back of one hand. Then she walks over and says, "Hi, honey," to Jane, bending down to kiss her on the side of the face. Jane manages to seem glad to see her. "You remember my friend Eveline from work," she says.

"I think I do, sure," Milly says.

"Maybe not," Eveline says.

"No, I think I do."

"I have one of those faces that remind you of somebody you never met," Eveline says.

Jane covers this with a laugh as Milly settles on her side of the booth.

"Do you hear that?" Milly says about the sirens. "I swear, it must be a big one. I wish I didn't hear the sirens. It makes me so jumpy and scared. Wally would never forgive me if I did, but I wish I could get up the nerve to go see what it is."

"So," Eveline says, blowing smoke, "how's the baby doing?"

Milly looks down at herself. "Sleeping now, I think."

"Wally — is it Wally?"

"Wally, yes."

"Wally doesn't let you chase ambulances?"

"I don't chase ambulances."

"Well, I mean — you aren't allowed to go see what's what when you hear sirens?"

"I don't want to see."

"I guess not."

"He's seen some terrible things. They all have. It must be terrible sometimes."

"Right," Eveline says. "It must be terrible."

Milly waves her hand in front of her face. "I wish you wouldn't smoke."

"I was smoking before you came," Eveline says. "I didn't know you were coming."

Milly looks confused for a second. Then she sits back a little and folds her hands on the table. She's chosen to ignore Eveline. She looks at Jane and says, "I had that dream last night."

Jane says, "What dream?"

"That Wally was gone."

Jane says nothing.

"But it wasn't the same, really. He'd left me, you know — the baby was born and he'd just gone off. I was so mad at him. And I had this crying little baby in my lap."

Eveline swallows the last of her beer and then gets up and goes out to stand near the line of wet pavement at the edge of the awninged sidewalk.

"What's the matter with her?" Milly asks.

"She's just unhappy."

"Did I say something wrong?"

"No — really. It's nothing," Jane says.

She pays for the beer. Milly talks to her for a while, but Jane has a hard time concentrating on much of anything now, with the sirens going and Eveline standing out there at the edge of the sidewalk. Milly goes on, talking nervously about Wally's leaving her in her dream, and how funny it is that she woke up mad at him, that she had to wait a few minutes and get her head clear before she could kiss him good morning.

"I've got to go," Jane says. "I came in Eveline's car."

"Oh, I'm sorry — sure. I just stepped in out of the rain myself."

They join Eveline outside, and Milly says she's got to go get her nephews before they knock down the ice cream parlor. Jane and Eveline watch her walk away in the rain, and Eveline says, "Jesus."

"She's just scared," Jane says. "God, leave her alone."

"I don't mean anything by it," Eveline says. "A little malice, maybe."

Jane says nothing. They stand there watching the rain and lightning, and soon they're talking about people at work, the salesmen and the boys in the parts shop. They're relaxed now; the sirens have stopped, and the tension between them has lifted. They laugh about one salesman who's apparently interested in Eveline. He's a married man — an overweight, balding, middle-aged Texan who wears snakeskin boots and a string tie, and who has an enormous fake-diamond ring on the little finger of his left hand. Eveline calls him Disco Bill. And yet Jane thinks her friend may be secretly attracted to him. She teases her about this, or begins to, and then a clap of thunder so frightens them both that they laugh about it, off and on, through the rest of the evening. They wind up visiting Eveline's parents, who live only a block from the café. Eveline's parents have been married almost thirty years, and, sitting in their living room, Jane looks at their things — the love seat and the antique chairs, the handsome grandfather clock in the hall, the paintings. The place has a lovely *tended* look about it. Everything seems to stand for the kind of life she wants for herself: an attentive, loving husband; children; and a quiet house with a clock that chimes. She knows this is all very dreamy and childish, and yet she looks at Eveline's parents, those people with their almost thirty years' love, and her heart aches. She drinks four glasses of white wine and realizes near the end of the visit that she's talking too much, laughing too loudly.

It's very late when she gets home. She lets herself in the side door of the house and walks through the rooms, turning on all the lights, as is her custom — she wants to be sure no one is hiding in any of the nooks and crannies. Tonight she looks at everything and feels demeaned by it. Martin's clean uniforms are lying across the back of the lounge chair in the living room. The TV and the TV trays are in one corner, next to a coffee table, a gift from Martin's parents, something they bought back in the fifties, before Martin was born. Martin's parents live on a farm ten miles outside town, and for the past year Jane has had to spend Sundays out there, sitting in that living room, with its sparse, starved look, listening to Martin's father talk about the weather, or what he had to eat for lunch, or the wrestling matches he watches on TV. He's a kindly man but he has nothing whatever of interest to say, and he seems to know it — his own voice always seems to surprise him at first, as if some profound inner silence had been broken; he pauses, seems to gather himself, and then continues with the considered, slow cadences of oration. He's tall and lean and powerful looking; he wears coveralls, and he reminds Jane of those pictures of hungry, bewildered men in the Dust Bowl thirties — with their sad, straight, combed hair and their desperation. Yet he's a man who seems quite certain about things, quite calm and satisfied. His wife bustles around him, making sure of his comfort, and he speaks to her in exactly the same soft, sure tones that he uses with Jane.

Now, sitting in her own living room, thinking about this man, her father-in-law, Jane realizes that she can't stand another Sunday afternoon listening to him talk. It comes to her like a chilly premonition, and quite suddenly, with a kind of tidal shifting inside her, she feels the full weight of her unhappiness. For the first time it seems unbearable, like something that might drive her out of her mind. She breathes, swallows, closes her eyes and opens them. She looks at her own reflection in one of the darkened windows of the kitchen, and then she finds herself in the bedroom, pulling her things out of the closet and throwing them on the bed. Something about this is a little frantic, as though each motion fed some impulse to go further, go through with it — use this night, make her way somewhere else. For a long time she works, getting the clothes out where she can see them. She's lost herself in the practical matter of getting packed. She can't decide what to take, and then she can't find a suitcase or an overnight bag. Finally she settles on one of Martin's travel bags, from when he was in the reserves. She's hurrying, stuffing everything into the bag, and when the bag is almost full, she stops, feeling spent and out of breath. She sits down at her dressing table for a moment, and now she wonders if perhaps this is all the result of what she's had to drink. The alcohol is wearing off. She has the beginning of a headache. But she knows that whatever she decides to do should be done in the light of day, not now, at night. At last she gets up from the chair and lies down on the bed to think. She's dizzy. Her mind swims. She can't think, so she remains where she is, lying in the tangle of clothes she hasn't packed yet. Perhaps half an hour goes by. She wonders how long this will go on. And then she's asleep. She's nowhere, not even dreaming.

She wakes to the sound of voices. She sits up and tries to get her eyes to focus, tries to open them wide enough to see in the light. The imprint of the wrinkled clothes is in the skin of her face; she can feel it with her fingers. And then she's watching as two men bring Martin in through the front door and help him lie down on the couch. It's all framed in the perspective of the hallway and the open bedroom door, and she's not certain that it's actually happening.

"Martin?" she murmurs, getting up, moving toward them. She stands in the doorway of the living room, rubbing her eyes and trying to clear her head. The two men are standing over her husband, who says something in a pleading voice to one of them. He's lying on his side on the couch, both hands bandaged, a bruise on the side of his face as if something had spilled there.

"Martin," Jane says.

And the two men move, as if startled at her voice. She realizes she's never seen them before. One of them, the younger one, is already explaining. They're from another company. "We were headed back this way," he says, "and we thought it'd be better if you didn't hear anything over the phone." While he talks, the older one is leaning over Martin, going on about insurance. He's a big square-shouldered man with an extremely rubbery look to his face. Jane notices this, notices the masklike quality of it, and she begins to tremble. Everything is oddly exaggerated — something is being said, they're telling her that Martin burned his hands, and another voice is murmuring something. Both men

go on talking, apologizing, getting ready to leave her there. She's
not fully awake. The lights in the room hurt her eyes; she feels
a little sick to her stomach. The two men go out on the porch
and then look back through the screen. "You take it easy, now,"
the younger one says to Jane. She closes the door, understands
that what she's been hearing under the flow of the past few moments is Martin's voice muttering her name, saying something.
She walks over to him.

"Jesus," he says. "It's awful. I burned my hands and I didn't
even know it. I didn't even feel it."

She says, "Tell me what happened."

"God," he says. "Wally Harmon's dead. God. I saw it happen."

"Milly —" she begins. She can't speak.

He's crying. She moves to the entrance of the kitchen and turns
to look at him. "I saw Milly tonight." The room seems terribly
small to her.

"The Van Pickel lumberyard went up. The warehouse. Jesus."

She goes into the kitchen and runs water. Outside the window
above the sink she sees the dim street, the shadows of houses
without light. She drinks part of a glass of water and then pours
the rest down the sink. Her throat is still very dry. When she
goes back into the living room, she finds him lying on his side,
facing the opposite wall.

"Martin?" she says.

"What?"

But she can't find anything to tell him. She says, "God — poor
Milly." Then she goes into the bedroom and begins putting away
the clothes. She doesn't hear him get up, and she's startled to
find him standing in the doorway, staring at her.

"What're you doing?" he asks.

She faces him, at a loss — and it's her hesitation that gives him
his answer.

"Jane?" he says, looking at the travel bag.

"Look," she tells him, "I had a little too much to drink tonight."

He just stares at her.

"Oh, this," she manages. "I — I was just going through what I
have to wear."

But it's too late. "Jesus," he says, turning from her a little.

"Martin," she says.

"What."

"Does — did somebody tell Milly?"

He nods. "Teddy. Teddy stayed with her. She was crazy. Crazy."

He looks at his hands. It's as if he just remembered them. They're wrapped tight; they look like two white clubs. "Jesus, Jane, are you —" He stops, shakes his head. "Jesus."

"Don't," she says.

"Without even talking to me about it —"

"Martin, this is not the time to talk about anything."

He's quiet a moment, standing there in the doorway. "I keep seeing it," he says. "I keep seeing Wally's face. The — the way his foot jerked. His foot jerked like with electricity and he was — oh, Christ, he was already dead."

"Oh, don't," she says. "Please. Don't talk. Stop picturing it."

"They gave me something to sleep," he says, "and I won't sleep." He wanders back into the living room. A few minutes later she goes to him there and finds that whatever the doctors gave him has worked. He's lying on his back, and he looks smaller somehow, his bandaged hands on his chest, his face pinched with grief, with whatever he's dreaming. He twitches and mutters something and moans. She turns the light off and tiptoes back to the bedroom. She's the one who won't sleep. She gets into the bed and huddles there, leaving the light on. Outside, the wind gets up — another storm rolls in off the plains. She listens as the rain begins, and hears the far-off drumming of thunder. The whole night seems deranged. She thinks of Wally Harmon, dead in the blowing, rainy dark. And then she remembers Milly and her bad dreams, how she looked coming from the downpour, the wet street, with the magazine held over her head — her body so rounded, so weighted down with her baby, her love, the love she had waited for, that she said had surprised her. These events are too much to think about, too awful to imagine. The world seems cruelly immense now, and remorselessly itself. When Martin groans in the other room, she wishes he'd stop, and then she imagines that it's another time, that she's just awakened from a dream and is trying to sleep while they all sit in her living room and talk the hours of the night away.

In the morning she's awake first. She gets up and wraps herself in a robe and then shuffles into the kitchen and puts coffee on.

For a minute it's like any other morning. She sits at the table to wait for the coffee water to boil. He comes in like someone entering a stranger's kitchen — his movements are tentative, almost shy. She's surprised to see that he's still in his uniform. He says, "I need you to help me go to the bathroom. I can't get my pants undone." He starts trying to work his belt loose.

"Wait," she says. "Here, hold on."

"I have to get out of these clothes, Jane. I think they smell like smoke."

"Let me do it," she says.

"Milly's in the hospital — they had to put her under sedation."

"Move your hands out of the way," Jane says to him.

She has to help him with everything, and when the time comes for him to eat, she has to feed him. She spoons scrambled eggs into his mouth, and holds the coffee cup to his lips, and when that's over with, she wipes his mouth and chin with a damp napkin. Then she starts bath water running, and helps him out of his underclothes. They work silently, and with a kind of embarrassment, until he's sitting down and the water is right. When she begins to run a soapy rag over his back, he utters a small sound of satisfaction and comfort. But then he's crying again. He wants to talk about Wally Harmon's death. He says he has to. He tells her that a piece of hot steel the size of an arrow dropped from the roof of the Van Pickel warehouse and hit poor Wally Harmon in the top of the back.

"It didn't kill him right away," he says, sniffling. "Oh, Jesus. He looked right at me and asked if I thought he'd be all right. We were talking about it, honey. He reached up — he — over his shoulder. He took hold of it for a second. Then he — then he looked at me and said he could feel it down in his stomach."

"Don't think about it," Jane says.

"Oh, God." He's sobbing. "God."

"Martin, honey —"

"I've done the best I could," he says, "haven't I?"

"Shhh," she says, bringing the warm rag over his shoulders and wringing it, so that the water runs down his back.

They're quiet again. Together they get him out of the tub, and then she dries him off, helps him into a pair of jeans.

"Thanks," he says, not looking at her. Then he says, "Jane."

She's holding his shirt out for him, waiting for him to turn and put his arms into the sleeves. She looks at him.

"Honey," he says.

"I'm calling in," she tells him. "I'll call Eveline. We'll go be with Milly."

"Last night," he says.

She looks straight at him.

He hesitates, glances down. "I — I'll try and do better." He seems about to cry again. For some reason this makes her feel suddenly very irritable and nervous. She turns from him, walks into the living room, and begins putting the sofa back in order. When he comes to the doorway and says her name, she doesn't answer, and he makes his way to the kitchen door.

"What're you doing?" she says to him.

"Can you give me some water?"

She moves into the kitchen and he follows her. She runs water, to get it cold, and he stands at her side. When the glass is filled, she holds it to his mouth. He swallows, and she takes the glass away. "If you want to talk about anything —" he says.

"Why don't you try to sleep awhile?" she says.

He says, "I know I've been talking about Wally —"

"Just, please — go lie down or something."

"When I woke up this morning, I remembered everything, and I thought you might be gone."

"Well, I'm not gone."

"I knew we were having some trouble, Jane —"

"Just let's not talk about it right now," she says. "All right? I have to go call Eveline." She walks into the bedroom, and when he comes in behind her, she tells him very gently to please go get off his feet. He backs off, makes his way into the living room. "Can you turn on the television?" he calls to her.

She does so. "What channel do you want?"

"Can you just go through them a little?"

She's patient. She waits for him to get a good look at each channel, waits for the commercials to end. Finally he settles on a rerun of *The Andy Griffith Show,* and she leaves him there. She fills the dishwasher and wipes off the kitchen table. Then she calls Eveline to tell her what's happened.

"You poor thing," Eveline says. "You must be so relieved. And I said all that bad stuff about Wally's wife."

Jane says, "You didn't mean it," and suddenly she's crying. She's got the phone held tight against her face, crying.

"You poor thing," Eveline says. "You want me to come over there?"

"No, it's all right — I'm all right."

"Poor Martin. Is he hurt bad?"

"It's his hands."

"Is it very painful?"

"Yes," Jane says.

Later, while he sleeps on the sofa, she wanders outside and walks down to the end of the driveway. The day is sunny and cool, with little cottony clouds — the kind of clear day that comes after a storm. She looks up and down the street. Nothing is moving. A few houses away someone has put up a flag, and it flutters in a stray breeze. This is the way it was, she remembers, when she first lived here — when she first stood on this sidewalk and marveled at how flat the land was, how far it stretched in all directions. Now she turns and makes her way back to the house, and then she finds herself in the garage. It's almost as if she's saying goodbye to everything, and as this thought occurs to her, she feels a little stir of sadness. Here, on the work table, side by side under the light from the one window, are Martin's model airplanes. He won't be able to work on them again for weeks. The light reveals the miniature details, the crevices and curves on which he lavished such care, gluing and sanding and painting. The little engines are lying on a paper towel at one end of the table; they smell just like real engines, and they're shiny with lubrication. She picks one of them up and turns it in the light, trying to understand what he might see in it that could require such time and attention. She wants to understand him. She remembers that when they dated, he liked to tell her about flying these planes, and his eyes would widen with excitement. She remembers that she liked him best when he was glad that way. She puts the little engine down, thinking how people change. She knows she's going to leave him, but just for this moment, standing among these things, she feels almost peaceful about it. She has, after all, no need to hurry. And as she steps out on the lawn, she realizes that she can take the time to think clearly about when and where; she can even change her mind. But she doesn't think she will.

He's up. He's in the hallway — he had apparently wakened and found her gone. "Jesus," he says. "I woke up and you weren't here."

"I didn't go anywhere," she says, and she smiles at him.

"I'm sorry," he says, starting to cry. "God, Janey, I'm so sorry. I'm all messed up here. I've got to go to the bathroom again."

She helps him. The two of them stand over the bowl. He's stopped crying now, though he says his hands hurt something awful. When he's finished, he thanks her, and then tries a bawdy joke. "You don't have to let go so soon."

She ignores this, and when she has him tucked safely away, he says, quietly, "I guess I better just go to bed and sleep some more."

She's trying to hold on to the feeling of peace and certainty she had in the garage. It's not even noon, and she's exhausted. She's very tired of thinking about everything. He's talking about his parents; later she'll have to call them. But then he says he wants his mother to hear his voice first, to know he's all right. He goes on — something about Milly and her unborn baby, and Teddy Lynch — but Jane can't quite hear him: he's a little unsteady on his feet, and they have trouble negotiating the hallway together.

In their bedroom she helps him out of his jeans and shirt, and she actually tucks him into the bed. Again he thanks her. She kisses his forehead, feels a sudden, sick-swooning sense of having wronged him somehow. That makes her stand straighter, makes her stiffen slightly.

"Jane?" he says.

She breathes. "Try to rest some more. You just need to rest now." He closes his eyes and she waits a little. He's not asleep. She sits at the foot of the bed and watches him. Perhaps ten minutes go by. Then he opens his eyes.

"Janey?"

"Shhh," she says.

He closes them again. It's as if he were her child. She thinks of him as he was when she first saw him, tall and sure of himself

in his reserves uniform, and the image makes her throat constrict.

At last he's asleep. When she's certain of this, she lifts herself
from the bed and carefully, quietly withdraws. As she closes the
door, something in the flow of her own mind appalls her, and
she stops, stands in the dim hallway, frozen in a kind of wonder:
she had been thinking in an abstract way, almost idly, as though
it had nothing at all to do with her, about how people will go to
such lengths leaving a room — wishing not to disturb, not to
awaken, a loved one.

RICHARD BAUSCH

A Kind of Simple, Happy Grace

FROM WIGWAG

THE REVEREND TARMIGIAN was not well. You could see it in his
face — a certain hollowness, a certain blueness in the skin. His
eyes lacked luster or brightness. He had a persistent, dry, deep
cough; he had lost a lot of weight. And yet on this fine, breezy
October day he was out on the big lawn in front of his church,
raking leaves. Father Russell watched him from the window of
his study, and knew that if he didn't walk over there and say
something, this morning — like so many recent mornings —
would be spent fretting and worrying about Tarmigian, seventy-
two years old and out raking leaves in the windy sun. He had
been planning to speak about it for weeks, but what could you
say to a man like that? An institution in Point Royal County, old
Tarmigian had been pastor of the neighboring church — Faith
Baptist, only a hundred yards away on the other side of Tallawaw Creek — for more than three decades. He referred to himself in conversation as Reverend Fixture. He was a tall, frail man
with wrinkled blue eyes and a wisp of fleecy blond hair above
each ear, and there were dimples in his cheeks. One of his favorite jokes — one of the many jokes he was fond of repeat-
ing — was that he had the eyes of a clown built above the natural
curve of a baby's bottom. He'd touch the dimples and smile, saying a thing like that. And the truth was he tended to joke too
much — even about the fact that he was apparently taxing himself beyond the dictates of good health for a man his age.

It seemed clear to Father Russell — who was all too often worried about his own health, though he was thirty years younger than Tarmigian — that something was driving the older man to these stunts of killing work: raking leaves all morning in the fall breezes, or climbing a ladder to clear drainspouts, or, as he did one day last week, lugging a bag of mulch across the road and up the hill to the little cemetery where his wife lay buried, as if there weren't fifteen people within arm's reach on any Sunday who would have done it gladly for him (and would have just as gladly stood by while he said his few quiet prayers over the grave). His wife had been dead twenty years, he had the reverential love and respect of the whole countryside, but something was driving the man, and, withal, there was often a species of amused cheerfulness about him almost like elation, as though he were keeping some wonderful secret.

It was infuriating: it violated all the rules of respect for one's own best interest. And today, watching him rake leaves, Father Russell decided that he would speak to him about it. He would find some way to broach the subject of the old man's health, and finally he would express an opinion about it.

He put a jacket on and went out and walked up the road to Tarmigian's church. The road went across a stone bridge over Tallawaw Creek and up a long incline. The air was blue and cool in the mottled shade, and there were little patches of steam on the creek when the breezes were still. The Reverend Tarmigian stopped raking, leaned on the handle of the rake, and watched Father Russell cross the bridge.

"Well, just in time for coffee."

"I'll have tea," Father Russell said, a little out of breath from the walk.

"You're winded," said Tarmigian.

"And you're white as a sheet."

It was true. Poor Tarmigian's cheeks were pale as death. There were two blotches on them, like bruises — caused, Father Russell was sure, by the blood vessels that were straining to break in the old man's head. He indicated the trees all around, burnished looking, still loaded with leaves, and even now dropping some of them, like part of an argument for the hopelessness of this task the old man had set for himself.

"Why don't you at least wait until they're finished?" Father Russell demanded.

"I admit, it's like emptying the ocean with a spoon." Tarmigian put his rake down and invited the other man into his kitchen for some hot tea. Father Russell followed him in, and watched him fuss and seem to worry, preparing it, and then he followed him into the study to sit among the books and talk. It was the old man's custom to take an hour every day in this book-lined room, though with this bad cold he'd contracted, he had lately done little of anything with regularity. He was too tired, or too sick. It was just an end-of-summer cold that he couldn't get rid of, he said, but Father Russell had observed the weight loss, the coughing; and the old man was willing to admit that lately his appetite had suffered.

"I can't keep anything down," he said. "Sort of keeps me discouraged from trying, you know? I'm sure when I get over this cold . . ."

"Medical science is advancing," said the priest, trying for sarcasm. "They have doctors now with their own offices, and instruments. It's all advanced to a sophisticated stage. You can get medicine for a cold."

"I'm fine. There's no need for anyone to worry."

Father Russell had seen denial before: indeed, he saw some version of it almost every day, and he had a rich understanding of the psychology of it. Yet Tarmigian's statement caused a surprising little clot of anger to form under the flow of his mind and left him feeling vaguely disoriented, as if the older man's blithe neglect of himself were a kind of personal affront.

Yet he found, too, that he couldn't come right out and say what he had come to believe: that the old man was jeopardizing his own health. The words wouldn't form on his lips. So he drank his tea and searched for an opening — a way of getting something across about learning to relax a little, learning to take it easy. There wasn't a lot to talk about beyond Tarmigian's anecdotes and chatter. The two men were not particularly close: Father Russell had come to his own parish from New York only a year ago, believing this little Virginia township to be the accidental equivalent of a demotion (the assignment, coming really like the draw of a ticket out of a hat, was less than satisfactory). He had felt almost immediately that the overfriendly elderly clergyman next door was a bit too southern for his taste — though Tarmigian was obviously a man of broad experience, having served in missions overseas as a young man, and it was true that he possessed a kind of simple grace. So, while the priest had in fact spent a lot of time in the first days trying to avoid him for fear of hurting the poor man's feelings, he had learned finally that Tarmigian was unavoidable, and had come to accept him as one of the mild irritations of the place in which he now found himself. He had even considered that the man had charm, was amusing and generous. He would admit that there had been times when he found himself surprised by a small stir of gladness when the old man could be seen on the little crossing bridge, heading down to pay another of his casual visits, as if there were nothing better to do than sit in Father Russell's parlor and make jokes about himself.

The trouble now, of course, was that everything about the old man, including his jokes, seemed tinged with the something awful that was clearly happening to him. And here Father Russell was, watching him cough, watching him hold up one hand as if to ward off anything in the way of advice or concern about it. The cough took him deep, so that he had to gasp to get his breath back; but then he cleared his throat and sipped more of the tea and, looking almost frightfully white around the eyes, smiled and said, "I have a good one for you, Reverend Russell. I had a couple — I won't name them — in my congregation, come to me yesterday afternoon, claiming that they were going to seek a divorce. You know how long they've been married? They've been married fifty-two years. Fifty-two years and they can't stand each other. I mean, can't stand to be in the same room with each other."

Father Russell was interested in spite of himself — and in spite of the fact that the old man had again called him Reverend. This would be another of Tarmigian's stories, or another of his jokes. He felt the need to head him off. "That cough," he said.

The other man looked at him as if he'd merely said a number, or recited the day's date.

"I think you should see a doctor about it."

"It's just a cold, Reverend."

"I don't mean to meddle —" said the priest.

"Yes, well. I was asking what you thought about a married couple, can't stand to be in the same room together after fifty-two years."

Father Russell said, "I guess I have to say I'd have trouble believing that."

"Well, believe it. And you know what I said to them? I said we'd talk about it for a while. Counseling, you know."

Father Russell said nothing.

"Of course," said Tarmigian, "as you well know, we permit divorce — when it seems called for."

"Yes," Father Russell said, feeling beaten.

"You know, I don't think it's a question of either one of them being interested in anybody else. Nobody's swept anybody off anybody's feet."

Father Russell waited for him to go on.

"I can't help thinking it's a little silly." Tarmigian smiled, sipped the tea, then put the cup down and leaned back, clasping his hands behind his head. "Fifty-two years of marriage and they want to untie the knot. What do you say, shall I send them over to you?"

The priest couldn't keep the sullen tone out of his voice. "I wouldn't know what to say to them."

"Well — you'd tell them to love one another. You'd tell them love is the very breath of living or some such thing. Just as I did."

Father Russell muttered, "That's what I'd have to tell them, of course."

"We concur." Tarmigian smiled again.

"What was their answer?"

"They were going to think about it. Give themselves some time to think, really. That's no joke." The Reverend Tarmigian laughed, coughing. Then it was just coughing.

"That's a terrible cough," said Father Russell, feeling futile and afraid and deeply irritable. His own words sounded to him like something learned by rote.

"Do you know what I think I'll tell them if they come back?"

Father Russell waited.

"I think I'll tell them to stick it out anyway, with each other."
Tarmigian looked at him and smiled. "Have you ever heard anything more absurd?"

Father Russell made a gesture he hoped the other took for
agreement.

Tarmigian went on: "It's probably exactly right — probably
exactly what they should do, and yet such odd advice to think of
giving two people who've been together fifty-two years. I mean,
when do you think the phrase 'sticking it out' would stop being
applicable?"

Father Russell indicated that he didn't know.

Tarmigian merely smiled.

"Very amusing," Father Russell said.

But the older man was coughing again.

From the beginning, there had been things Tarmigian said
and did which unnerved the priest. Father Russell was a man
who could be undone by certain kinds of boisterousness, and
there were matters of casual discourse he simply would never
understand. Yet, often enough over the seven months of their
association, he had entertained the suspicion that Tarmigian was
harboring a bitterness, and that his occasional mockery of himself was some sort of reaction to it, if it wasn't in fact a way of
releasing it.

Now Father Russell sipped his tea and looked out the window.
Leaves were flying in the wind. The road was in blue shade, and
the shade moved. There were houses beyond the hill, but from
here everything looked like a wilderness.

"Well," Tarmigian said, gaining control of himself. "Do you
know what my poor old couple say is their major complaint?"

Father Russell waited for him to go on.

"Their major complaint is they don't like the same TV programs. Now, can you imagine a thing like that?"

"Look," the priest blurted out, "I see you from my study window — You're — you don't get enough rest. I think you should
see a doctor about that cough."

Tarmigian waved this away. "I'm fit as a fiddle, as they say.
Really."

"If it's just a cold," said Father Russell, giving up. "Of course —"
He could think of nothing else to say.

"You worry too much," Tarmigian said. "You know, you've got bags under your eyes."

True.

In the long nights, Father Russell lay with a rosary tangled in his fingers and tried to pray, tried to stop his mind from playing tricks on him: the matter of greatest faith was, and had been for a very long time now, that every twist or turn of his body held a symptom; every change signified the onset of disease. It was all waiting to happen to him, and the anticipation of it sapped him, made him weak and sick at heart. He had begun to see that his own propensity for morbid anxiety about his health was worsening, and the daylight hours required all his courage. Frequently, he thought of Tarmigian as though the old man were in some strange way a reflection of his secretly held, worst fear. He recalled the lovely, sunny mornings of his first summer as a curate, when he was twenty-seven and fresh, and the future was made of slow time. This was not a healthy kind of thinking. It was middle age, he knew. It was a kind of spiritual dryness he had been taught to recognize and contend with. Yet each morning his dazed waking — from whatever fitful sleep the night had yielded him — was greeted with the pall of knowing that the aging pastor of the next-door church would be out in the open, performing some strenuous task. When the younger man looked out the window, the mere sight of the other building was enough to make him sick with anxiety.

On Friday, Father Russell went to St. Celia Hospital to attend to the needs of one of his own older parishioners, who had broken her hip in a fall, and while he was there a nurse walked in and asked that he administer the sacrament of extreme unction to a man in the emergency room. He followed her down the hall and the stairs to the first floor, and while they walked she told him the man had suffered a heart attack, that he was already beyond help. She said this almost matter-of-factly, and Father Russell looked at the delicate curve of her ears, thinking about design. This was, of course, an odd thing to be thinking about now, but he cultivated it for just that reason. Early in his priesthood, he had learned to make his mind settle on other things during moments requiring him to look on sickness and death — small things, outside the province of questions of eternity and salvation, and the common doom. It was what he had always managed as a protection against too clear a memory of certain daily horrors — images that could blow through him in the night, like the very winds of fright and despair — and if over the years it had mostly worked, it had recently been in the process of failing him. Entering the crowded emergency room, he was concentrating on the coils of a young woman's ear as an instrument of hearing when he saw Tarmigian sitting on one of the chairs near the television, his hand in a bandage, his white face sunk over the pages of a magazine.

Tarmigian looked up, then smiled, held up the bandaged hand. There wasn't time for the two men to speak. Father Russell nodded at him and went on, following the nurse, feeling strangely precarious and weak. He looked over his shoulder at Tarmigian, who had simply gone back to reading the magazine, and then he was attending to what the nurse had brought him to see: she pulled a curtain aside to reveal a gurney with two people on it — a man and a woman of roughly the same late middle age, the woman cradling the man's head in her arms and whispering something to him.

"Mrs. Simpson," the nurse said, "here is the priest."

Father Russell stood there while the woman looked at him. She was perhaps fifty-five, with iron-gray hair and small, round wet eyes. "Mrs. Simpson," he said to her.

"He's my husband," she murmured, rising, letting the man's head down carefully. His eyes were wide, as was his mouth. "My Jack. Oh, Jack, Jack."

Father Russell stepped forward and took her hands, and she cried, staring down at her husband's face.

"He's gone," she said. "We were talking, you know. We were thinking about going down to see the kids. And he just put his head down. We were talking about how the kids never come to visit and we were going to surprise them."

"Mrs. Simpson," the nurse said, "would you like a sedative? Something to settle your nerves —"

"No," said Mrs. Simpson. "I'm fine."

Father Russell began to say the rite, and she stood by him, gazing down at the dead man.

"He just put his head down," she said. Her hands trembled over the cloth of her husband's shirt, which was open wide at the

chest, and it was a moment before Father Russell understood
that she was trying to button the shirt. But her hands were shaking too badly. She patted the shirt down, then bowed her head
and sobbed. Somewhere in the jangled apparatus of the room
something was beeping, and he heard air rushing through pipes;
everything was obscured in the intricacies of procedure. He was
simply staring at the dead man's blank countenance, all sound
and confusion and movement falling away from him. It was as
though he had never looked at anything like this before; he remained quite still, in a profound quiet, for some minutes before
Mrs. Simpson got his attention again. She had taken him by the
wrist.

"Father," she was saying. "Father, he was a good man. God
has taken him home, hasn't He?"

Father Russell turned to face the woman, to take her hands
into his own, and to whisper the words of hope.

"I think seeing you there, at the hospital —" he said to Tarmigian. "It upset me in a strange way."

"I cut my hand opening the paint jar," Tarmigian said. He
was standing on a stepladder in the upstairs hallway of his rectory, painting the crown molding. Father Russell had walked out
of his church in the chill of the first frost and made his way
across the little stone bridge and up the incline to the old man's
door, had knocked and been told to enter, and, entering, finding no one, had reached back and knocked again.

"Up here," came Tarmigian's voice.

And the priest had climbed the stairs in a kind of torpor, his
heart beating in his neck and face. He had blurted out that he
wasn't feeling right, hadn't slept at all well, and finally he'd begun to hint at what he could divine as to why. He was now sitting
on the top step, hat in hand, still carrying with him the sense of
the long night he had spent, lying awake in the dark, seeing not
the dead face of poor Mrs. Simpson's husband but Tarmigian
holding up the bandaged hand and smiling. The image had
wakened him each time he had drifted toward sleep.

"Something's happening to me," he said now, unable to believe himself.

The other man was reaching high, concentrating. The ladder
was rickety.

"Do you want me to hold the ladder?"

"Pardon me?"

"Nothing."

"Did you want to know if I wanted you to hold the ladder?"

"Well, do you?"

"You're worried I'll fall, right?"

"I would like to help."

"And did you say something was happening to you?"

Father Russell said nothing.

"Forget the ladder, son."

"I don't understand myself lately," said the priest.

"Are you making me your confessor or something there, Reverend?" Tarmigian asked.

"I — I can't —"

"I don't think I'm equipped."

"I've looked at the dead before," said Father Russell. "I've held them in my arms. I've never been very much afraid of it. I mean, I've never been morbid."

"Morbidity is an indulgence."

"Yes, I know."

"Simply refuse to indulge yourself."

"I'm forty-three —"

"A difficult age, you know, because you don't know whether you fit with the grown-ups or the children." Tarmigian paused to cough. He held the top step of the ladder with both hands, and his shoulders shook. Everything tottered. Then he stopped, breathed, wiped his mouth with the back of one hand.

Father Russell said, "I meant to say I don't think I'm worried about myself."

"Well, that's good."

"I'm going to call and make you an appointment with a doctor."

"I'm fine. I've got a cold. I've coughed like this all my life."

"Nevertheless."

Tarmigian smiled at him. "You're a good man, but you're learning a tendency."

No peace.

Father Russell had entered the priesthood without the sort of fervent sense of vocation that he believed others had. In fact, he had been troubled by serious doubts about it right up to the last year of seminary — doubts that, in spite of his confessor's reassurances to the contrary, he felt were more than the normal upsets of seminary life. In the first place, he had come to it against the wishes of his father, who had entertained dreams of a career in law for him; and while his mother applauded the decision, her own dream of grandchildren was visibly languishing in her eyes as the time of his final vows approached. Both parents had died within a month of each other during his last year of studies, and so there had been times when he'd also had to contend with an apprehension that he might unconsciously be learning to use his vocation as a form of refuge. But finally, nearing the end of his training, seeing the completion of the journey, something in him rejoiced, and he came to believe that this was what having a true vocation was: no extremes of emotion, no real sense of a break with the world, though the terms of his faith and the ancient ceremony that his training prepared him to celebrate spoke of just that. He was even-tempered and confident, and when he was ordained he set about the business of being a parish priest. There were things to involve himself in, and he found that he could be energetic and enthusiastic about most of them. The life was satisfying in ways he hadn't expected, and if in his less confident moments some part of him suspected that he was not progressing spiritually, he was also not the sort of man to go very deeply into such questions: there were things to do. He was not a contemplative.

Or hadn't been. Something was shifting in his soul.

Nights were awful. He couldn't even pray now. He stood at his rectory window and looked at the light in the old man's window, and his imagination presented him with the belief that he could hear the faint rattle of the deep cough, though he knew it was impossible across that distance. When he said the morning mass, he leaned down over the host, and had to work to remember the words. The stolid, calm faces of his parishioners were almost ugly in their absurd confidence in him, their smiles of happy expectation and welcome. He took their hospitality and their care of him as his due, and felt waves of despair at the ease of it, the habitual taste and lure of it, and all the time his body was aching in ways that filled him with dread, and reminded him of Tarmigian's ravaged features.

Sunday morning early, it began to rain. Someone called, then hung up before he could answer. He had been asleep; the loud ring at that hour frightened him, changed his heartbeat. He took his own pulse, then stood at his window and gazed at the darkened shape of Tarmigian's church. That morning, after the second mass, exhausted, miserable, he crossed the bridge in the rain and knocked on the old man's door. There wasn't any answer. He peered through the window on the porch and saw that there were dishes on the table in the kitchen, which was visible through the arched hallway off the living room. Tarmigian's Bible lay open on the arm of the easy chair. Father Russell knocked loudly, and then walked around the building, into the church itself. It was quiet. The wind stirred outside, and sounded like traffic whooshing by. Father Russell could feel his own heartbeat in the pit of his stomach. He sat down in the last pew of Tarmigian's church and tried to calm himself down. Perhaps ten minutes went by, and then he heard voices. The old man was coming up the walk outside, talking to someone. Father Russell stood, thought absurdly of trying to hide, but then the door was opened and Tarmigian walked in, accompanied by an old woman in a white woolen shawl. Tarmigian had a big umbrella, which he shook down and folded, breathing heavily from the walk and looking, as always, even in the pall of his decline, amused by something. He hadn't seen Father Russell yet, though the old woman had. She nodded, and smiled broadly, her hands folded neatly over a small black purse.

"Well," Tarmigian said, "to what do we owe this honor, Reverend?"

It struck Father Russell that they might be laughing at him. He dismissed this thought, and, clearing his throat, said, "I — I wanted to see you." His own voice sounded stiff and somehow foolish to him. He cleared his throat again.

"This is Father Russell," Tarmigian said, loud, to the old woman. Then he touched her shoulder and looked at the priest. "Mrs. Aldenberry."

"God bless you," Mrs. Aldenberry said.

"Mrs. Aldenberry wants a divorce," Tarmigian murmured.

"Eh?" she said. Then, turning to Father Russell: "I'm hard of hearing."

"She wants to have her own television set," Tarmigian whispered.

"Pardon me?"

"And her own room."

"I'm hard of hearing," she said cheerfully to the priest. "I'm deaf as a post."

"Irritates her husband," Tarmigian said.

"I'm sorry," said the woman. "I can't hear a thing."

Tarmigian guided her to the last row of seats, and she sat down there, still clutching the purse. She seemed quite content, quite trustful, and the old minister, beginning to stutter into a deep cough, winked at Father Russell — as if to say this was all very entertaining. "Now," he said, taking the priest by the elbow, "let's get to the flattering part of all this — you walking over here getting yourself all wet because you're worried about me."

"I just wanted to stop by," Father Russell said. He was almost pleading. The old man's face, in the dim light, looked appallingly bony and pale.

"Look at you," said Tarmigian. "You're shaking."

Father Russell could not speak.

"Are you all right now?"

The priest was assailed by the feeling that the older man found him somehow ridiculous — and he remembered the initial sense he'd had, when Tarmigian and Mrs. Aldenberry entered, that he was being laughed at. "I just wanted to see how you were doing," he said.

"I'm a little under the weather," Tarmigian said, smiling.

And it dawned on Father Russell, with the force of a physical blow, that the old man knew quite well he was dying.

Tarmigian indicated Mrs. Aldenberry with a nod of his head. "Now I have to attend to the depths of this lady's sorrow. You know, she says she should've listened to her mother and not married Mr. Aldenberry fifty-two years ago. Now, you think about that a little. Imagine her standing in a room slapping her forehead and saying, What a mistake! Fifty-two years! Oops! A mistake. She's glad she woke up in time. Think of it. And, I'll tell you, Reverend, I think she feels lucky."

Mrs. Aldenberry made a prim, throat-clearing sound, then turned in her seat, looking at them.

"Well," Tarmigian said, straightening, wiping the smile from his face. He offered his hand to the priest. "Shake hands. No, let's embrace. Let's give this poor woman an ecumenical thrill."

Father Russell shook hands, then walked into the old man's extended arms. It felt like a kind of collapse. He was breathing the odor of bay rum and talcum, and of something else, too, something indefinable and dark, and to his astonishment he found himself fighting back tears. The two men stood there while Mrs. Aldenberry watched, and Father Russell was unable to control the sputtering and trembling that took hold of him. When Tarmigian broke the embrace, the priest turned away, trying to compose himself. Tarmigian was coughing again.

"Excuse me," said Mrs. Aldenberry. She seemed a little confused.

Tarmigian held up one hand, still coughing; his eyes had grown wide with the effort.

"Hot toddy — honey with a touch of lemon and whiskey," she said, to no one in particular. "Works like a charm."

Father Russell thought about how someone her age would indeed learn to feel that small folk remedies were effective in stopping illness. It was logical, and reasonable, and he was surprised by the force of his own resentment of her for it. He stood there wiping his eyes and felt his heart constrict with hatred.

"There," Tarmigian said, getting his breath back.

"Hot toddy," said Mrs. Aldenberry. "Never knew it to fail." She was looking from one to the other of the two men, her expression taking on something of the look of tolerance. "Fix you up like new," she said, turning her attention to the priest, who could not stop blubbering. "What's — what's going on here?"

Father Russell had a moment of sensing that everything Tarmigian had done or said over the past year was somehow freighted with this one moment, and it took him a few seconds to recognize the implausibility of such a thing. No one could have planned it, or anticipated it: this one aimless gesture of humor — out of a habit of humorous gestures, and from a brave old man sick to death — that could feel so much like health, like the breath of new life.

He couldn't stop crying. He brought out a handkerchief and covered his face with it, then wiped his forehead. It was quiet. The other two were gazing at him. He straightened, caught his breath. "Excuse me."

"No excuse needed," Tarmigian said, looking down. His smile seemed tentative and sad now. Even a little afraid.

"What's going on here?" the old woman wanted to know.

"Why, nothing out of the ordinary," Tarmigian said, shifting the weight of his skeletal body, clearing his throat, managing to speak very loudly, very gently, so as to reassure her, but making certain, too, that she could hear him.

MADISON SMARTT BELL

Finding Natasha

FROM ANTAEUS

"HEY, CAPTAIN," Stuart said. He'd seen the dog as soon as he turned the corner, stretched over the doorsill of the bar in a wide amber beam of the afternoon sun. "Hey, babe, you still remember me?" He hesitated, just outside the doorway, in case the big German shepherd did not remember him after all. No doubt that Captain was a lot older now, shrunken into his bagging skin, the hair along the ridge of his back turning white. A yellow eye opened briefly on Stuart and then drowsed slowly back shut. Stuart took a long step over the dog and was inside the shadowy space of the bar.

He had expected Henry to be behind the counter and he felt a pulse of disappointment when he saw it was Arthur instead. On Saturday nights Arthur would often cover the bar while Henry and Isabel went out to dinner, but ordinarily they wouldn't have left so early, not at midafternoon. Stuart sat down at the outside corner of the bar. When Arthur got over to him Stuart could see he didn't remember who he was.

"Short beer," Stuart said, not especially wanting to get into it just yet. There were two people sitting at the far end of the counter, he couldn't quite make out their faces in the shadows, and nobody else in the place. He swiveled his stool back toward the door and as his eyes adjusted to the dim he saw the new paint, new paneling. It had all been done over, the broken booths and tables all replaced, a new jukebox right where the pay phone used to be. The opposite wall was practically papered with portrait sketches of the Mets.

"Hey, what's going on?" Stuart said. Arthur had put down the glass of beer and picked up the dollar Stuart had laid on the bar. "Hey, you even got new glasses too? Henry and Isabel do all this work?"

"They retired," Arthur said, staring at Stuart, like he knew he ought to recognize him now. "What, you haven't been around in a while, right? You move in Manhattan?"

"Further than that," Stuart said. He pushed the beer glass a little away from him. A weird little bell-shaped thing, nothing like the straight tumblers Henry had used.

"Who would it be but Stuart?" said one of the men at the far end of the bar. Stuart peered back into the dim. "Give him a shot on me, Arthur."

"Clifton," Stuart said. Arthur was reaching behind him for a bottle of Jack, he'd remembered that much now, at least.

"Nah," Stuart said. "No thanks."

"What, you don't drink anymore either?" Clifton said.

"I drink," Stuart said. "It's a little early." Clifton was on his feet, walking up into the light toward him now. He looked like he'd had little sleep and there was reddish stubble on his face. Stuart shifted to the edge of his stool and put one foot on the floor.

"You're back, hey?" Clifton said.

"Righto," Stuart said.

Clifton parted T-shirt from jeans to scratch at his shriveled belly.

"Miss your old friends?"

"Some of them," Stuart said. "Any of them still around?"

"Like the song goes," Clifton said. "They're all dead or in prison."

"Ah, but I see you're still here, though."

"Yeah. Partially."

"What about Ricky?"

"He's around, sometimes. Moved over to Greenpoint, though."

"And Rita?"

"I don't know, I heard she went to L.A."

"Thought I saw Tombo over around Tompkins Square . . ."

"Probably you did. He's still around there as far as I know."

"What about Natasha, then?"

"Ah," Clifton said. "You know I can't remember when I last saw Natasha."

"She still doing business with Uncle Bill, you think?"

"Uncle Bill got sick and died," Clifton said, and glanced up at the clock. "Speaking of which, I got to make a little run . . ."

"Yeah, well," Stuart said. "Great to see you and everything."

"Yeah," Clifton said. "What do you need?"

"Man," Stuart said. "You can't talk about that in Henry's place."

"You been away quite a while, babe," Clifton said. "It's not Henry's place anymore. So, you know. I can be back in a hour."

"Not to see me," Stuart said. "No more."

"Yeah? We'll see you," Clifton said. "Dig you later, babe." He stepped over the dog and went out through the bar of sunlight reddening in the doorway.

Stuart raised his hand and let it drop on the counter.

"They moved too?" he said. "They moved out of upstairs?"

"Yeah," Arthur said. "Out to Starrett City."

"Man," Stuart said. "Can't quite get used to it."

"The new guy opens the kitchen back up," Arthur said. "That should really make a difference."

"What now?" Stuart got up and went toward the back. A half partition had been raised in front of the area where Henry and Isabel used to have their own meals, and now there were four small tables set up as for a restaurant. Stuart turned back to Arthur.

"Captain lets people go back in there now?" Stuart walked back to his stool and sat. "Man, used to be if you just stepped over that line he was right there ready to take your leg off for you."

"I think he'll have to get over that," Arthur said. "He's old for all that, anyhow." The dog heaved himself up from the doorsill, walked back into the room, and lay stiffly down again.

"Yeah, Captain, getting cold, you're right," Arthur said. Then to Stuart: "Want to shut that door?"

Stuart got up. It had been a mild fall day but now the air had a winter bite. He pushed the door shut and stayed for a minute, squinting through the window at the dropping sun, across the VFW decal on the pane.

"Can't believe they'd of left the dog here," he said, turning back toward the counter.

"Henry comes by to see him," Arthur said. "You couldn't take him out of this place, though. He would just die."

Upstate, the week before, it had turned cold early, and alongside the railroad track the river was choked with ice. Stuart had bought papers at the station, the *News,* the *Post,* but he couldn't seem to focus on the print. From the far shore of the Hudson, chilly brown bluffs frowned over at him, sliding back and back. The train ran so low on the east bank it seemed that one long step could have carried him onto the surface of the river, though solid as the ice appeared it could hardly have held anybody's weight so early in the season. He stared through the smutty window of his car, the view infrequently broken up by a tree jolting by, or a building, or the long low sheds at the stations: New Hamburg, Beacon, Cold Spring. Opposite West Point the ice vanished and the river's surface turned steel smooth and gray.

If he'd been a fish, Stuart caught himself wondering, how much farther down could he swim without dissolving? Chemicals warmed the water down here, as much as and more than any freaks of weather. What fish would swim into that kind of trouble? He'd slept little the night before, his last night in Millbrook, so maybe that and too much coffee accounted for the jitters that worsened as Tarrytown and Yonkers fell back by, and rose toward actual nausea when the George Washington Bridge, almost a mirage downriver, floated into clearer view. If he'd been a fish he could breathe water, though the water here might kill or change him. He was headed into a hostile element, a diver for what pearl he couldn't say. The train dragged toward 125th Street like a weight pulling him under. The couple of years he'd been away were long enough he should have stayed forever. No point to come back now, so late, unless to recover something, what? The train dropped along the dark vector of the tunnel to Grand Central, and Stuart, like a hooded hawk, grew calm.

An hour or two and he'd remembered how to swim again, or glide. A thermal carried him up into a Times Square hotel, one of the kind where they did a take when he said he wanted the room all night, but by the week it turned out to be a bargain. Suspended in some other current, Stuart lazed back out into the street and drifted, from a bar to a street-corner stand to one of the old needle parks to another bar, and so on. *Don't go where you used to go,* they'd told him at the center, *don't see those same old people, or you'll fall.* No doubt that bigger, meaner fish still eyed him from their neighbor eddies, but he wasn't bleeding anymore, and a flick of tail or fin shot all of them away.

The weather was still bland down here, much milder than upstate, though it began to have its bitter aftertaste of cold. Stuart cruised up into the chill of the evening, watching whores and dealers check him over before they swirled away, always wondering if he might run into Natasha. He was not exactly looking yet, but developing a ghost of an intention. If he had asked himself, *Why her?* he would have had no answer. Just . . . Natasha. He had written her a time or two from Millbrook, hadn't had anything back, not that he'd expected it. Why Natasha? Others had been as close, or closer, and he didn't want to look for them. He wasn't looking for Natasha either. It had been spontaneous at first, this feeling that she was about to appear.

Clifton had been wrong about Rita, Stuart eventually found out. She wasn't in L.A. after all, she was in Bellevue getting over hepatitis A. They made him take a shot of gamma globulin when he went in to see her, even though he tried to tell them how long he'd been upstate. He also tried a joke about needles, but the nurses didn't laugh. When Rita invited him to sit down he had to tell her no.

"Funny, almost everybody seems to say that," Rita said. Her smile was not particularly bright. She was on a big ward, but curtains ran on tracks between the beds, and there were a couple of chairs pulled up to her nightstand, with magazines piled on the seats. The whites of her eyes were still a funny color and she was so thin that Stuart had trouble telling what were the lines of her body and what were only wrinkles in the sheet.

"Well, now," Stuart said. "You look good."

"Don't give me that," Rita said. "I look like I'm gonna die."

"You're not," Stuart said.

"Not this time," Rita said.

Stuart groped for a commonplace.

"Clifton told me you went west."

"No way," Rita said, patting the mattress with a bony hand. "I been right here."

"When do you get out?" Stuart said.

"I don't know. Two weeks more maybe. They don't want to give me a date."

Rita's folding alarm clock ticked loudly across the next patch of silence.

"You need anything?" Stuart said.

"Not that I can get."

"Well, let me know, O.K.?" Stuart pulled the curtain back and paused in the gap. "Hey. I been kind of trying to get hold of Natasha. You wouldn't know what she's been up to, would you?"

"I know she hasn't been up here," Rita said. "Not a whole lot else. Last I heard she was tricking for Uncle Bill."

"My God," Stuart said. "That sounds like a losing proposition."

"You know how it is," Rita said. "She's got a nice big nut to make every day."

"I guess," Stuart said. "Hey, but Clifton told me Uncle Bill was dead."

"Is that right," Rita said. "Clifton seems to be kind of full of bad information these days."

Bars and coffee shops, coffee shops and bars. Stuart circled the island from end to end of the old boundaries: the Marlin, McCarthy's, Three Roses, the Chinatown spots, anywhere she might have come in for any reason, rest her feet, get out of the weather, kill time waiting to score. Some places they remembered what he drank, but mostly not, and every now and then he'd meet somebody else who hadn't seen Natasha.

"Nah, man, she ain't been around *here*."

"Didn't I hear she went to Chicago? I can't think if it was her or somebody else. Memory slips a little on the fourth one . . ."

"Haven't seen her in about eight months. Maybe not since last summer . . ."

"Hey Stuart, what ever happened to that snippy little black-haired girl you used to hang around with?"

Wish I knew . . . On sleepless nights, he'd eat small-hour breakfasts at the Golden Corner or someplace just about like it, hunched down behind a newspaper, eavesdropping on the booths around him full of hookers on break, waiting for the voice or the name. By the time winter set hard in the city he'd started on the false alarms, recognizing Natasha in just about any middle-sized dark-haired white girl. It happened more than once a night sometimes, he'd have to walk right up to whomever he'd spotted and then at the last minute veer away. He did that so many times that the hookers started calling him Mr. No-Money Man.

Uncle Bill's place was up at 125th Street near the Chinese restaurant, just past the train trestle. A black kid with his hair done up in tight cornrows was waiting by the entry when Stuart arrived, one leg cocked up on the railing, the loose foot swinging to its limit like the pendulum of a clock. Stuart stood sideways to keep one eye on him while he studied the row of bells. The third one now said "Childress" instead of "B.B." like it should have, but he reached to ring it anyway.

"Man done gone," the black kid said. Stuart turned all the way toward him.

"What man is that?"

"Billbro, who else?"

"Know where he went?"

The kid spat over the railing.

"You got a cigarette on you, man?"

Stuart passed him a single Marlboro.

"He in the trench," the kid said. "There's a place just about ten blocks up can fix what it is you need."

Stuart laughed briefly.

"You think I'm the right color to be going about ten blocks up from here?"

The kid grinned and blew some smoke.

"Long's you go with *me* you are."

"Thanks anyway," Stuart said. "It was a personal visit kind of thing. What was this trench you were talking about?"

"Out on one of them islands, I forget." The kid's tennis shoe, fat with thick lacing and white as new bones, beat back and forth on the hinge of his knee. "You know, when you die without no money, then they shove you in the trench."

"Oh," Stuart said. "That trench. Do you get a box at least?"

"I don't think so, bro," the kid said. "Maybe you might get a bag."

Up at Millbrook, Stuart's image of Natasha had been clear as a photograph tacked to the wall, but once he was back in the city it began to blur and fade and run together in a swamp of other faces: magazine covers, or actresses on posters outside the movies, and always and especially the dozens of near-misses that kept on slipping past him. Now her memory was less a face and figure than just a group of gestures, and these too began to dissipate and dissolve, until when he thought of Natasha he often thought of a painting he'd once seen by Manet: a full-length portrait of a woman in a gray dustcoat down to her feet, one hand lightly extended toward what — a birdcage? He couldn't even remember the painting all that well. The woman in the portrait was nothing like Natasha, she had a totally different face, was taller, heavier, had red hair. Yet the cool repose of her expression also managed to suggest that she was poised at the edge of something. Stuart began to doubt if he would recognize Natasha when he found her, and what if he'd already passed her by? He recognized people who *weren't* her frequently enough, that much was for sure.

Stuart was trying to outlast a drunk with a three A.M. breakfast at the Golden Corner when a hooker slid into the booth across from him.

"I been thinking about you, Mr. No-Money Man," she said. "I been thinking, if you ate a little bit less breakfast, you might have a little bit more money." When she laughed, her eyes half disappeared into warm crinkles at their corners. Stuart saw she was a lot older than she wanted to appear, but not bad looking still, in a stringy kind of way. He sort of liked her face, under all the make-up. She was wearing white lipstick and white eye shadow, on skin the shade of tan kid leather. The wig she had on was a color no hair had ever been.

"I bet you got fifty cent right now," she said. "Buy me a cup of coffee."

"Get the number ten breakfast if you want it," Stuart said. "Or anything else they got." He was in a slightly reckless condition and a lot of his concentration was being spent on keeping her from splitting into twos and fours.

"*Hell,* yes," she said, and shouted an order toward the counter. "I knew you had that money all along."

"Not that much," Stuart said, laying down his fork.

"Enough," she said, aiming a long fingernail at his nose. "Your trouble is you think you can't find what you need. You know I seen you looking. Up and down and up and down —" She slapped the table. "You might not think it but I can do it all myself, do it real well too."

"Breakfast only," Stuart said, and as if those were the magic words, an oblong plate of hash and eggs came skidding into the space between her elbows.

"I got it now," she said, biting into a triangle of damp toast. "You not looking for some*thing.* You looking for some*body,* right?"

"Yeah," Stuart said. "Right."

"Have to be a girlfriend."

"As a matter of fact, no," Stuart said. "Just somebody I used to know."

"What for, then?"

"I don't know," Stuart said. "I think I got survivor syndrome."

"Say what?"

"I feel responsible," Stuart said, hearing his words begin to slur. "For like . . . for everybody. Don't ask me why but I always felt like she'd be the only one I could do anything about." He elbowed his plate out of the way and clasped his hands in front of him. "It's got to be like a long chain of people, see? I take hold of her and she takes hold of somebody else and finally somebody takes hold of you maybe, and then if everybody holds on tight we all get out of here."

The hooker shoveled in a large amount of hash and eggs with a few rapid movements and then looked back up.

"Out of where?"

"Ah, I can't explain it," Stuart said, fumbling out a cigarette. "Whose idea was this, anyway?"

The hooker stared at him, not smiling so much now.

"You be knee-walking drunk once you stand up, won't you?" she said after a while. "Man, where you coming from with this kind of talk?"

"Straight out of hell," Stuart said, trying to get his cigarette together with his match. "You familiar with the place?"

Over the winter he started going to the kung fu movies, across 42nd Street and around Times Square. It was a better time killer than drinking for him now; he'd tried getting drunk a few more times but he didn't much like where it took him. He went to the movies at night or sometimes in the afternoons, wearing a knit cap pulled down to his eye sockets so others couldn't tell much about him in the dark. It would take him a while, sometimes, to find a seat. Often whole sections had been ripped out, and also he liked to get one that put his back to a post or some other barrier. In the half-light reflected back from the screen, the rest of the audience milled through clouds of dope smoke, dealing for sinsé or street ludes or dust, each cluster playing a different boom box, usually louder than the soundtrack. They only turned to the screen when there was fighting, but the fight scenes always got their whole attention, bringing screams of approval from every cranny of the huge decaying theaters.

Stuart, on the other hand, always watched all the way through, even the tedious love scenes. He was not very discriminating, could watch the same picture again and again, often staying so long he would have forgotten whether it was day or night by the time he returned to the street. The movies were all so similar that there was not much to choose among them, if you were going to bother to watch them at all. He observed that the theme of *return* was prevalent. What the returning person usually did was kill people, keeping it up until there was no one left or he was killed himself.

Twisted among the lumps and rickets of his moldy ricket of a bed, Stuart falls into a dream so deep and profoundly revealing that at every juncture of it he posts his waking self a message: You *must* remember this. The dream is room within room within room, each suppressing its breathless secret, and on every threshold, Stuart swears he will remember. Each revelation has sufficient power to make him almost weep. When he sits up suddenly awake, the message is still thinly wrapped around him, bound up in a single word, a name.

Clifton. Stuart stared at a gleaming crack in the gritty window-pane, an arm's reach across the space between the bedstead and the wall. *Clifton,* that was nothing but nothing, and the dream was entirely gone. He flopped back over onto his side, eyes falling back shut, fingers begin to twitch, and a shard of the dream returns to him. The self of his dream comes hurrying from a building and in passing glances at a peddler on the sidewalk, a concrete-colored man propping up a dismal scrap of a tree. Its branches are hung with little figurines carved in wood and stone, and Stuart, hastening on his way, takes in as a matter of course that each of them astonishingly lives, is animate, moving toward the others, or away. In the dream he rushes past as though it were completely ordinary, but now he is transfixed by the gem-like movement of the tree, this nonsense miracle, a mere wonder outside the context of the dream, and uninterpretable. Stuart sat back up in the knot of his grimy blanket, muttering, *Clifton.* Surely, somewhere in all of this there must be something to extract.

Back in Brooklyn, Stuart checked in Henry's old bar to see if anyone knew where Clifton was living now and found that no one did. He tried the old place up on Broadway and the super sent him back around the corner to a half-renovated building between two shells on South 8th Street. It was a sunny day, though cold, and even the well to the basement door was full of light. Stuart rolled his newspaper tighter in his right hand and rapped on the door with his left. It took five or ten minutes of off-and-on knocking before the door pulled back on the chain, then re-closed and opened all the way.

"You been a long time coming," Clifton said. Inside, the light that leaked down from the street level was thin and watery. Clifton shimmered vaguely as he yawned and stretched; it looked like he'd been caught asleep, though it was well past noon. There was something that smelled to Stuart a little like old blood. He followed Clifton into the room and kicked the door shut behind him with his heel.

"The worried man," Clifton said, bending away from Stuart to get a T-shirt from the bed. "Well, babe, you ready for me to make your troubles go away?"

"Can you?" Stuart said. "Clifton?" When Clifton began to turn toward him, Stuart lashed at him with the rolled newspaper, and the heavy elbow of pipe he'd furled inside it knocked Clifton all the way over and sent him sliding into the rear wall.

"What in hell is the matter with you?" Clifton said. He sat up against the wall and stroked at the side of his mouth, his finger coming away red from a little cut. "Have you gone crazy or what?" Stuart looked down at him, trying to feel something, anything, but could not. He thought for no reason of the trench, bags jumbled into it, barely covered with a damp film of dirt.

"Just curious," he said haltingly.

"Yeah, well, are you satisfied now?"

"Not really," Stuart said. The newspaper hung at the full length of his arm, pointed at the floor. "I was thinking I might beat your face out the back of your head, but I don't really feel like it now."

"That's real good, Stuart," Clifton said. "I'm glad you don't feel like it now. You don't maybe want to tell me why you felt like it a minute ago?"

"I don't know why," Stuart said. "What happened to Natasha?"

"Man, are you kidding me, man?" Clifton said. "I'm going to tell you the truth now, O.K. *I don't freaking know.*"

Stuart took a step forward, hefting the newspaper. Clifton raised one hand more or less in front of his face and pushed up into a crouch with the other.

"Hey, I would tell you now if I knew, man," he said. "You got the edge on me, O.K.? Besides, what would I want to hide it for? I don't know any more than you do, man."

"O.K.," Stuart said, and let the newspaper fall back to rest against his thigh. Clifton reached into the side of his mouth and took something out and looked at it.

"This is my tooth I got here, man," he said. "I cannot believe you did this over that dumb freaking chick."

"I had a dream," Stuart said, "but maybe this wasn't what it was supposed to be about."

Clifton pushed himself up off the floor and stood, pressing the T-shirt over the bleeding edge of his mouth.

"Yeah, well, thanks for stopping by," he said, words a little slurred by the cloth. "Next time I see you I'm going to kill you, you do know that, I hope."

"No you won't," Stuart said.

"Maybe, maybe not." Clifton said. "Don't turn your back."

Almost every day he bought a paper and almost every day he didn't read much of it. He'd glance through quickly and then roll it and carry it all day, till the front pages began to curl and tatter and the ink started to bleed off on his fingers. After a while the feel of the rolled newspapers stopped reminding him directly of Clifton and only made him uncomfortable in a dull way he couldn't identify.

There was always too much news about missing people, and too many of the ones who weren't missing were dead. Every time he heard about someone else missing he wondered how many just vanished without being missed. Every third person he passed on the street was probably missing from somewhere.

"Missing" was no more than a whitewash; a better word would be "gone." *Gone people.* Whenever Stuart looked at the faces on the milk cartons, he had a deep feeling the children were dead. He didn't own a picture of Natasha, but all the same he was convinced that if she'd died he would have known that too.

When it got warm enough to sit outside again Stuart sat in Tompkins Square with one more unread newspaper flattened on the bench beside him and watched Tombo coming across from the east side. He would have let him go on by, but Tombo saw him before he could get the paper up, came over, and sat down.

"Long time," Tombo said. "I wasn't even sure you were still around."

"I'm here," Stuart said. Tombo leaned back on the bench, shooting his long legs out before him. He had on a nice pair of gray pleated pants, expensive looking. None of it ever seemed to age or even touch him. He still had his dark and vaguely for-eign prettiness, perfect skin, red pouty mouth, long eyelashes like a girl's. Stuart watched him blink his eyes and sniffle.

"Hey, you know Clifton's been talking you down a lot," Tombo said, shifting around in Stuart's direction. "He keeps on telling everybody he's gonna fix your business."

"Good," Stuart said. "If he's talking about it then he won't do anything."

"You think?"

"Clifton's got a temper," Stuart said. "But he'll never let it take him all the way to jail."

"Maybe not," Tombo said. He snorted, pulled out a handkerchief, and blew his nose. "Allergies, man," he said. "It always gets to me around this time of year."

"What are you giving me that line for?" Stuart said. "I'm not a cop."

"Right, I forgot," Tombo said, glancing over at him under his eyelashes. "You still clean?"

"Yeah," Stuart said.

"They do a pretty good job on you up at Millbrook, huh? It sticks?"

"So far," Stuart said. "One day at a time and all that kind of thing."

Tombo shifted around on the bench.

"I'd been thinking maybe I might go up there sometime myself," he said.

"Well," Stuart said. "When you decide to go, then you'll go."

"People tell me you're looking for Natasha," Tombo said.

"Do they," Stuart said. "Everybody likes to talk to you about my business, seems. Why, you haven't seen her, have you?"

"Not in a year at least, nope. Sorry, bud . . . What are you looking for her for?"

"I quit looking for her," Stuart said. "You can't look for somebody around here, it's ridiculous. I'm just . . . I'm just waiting to find her, that's all."

"Interesting strategy," Tombo said, standing up. "Well, good luck."

Stuart started making trips to Brooklyn, back to what had been Henry's place, though he didn't much like the feel of it, not after the remodeling. Why he kept going out there he didn't really know, maybe just for the inconvenience of it, for the journey. Clifton had stopped coming in, the new bartender was a stranger, there was seldom anyone he knew there except the dog. They still hadn't opened up the restaurant section. Sometimes Stuart's visit would coincide with Henry's, who tended to drop in most Thursday and Friday afternoons. He'd take Captain out around the block and then come back and sit at the bar, drinking white wine on ice from one of the old straight glasses they'd apparently saved just to serve him with. It pleased Stuart that this one little thing was still the same, and he felt happier in the place when Henry was in there too, though they didn't have much to say to each other past hello, and though the old man looked all wrong, sitting on the outside of the bar.

Whenever the weather was good enough he walked back across the bridge and caught the subway at Delancey Street on the Manhattan side. He was in a lot better shape than he'd been in the old days, but it was still enough of an effort that doing it fast set his heart slamming. That sense of an urge out in front of him was familiar, though now he wasn't going for a fix; the energy he set out ahead of him had become its own point. The walkway was a little more run-down than he remembered it. A lot of the tiles had come loose and blown away, and now he could look through cracks in the steel plating and see all the way down to the place far below the roadway where the water slowly turned and moiled. But the rise of excitement was the same as it always had been, as he pushed himself up to the crux of the span, where the howling of the traffic stopped being a scream and became a sigh. Arrived just there, with the afternoon barely past its daily crisis, he stopped and looked farther across at the tall buildings limned explosively with light, exultant, thinking, *This is what you always will forget, this is what you never can remember, this is what you have to be here for.*

It's not the first but the fifth or sixth day of spring when Stuart finally finds Natasha. All winter he's felt old and moribund, frozen half through, but now a new green shoot of youth begins to uncurl inside of him. It's a fresh and tingling day, the weather so very fine that it alone would be enough to make you fall in love. The people in Washington Square have bloomed into their summer clothes and they all look almost beautiful. Stuart walks around the rim of the fountain, hands in his pockets, a cigarette guttering at the corner of his mouth, smiling a little as the fair breeze ruffles his hair. He's headed straight for Natasha before he's even seen her, and then he does: she's tapped out there on one of the benches just at the bottom edge of the circle, head lolled back, mouth a little open, hands stretched palms-up on her knees. When he gets a little closer, he can even see her eyes darting under the closed lids, looking at the things she's dreaming of. Man, she's way too thin, she's got bad-looking tracks, infected, and it's a fifty-fifty chance she's dying, but Stuart won't think about any of that right now, just keeps on walking, up into the moment he's believed in for so long.

for Wyn Cooper

C. S. GODSHALK

The Wizard

FROM THE AGNI REVIEW

"HEY, LOOK AT THAT! You know what that is?" the Wizard says.
"That's a goddamn red-winged blackbird. Miss Watts saw four
of 'em last week at her feeder. You know what that means?"

Rensselaer blinks and checks his jockstrap, where he has stuffed
two small brown packages. He is an unbelievably skinny twelve-
year-old with a dreamy smile and a fine, caramel-colored face.
It makes the older boy's face look almost blue.

" 'Spring,' asshole."

"Where is the old witch?" Rensselaer asks mildly. They are in
Miss Watts's back yard, but she isn't around and he can't feel her
little beady eyes creeping out at them from a window.

"She's at Boston City Hospital right this goddamn minute. She's
got a dropped bladder and they're tying the whole thing up,"
the Wizard says.

"Miss Watts is crippled," he told Rensselaer the year before. "Walks
with a cane, but she ain't old. She sees you buying or selling, she
hit you with a cane. Wham! Broke Bama Aguilar's windshield.
Ain't afraid of nobody! She teaches eighth grade. She was my
last teacher. She say, 'George Albert, you have a gift for numbers. You don't need prealgebra. You don't need *pre* anything.'
We finished these two books, her and me. One was the tenth-
grade math book and one was a little green book, *Amusements in
Mathematics*. It was full of weird stuff. It told about this one guy,
Fibonacci. Fibonacci figured, if he put a pair of rabbits in a box,
how many pairs of babies from that first pair would be made in

a year if every month each pair had a new pair that could make babies when it was two months old. It goes: 1 2 3 5 8 13 21 34 55, like that. The rabbits are immortal."

He does not know why he does this, explains stuff like this to Rensselaer, whose soft smile may well have roots in retardation. But Rensselaer, though inappropriate in age and intelligence, is a friend, and the Wizard is now in a zone between friends, between the possibilities of friendship. At sixteen, he has become a dealing power on Homestead Street, and so not a child. He is no man, though he is wily and moving up.

"Miss Watts told about hundreds of things," the Wizard says. "The Constitution. Goiter belts. She told about Monticello, Jefferson's mansion. And I know I got to see that place. I sold two kilos in four days and took a Trailways bus. Just me. I brought her back a pen back with a little plastic Monticello floatin' inside.

"What a place. That dude *hid* everything. He hid the slave quarters under the house. He had dumbwaiters, little chimneys for food to go up and down, hot food coming up from the kitchen and revolving doors so he don't have to be bothered with servants while he is conversing in his dining room. He just pulled the food out of the walls and stuck in the dirty plates.

"He had a chair with this arm. An extension. You copy something small, trace it over with a pen, but the pen is attached to a rod and a lot of crap and then to another pen, which is making a huge fucking picture of the same thing you are at that moment drawing little. Goddamn! You look up at this dial over the doorway *inside,* and it tells you the wind, where it's coming from and how strong, *outside.* He had a clock that could tell the time any which way. All the hours, days, months, and moons. And flowers! Yellow tulips like a blanket. 'Herbs.' Miss Watts liked her pen. She say, 'What do you know!' tiltin' it to make the little house float."

Corinna Watts lives at 49 Homestead. Homestead is a heavy dealing street that still has a few crazy genteel pockets. In between is a quarter mile of empty, boarded-up houses with hundreds of places to deal and disappear. Miss Watts owns her house. She has a small garden in the back. That's how the Wizard met her outside school. He was checking out the flowers. Actually, he and another kid were setting up their scales, just chickenshit stuff in the sixth grade, and they noticed all these flowers on the other side of the fence. Roses. They picked off a couple and started throwing them at each other.

She came out waving these huge scissors and they grabbed their stuff and ran. But she yelled, "Come back! Come back! You boys like flowers? Here!" she held up the scissors. "Pick yourselves some." They looked at each other and put their stuff in the grass and crept back and took the scissors and thanked her and she went inside. They picked every flower she had. Some they just knocked the tops off, swatting them with the closed blades. Whap! Whap! Whap! When she came out, they ran. She stood with her arms hanging in the middle of that little headless garden. It looked like a war zone.

Walking up Humboldt, the Wizard didn't feel so great. He twisted a few gas caps off parked cars and dropped them into the drain at the corner, but he didn't feel any better. They finished their packages behind Baby Lyle's Deli and split. Walking home, he felt an itch in his collar and it was the tiny head of a rose caught inside. It was tight like a little umbrella, with no smell because it was still shut. He split it open with his nails and felt the hundreds of pink, silky layers, like a little body not born.

The next day, he took the MBTA to Quincy Market and bought two boxes of flowers from a ripoff plant store under a glass dome. He made fifty bucks off Earl Johnson for a crack delivery and he took it, the whole thing, and bought these red flowers in flat boxes. They at least looked like something; the roses this guy had were just sticks in pots with pictures of roses stuck on. The guy said it wasn't the season for roses. You pay and wait for them to *appear* from these sticks. He couldn't believe people bought that line. He took the red ones. Salvia, the guy called them. He took them back on the MBTA, these two flat boxes taking up four seats, with all these old farts standing. He enjoyed it. He shuffled down the back alley with a box on each shoulder. He waited a while to see if anyone was around and then cut into Miss Watts's yard and took out Selma's soup spoon and began to dig. He put the plants in carefully, not in rows but in spirals of 'increasing radii.' When he finished the little spirals, he took a pail by the basement steps and ran some water in it but she heard that. She came leaping out, swinging her cane. It came down like lead, and he thought she broke his back. He grabbed it up where it was high, ready to slam down again, only she froze, her arm in the air, her eyes bouncing around the ground.

"Salvia," she said softly. "My Lord."

The salvia didn't do so hot, but the Wizard came by regularly to take care of it. He lived eleven houses down, at number 28.

"A perfect number," he said to Rensselaer the night he moved in his stuff.

"What's so perfect?" the child asked.

"Twenty-eight is the sum of its own divisors, if you count one but don't count *it*. It's the second perfect number."

"What's the first?" Rensselaer asked, smiling wide.

"Six. Your IQ."

Number 28 is a three-story building with six apartments, the Wizard's and the other five which are boarded up. It has no electricity and no phone, "just sunlight and direct communication," he says, although he does have two little battery lamps from K mart. He has a sleeping bag, an impressive collection of *Penthouse*s, a bear statue in a bathrobe with holes in his paws for toothbrushes that Selma bought him, and a giant ficus tree he also got at K mart and which is amazingly healthy. When it gets too cool for the tree, he covers it with plastic garbage bags and tapes it and moves back to his mother's. He doesn't live with Selma unless it's freezing. "Her house is shit-dirty both ways," he says. "Crap all over, and dealing round the clock. When I lived there, I went to school a lot. It was a fucking relief.

"At school I got ninety-ninth percentile in 'conceptual mathematical ability.' I did out of sight in the ERBs, these five days of tests of which days I did not miss one. I am 'bright.' Bright like a nuclear bomb."

The Wizard's real name is George Albert Cantrell. Earl calls him the Wizard because he can figure street price in a flash. "You got to figure your flat cost," the Wizard says, "then things like bail money, dealing time lost if you're picked up, runners, eyes. This is not easy, it's fucking calculus. It is also work under pressure. Earl is thirty-two years old but he don't go nowhere without me no more. We never carry much. 'We light,' he says, 'we are two feathers.' Earl weighs about 250 pounds. He's got this huge smile, his whole face gets into the act. But he's a mean son of a bitch. Even if he is my brother, which he ain't. Not by the latest which Selma tells me. But Selma, she is a great storyteller."

Earl is always polite to certain people. To Bama, his main supply. And to people like Miss Watts. He teaches school, too, and he is good at it. "This is a good place," he says to the new payroll of baby runners. "We should take care of it. No molesting innocent people. Keep a nice clean street. We are doing business and we don't need no crap. We deal clean and we move. Don't hurt nobody. They our cover. They our 'ticket.' These are Queen Elizabeths," he says to the small child Toussaint, handing him a bunch of bright pink roses in cellophane with a twenty-dollar bill for delivery. "They for Miss Watts. *I* give them to her, she crack my skull!" he laughs. "You say they from Mr. Earl Johnson. Then run."

The Wizard and Earl really didn't know each other, even though they were half-brothers, or fourths or something, and then one day Earl's up at Anne Marie's, his "mother-in-law's" dealing, and the Wizard sees 5-o come down the street, and then another car, slow, the wrong way, and he checks and sees Earl's got nobody looking out so he runs up and says, "The Man's coming down both ways." Earl streaks out, he is big but he can move, then he comes back fast and shoves the Wizard a hundred. So they get to know each other.

Miss Watts doesn't speak of Earl. Her time, she says, is not to be wasted on shit. She talks about other things. "Out of the blue," the Wizard says, "I am watering the salvia, which later I found out was too much and rotting the roots and killing them but she just let me do it because I believe she likes to see me. I am in many ways entertaining, and out of the blue she looks up from her aluminum chair and her Sunday *Globe* and says, 'George Albert, you take the Secondary School Admission Test. Take it three, four times till you get the hang. We get you into Alden Hill. That school is this island,' she says, 'in the jungle of life.' That was one of her expressions, 'the jungle of life.' She says things like 'the jungle of life' and 'with the help of God and eighty-

five policemen,' and, when she looks in a mirror sometime she
say, 'I look like the wreck of the *Hesperus*,' which I believed for a
long time was some prehistoric animal, but it turns out to be a
fucking boat."

"Miss Watts says take this test. I say, 'Miss Watts, I don't mind.
How do I take it?' And I take it. I go to school, another school,
on a Saturday morning and blow my brains out over this fucking
long test. You go in with two number 2 pencils — it has to say
number 2 on the side of the pencils or you can't use them. You
can't take food, no 'artificial aids' like calculators or calculator
watches, my jacket has thirteen because people sometimes like a
little extra and I had not yet hit the street, so I left the jacket on
and I was *warm*. There was this dude watchin' everybody all the
time. One girl, fat, white, was crying. She was getting her test
wet. She had big breasts and no bra and a little girl dress and I
said, I whispered, 'Hey baby, don't do that, you get your test all
wet,' and the guy almost threw me out. I didn't do so good that
time. Miss Watts, she says take it again, so I do. And a third time.
'That's enough!' she say. The score I got was, you know, in outer
space.

"Alden Hill *is* a fucking hill. Green. All these big brick buildings and neat little paths at the top. It has great 'sports facilities,'
big flat fields where you play games that needs tons of 'equip-
ment,' which means the place is ass-deep in cash. It's got extremely smart, rich students. Miss Watts set me up for the inter-
view. The junior high sent my record and she set me up. They
had this Chinese kid show me around. It was funny they picked
a Chinese. They got brothers there, too. Black and beautiful as
me, jackets and ties you'd put on a corpse, big blue book bags
with the name of the school all over. You wonder how the fuck
they got there. They'd have to be airlifted from Homestead. But,
as the man says, they 'do.' We ate lunch in this room entirely of
natural wood, even the ceiling. Gordon Ho plays the violin and
lacrosse. Lacrosse is this Indian game with big salad spoons. I
stuck around and watched the practice in which he was pretty
lousy and then I tried it. I did all right. I got the walk for it, and
I got the run.

"The Hill gets tons of money from everywhere because it does a fucking good job as a school. After you finish you are made. You just slide cross the river to Harvard, I mean your ass is greased forever. You're a lawyer, you get the richest, evilest cases. You be a business man, you got yourself a direct South American pipeline. You got yourself an education.

"Ho dropped me at Admissions and this guy Crosby interviewed me. He sat on the side of his desk. Friendly. Sly. Ask you nothing right out. A cruisin' shark. He says, 'We encourage inner city boys.' Then he zones in. 'George, what kind of a boy would you say you are?'

"I don't know how to answer this.

" 'You've been out of school this year. What do you do with your time?'

"I decide to tell the truth, but not about working for Earl which takes up most of my time. I tell him about 'Miss Watts days.' And these exist. She used to actually come, but lately she don't. She's got this bladder and we just get started and I have to bring her back. So I have Miss Watts days without her.

"I tell Crosby about Miss Watts days. I go to the aquarium a lot. It's this gigantic tube of water standing on end with a ramp wrapped around it so you can look in at the fish as you climb up. The fish look out. At eleven o'clock and four this guy in a rubber suit jumps in and feeds them. He even feeds the sharks. The fish don't eat each other. And that's amazing. I mean all these fish, natural enemies, and they just cruise around looking at the people. They don't 'molest' each other. They got so much fucking food, they don't need to. They're bored.

"I get to the aquarium on the T. You can get anywhere in Boston on the T. 'Boston is a cultural mecca,' Miss Watts says. 'Walk in! Walk on in like you strut into my garden and whack my flowers!' I do.

"I find you can cruise into some pretty good places. For instance, you can get off at Central Square and cut into MIT. I found this out when I ran stuff to a candy factory next door. You can walk right into those big stone buildings. You carry a book and look like you're late for something. Sometimes, you can actually walk into rooms where guys are working and they don't give a shit. That's how I met Stoltz. I stepped out of a hall when all these Japs come walking towards me and then I was in

this big room. I mean *big*. The ceiling was about thirty feet high
and it had these extremely shiny aluminum pillars everywhere.
I hear music, a twinkly music like the kind they play for Rensselaer's sister when she dances at BoJo's, and then it stops. *No
one* is there. I mean, this is a really big room with only me in it
and then this twinkly music that just stops. I start to leave and
the music starts again. When I stop, it stops. A light comes on
but only over me. I start walking again and the light follows me
and the twinkly music starts and I walk real fast and the music
goes crazy and the light turns red. I freeze. It all stops. I tap one
foot. The music jangs once. So then I go into my moves. I jive
slow, and then I take off. I leap and scrouch down and come up
wild, and the room is filled with this Martian music. I stop and
head for the door and this white guy comes out, really *white*, like
somebody who lives in the dark all the time. He says, 'Wow. Wow.
I didn't know it could do that.' It turns out this is art. The music
and lights are connected to the fucking floor. He shows me my
moves on video and I look spectacular. It's 'audio kinetic art.'
Some of the stuff is great, but some is shit. I mean, one whole
room is somebody's 'dream,' right? I check in with Stoltz every
once in a while, though. He is a patient dude.

"I also touch down also at BoJo's and the Fine Arts, usually on
the same day because you can change lines easy at the Combat
Zone and head out Huntington Avenue to the museum. The
museum is this palace. Outside they got a stone Indian on a horse
with his arms spread out and his face looking up at the sky, a
natural six-time loser. They got thousands of pictures and museum cops who don't do anything but let you float along. The
thing I like about this place is, after you come out, you can be
anywhere, sleeping, eating, and still know the stuff is there if
you want to go back and check it out again. Sometimes they get
new stuff which stays for only a little while so you got to look
good. There is one thing I always check out when I go. It is a
picture called *The Fantastic Beast*. It is an 'etching,' a drawing of
a monster. But a goddamn genius monster. It's from the Bible.
When I saw it the first time, I'm turning this corner by the Egyptian stuff, and there it is, like an enemy you see in the street. It
was all the crap in the world in a face. The eyes were good eyes
that look like they know you and maybe even love you, but the

lips could kiss you or eat you. There are these little Walkmen
you rent that tell you about the picture, only Wiley, the black
dude in a brown uniform who rents them, give me mine free. I
listen for the part coming up about *The Fantastic Beast,* but it
don't say much. Early Renaissance, some other stuff. I didn't use
the box again because it wrecks looking. Your ears take the energy from your eyes, I find.

"Wiley is a friendly man. He looks old, but when he laughs he
looks young. 'Nobody know how old a black man is,' he says. 'I
can be a senior citizen at the movies, and I still got the moves for
sweet young ass.' He knows a lot about art. He's got his favorite
stuff too. His favorite thing of all is a room. It's a big empty
room they got on the second floor. All polished wood, soft and
quiet. The whole ceiling is carved and set in like it belongs, but
it don't. It belongs in Japan. They got houses like this in Japan
with nothing in them. Except they're filled up with something.
They're filled up with 'quiet.' On the sides of this room they got
huge cardboard pictures, folded and standing up, each one bigger than ten men shoulder to shoulder. There's a bench in the
middle of the room with nobody ever on it and I sit there sometimes and jiggle numbers for the evening action. One cardboard
has a warrior chasing another on horseback, with armor like you
wouldn't believe. He makes Robocop look like Mickey Mouse.
The guy he's chasing is crossing a river and you can see by his
expression and the swirly lines in the water that that river is fuckin'
movin'! You think, 'Sucker! You're caught! If the guy behind
don't get you, the river will.' The first time, I walked all the way
out of that room and down the stairs and outside to the T stop
and then I come back and look at that guy in the river again.
And he don't look afraid. He looks like he knows something.
And then I don't know which one is chasing which, for he looks
like he's just waiting in that river for the other dude to follow.
Now *that's* a picture. I told Miss Watts about it. She says there is
this movie at Coolidge Corner, that if I like that picture I should
see this movie. We go. It turns out to be one hell of a movie. It's
about an old Jap king who decides to be nice to his sons because
he's getting old and so he 'abdicates' before dying, to let them all
sort of get their feet wet in ruling, and they go nuts. It doesn't
sound like a good story, but it is. Especially in the beginning,

when everything is real quiet. There is a long time when you just look at all these green mountains with wind blowing in the grass and these horsemen, quiet, looking, looking, and you wonder what the fuck they're looking for but you know it's something because you hear weird Stoltz-type music in the background. And then the whole thing explodes because this animal, this fucking monster, a wild boar, busts out of the grass and the horsemen charge after it, even this old guy who is a very good horseback rider. It is really not Japanese at all, Miss Watts says. It is a story by 'Shakespeare.' She give me the book and I try a couple of pages but it don't make sense. It's in another language with just bits of English thrown in, although I can see the guy is no dope.

"I tell Crosby about the aquarium and the museum and some of the other places I go and he listens and I think it's going O.K., but then he hits me again with a bunch of those 'loose' questions.

" 'Look, Mr. Crosby,' " I say finally. 'What do you want to know? Am I a smart boy? Yes I am. Am I a good boy? I am a good boy, but I don't take no shit.'

"He looks out the window. 'Good in what way, George?'

"I look out, too. 'It depends. Just good or good *at*. When I'm good, I know it. I can say, "I am being good right now," and I think if you can say that, I mean if you *know* that, I don't think you really are. 'Good.' Not like Rensselaer Charles is good, I think. He's good and he don't know it. It's just like breathin' to him. Like when he stood up and yelled to me, he knew Bama's gorillas were coming across Franklin Field just a hundred yards behind, and he stands up, *stands up* in that purple shirt with the singing raisins and yells to me. 'That's good,' I think to myself. 'And fucking stupid.'

" 'What are you good *at*?' Crosby asks.

" 'Mathematics, reading, auto mechanics . . .' Pussy, I might add. Whistlin'. I am, in fact, an extremely good whistler.

" 'In that order?' he says.

" 'All equal. I'm Superman.' I get up and walk to the door. 'What are you good at, Mr. Crosby? It sure as hell isn't interviewing.' But I don't say that either, because at the door, or half behind it, I see it. A picture of a man, young, with half his arm exposed, the skin is lifted back, and all the veins and muscles inside are drawn perfect. His face, or half a face because the rest isn't drawn, is beautiful, like a woman's, and I know in the whole world the same fucking guy made it that made *The Beast.*

" 'Dürer,' Crosby says. 'One of his earlier drawings. It was given to the school by the Alden family. There's another outside the infirmary. Do you like it?'

" 'Yeah. But not as much as some of his other stuff.'

"His eyes light up. He's kind of leaning over me, his arm high up on the door. 'What else do you like?'

" *'The Fantastic Beast,'* I say.

"He looks pink and happy. 'A masterpiece,' he whispers."

Miss Watts got the call. The Wizard walked up those rickety back steps and she opened the door and yanked him in and he had to hold her shoulders to stop her from jumping. "They like you fine! You are *in!*" she yelled. "Full scholarship! They say they just hope they can keep up the caliber of your education!" They "juked," she called it, holding on to him and jumping up and down like a monkey. Afterwards, he put her to bed like an old baby. He felt somehow great and no one to tell but this old baby.

He planned to work solid with Earl the five months before school started. You couldn't live on a scholarship and he wasn't going to screw things up by dealing at the Hill. Earl would ask it, demand it in his pig way when he found out. But by then, he figured, he could handle Earl.

By then, Earl might not even be around. He was doing some pretty stupid things. He was doing almost all his business in one place, for one thing. Anne Marie's had already been busted twice, and an apartment busted three times could be padlocked. Most regulars moved before this happened, but Anne Marie couldn't move anywhere.

"How the hell she gonna move with that tribe?" the Wizard asked, but Earl just said to meet him. The Wizard didn't like Anne Marie's for another reason. He didn't like the 'atmosphere.' The family was pure women, a hundred percent. All kinds of women. There were Shirley and her baby and La Toya, Daryl's baby girl, back to roost, and Francine and Kendra, who went to hairdressing school now and then. Six fucking women. Daryl, Anne Marie's only boy, was caught dealing, and they were "upgrading" the project so a known dealer could not visit his mama, and she had to sign that he wouldn't and she did that.

Anne Marie was everything in life a female could be. She was sweet and she was mean as hell. She was skinny like sticks in her arms and legs, and fat, really big, round her middle. She was — but only in the soft light coming up from the courtyard around ten in the morning in her old rose robe — pretty. She had a magic. She could get real funny in the blackest times. When Daryl was hit she was so sad, she looked at the cop who came in the morning and told her about Daryl at the door. He told her and she died. Then she made the fucking cop laugh. He told her about Daryl and she died for a while in the doorway and then turned around and made him laugh. She was a daughter and a mother and a grandmother and a sister, but she was no friend. Sometimes she was a shrieking witch and sometimes she was an angel of light. The only thing she always was, was tired. She was, to her older daughters, Shirley and Francine, disappearing in bits, like an old screw doll. All that would be left some morning, Shirley felt, was Anne Marie's raging heart in her ashtray on the kitchen table. Yet in that dim debacle of a life of hers, she had one ironbound claim to fame: She had never killed a child. No baby ever started in her or in one of hers was ever cut out. Anne Marie held on to that like a rope thrown to a drowning man and none of her children was going to wrench it from her hands. There were filthy diapers everywhere.

Shirley is usually not home when the Wizard shows up to wait for Earl. This time she is, but she looks like she's leaving. Tall, hair down to her ass. Looks like a model. She's Earl's girl, and has one baby by him — yet another girl, the five hundredth or something. Georgia Delight. That is a gorgeous name, and the kid is too. Dark and gorgeous like a bug-eyed doll. Earl bought her a huge pink bear almost as big as himself last Christmas. When he was carrying it up the stairs, it looked like this gorilla and giant bear come up fighting.

Earl likes to give presents. On Shirley's birthday, he gave her a fifty-thousand-volt sting gun in a blue velvet box. She said, "What the hell am I supposed to do with this? Earrings! You give a girl *jewelry*, asshole!" Only Shirley can talk to Earl like this.

"Hey, baby," he says, the phone wedged into his bull neck. "You're mine. Sooner or later you'll need it." He reaches over and wiggles her ear. Earl is accurate. He's connected direct with a Miami supply, and that is a jumping game.

"Watch Delight for me, baby," Shirley says to the Wizard. And she is gone.

He finds *Square One* on the tube, a program he likes, and sits down with Delight, who is balled up at her end of the sofa. Delight's "inner home" in the apartment is the maroon sofa or the right-hand corner of it, where she is usually asleep or looking at the tube or somewhere in between. She doesn't get up, at two, to go to the bathroom. She smells all the time like Delight.

A bunch of colored triangles dance around the screen and fall into a dazzling design. "Tessa-laaation" peels out on a salsa beat.

"Hey, little bean bag," the Wizard says, grabbing the tiny wrists, gently jamming his nose into hers. "You are looking at a 'secret yuppie.' Soon nobody gonna see nothing but my fucking dust." Delight laughs and reaches for his nose and he pulls her, smell and all, into his lap. He liked watching TV with this baby. He thinks, holding her wondrous warmth, and then rejects the revelation with bitterness, that his only friends in the world are an old woman and a retarded boy and this baby. Earl arrives with his customer. His stupidity is becoming phenomenal.

Half the time, he doesn't show at all. There is one time the Wizard came up and the place was totally deserted. This was good. It is the way it's supposed to be, professionally speaking. Even Delight is not in her corner. "What would happen," he thinks, switching on the TV and easing into the sofa, "to that baby *outside*? Her skin would split. Fresh air and sunlight would shatter her insides with surprise."

Little mousy sounds come from the bedroom. He checks in and sees Delight in one bed and in the other, wide-eyed, spaced out, is Francine, a baby face on a long woman's body with butterflies on her panties. "Hey, Wizard," she says. Delight makes small, cranky sounds, curling up like an elbow noodle and spiking out. Two pillows keep her from falling on the floor.

"She's all right," Francine says, "she'll go back to sleep. Come here, baby. Sit down." He does. And through, above, and below

Delight's murmurings, her tiny wails and fitful sleep, he gets to know Francine. Later, easing down the stairs, away from that universe of women, he reflects on how there might now be another exotically named star, shining just for him, already pressing against those butterfly wings with a steady beat.

"You fucking going to do the right thing," Earl says. It's the day after Christmas and he is holding a beer. His watch, a present from Shirley, is bleeping, bleeping red.

"What's the right thing?" the Wizard asks politely, raising his eyebrows. "A sting gun? A hundred-pound pink bear?"

Earl's face levels menacingly. Then it suddenly cracks into its wide smile. "You got balls, my man."

Francine is carrying a little ball. She carries it every Tuesday and Thursday morning to hairdressing class and then over to Bama Aguilar's, who pats it afterwards for good luck. She likes hairdressing, but she also carries an ad in her curler case for the Ryco Travel Agent School in Brighton. She is an ambitious child. She is quick and can predict most things, but she is mildly amazed at the Wizard. He is a baby boy who makes a hell of a lot of money. There is no reason not to tuck him under her wing. But he resists like a full-grown son of a bitch.

"Do you believe I am that fucking dumb!" he says when she tells him. "You get rid of it, maybe it's mine. Only way." Yet even as he hurls this at her, he knows, in rising despair, that Francine will be true to Anne Marie, that preserver of life.

"It's no fucking deal," Francine says. She has a lovely, easy smile. "There's Delight's clothes and her playpen which she'll outgrow soon. Nothing will change. If you put up regular. And you do, baby," she kneads him softly. "You do."

He does not. His last run to Miami with Earl is in late August and he gets back to Homestead on a broiling Saturday afternoon and visits no one, not Francine or Selma or Miss Watts, distributing no wealth. He climbs the stairs with his three white shirts and two dead ties in a shopping bag and opens the door to that cool, boarded-up apartment, and finds that the essence of death is air. The ficus is a brown cornstalk. He crumples a leaf and fills a thin shaft of light with golden motes.

On Monday, climbing Anne Marie's ammonia-scented stairwell, that endless spiral of information and gratification, he is told that the family is not at home. They're all down at J. Arnold Moon & Sons, where Delight has gone and gotten her baby hair done up in four white plastic barrettes and a pink nylon party dress smoothed down in a satin-lined box. Moon's, a cockeyed, gaily austere funeral home at the corner of Columbia Avenue, is packed. He pushes through the crowd but seems to get nowhere, then suddenly stares down at a doll in a shoebox. He passes back, underwater, not breathing, into the sudden, merciful jolt of daylight and traffic.

Shirley is standing on a patch of grass. "The little bitch should have complained!" she screams. Earl has her arms pinned. It was true, he thinks: If they couldn't hear her, how could they know? Those stupid little "mumbles"! Francine waddles down the stairs behind him in high heels and a shiny black dress and Shirley lunges for her. "You were in the next fucking bed! Day in, day out!"

The patch of grass in front of Moon's is the same homogeneous green of the grass on the Hill. The Wizard's sneakers leave soft half-moons as he traverses, scanning the future. Francine's ball, this "Julep Jill" or "Spring Fantana," for these are names she has considered, will be placed in Delight's playpen and Francine will be her own first customer in the travel business. He knows this. Yet it is not "Julep Jill" or "Spring Fantana" or even "Shannon Hussein" he sees, but Delight, aglow with fever, her small sounds rising, and all he wants in the world is to get that elbow-noodle body in his arms and run.

Miss Watts is not in her chair. He does not expect her to be. Twice she has gone to the hospital for her rotting bladder, and now they've got her in some kind of home. The aluminum chair is there, open and jammed into the earth like always, its dirty white and green webbing loose at the back. He sits in it and looks around. The yard looks good. He pays Rensselaer to take care of it. He pays him an insane amount, same as a courier. He would like to keep Rensselaer in this yard forever.

The next day he finds it, he is good at finding things in this city, a concrete, convalescent bunker across from Franklin Park. He has three of her Magenta Queens in waxed paper. A fat woman in a dirty uniform lets him in and suspiciously parks him outside a little room with four beds. He finds her in the one behind the door. It looks like they made a dummy Miss Watts out of her old green sweater and a dried peach for her head. She looks at him, a long look with nothing in it, but he sits down anyway and begins to talk. He talks and talks, like he has never talked before to anyone. He can actually watch himself talking, but he can't stop. He talks about everything: Francine, Selma, Earl, Crosby, everything except Delight. He circles round that baby like a rock in a stream. He knows Miss Watts is listening because every once in a while her mouth does a little jerk. She looks "light," as if something has all but eaten her up inside, but when she speaks, it flops to the floor and slithers under the door.

"You are a shining star!" she says with amazing volume and venom. "Stick to your plan!" This explosion caves her in or maybe kills her. Through the blinds, he watches Franklin Park disappear in the oncoming night.

"A baby," Miss Watts says, her eyes closed. "Most precious, precious thing." At the T, he is still holding the Magenta Queens. He vows he will never go back.

But the next time is better. Miss Watts has managed to concentrate a nut of energy, enough to sustain almost five minutes of her original self. "They will remove me, George Albert," she says calmly. "Don't look for me. There's no point. I won't be there. I'm not even here!" Her face looks almost cheerful. "Right now I'm in my chair in my yard and the sun is shining and you are rotting the roots of my salvia. I can see the little rainbows in the spray from your can. I can be any goddamned place I want!"

He rises, smiling.

"You'll do the right thing," she says, a claw grasps his wrist hard, painfully. "And it sure as hell isn't supporting some whore."

Sometimes the Wizard liked to think that he was physically made up of a lot of little clocks. Ping, ping. Clocks for dealing, when and how much, where, the time to expand, when to pull back, sit tight, move again. Ping. Time to fertilize the ficus. The ping he heard was a new one. He had set that clock five months before, the alarm for the first day of class. He rose in the darkness and put on the white shirt and dead tie and jacket and pants and softly flopped down the stairs into the silent, almost beautiful street.

He got to the Hill just before dawn, and he pulled his jacket together and sat down. The air was cool and amazingly still, like sitting under a big blue bell, and he lay back and closed his eyes. After a while, a soft shaft of light glided up the slope, gilding his hands, then his face. A car door slammed.

Five or six boys passed by, their voices melding into the early light. He sat up and watched half a dozen more cars pull up, then he got up and walked back down the narrow path, out across St. Francis Avenue and down to the T.

The train was jammed with early commuters. He stood in the middle of the car, not having to brace himself on anything, supported upright and propelled along at roaring speed. He changed at Park and took an emptier car west. Wiley would not be working today. He didn't want to run into him anyway. He would wait until the glass doors opened and climb up to the second floor and walk down the long corridor, passed the store and cafeteria and the Egyptian stuff in cases, and look at it, its several horns and teeth, its stupid, menacing, ardent eyes, the consummate genius of the hand that drew it, and know he didn't have to see it again. He could remember it. He could draw it perfectly from memory. If he had Jefferson's chair, he could draw it as big as it really was. And it was enormous, bigger than the world.

PATRICIA HENLEY

The Secret of Cartwheels

FROM THE ATLANTIC MONTHLY

THE WINESAP TREES along the road were skeletal in the early evening light. I stared out the school bus window and cupped like a baby chick the news I looked forward to telling Mother: I'd decided on my confirmation name.

"What's nine times seven?" my sister Jan Mary said.

"Sixty-three," I said. *Joan.* That was Mother's confirmation name, and I wanted it to be mine as well. She'd told me it was a name of strength, a name to carry you into battle.

"I tore my corduroys," my brother, Christopher, said. He stood in the aisle, bracing himself with one hand on the chrome pole beside the driver, who wore a baseball cap and a big plaid mackinaw.

The bus driver sang, "Don't sit under the apple tree with anyone else but me." I knew we were nearing our stop, the end of the route, when the driver sang this song. We were the last ones on the bus. Although the heater was chuffing hard, frost in the shape of flames curled along the edges of the windows.

"Sweet dreams," the driver said, as we plodded down the slippery steps of the school bus.

Aunt Opal's pale green Cadillac was parked at an odd angle near the woodshed. I knew something was wrong — she never drove out from Wenatchee to visit in the winter. I remembered what our mother had told me the night before. Before bedtime we all lined up to kiss her good night, and when my turn came, she said, "There are signs in life. Signs that tell you what you have to do." Her voice had frightened me. I didn't want to hear what she had to say.

Jan Mary said, "Who's that?" Her knit gloves were soggy, her knees chapped above slipping-down socks.

"Aunt Opal," Christopher said. His voice was dead, and I knew he knew and understood.

Our breath came in blue blossoms in the cold, cutting air, and a light went on in the living room. I didn't want to go in, but I kept trudging through the snow.

Inside, everything was in its place, but our mother was gone, which made the house seem cold and empty. Four-year-old Suzanne stood on the heat register, her grubby chenille blanket a cape around her shoulders. Her hair had been recently brushed, and she wore plastic barrettes — a duck on one side, a bow on the other. When I remember those years at home, this is one of the things I focus on: how nothing ever matched — not sheets, not barrettes, not cups and saucers, not socks. And sometimes I think the sad and petty effort to have matching things has been one of the chief concerns of my adult life. Aunt Opal perched uneasily on a ladderback chair, with the baby, Katie Jean, on her lap. Katie Jean, eyes roving, held her own bottle of milk, and when she saw me, her look latched on to me and she stopped sucking and squirmed and kicked. Her plastic bottle clunked onto the floor. Aunt Opal's white wool pant suit stretched tightly across her fat thighs. Her teased hair stood hard and swirled. Ill at ease, she shifted her weight gingerly, as though she might get dirty. I thought I saw pity in her eyes, and I looked away. Christopher and Jan Mary hung back by the kitchen door, Christopher banging his metal lunch box softly against his leg.

"Where's our mother?" I said, scooping up Katie Jean.

"Now, I hate to have to be the bearer of bad tidings," she began. "I know this will be hard on you children. I don't know what your mother was thinking of." She got up and stalked over to Suzanne, her spike heels dragging on the linoleum.

"Just tell me where she is." The baby stiffened in my arms. This was the first time I'd ever issued a command to a grownup, and I felt both powerful and worried. Without our mother there, I was suddenly older.

Aunt Opal took a few seconds to adjust one of Suzanne's barrettes. "At the VA hospital," she said. "She's sick. Surely you must have known? She needs a rest. She's gone away and left you."

Meek as old dogs, Christopher and Jan Mary went into the living room and turned on the television. I snugged the baby into her high chair, tucked a receiving blanket around her bare legs, and began peeling potatoes for supper. Suzanne sat in her miniature rocker, holding a Dr. Seuss book upside down and mouthing the words she knew by heart. I remember thinking that if we could just have an ordinary supper, do our homework, fold the laundry, say our prayers, then we could manage with Mother away. We might feel as though she'd just gone through the orchard to visit a neighbor, and that she might return at any moment.

"You'll have places to go, of course," Aunt Opal said, lighting the gas under the stale morning coffee. The sulfurous smell of the match lingered.

"Places?"

"Christopher can stay with Grandma and Grandpa. Janice will take the baby."

"We'll stay here together," I said.

"Roxanne," she said, pouring coffee into a flowered teacup. "You're too young to stay here alone with all these children."

I remember feeling small and powerless then, and I saw that I still needed to be taken care of — in fact, wanted to be taken care of — but I did not think I would be. I had no trust in anyone, and when you are a child, feeling this way, every day becomes a swim through white water with no life jacket. Many years went by before I allowed myself to wonder where my father was during this time.

"How long will we be gone?" I said.

"It's hard to say," Aunt Opal said, sighing. "It's really hard to say."

I was thirteen, Christopher twelve, and Jan Mary eight. We went to St. Martin's and rode the public school bus home, aware of our oddity — Christopher's salt-and-pepper cords instead of jeans, the scratchy scapulars against our chests, the memorization of saints' names and days and deeds. The week before our mother went away, I had stayed home from school twice, missing play auditions and report-card day. She had written excuses on foolscap: *Please excuse Roxanne from school yesterday. I needed her at home.*

Our father worked in another state. The house was isolated, out in the country; our nearest neighbor lived a mile away. During the summer I loved where we lived — the ocean of apple blooms, the muted voices of the Spanish-speaking orchard workers, the wild berries, like deep black fleece along the railroad tracks. Winters were another story. We heated with wood, and the fine wood ash smudged our schoolbooks, our clothes and linens, our wrists and necks. The well was running dry, and we children shared our bath water. By my turn the water was tepid and gray. Our mother fed the fire, waking sometimes twice in the night to keep it going, and her hands and fingers were cracked, swollen. I wanted to cry whenever I looked at them. The loneliness was like a bad smell in the house.

In the evening, while the others, the younger ones, watched *I Love Lucy*, she sipped Jack Daniel's from a jelly glass and told me her secrets, plucking me from childhood's shore. Very late, when the others had gone to bed, she'd curse our father in a whisper. One night, when she had filled that jelly glass for the third time, and wanted company, she told me about her true love, a woman she'd known in the WACs during the war, when they worked together in the motor pool in Dayton, Ohio. You can learn too much too soon about your mother's past. The weight of her concerns made me turn from her and wish that something would save us from the life we shared with her. I couldn't make the wish while I was watching her split and bleeding hands light a cigarette. But later, lying confused and rigid in the double bed I shared with cuddling Jan Mary and Suzanne, I wished that our mother would go away.

All of the moving took place at night. Aunt Opal drove Suzanne, Jan Mary, and me up the Entiat River to Entiat Home, a place local people called the orphans' home, though in truth the children there were not orphans but children whose parents could not care for them. The frozen river glittered in the moonlight. The fir trees rode in dark procession along the far bank. I sat in the front seat, a privilege of the oldest. The car was vast and luxurious and exotic. Most of the way, no one spoke.

Finally, from the cavernous back seat, Suzanne said, "Where's the baby?"

Don't ask, I thought, don't ask. I tried to send this silent message to Suzanne, but she didn't get it. Blood beat in my head.

"Katie Jean might need us," she said.

"Katherine will be fine," Aunt Opal said. "Fine, fine. She's with your cousin Janice, who has another baby for her to play with."

Her jolly voice made me feel as though someone were hugging me too hard, painfully. When we'd left Christopher at Grandma and Grandpa Swanson's, I'd felt sick to my stomach, not because I would be separated from him — no — but because I wanted to stay there too. I wanted to cling to Grandma Swanson and say, Take me, keep me. But I was the oldest. I didn't cling and cry.

I would miss Christopher. We had fallen into the habit of sitting in the unfinished knotty-pine pantry, after our baths and the dishes were done, listening to the high school basketball games on the staticky radio. We knew the players' names and numbers. Together we had anticipated the mystery of going to high school.

Aunt Opal turned slowly into the uphill drive, which was lined with billows of snow. The dark was my comfort — I didn't want to see everything at once. We parked in front of a red-brick house with two wrought-iron lamps beside the neatly shoveled steps. Silence leaped at us when Aunt Opal shut off the engine. The place seemed a last outpost before the black and convoluted mountains, the Cascades, which, I imagined, went slanted and ragged to the sea. Then quickly, nimbly, a man and a woman came coatless down the steps and opened the car doors, greeting us as though we were their own children returning home. The woman was thin and wore pearls and a skirt and sweater. The man had hair as black as an eggplant. Their voices were cheerful, but they kept their hands to themselves, as though they knew we would not want to be touched by strangers.

One moment we were in the dark, the car, the winter mountain air; the next, all three of us were ushered into a blinding white place that was like a hospital room, with white metal cupboards, white metal cots, and everything amazingly clean and shiny under the fluorescent lights, cleaner even than Grandma Swanson's house.

We sat on the edge of a cot without speaking to one another. Snow dripped in dirty puddles from our saddle oxfords. The floor was black and white like a checkerboard. In the hallway, out of sight, Aunt Opal spoke with the man and woman — "Well behaved," I heard her say — and then she departed with all the speed and indifference of a UPS driver. Through a tall window in the room I watched her headlights sweep across the cinnamon bark of a ponderosa pine. From someplace far away in the house came Christmas carols, wreathed in pure recorded voices. My body played tricks on me: my head hurt, and my stomach knotted in an acid snarl.

Suzanne growled in a baby way she had when she was tired or angry. I pulled her onto my lap and she sucked her thumb. Consoling her was my only source of reassurance.

Jan Mary stamped the dirty puddles with the toe of her shoe. "How will we get to school?" she said.

"We'll go to a different school."

"I don't want to."

"We don't always get to do what we want," I said, shocked at the way I parroted our mother.

The woman in the pearls came into the bright room and leaned over us, one arm around Jan Mary's back.

"I'm Mrs. Thompson," she said. Her words were stout with kindness, which seemed a warning to me, as though she could hurt me, and she smelled good, like flowery cologne. She's someone's perfect mother, I thought.

"You'll need baths before bedtime, girls," she said. She strode to the oak door across the room and opened it, and then switched on the bathroom light. "You have your own pajamas?"

"Yes," I said, nodding in the direction of the cardboard Cream of Wheat carton that held my clothes. Each of us had packed a carton with our best things.

"You can help your sisters bathe, Roxanne," she said. "Then I'll check your heads for lice."

"Our mother wouldn't allow that," I said.

"What did you say?"

"Our mother wouldn't allow us to have lice," I said. My voice seemed inordinately loud.

"It's just our policy," she said. "Now get moving. It's late."

We bedded down the first night in that same room, on the single cots made up with coarse cotton sheets and cream-colored

wool blankets with a navy stripe around the edge. The light from
the hallway bridged the high transom of the closed door, and I
didn't sleep for a long time. Our presence there rebuked our
mother, and I felt that humiliation as keenly as though I were
she. I kept thinking, We'll be better when we go home — we'll
work harder, knock down the cobwebs more often, check Jan
Mary's homework, throw out the mismatched socks. Keeping
domestic order was, inexplicably, bound up with being good,
blessed. The fantasies that lulled me to sleep were of cupboards
packed with thick folded towels, full cookie jars, an orderly
abundance, like perpetual fire against the night.

The next morning I lay there, warm but wet, with the covers
up to my neck. Suzanne and Jan Mary were still asleep. A cat
meowed urgently in the hallway. The windows were long and
divided into panes of wavery old glass. Outside it was snowing,
the dry, fine net of winter. An old cottonwood tree in the yard
had been struck by lightning some time ago. The split in the
main trunk had been girdled with an iron band; it had healed,
and now the scar tissue bloomed over the edge of the metal ring.
I wondered what time it was and what would happen next. The
procedure of moving, being dropped off like a litter of kittens,
had been bad enough, and now I had to admit I had wet the
bed. I dreaded telling someone, but wanted to get it over with.

I thought of Mary in *The Secret Garden* and the way her spite
protected her. I remembered the places I'd read the book: on
the school steps at recess in second grade, under the cooling
arms of a juniper tree when I was eleven. My own spite and
anger could not protect me. They were repulsive feelings I
couldn't bear to admit to myself, because then I'd have to admit
them to the priest. I'd told him once that I'd wished our mother
would go away. I'd wished it for my birthday, which seemed to
magnify the sin. He did not understand the power of wishes,
and for penance he gave me a mere five Hail Marys. Now our
mother *was* gone, and I tried to imagine her inside the VA hospital, but I could only picture the rusted iron bars, the flaking
pink-stucco walls. The hospital was down by the Columbia River.
The summer I was ten, a male patient people called "a crazy"
had deliberately walked into the river and drowned.

The door opened, Mrs. Thompson peeked in, and Jan Mary

and Suzanne sat up in their cots, their choppy hair all askew, eyes puffy with sleep.

"Time to get up, ladies," Mrs. Thompson said. She wore a robe of some soft peach fabric.

"Snow," Suzanne announced.

I threw back the covers, and the cool air sliced through my wet pajamas and chilled me. I forced myself to slither across the floor.

"Mrs. Thompson," I said officiously, as though I spoke of someone else, "I've wet the bed."

"Oh?"

"What shall I do?"

She stepped into the room and closed the door. "Does this happen often?" She walked to my cot, with me close behind.

"Roxie wet the bed, Roxie wet the bed," Jan Mary sang.

I flung her a murderous glare, which silenced her at once.

"Sometimes," I said vaguely. By this time I had no feelings in the matter. I'd killed them, the way you track down a mud dauber and squash him.

Mrs. Thompson quickly jerked the sheets from the bed and carried them into the bathroom, holding them at arm's length from her peachy robe.

"Please," I said. "Let me."

She dumped the sheets in the tub. "Run cold water on them. Add your pajamas. Rinse them good. Ask your sister to help you wring them out and then hang them over this shower curtain. When they dry, we'll put them in the dirty laundry." I felt I'd depleted whatever good will had existed between us.

The entire six months at Entiat I followed this routine. I managed to keep from wetting the bed four times in those six months, by what miracle I could not tell. I tried prayers and wishes, not drinking after six in the evening. Nothing worked. I lived in the Little Girls' House, though my age was borderline — they could have assigned me to the Big Girls' House. And every day all the little girls knew what I'd done when they saw my slick and gelid sheets hanging like Halloween ghosts in the bathroom.

Mrs. Hayes, the dorm mother of the Little Girls' House, had two immense tomcats, Springer and Beau, whose claws had been removed. They lived like kings, always indoors. Everyone called the dorm mother Gabby Hayes behind her back. She was in her fifties and smelled of gardenias and cigarette smoke. Her lipstick was thick and cakey, the color of clay flowerpots. She prided herself on her hair — it was coppery and resembled scrubbing pads we used in the kitchen. If someone broke the rules, she would announce to the group at large, "That's not allowed here." The chill in her voice always arrested the deviant.

Life in the Little Girls' House was orderly, neat, regulated. Before school in the morning we did our chores, young ones polishing the wooden stairs, older ones carting the laundry in duffel bags to the laundry building. Some were assigned kitchen duty, others bathrooms. Everyone, down to the four-year-olds, had work to do. I was impressed with the efficiency and equanimity with which work was accomplished. I wrote letters to our mother, in my experimental, loopy left-hand slant, suggesting job charts on the refrigerator, new systems we could invent to relieve her of her crushing burden.

The house sheltered twenty-three of us. Jan Mary and Suzanne naturally gravitated toward others their age. They slept away from the oldest girls, in a drafty long hall near Mrs. Hayes's apartment. Our family ties were frayed, and I was genuinely surprised when I met Jan Mary's musing blue eyes in recognition across the dinner table. She seemed to be saying, How in the world did we get here?

The first day at the new school I was issued a pair of faded blue cotton bloomers for PE. At St. Martin's, PE had meant softball on the playground. At the new school the locker room was my personal hell: the body smells, the safety-pinned bras, the stained slips, the hickeys, the pubic hair growing wild above our thighs. Sister Michael had always told us not to look at ourselves when we bathed, to be ashamed and vigilant. In the locker room we girls were elbow to elbow in the narrow aisle beside the dented pink lockers.

"What is your *prob*lem?"

"The F word. That's all he knows thesé days."

"My mother won't let me."

"Bud's getting a car for his birthday."

Their conversations shimmered around me like a beaded curtain. We couldn't help but see one another — our new breasts, our worn underwear — but the talk kept us on another plane, a place above the locker room, where we could pretend we weren't totally vulnerable, absolutely displayed.

Georgia Cowley, a squat, freckled woman, ruled that class with a cruel hand. When I entered the gym for the first time, she waved sharply in my direction and I went over to her.

"Name?"

"Roxanne Miller."

"We're tumbling, Roxanne Miller," she said, writing something on her clipboard. "You ever tumbled?"

"No, ma'am." I looked at the girls casually turning cartwheels, blue blurs, on the hardwood floor. My hopes of fading into the wrestling mats for the hour fluttered like a candle in a storm.

"Come out here with me," she said.

I followed her to the red mat in front of the stage.

"We start with forward rolls. Squat down."

I squatted, glancing desperately around to find someone I could imitate. All motion had wound down, and the girls were gathered in gossip knots, chattering and watching me with slitted eyes. I remember staring at Miss Cowley's gym shoes and noting a splat of dried tomato seeds on the toe of one of them.

"Tuck your head. Now one foot forward, hands on the mat."

She gave me a little shove to propel me forward. I fell sideways, my pale thigh plopping fishlike on the floor. The girls giggled, and hot tears swelled in my head. The seconds on the floor expanded, seemed to go on forever.

"Get up," she said. "Sit over there on the bleachers for a while and watch. You'll get the hang of it." Then she blew her chrome whistle, and the girls lined up to do their forward rolls.

On the bleachers a Negro girl from Entiat, Nadine, slid next to me, sighing hard. "Got the curse," she said. "I'm sitting out."

"You can sit out?"

"Sure 'nough." She scratched her skinny calf. "You know the secret of cartwheels, Roxanne?"

"No," I said, interested, thinking her words might contain some secret I could learn, some intellectual knowledge that I could translate into body knowledge.

"Catch yourself before you kill yourself," she whispered, as she retied her sneaker. "Catch yo*self.*" And then she leaped up and turned a few, flinging herself into them with her own peculiar flick of her pink palms above her nappy head.

"Jefferson," Cowley barked. "Sit down and keep quiet."

For the rest of the gym period Nadine and I wrote messages on each other's backs, using our index fingers like pencils through the scratchy blue blouses.

At Christmas we were farmed out. I don't know how these decisions were made. Certainly I don't remember being asked where I would like to go for Christmas. Suzanne went with Mr. and Mrs. Thompson. Jan Mary was taken by Aunt Opal. I went to stay with the family of Darla Reamer, who had been our neighbor for five years. Darla was two years older than I was. When I'd been in fifth grade and Darla in seventh, we rode the school bus together and wrote love notes to each other using a special language we'd developed, a lispish baby talk in writing. Later that year she chose another girl as her best friend and left me miserable. Going to spend Christmas with her and her family, enduring their charity, was like an arduous school assignment I had to survive to attain the next grade. Her mother gave me a Shetland sweater and a jar of Pacquin hand cream. Her father took me out in the wind-crusted snowy field to see his apiary. We went to church, and those brief moments kneeling in the oak pew and at the altar, with its starlike poinsettias, were the only familiarity and peace I experienced. Darla spent many hours on the telephone with Julia, the one who'd taken my place. I was relieved when Mr. Reamer drove me back to Entiat on Christmas night. Many girls were still away and Mrs. Hayes let me stay up late. I drank hot chocolate alone in the dining room and wrote our mother a letter full of false cheer and fantasy about the future.

In our sleeping quarters, after lights out, under cover of dark, some girls took turns revealing fears, shames, wishes expressed as truth. When this talk began, their voices shifted from the usual shrill razzmatazz repartee about hairstyles, boys at school, and who'd been caught smoking. They spoke in church whispers.

"My mother tore my lip once. I had five stitches."

"My father's coming to get me on my birthday."

I didn't participate in this round robin but instead lay on my stomach, my pillow buckled under my chest, and watched the occasional gossamer thread of headlights on the river road. Night travel seemed to involve so much freedom and purpose — a will at work. Their talk was sad and low, and I, in my isolation, dreamed of going away, of having the power, the inestimable power, to say *I'm leaving*. Boys could somehow run away and make it, survive. But everyone knew that a girl's life was over if she ran away from home — or whatever had become home, whatever sheltered her from ruin.

Some nights, if we heard the rush of Mrs. Hayes's shower, we would sing in our thin voices a maudlin song that was popular at the time, "Teen Angel." One night the community of singing gave me courage, and after the song faded, I said, "I saw my mother hit my father with a belt."

As one, they sucked in their breath. Then Nadine said, "No *wonder* your mama in the hospital, girl."

They laughed, a false, uncertain snicker. I hated Nadine at that moment, and felt heartbroken in my hate. I'd always tried to be nice to her, because our mother had said they were just like everyone else inside.

On Valentine's Day we received a crumpled package wrapped in a brown grocery sack and tied with butcher's twine. Inside was a cellophane bag of hard candy hearts stamped "Be Mine" and "I Love You." Our mother had enclosed three penny valentines, and on mine she wrote, "I'm home now with Katie Jean and Christopher. See you soon." She was home! I'd given up on mail from her, but I'd kept writing. I tried to imagine her there with Christopher and the baby, without me to help her, and the thought made me feel invisible, unnecessary in the world. Don't think about it, I said to myself, and I began then the habit of blocking my thoughts with that simple chant. *Don't think about it.*

In April we were allowed to go home for a weekend.

"Your neighbor's here," Mrs. Hayes whispered in my ear, early that Saturday morning. "Help your sisters dress. I'll give him a tour while he's waiting."

I had a great deal to be excited about: seeing Christopher,

going to our old church, being with our mother. Our mother. Her life without me was a puzzle, with crucial pieces missing. I had high hopes about going home. Our mother was well; everyone — Mrs. Hayes, Mr. Reamer — said so.

We met him by his pickup truck. His khakis were spattered with pastel paint; he said he'd been painting his bee boxes. We fell into silence on the drive home. The thought surfaced, like the devil's tempting forefinger, that though we were only an hour's drive from our mother, we hadn't seen her since that morning in December when we went to school not knowing life would be irrevocably changed by the time we returned home. Did she know that morning that she wouldn't see us for four months?

Spring was alive down in the valley. The daffodil leaves were up along the driveway, though the flowers were still just pale shadows of memory, tightly curled and green. Mr. Reamer parked his pickup truck and sat hunched, arms folded across the steering wheel, waiting for us to get out.

We were all shy, bashful, and I hung back, urging Jan Mary and Suzanne forward with little pushes on their shoulder blades.

Jan Mary flinched and said meanly, "Don't push."

"Don't spoil it, now," I said.

And we three walked forward in a solemn row down the gravel drive toward the house. We wore our next-best dresses. Mine was a taffeta plaid with a smocked bodice and a sash, and I'd worn my cream-colored knee socks, saving my one pair of nylons for Sunday morning. I hadn't wanted to go home in nylons — they were a new addition to my sock drawer, and I was afraid our mother would say I was growing up too fast. The house looked the same, sagging at the corners of the roof, the gray paint blistering along the bottom of the door. It was a sunny day. Darla Reamer's cocker spaniel came yapping out the drive, flipping and bouncing the way cockers do. As we drew near the house, I saw that Darla was sitting with our mother in that small patch of grass in front of the house. Someone had put a wooden cable spool there for a table, and Darla and Mother sat near each other in lawn chairs. Darla was painting Mother's fingernails.

"Here come my girls," Mother said, waving her free hand.

Music was on inside the house, and we could hear it through the open window: *"You made me love you."* I didn't know what to do with Darla there. I'd imagined our mother embracing us, welcoming us, with significance. My heart shrank in disappointment, a rancid feeling, everything going sour at once. Suzanne, being only four, went right up to Mother and slipped her little arms around her neck and kissed her cheek. Jan Mary said, "Will you do mine, too, Darla?"

Katie Jean started crying from somewhere in the house. Mother, startled, rose partway from her chair and then sank back, waving her wet fingernails and looking helplessly at Darla. A raw, clean smell filled the yard, like cornsilk when you go outside to shuck corn in the summer dusk. Darla looked older, in a straight linen skirt with a kick pleat in the back. She had on slim flats and tan-tinted nylons. Her hair was in a French roll.

"I'll get her," Darla said, and she went into the house, letting the screen door slam. Suzanne was close on her heels.

Mother pulled me near, her arm around my waist. "How's my big girl?" she asked. She'd had her black hair frizzed in a permanent wave and her nails were painted fire-engine red. With one hand she shook a Lucky from the pack on the table. A glass of whiskey and melting ice was on the ground beside her chair. Her knuckles looked pink, but the cuts and splits were healed.

"Fine," I said.

"Darla's been helping me," she said. I held my breath to keep from crying.

I felt exhausted, not the clean exhaustion of after-dark softball but a kind of weariness; I was worn out with the knowledge that life would be different, but not in the way I had imagined or hoped. I didn't want to forgive her for being the way she was, but you have to forgive your mother. She searched my eyes and tried to make some long-ago connection, sweet scrutiny, perhaps the way she'd looked at me when I was a new baby, her first baby. I looked away. Jan Mary gnawed delicately at her cuticles. Christopher came around the corner of the house swinging his Mickey Mantle bat, his leather mitt looped on his belt. The new spring leaves were so bright they hurt my eyes.

PAM HOUSTON

How to Talk to a Hunter

FROM QUARTERLY WEST

WHEN HE SAYS "Skins or blankets?" it will take you a moment to
realize that he's asking which you want to sleep under. And in
your hesitation he'll decide that he wants to see your skin wrapped
in the big black moosehide. He carried it, he'll say, soaking wet
and heavier than a dead man, across the tundra for two — was
it hours or days or weeks? But the payoff, now, will be to see it
fall across one of your white breasts. It's December, and your
skin is never really warm, so you will pull the bulk of it around
you and pose for him, pose for his camera, without having to
narrate this moose's death.

You will spend every night in this man's bed without asking
yourself why he listens to top-forty country. Why he donated
money to the Republican party. Why he won't play back his messages while you are in the room. You are there so often the messages pile up. Once, you noticed the bright green counter reading as high as fifteen.

He will have lured you here out of a careful independence
that you spent months cultivating; though it will finally be winter, the dwindling daylight and the threat of Christmas, that makes
you give in. Spending nights with this man means suffering the
long face of your sheep dog, who likes to sleep on your bed, who
worries when you don't come home. But the hunter's house is
so much warmer than yours, and he'll give you a key, and just
like a woman, you'll think that means something. It will snow
hard for thirteen straight days. Then it will really get cold. When
it is sixty below there will be no wind and no clouds, just still air

and cold sunshine. The sun on the windows will lure you out of bed, but he'll pull you back under. The next two hours he'll devote to your body. With his hands, with his tongue, he'll express what will seem to you like the most eternal of loves. Like the house key, this is just another kind of lie. Even in bed; especially in bed, you and he cannot speak the same language. The machine will answer the incoming calls. From under an ocean of passion and hide and hair you'll hear a woman's muffled voice between the beeps.

Your best female friend will say, "So what did you think? That a man who sleeps under a dead moose is capable of commitment?"

This is what you learned in college: A man desires the satisfaction of his desire; a woman desires the condition of desiring.

The hunter will talk about spring in Hawaii, summer in Alaska. The man who says he was always better at math will form the sentences so carefully it will be impossible to tell if you are included in these plans. When he asks you if you would like to open a small guest ranch way out in the country, understand that this is a rhetorical question. Label these conversations future perfect, but don't expect the present to catch up with them. Spring is an inconceivable distance from the December days that just keep getting shorter and gray.

He'll ask you if you've ever shot anything, if you'd like to, if you ever thought about teaching your dog to retrieve. Your dog will like him too much, will drop the stick at his feet every time, will roll over and let the hunter scratch his belly.

One day he'll leave you sleeping to go split wood or get the mail and his phone will ring again. You'll sit very still while a woman who calls herself something like Patty Coyote leaves a message on his machine: she's leaving work, she'll say, and the last thing she wanted to hear was the sound of his beautiful voice. Maybe she'll talk only in rhyme. Maybe the counter will change to sixteen. You'll look a question at the mule deer on the wall, and the dark spots on either side of his mouth will tell you he shares more with this hunter than you ever will. One night, drunk, the hunter told you he was sorry for taking that deer, that every now and then there's an animal that isn't meant to be taken, and he should have known that deer was one.

Your best male friend will say, "No one who needs to call herself Patty Coyote can hold a candle to you, but why not let him sleep alone a few nights, just to make sure?"

The hunter will fill your freezer with elk burger, venison sausage, organic potatoes, fresh pecans. He'll tell you to wear your seat belt, to dress warmly, to drive safely. He'll say you are always on his mind, that you're the best thing that's ever happened to him, that you make him glad that he's a man.

Tell him it don't come easy, tell him freedom's just another word for nothing left to lose.

These are the things you'll know without asking: The coyote woman wears her hair in braids. She uses words like "howdy." She's man enough to shoot a deer.

A week before Christmas you'll rent *It's a Wonderful Life* and watch it together, curled on your couch, faces touching. Then you'll bring up the word "monogamy." He'll tell you how badly he was hurt by your predecessor. He'll tell you he couldn't be happier spending every night with you. He'll say there's just a few questions he doesn't have the answers for. He'll say he's just scared and confused. Of course this isn't exactly what he means. Tell him you understand. Tell him you are scared too. Tell him to take all the time he needs. Know that you could never shoot an animal, and be glad of it.

Your best female friend will say, "You didn't tell him you loved him, did you?" Don't even tell her the truth. If you do, you'll have to tell her that he said this: "I feel exactly the same way."

Your best male friend will say, "Didn't you know what would happen when you said the word 'commitment'?"

But that isn't the word that you said.

He'll say, "Commitment, monogamy, it all means just one thing."

The coyote woman will come from Montana with the heavier snows. The hunter will call you on the day of the solstice to say he has a friend in town and can't see you. He'll leave you hanging your Christmas lights; he'll give new meaning to the phrase "longest night of the year." The man who has said he's not so good with words will manage to say eight things about his friend without using a gender-determining pronoun. Get out of the house quickly. Call the most understanding person you know that will let you sleep in his bed.

Your best female friend will say, "So what did you think? That he was capable of living outside his gender?"

When you get home in the morning there's a candy tin on your pillow. Santa, obese and grotesque, fondles two small children on the lid. The card will say something like, From your not-so-secret admirer. Open it. Examine each carefully made truffle. Feed them, one at a time, to the dog. Call the hunter's machine. Tell him you don't speak chocolate.

Your best female friend will say, "At this point, what is it about him that you could possibly find appealing?"

Your best male friend will say, "Can't you understand that this is a good sign? Can't you understand that this proves how deep he's in with you?" Hug your best male friend. Give him the truffles the dog wouldn't eat.

Of course the weather will cooperate with the coyote woman. The highways will close, she will stay another night. He'll tell her he's going to work so he can come and see you. He'll even leave her your number and write "Me at Work" on the yellow pad of paper by his phone. Although you shouldn't, you'll have to be there. It will be you and your nauseous dog and your half-trimmed tree all waiting for him like a series of questions.

This is what you learned in graduate school: in every assumption is contained the possibility of its opposite.

In your kitchen he'll hug you like you might both die there. Sniff him for coyote. Don't hug him back.

He will say whatever he needs to to win. He'll say it's just an old friend. He'll say the visit was all the friend's idea. He'll say the night away from you has given him time to think about how much you mean to him. Realize that nothing short of sleeping alone will ever make him realize how much you mean to him. He'll say that if you can just be a little patient, some good will come out of this for the two of you after all. He still won't use a gender-specific pronoun.

Put your head in your hands. Think about what it means to be patient. Think about the beautiful, smart, strong, clever woman you thought he saw when he looked at you. Pull on your hair. Rock your body back and forth. Don't cry.

He'll say that after holding you it doesn't feel right holding anyone else. For "holding," substitute "fucking." Then take it as a compliment.

He will get frustrated and rise to leave. He may or may not be bluffing. Stall for time. Ask a question he can't immediately answer. Tell him you want to make love on the floor. When he tells you your body is beautiful, say, "I feel exactly the same way." Don't, under any circumstances, stand in front of the door.

Your best female friend will say, "They lie to us, they cheat on us, and we love them more for it." She'll say, "It's our fault. We raise them to be like that."

Tell her it can't be your fault. You've never raised anything but dogs.

The hunter will say it's late and he has to go home to sleep. He'll emphasize the last word in the sentence. Give him one kiss that he'll remember while he's fucking the coyote woman. Give him one kiss that ought to make him cry if he's capable of it, but don't notice when he does. Tell him to have a good night.

Your best male friend will say, "We all do it. We can't help it. We're self-destructive. It's the old bad-boy routine. You have a male dog, don't you?"

The next day the sun will be out and the coyote woman will leave. Think about how easy it must be for the coyote woman and a man who listens to top-forty country. The coyote woman would never use a word like "monogamy"; the coyote woman will stay gentle on his mind.

If you can, let him sleep alone for at least one night. If you can't, invite him over to finish trimming your Christmas tree. When he asks how you are, tell him you think it's a good idea to keep your sense of humor during the holidays.

Plan to be breezy and aloof and full of interesting anecdotes about all the other men you've ever known. Plan to be hotter than ever before in bed, and a little cold out of it. Remember that necessity is the mother of invention. Be flexible.

First, he will find the faulty bulb that's been keeping all the others from lighting. He will explain in great detail the most elementary electrical principles. You will take turns placing the ornaments you and other men, he and other women, have spent years carefully choosing. Under the circumstances, try to let this be a comforting thought.

He will thin the clusters of tinsel you put on the tree. He'll say something ambiguous like, Next year you should string popcorn and cranberries. Finally, his arm will stretch just high enough to place the angel on the top of the tree.

Your best female friend will say, "Why can't you ever fall in love with a man who will be your friend?"

Your best male friend will say, "You ought to know this by now: Men always cheat on the best women."

This is what you learned in the pop psychology book: Love means letting go of fear.

Play Willie Nelson's "Pretty Paper." He'll ask you to dance, and before you can answer he'll be spinning you around your wood stove, he'll be humming in your ear. Before the song ends he'll be taking off your clothes, setting you lightly under the tree, hovering above you with tinsel in his hair. Through the spread of the branches the all-white lights you insisted on will shudder and blur, outlining the ornaments he brought: a pheasant, a snow goose, a deer.

The record will end. Above the crackle of the wood stove and the rasp of the hunter's breathing you'll hear one long low howl break the quiet of the frozen night: your dog, chained and lonely and cold. You'll wonder if he knows enough to stay in his dog house. You'll wonder if he knows that the nights are getting shorter now.

SIRI HUSTVEDT

Mr. Morning

FROM THE ONTARIO REVIEW

SOMETIMES even now I think I see him in the street or standing in a window or bent over a book in a coffee shop. And in that instant, before I understand that it's someone else, my lungs tighten and I lose my breath.

I met him eight years ago. I was a graduate student then at Columbia University. It was hot that summer and my nights were often sleepless. I lay awake in my two-room apartment on West 109th Street listening to the city's noises. I would read, write, and smoke into the morning, but on some nights when the heat made me too listless to work, I watched the neighbors from my bed. Through my barred window, across the narrow air shaft, I looked into the apartment opposite mine and saw the two men who lived there wander from one room to another, half dressed in the sultry weather. On a day in July, not long before I met Mr. Morning, one of the men came naked to the window. It was dusk and he stood there for a long time, his body lit from behind by a yellow lamp. I hid in the darkness of my bedroom and he never knew I was there. That was two months after Stephen left me, and I thought of him incessantly, stirring in the humid sheets, never comfortable, never relieved.

During the day, I looked for work. In June I had done research for a medical historian. Five days a week I sat in the reading room at the Academy of Medicine on East 102nd Street, filling up index cards with information about great diseases — bubonic plague, leprosy, influenza, syphilis, tuberculosis — as well as more obscure afflictions that I remember now only because of their names — yaws, milk leg, green sickness, rhinitis, rag-sorter's disease, housemaid's knee, and dandy fever. Dr. Rosenberg, an octogenarian who spoke and moved very slowly, paid me six dollars an hour for all those index cards, and although I never understood what he did with them, I didn't ask him, fearing that an explanation might take hours. The job ended when my employer went to Italy. I had always been poor as a student, but Dr. Rosenberg's vacation made me desperate. I hadn't paid the July rent, and I had no money for August. Every day I went to the bulletin board in Philosophy Hall where jobs were posted, but by the time I called, they had always been taken. Nevertheless, that was how I found Mr. Morning. A small handwritten notice announced the position: "Wanted. Research assistant for project already under way. Student of literature preferred. Herbert B. Morning." A phone number appeared under the name and I called immediately. Before I could properly introduce myself, a man with a beautiful voice gave me an address on Amsterdam Avenue and told me to come over as soon as possible.

It was hazy that day, but the sun glared and I blinked in the light as I walked through the door of Mr. Morning's tenement building. The elevator was broken, and I remember sweating while I climbed the stairs to the fourth floor. I can still see his intent face in the doorway. He was a very pale man with a large handsome nose. He breathed loudly as he opened the door and let me into a tiny stifling room that smelled of cat. The walls were lined with stuffed bookshelves and more books were piled in leaning towers all over the room. There were tall stacks of newspapers and magazines as well, and beneath a window whose blind had been tightly shut was a heap of old clothes or rags. A massive wooden desk stood in the center of the room and on it were perhaps a dozen boxes of various sizes. Close to the desk was a narrow bed, its rumpled sheets strewn with more books. Mr. Morning seated himself behind the desk, and I sat down in an old folding chair across from him. A narrow ray of light that had escaped through a broken blind fell to the floor between us, and when I looked at it, I saw a haze of dust.

I smoked, contributing to the room's blur, and looked at the skin of his neck; it was moon white. He told me he was happy I had come and then fell silent. Without any apparent reserve, he looked at me, taking in my whole body with his gaze. I don't know if his scrutiny was lecherous or merely curious, but I felt assaulted and turned away from him, and then when he asked me my name, I lied. I did it quickly, without hesitation, inventing a new patronym: Davidsen. I became Iris Davidsen. It was a defensive act, a way of protecting myself from some amorphous danger, but later that false name haunted me; it seemed to move me elsewhere, shifting me off course and strangely altering my whole world for a time. When I think back on it now, I imagine that lie as the beginning of the story, as a kind of door to my uneasiness. Everything else I told him was true — about my parents and sisters in Minnesota, about my studies in nineteenth-century English literature, my past research jobs, even my telephone number. As I talked, he smiled at me, and I thought to myself, It's an intimate smile, as if he has known me for years.

He told me that he was a writer, that he wrote for magazines to earn money. "I write about everything for every taste," he said. "I've written for *Field and Stream, House and Garden, True Confessions, Reader's Digest.* I've written stories, one spy novel, poems, essays, reviews — I even did an art catalogue once." He grinned and waved an arm. "Stanley Rubin's rhythmical canvases reveal a debt to mannerism — Pontormo in particular — the long undulating shapes hint at . . ." He laughed. "And I rarely publish under the same name."

"Don't you stand behind what you write?"

"I am behind everything I write, Miss Davidsen, usually sitting, sometimes standing. In the eighteenth century, it was common to stand and write — at an escritoire. Thomas Wolfe wrote standing."

"That's not exactly what I meant."

"No, of course, it isn't. But you see, Herbert B. Morning couldn't possibly write for *True Confessions,* but Fern Luce can. It's as simple as that."

"You enjoy hiding behind masks?"

"I revel in it. It gives my life a certain color and danger."

"Isn't danger overstating it a bit?"

"I don't think so. Nothing is beyond me as long as I adopt the correct name for each project. It isn't arbitrary. It requires a gift, a genius, if I may say so myself, for hitting on the alias that will unleash the right man or woman for the job. Dewitt L. Parker wrote that art catalogue, for example, and Martin Blane did the spy novel. But there are risks, too. Even the most careful planning can go awry. It's impossible to know for sure who's concealed under the pseudonym I choose."

"I see," I said. "In that case, I should probably ask you who you are now?"

"You have the privilege, dear lady, of addressing Herbert B. Morning as himself, unencumbered by any other personalities."

"And what does Mr. Morning need a research assistant for?"

"For a kind of biography," he said, "for a project about life's paraphernalia, its bits and pieces, treasures and refuse. I need someone like you to respond freely to the objects in question. I need an ear and an eye, a scribe and a voice, a Friday for every day of the week, someone who is sharp, sensitive. You see, I'm in the process of prying open the very essence of the inanimate world. You might say that it's an anthropology of the present."

I asked him to be more specific about the job.

"It began three years ago when she died." He paused as if thinking. "A girl — a young woman. I knew her, but not very well. Anyway, after she died, I found myself in possession of a number of her things, just common everyday things. I had them in the apartment, this and that, out and about, objects that were lost, abandoned, speechless, but not dead. That was the crux of it. They weren't dead, not in the usual way we think of objects as lifeless. They seemed charged with a kind of power. At times I almost felt them move with it, and then after several weeks, I noticed that they seemed to lose that vivacity, seemed to retreat into their thingness. So I boxed them."

"You boxed them?" I said.

"I boxed them to keep them untouched by the here and now. I feel sure that those things carry her imprint — the mark of a warm, living body on the world. And even though I've tried to keep them safe, they're turning cold. I can tell. It's been too long, so my work is urgent. I have to act quickly. I'll pay you sixty dollars per object."

"Per object?" I was sweating in the chair and adjusted my position, pulling my skirt down under my legs, which felt strangely cool to the touch.

"I'll explain everything," he said. He took out a small tape recorder from a drawer in his desk and pushed it toward me. "Listen to this first. It will tell you most of what you want to know. While you listen, I'll leave the room." He stood up from his chair and walked toward a door. A large yellow cat appeared from behind a box and followed him. "Press play," he commanded and vanished.

When I reached for the machine, I noticed two words scrawled on a legal pad near it: "woman's hand." When I turned on the machine, a woman's voice whispered, "This belonged to the deceased. It is a white sheet for a single bed . . ." What followed was a painstaking description of the sheet. It included every tiny discoloration and stain, the texture of the aged cotton and even the tag from which the words had disappeared in repeated washings. It lasted for perhaps ten minutes; the entire speech was delivered in that peculiar half voice. The description itself was tedious and yet I listened with anticipation, imagining that the words would soon reveal something other than the sheet. They didn't. When the tape ended, I looked over to the door behind which Mr. Morning had hidden and saw that it was now ajar and half of his face was pressed through the opening. He was lit from behind, and I couldn't see his features clearly, but the pale hair on his head was shining, and again I heard him breathe with difficulty as he walked toward me. He reached out for my hand. Without thinking, I withdrew it.

"You want descriptions of that girl's things, is that it?" I could hear the tightness and formality in my voice. "I don't understand what a recorded description has to do with your project as a whole or why the woman on the tape was whispering."

"The whisper is essential, because the full human voice is too idiosyncratic, too marked with its own history. I'm looking for anonymity so the purity of the object won't be blocked from coming through, from displaying itself in its nakedness. A whisper has no character."

The project seemed odd, even eccentric, but I found myself drawn to it. Chance had given me this small adventure and I was pleased. I also felt that beneath their eccentricity, Mr. Morning's ideas had a weird kind of logic. His comments about whispering, for example, made sense.

"Why don't you write out the descriptions?" I said. "Then there will be no voice at all to interfere with the anonymity you want." I watched his face closely.

He leaned over the desk and looked directly at me. "Because," he said, "then there's no living presence, no force to prompt an awakening."

I shifted in my chair again, gazing at the pile of rags under the window. "What do you mean by awakening?"

"I mean that the objects in question begin to stir under scrutiny, that they, mute as they are, can nevertheless bear witness to human mysteries."

"You mean they're clues to this girl's life? You want to know about her, is that it? Aren't there more direct routes for finding out biographical information?"

"Not the kind of biography I'm interested in." He smiled at me, this time opening his mouth, and I admired his large white teeth. He isn't old, I thought, not even fifty. He leaned over and picked up a blue box from the floor — a medium-sized department store box — and handed it to me.

I pulled at its lid.

"Not now!" He almost cried out. "Not here."

I pushed the lid back down.

"Do it at home alone. The object must be kept wrapped and in the box unless you are working. Study it. Describe it. Let it speak to you. I have a recorder and a new tape for you as well. Oh yes, and you should begin your description with the words 'This belonged to the deceased.' Could you have it for me by the day after tomorrow?"

I told him I could and then left the apartment with my box and tape recorder, rushing out into the daylight. I walked quickly away from the building and didn't look into the box until I had turned the corner and was sure that he couldn't see me from his window. Inside was a rather dirty white glove lying on a bed of tissue paper.

I didn't go home until later. I fled the heat by going into an air-conditioned coffee shop, sitting for hours as I scribbled notes to myself about the glove and made calculations as to the number of objects I needed to describe before I could pay my rent. I imagined my descriptions as pithy, elegant compositions, small literary exercises based on a kind of belated nineteenth-century positivism. Just for the moment, I decided to pretend that the thing really can be captured by the word. I drank coffee, ate a glazed donut, and was happy.

But that night when I put the glove beside my typewriter to begin work, it seemed to have changed. I held it, felt the lumpy wool and then very slowly pulled it over my left hand. It was too small for my long fingers and didn't cover my wrist. As I looked at it, I had the uncanny feeling that I had seen the same glove on another hand. I began to tug abruptly at its fingers until it sailed to the floor. I let it lie there for several minutes, unwilling to touch it. The small woolen hand covered with smudges and snags seemed terrible to me, a stranded and empty thing, both nonsensical and cruel. Finally I snatched it up and threw it back into the box. There would be no writing until the next day. It was too hot; I was too tired, too nervous. I lay in bed near the open window, but the air stood still. I touched my clammy skin and looked over at the opposite apartment, but the two men had gone to sleep and their windows were black. Before I slept I moved the box into the other room.

That night the screaming began. I woke to the noise but couldn't identify it and thought at first that it was the demented howling of cats I had heard earlier in the summer. But it was a woman's voice — a long guttural wail that ended in a growl. "Stop it! I hate you! I hate you!" she screamed over and over. I stiffened to the noise and wondered if I should call the police, but a long time I just waited and listened. Someone yelled "Shut up" from a window and it stopped. I expected it to begin again, but it was over. I wet a washcloth with cold water and rubbed my neck, arms, and face with it. I thought of Stephen then, as I had often seen him, at his desk, his head turned slightly away from me, his large eyes looking down at a paper. That was when his body was still enchanted; it had a power that I battled and raged against for months. Later that enchantment fell away, and he passed into a banality I never would have thought possible.

The next morning I began again. By daylight the small box on the kitchen table had returned to its former innocence. Using my notes from the coffee shop, I worked steadily, but it was difficult. I looked at the glove closely, trying to remember the words for its various parts, for its texture and the color of its stains. I noticed that the tip of the index finger was blackened, as if the owner had trailed her finger along a filthy surface. She was probably left-handed, I thought, that's a gesture for the favored hand. A girl running her finger along a subway railing. The image prompted a shudder of memory: "woman's hand." The words may have referred to her hand, her gloved hand, or to the glove itself. The connection seemed rife with meaning, and yet it spawned nothing but a feeling vaguely akin to guilt. I pressed on with the description, but the more I wrote, the more specific I was about the glove's characteristics, the more remote it became. Rather than fixing it in the light of scientific exactitude, the abundance of detail made the glove disappear. In fact, my minute description of its discolorations, snags and pills, its loosened threads and stretched palm, seemed alien to the sad little thing before me.

In the evening I edited my work and then read it into the machine. Whispering bothered me; it made the words clandestine, foreign, and when I listened to the tape, I didn't recognize my own voice. It sounded like a precocious child lisping absurdities from some invisible part of the room, and when I heard it, I blushed with a shame I still don't understand.

Late that night I woke to the screaming again, but it stopped after several minutes, just as before. This time I couldn't get back to sleep and lay awake for hours in a vague torment as the shattered images of exhaustion and heat crowded my brain.

Mr. Morning didn't answer the bell right away. I pressed it three times and was about to leave when I heard him shuffling to the door. He paused in the doorway, looked me directly in the eyes, and smiled. The beautiful smile startled me, and I turned away from him. He apologized for the delay but gave no explanation. That day the apartment seemed more chaotic than on my first visit; the desk in particular was a mass of disturbed papers and boxes. He asked me for the tape; I gave it to him, and then he ushered me from the room, gently pushing me behind the door where he had concealed himself the last time.

I found myself in the kitchen, a tiny room, even hotter and

smellier than the other. There were a few unwashed dishes in
the sink, several books piled on the counter, and one large, white
box. From the next room I could just manage to hear the sound
of the tape and my soft voice droning on about the glove. I paged
through a couple of books, a world atlas and a little copy of *The
Cloud of Unknowing*, but I was really interested in the box. I stood
over it. The corners of the lid were worn, as if it had been opened
many times; two of the sides were taped shut. I ran my finger
over the tape to see if I could loosen it. I picked at the tape's
yellow skin with my nail, but my efforts made it pucker and tear,
so I stopped, trying again on the other side. My head was bent
over the box when I heard him coming toward the door, and I
leapt backwards, accidentally pushing the box off the counter.
It fell to the floor but didn't open. I was able to return it to its
place before Mr. Morning appeared in the doorway. Whether
or not he saw my hands dart away from the box, I still don't
know, but when the box fell, whatever was inside it made a loud,
hollow, rattling noise, and he must have heard that. Yet he said
nothing.

We walked into the other room and sat down. He looked at
me and I remember thinking that his gaze had a peculiar strength
and that he seemed to blink less often than most people.

"Was the tape O.K.?" I asked.

"Fine," he said, "but there was one aspect of the thing you
neglected to describe and I think it's rather important."

"What's that?"

"The odor."

"I didn't think of it," I said.

"No," he said, "many people don't, but without its smell, a
thing loses its identity; the absence of odor cripples your description, makes it two-dimensional. Every object has its own scent
and carries the odor of its place as well. This can be invaluable
to an investigation."

"How?" I said it loudly.

He paused and looked at the window. "By evoking something
crucial, something unnoticed before, a place or time or word.
Just think of the things we forget in closets and attics, the mil-
dew, the dust, the crushed dry bodies of insects — these odors
leave their traces. My mother's trunks smelled of wet wool and

lavender. It took me a long time to realize what that odor was, but then I identified it, and I remembered events I had forgotten."

"Is there something you want to remember about this girl who died?" I asked.

"Why do you say that?" He jerked his head toward me.

"Because you obviously want something out of all this. You want these descriptions for a reason. When you mentioned those trunks, I thought you might want to trigger a memory."

He looked away again. "A memory of a whole world," he said.

"But I thought you hardly knew her, Mr. Morning."

He picked up a pencil and began to doodle on a notebook page. "Did I tell you that?"

"Yes, you did."

"It's true. I didn't know her well."

"What is it you're after, then? Who was this person you're investigating?"

"I would like to know that, too."

"You're evading my questions. She had a name, didn't she, this girl?"

"Her name won't help you, Miss Davidsen." His voice was nearly a whisper.

"Well, it won't hurt me either," I said.

He continued to move the pencil idly on the page in front of him. I craned to see it, trying to disguise the gesture by adjusting my skirt. There were several letters written on the paper — what looked like an *I,* a *Y,* a *B,* an *O,* an *M,* and a *D.* He had circled the *M.* If those markings were intended to form some kind of order, it was impossible to make it out, but even then, before I suspected anything, those letters had a strange effect on me. They stayed with me like the small but persistent aches of a mild illness.

Putting the pencil down, he looked up at me and nodded. He patted his chest. "The heat has given you a rash — here."

"No, it's my birthmark." I touched the skin just below my collarbone.

"A port wine stain," he said. "It has character — a mark for life. If you'll forgive me for saying so, I've always found flaws like that poignant, little outward signs of our mortality. I used a birthmark in something I wrote once . . ."

I interrupted him. "You aren't going to tell me anything, are you?"

"You're referring to our subject, I take it?"

"Of course."

"I think you've failed to understand the nature of your task. I hired you precisely because you know nothing. I hired you to see what I cannot see, because you are who you are. I don't pretend that you're a blank slate. You bring your life with you, your nineteenth-century novels, your Minnesota, the fullness of your existence in every respect, but you didn't know her. When you look at the things I give you, when you write and then speak about them, your words and voice may be the catalysts of some undiscovered being. Knowledge of her will only distract you from your work. Let us say, for the sake of an example, that her name was Allison Hart and that she died of leukemia. Something appears before you, an image. A row of hospital beds, perhaps, in a large room lit by those fluorescent tubes, and you see her, I'm sure you do. Allison — it's a romantic name — pale and emaciated, once beautiful, she lies under white sheets . . . And what you see will not only be shaped by my words, but by my inflections, my expression, and then you will lose your freedom."

I began to speak, but he stopped me.

"No, let me say my piece. Let us say that I tell you her name was," he paused, "Maxine Robinson and that she was murdered." He looked out past me toward the door and squinted as if he were trying to see something far away. He took several deep breaths. "That she was killed right here in this building. What would you compose then, Miss Davidsen, when you look inside my boxes? You'd be suffocated by what you know, just as I am. It wouldn't do; it just wouldn't do."

"It doesn't make sense. I still don't understand why I shouldn't know the facts of her life and death."

"Because," he almost shouted. "Because we are about the business of discovery, of resurrection, not burial." He grabbed the edge of the desk and shook it. "Atonement! Miss Davidsen. Atonement!"

"Good God," I said, "atonement for what?"

He was suddenly calm. He pushed his chair back, crossed his legs, folded his arms, and cocked his head to one side. These movements seemed self-conscious, almost theatrical. "For the sins of the world."

"What does that mean?"

"It means exactly what the words say."

"Those words, Mr. Morning," I said, "are liturgical. You've gone into a religious mode all of a sudden. What am I to think? You seem to have a talent for saying nothing with style."

"Be patient and I think you'll begin to understand me." He was smiling.

I had no reply for him. The hot room, the darkness, his outburst, and incomprehensible speech had robbed me of the will to answer. Exhaustion had come over me in a matter of seconds. My bones hurt. Finally I said, "I should leave now."

"If you stay, I'll make tea for you. I'll feed you crumpets and tell you stories. I'll dazzle you with my impeccable manners, my wit and imagination."

I shook my head. "I really have to go."

He paid me then with three twenty-dollar bills and gave me another box — this time a small white jeweler's box. He told me he didn't need the description until Monday of the following week. I had four days. We shook hands and then just before I walked through the door, he patted my arm. It was a gesture of sympathy and I accepted it as if it were owed to me.

Inside the second box was a stained and misshapen cotton ball. I found myself hesitant to touch it, as if it were contaminated. The wad of fiber was colored with make-up or powder that looked orange in the light and was also marked with an unidentifiable clot of something dense and brown. I drew away from the little box. Had he salvaged this thing after her death? I imagined him in a bathroom bending over a wastebasket to retrieve the used cotton ball. How had he found these things? Had he hoarded more of her refuse in boxes? I saw him alone, his fingers tracing the outlines of an object as he sat in his chair in front of the window with the closed blinds. But in the daydream I couldn't see what he held. I saw only his body hunched over it.

In those four days between visits to Mr. Morning, I was never free of him. Bits and pieces of his conversation invaded my thoughts, appearing unsummoned at all hours, especially at night. The idea that the girl had been murdered in his building took hold of me, and I began to imagine it. He had taunted me with it; he had intended to entice me with it as just another possible death, but once it was said, I felt that I had known it from the beginning. Resurrection. Atonement. He had seemed genuinely passionate. I remembered his troubled breathing as he spoke, the letters on the page, the white box falling, his hand on my arm. At the same time, I told myself that the man was a charlatan, someone who loved games, riddles, innuendo. Nothing he said could be believed. But in the end, it was his posing that made me suspect that he had hidden the truth among the lies and that he was in earnest about his project and the girl.

That night I worked for hours on the description. I held the cotton ball with a pair of tweezers up to the light, trying to find the words that would express it, but the thing was lost to language; it resisted it even more than the glove. And when I tried metaphors, the object sank so completely into the other thing that I abandoned making comparisons. What was this piece of waste? As I sat sniffing fibers and poking at the brown stain with a needle, I was overwhelmed by a feeling of disgust. The cotton ball told me nothing. It was a blank, a cipher; it probably had no connection to anything terrible, and yet I felt as if I had intruded on a shameful secret, that I had seen what I should not have seen. I composed slowly and my mind wandered. It was a night of many sounds: a man and a woman were fighting in Spanish next door; fire sirens howled and I heard a miserable dog crying somewhere close. I thought of the summers in Minnesota, hot, muggy, but open to the air. At around two o'clock, in the baking confines of my bedroom, I whispered the description into the machine. After it was recorded, I put the cotton ball back into its box and hid it and the tape inside a cupboard in the other room. As I shut the door, I realized that I was behaving like a person with a guilty conscience.

For the third time I stood outside Mr. Morning's door in the dim hallway. A noise was coming from the apartment; it was as if a wind were gusting through it, a rush of sound. I put my ear to the door and then I understood what it was — the tapes, one breathy voice on top of another. He was playing the descriptions. No one voice could be distinguished from another, but I felt sure that mine was among them; I backed away from the door. At that moment I considered running, leaving the box and tape recorder outside the door. Instead I knocked. It may have been that by then I had to know about Mr. Morning, that I had to know what he was hiding. I listened to the sound of the machines being turned off and rewound one by one and then to the sound of drawers being opened and shut.

When he came to the door, he was disheveled. His hair, moist with sweat, stuck up from his head and two buttons on his shirt were unbuttoned. I avoided looking into his flushed face and turned instead to the now familiar room. The blinds were still tightly shut. How can he stand the darkness? I thought. He leaned toward me and smiled.

"Excuse my appearance, Miss Davidsen, I was sleeping and forgot the time altogether. You see me in my Oblomovian persona — only half awake. You'll have to imagine the brocade dressing gown, I'm afraid. And there's no Zakhar, to my infinite regret."

He went on, "Let me have the description and I'll shoo you into the other room right away and then we can talk. I've looked forward to your coming. You brighten the day."

In the kitchen I looked for the box, but it wasn't there. He's moved it, I thought, so I can't see what's in it. The low sound of my voice came from the other room as I waited. How many people had he hired to read those descriptions onto tapes? What were they really for? For an instant, I imagined him lying in the unmade bed listening to that chaos of whispers, but I pushed the image away. Then he was at the door, motioning for me to follow him into the other room.

"You did a good job with a difficult object," he said.

"Where did you get it?" I said. "It doesn't seem like a very revealing thing to me, a bit of discarded fluff."

"She left it here," he said.

"Who was she? What was she to you?"

"You can't resist, can you? You're dying of curiosity. I suppose it's to be expected from a smart girl like you. I honestly don't know who or what she was to me. If I did, I wouldn't be working on this problem. But that won't satisfy you, will it?"

I heard myself sigh and turned away from him. "I feel that there's something wrong with what you've told me, that there's something hidden behind what you say. It makes me uneasy."

"I will tell you what you want to hear, what you already think you know — that she was murdered. She was killed in the basement laundry room of this building. She lived here."

"And her name was Maxine Robinson."

"No," he said. "I made that up."

"Why?" I said. "Why do that?"

"Because, my friend, I wasn't giving you the facts at the time. I was just giving you a story — one story among a host of possible stories — a little yarn to amuse you and keep you coming back." He looked at his hands. "And keep me alive. A thousand and one tales."

"It would relieve me enormously if you could keep books out of this for once."

"I can try, but they keep popping up like a tic, one after another, rumbling about in my brain, all those people, all that talk. It's a madhouse in there." He pointed to his head and grinned.

"What was her real name?"

"It doesn't matter. I mean that. It doesn't matter for what you're doing. A name can evoke everything and nothing, but it's always a boulder that won't let you pass. I know. I'm a specialist. I want to keep you pure and her nameless." He stared at me. "I'm not fooling you. I need you. I need your help and if you know too much, I'll lose you. You won't be able to do the descriptions anymore."

The emotion in his voice affected me. It was as if he had revealed something intimate, unseemly. I could feel the heat in my face. When I spoke there was a tremor in my voice. "I don't understand you."

"I'm trying to understand a life and an act," he said. "I'm trying to piece together the fragments of an incomprehensible being and to remember. Do you know that I can't even remember her face? Try as I may, it will not be conjured. I can tell you what she looked like; I can recite a description of her features, part by part, but I cannot evoke the whole face."

"Don't you have a photograph?"

"Photographs!" He spat out the word. "I'm talking about true recollection — seeing the face."

The cat rubbed against Mr. Morning's legs and I looked at it. The room was cooler. "Could you open the window?" I said.

He stood up and pulled at the blind, raising it halfway. It was darker outside; a gray cloud cover had replaced the stifling yellow haze. I looked at his profile in front of the window. He stood there in his loose shirt and pants, his hand in one pocket, and I found him elegant. It's in his shoulders, I thought, and the narrowness of his hips. He must have loved her or hated her.

"I should get going," I said.

"You will do another description for me, won't you?"

I nodded. He gave me another small box and three twenty-dollar bills and asked me to return in two days. I pushed the money into my pocket without looking at it and stood up. A breeze came from the window. The weather was changing. At the door, he extended his hand and I took it. He held it for a few seconds longer than he should have, and as I pulled it away, he pressed his thumb into my palm. It startled me, but I felt a familiar shudder of excitement.

It had grown cool with remarkable speed. The sky was darkly overcast and I turned my face upward to feel the first drops of rain as I strode home. I ran into my apartment to open the box, pulling up its lid and pushing aside tissue paper. The third object lay before me on the table. It was a mirror, unadorned, a simple rectangle without even a frame. I picked it up and examined my face, removing a bit of sleep from the inside corner of my eye, studied my mouth, the line of my chin, and then moved the mirror away to see more. I still can't understand it, but as I looked, I was overcome with nausea and faintness. I sat down, put my head between my knees, and took deep breaths. It's possible that the dizziness had nothing to do with the mirror. I had had very little to eat that day and the day before. I scrimped on food for cigarettes, trying to keep my expenses down, and it may have been simple hunger, and yet when I think of that mirror now, it disturbs me, as if there were something wrong with it, something sickening.

Still unstable on my feet, I went to my desk and began to make notes. I was writing to myself, typing out questions about Mr. Morning and the project, but I couldn't put anything together. His remarks about memory, whispering, resurrection returned to me as scraps of some inscrutable idea, some bizarre plan. And then I thought of the noise of the tapes behind the door, his touch and his slender figure in front of the window. Those letters, I thought, those letters on the page. What did they mean? A name. Her name. I moved the letters around, trying to arrange them into a coherent order. I found *mob*, *boy*, *dim*, and then *body*. The word coursed through me — a tiny seizure in my nerves. But it was absurd; a man doodles on a paper and I decode his meaningless scribbles. Besides, there were letters that could not be incorporated. *I. M.* He had circled the *M*. The suspicion did not leave me, and I began to imagine that rather than hiding, Mr. Morning really wanted to talk, wanted to tell me something, that the letters, the hints, were revelations, part of a circuitous confession. "If you know too much, I'll lose you." I took my umbrella and went out into the rain.

Within five minutes, I was standing in the entryway of Mr. Morning's building. I buzzed the super. After a considerable wait, a small fat man came to the door. He yawned and then raised his eyebrows, an expression apparently intended to replace the question What do you want?

"I'm looking for an apartment," I said. "Do you have anything vacant?" This was my first ploy, and to my surprise, the building had one empty apartment.

"Three seventy-five a month." He raised his brows again.

"I'd like to see it."

He took me to the third floor and opened the door of a small apartment identical to Mr. Morning's. I walked through the rooms as if I were inspecting them. The man leaned against the open door with a look of belligerent boredom.

"I was told there was a murder in this building," I said.

"That was three long years ago. There hasn't been nothing in that way since."

I walked toward him. "What was her name?"

"Your umbrella's dripping on me, sweetheart."

I moved it away and repeated the question. "Was it Maxine, Maxine Robinson?"

"Hey, hey, hey," he lifted up his hands and backed away from

me. "What's going on here? The name was Zalewski, Sherri Zalewski. It's no secret. It was in all the papers."

Tears were in my eyes and I turned away from him.

"What's the matter, kid?" he said.

"Please, tell me," I said. "Did they find the person who did it?"

"You got some kind of special interest here?" he said.

"There can't be any harm in telling me the story," I said.

He did tell me then. I think he was sorry for me or embarrassed by my emotion. Sherri Zalewski had been a nurse who
lived in the building. She was knifed to death on a February
night while doing her laundry. No one had seen or heard anything. A woman who moved out shortly afterward had found
her the next morning. "Real ugly," he said. "Real bad." The
woman had vomited in the hallway. The police never found the
killer. "They snooped around here for months," he said. "Nothing came of it. They were after the guy in 4F for a while, a real
weirdo, Morning. Even took him down to the station. All the
tenants were calling and bitching about him. They let him go.
Didn't have a thing on him."

"Do you think he killed her?"

"Nah," he said, "he's not the type."

From there I went to Butler Library to check the papers, but
there was little new in them. Sherri Zalewski had grown up in
Greenpoint. Her mother was dead; her father was a mailman;
she had one sister. A friend, quoted in the *Times,* called her "an
angel of mercy." Mr. Morning was not mentioned. According to
the articles, the police had no suspects. Sherri Zalewski vanished
from print for months; her name appeared only once again, in
a story run by the *Times* on unsolved murders in New York City.
I found a single photograph of her — a grainy block of newsprint that was probably taken from a high school graduation
portrait. I stared at the picture, looking for a way in, but it was
unusually blank: a girl, neither pretty nor homely, with small
eyes and a full mouth.

I carefully attached the chain lock on my door and turned on
every light in my apartment before I sat down at the typewriter.
I decided to write and record a letter to Mr. Morning. I did
describe the mirror briefly but there was little to say. Its surface
was unscratched; it had no discernible odor; it was at the same

time a full and empty thing, dense with images in one place,
vacant in another. Except for the steady sound of the rain outside, my building and street were uncommonly quiet that night,
but the noises I did hear made me jump, and I understood that
I was listening for someone, waiting, expecting the sound of an
intruder. He was in my head. Fragments of our conversation
came back to me: Fern Luce, what he had said about remember-
ing the girl's face, the smell of wool and lavender in his mother's
trunk. I wrote, and as I wrote, I saw her body on the floor in the
vacant apartment I had visited. I always see it there, for some
reason — bloodied and torn apart. I see the corpse as in a photograph, in black and white, illuminated by a dim light bulb.
Even now when it comes to me, I can't examine it closely. I push
it away.

Evening became night. The room turned dusky and a chill
made the blond hair on my arms stand up. I wrapped myself in
a blanket and wrote one page after another and threw them away.
When I finished I had just one page. The mirror lay beside me
shining in the lamplight. At around one o'clock in the morning,
I spoke the words I had written into the tape recorder but didn't
listen to them. The wind blew over my bed, and I fell into a
deep, empty sleep.

Mr. Morning's rooms were cool and wet that day. His windows
were open for the first time, and the wind blew in, ruffling a
newspaper that lay on top of a pile. His usually pale cheeks were
rosy and he seemed to be breathing more easily. I am quite sure
that he sensed my apprehension immediately, because he said
so little to me, and in his face there was sorrow or maybe regret.
Before I secluded myself in the kitchen, I noticed that there was
a tall stack of papers that looked like a manuscript on the desk.

I didn't close the door to the kitchen; I let it stand open slightly
and put my eye to the crack. I watched him as he placed the tape
recorder in front of him on the desk and turned it on. He leaned
back in his chair, let his arms hang limply at his sides, and closed
his eyes. After a brief interval of static from the machine, I heard
my voice come from the other room. I listened to the short description of the mirror that I had dutifully whispered onto the
tape. Then I heard my full voice and saw Mr. Morning look

sharply in my direction. I quickly shut the door. As I listened to
the high, childlike voice that must have been mine, I clenched
my teeth so tightly that later my jaw was sore.

"I know who she was. Her name was Sherri Zalewski. I wondered for a while if you hadn't invented her, but now I know
that she existed and that she lived and died in your building. A
glove, a stained cotton ball, a mirror. Why these things? Where
did you find them? You must have known that I would ask these
questions. I suspect that you have invited them, that you knew I
would find out about her and about you. You should have told
me the story, Mr. Morning. You should have told me directly
rather than hinting at it. I do believe that, for you, this project is
somehow an attempt to undo what happened that night, that
these things of hers are a part of some elaborate idea that I can't
make out." There was a pause on the tape, and I listened for a
noise from him, but there was nothing. "The things, the tapes,
all your talk. I don't know what to do with them, how to understand them, how to understand you. I do know that the dead do
not come back to life." I heard a loud scraping noise. He must
have moved his chair. But the tape was still on. I pressed myself
against the door as if the weight of my body could shut him out.
"I know that the police questioned you, that they suspected you.
I am not saying that you killed her; I'm asking you to tell me the
truth. That is all." It was over. He was walking to the door and
I heard him turn the knob on the other side. I stepped back. He
was breathing loudly and a wheezing sound seemed to come from
deep in his chest. He stood in the open doorway and stared at
me, his face deeply flushed. He looked as if he were about to
speak, but then he closed his mouth and gained control of his
breathing.

He said, "What is there to say? You expect me to confess, don't
you, to fall down before you and tell you that I murdered her.
But that isn't going to happen. It can't happen."

"What are you saying?" My voice was choked.

"I have already explained everything to you." He looked past
me and pressed his lips together in a spasm of emotion. "There
is nothing more to say. The story is yours. Not mine."

"What do you mean?"

"I mean that you've invented the story yourself. It belongs to you, not to me. You've already chosen an ending, a way out. I suppose it's inevitable that you should want satisfaction." He looked at me. " 'The evil wizard turned to stone.' 'The King and Queen lived happily ever after.' 'He died in prison, a broken man.' Whatever. What you've forgotten is that some things are unspeakable. That's what you've left out. Words may cover it up for a while, but then it comes howling back. A storm. A plague. Only half remembered. The difference between you and me is that I know I've forgotten. You don't." He turned around and faced the other room.

I spoke to his back. "That's what you have to say to me? I ask you to tell me the truth and you tell me that?"

"Yes," he said.

"I don't understand you. I don't understand you at all. Tell me that you didn't kill her." My voice was shrill.

"No," he said.

Mr. Morning walked toward his desk, and I heard the blinds rattle. There was a gust of wind from outside, and the papers on the desk were whipped into the air — hundreds of white pages flapped noisily against the bookshelves and walls, blew over the chairs and stacks of newspapers, sliding across the wood floor. Mr. Morning scrambled to retrieve them.

"Listen, Iris," he said. "I know things have changed, but I don't want to lose you. I want you to stay with me and do some more work. I want you to talk with me the way you've done these last two weeks. You will stay, won't you?"

I said yes to him. I thought to myself that if I did one more description, I could press him again, that he would tell me the truth, but now I wonder if that was really the reason.

He opened the desk drawer and took out another small white box. He held it out to me with both hands. "For tomorrow. Tomorrow at two." He gave me the tape recorder, and then, after explaining that he was short of cash, he wrote out a check to Iris Davidsen.

"I can't accept it," I said.

"Please, I insist."

I took it, knowing that I could never cash it. I walked to the door, picking my way among the fallen pages. He walked beside me.

At the door, he took my hand in both of his. "There's one last thing. Before you go, I want you to leave me something of yours." His eyes were shining.

"No."

"Why not?"

I released my hand from his grip. "No."

"One small thing." He leaned closer to me, and in the opening of his shirt I saw the cleft of his collarbone. There was a vague scent of cologne.

I opened my purse and began to search it, roughly pushing aside books, envelopes, and keys until I found an old green eraser, blackened with lead smudges, and thrust it into his hand, saying that I had to leave for an appointment.

I imagine that he stood in the doorway and watched me rush to the stairs and that he continued to stand there as I ran down one flight after another, because I never heard the door close.

I ran into the street and began to walk toward Broadway. When I reached the corner, I paused. It had stopped raining and the sky was breaking into vast, blank holes of blue. I watched the clouds move and then looked into the street. The sidewalk, buildings, and people had been given a fierce clarity in the new light; each thing appeared radically distinct, as if my eyesight had suddenly been sharpened. It was then that I decided to get rid of the things. I opened my bag, took out the check, ripped it to pieces, and threw it into a large trash bin. Then I threw away the tape recorder and the unopened box. I can still see the small black machine lying askew on the garbage heap and the smaller box as it tumbled farther into the bin. It upset a Styrofoam cup as it fell, and I turned away just as a stream of pale brown coffee dregs ran over its lid. My memory of those discarded objects, lying among the other waste, is vivid but silent, as if I had been standing in the noiseless city of a movie or a dream. I saw them for only an instant, and then I ran from those things as if they were about to rise up and pursue me.

I didn't think that would be the end of it. Mr. Morning had my telephone number, after all, and there was nothing to prevent him from finding me. I waited for months, but I never heard from him. When the telephone rang, it was always someone else.

DENIS JOHNSON

Car-Crash While Hitchhiking

FROM THE PARIS REVIEW

A SALESMAN who shared his liquor and steered while sleeping
. . . A Cherokee filled with bourbon . . . A VW no more than
a bubble of hashish fumes, captained by a college student . . .

And a family from Marshalltown who head-onned and killed
forever a man driving west out of Bethany, Missouri . . .

. . . I rose up sopping wet from sleeping under the pouring
rain, and something less than conscious, thanks to the first three
of the people I've already named — the salesman and the Indian and the student — all of whom had given me drugs. At the
head of the entrance ramp I waited without hope of a ride. What
was the point, even, of rolling up my sleeping bag when I was
too wet to be let into anybody's car? I draped it around me like
a cape. The downpour raked the asphalt and gurgled in the ruts.
My thoughts zoomed pitifully. The traveling salesman had fed
me pills that made the linings of my veins feel scraped out. My
jaw ached. I knew every raindrop by its name. I sensed everything before it happened. I knew a certain Oldsmobile would
stop for me even before it slowed, and by the sweet voices of the
family inside of it I knew we'd have an accident in the storm.

I didn't care. They said they'd take me all the way.

The man and the wife put the little girl up front with them,
and left the baby in back with me and my dripping bedroll. "I'm
not taking you anywhere very fast," the man said. "I've got my
wife and babies here, that's why."

You are the ones, I thought. And I piled my sleeping bag against
the left-hand door and slept across it, not caring whether I lived

or died. The baby slept free on the seat beside me. He was about nine months old.

. . . But before any of this, that afternoon, the salesman and I had swept down into Kansas City in his luxury car. We'd developed a dangerous cynical camaraderie beginning in Texas, where he'd taken me on. We ate up his bottle of amphetamines, and every so often we pulled off the interstate and bought another pint of Canadian Club and a sack of ice. His car had cylindrical glass-holders attached to either door and a white, leathery interior. He said he'd take me home to stay overnight with his family, but first he wanted to stop and see a woman he knew.

Under midwestern clouds like great gray brains we left the superhighway with a drifting sensation and entered Kansas City's rush hour with a sensation of running aground. As soon as we slowed down, all the magic of traveling together burned away. He went on and on about his girlfriend. "I like this girl, I think I love this girl — but I've got two kids and a wife, and there's certain obligations there. And on top of everything else, I love my wife. I'm gifted with love. I love my kids. I love all my relatives." As he kept on, I felt jilted and sad. "I have a boat, a little sixteen-footer. I have two cars. There's room in the back yard for a swimming pool." He found his girlfriend at work. She ran a furniture store, and I lost him there.

The clouds stayed the same until night. Then, in the dark, I didn't see the storm gathering. The driver of the Volkswagen, a college man, the one who stoked my head with all the hashish, let me out beyond the city limits just as it began to rain. Never mind the speed I'd been taking, I was too overcome to stand up. I lay out in the grass off the exit ramp and woke in the middle of a puddle that had filled up around me.

And later, as I've said, I slept in the back seat while the Oldsmobile — the family from Marshalltown — splashed along through the rain. And yet I dreamed I was looking right through my eyelids, and my pulse marked off the seconds of time. The interstate through western Missouri was, in that era, nothing more than a two-way road, most of it. When a semi truck came toward us and passed going the other way, we were lost in a blinding spray and a warfare of noises such as you get being towed through an automatic car wash. The wipers stood up and lay down across the windshield without much effect. I was exhausted, and after an hour I slept more deeply.

I'd known all along exactly what was going to happen. But the man and his wife woke me up later, denying it viciously.

"Oh — *no!*"

"NO!"

I was thrown against the back of their seat so hard that it broke. I commenced bouncing back and forth. A liquid which I knew right away was human blood flew around the car and rained down on my head. When it was over I was in the back seat again, just as I had been. I raised up and looked around. Our headlights had gone out. The radiator was hissing steadily. Beyond that, I didn't hear a thing. As far as I could tell, I was the only one conscious. As my eyes adjusted I saw that the baby was lying on its back beside me as if nothing had happened. Its eyes were open and it was feeling its cheeks with its little hands.

In a minute the driver, who'd been slumped over the wheel, sat up and peered over at us. His face was smashed and dark with blood. It made my teeth hurt to look at him — but when he spoke, it didn't sound as if any of his teeth were broken.

"What happened?"

"We had a wreck," he said.

"The baby's O.K.," I said, although I had no idea how the baby was.

He turned to his wife.

"Janice," he said. "Janice, Janice!"

"Is she O.K.?"

"She's dead!" he said, shaking her angrily.

"No she's not." I was ready to deny everything myself now.

Their little girl was alive, but knocked out. She whimpered in her sleep. But the man went on shaking his wife.

"Janice!" he hollered.

His wife moaned.

"She's not dead," I said, clambering from their car and running away.

"She won't wake up," I heard him say.

I was standing out here in the night, with the baby, for some reason, in my arms. It must have still been raining, but I remember nothing about the weather. We'd collided with another car on what I now perceived was a two-lane bridge. The water beneath us was invisible in the dark.

Moving toward the other car I began to hear rasping, metallic snores. Somebody was flung halfway out the passenger door, which was open, in the posture of one hanging from a trapeze by his ankles. The car had been broadsided, smashed so flat that no room was left inside of it even for this person's legs, to say nothing of a driver or any other passengers. I just walked right on past.

Headlights were coming from far off. I made for the head of the bridge, waving them to stop with one arm, and clutching the baby to my shoulder with the other.

It was a big semi, grinding its gears as it decelerated. The driver rolled down his window and I shouted up at him. "There's a wreck. Go for help."

"I can't turn around here," he said.

He let me and the baby up on the passenger side, and we just sat there in the cab, looking at the wreckage in his headlights.

"Is everybody dead?" he asked.

"I can't tell who is and who isn't," I admitted.

He poured himself a cup of coffee from a thermos and switched off all but his parking lights.

"What time is it?"

"Oh, it's around quarter after three," he said.

By his manner he seemed to endorse the idea of not doing anything about this. I was relieved and tearful. I'd thought something was required of me, but I hadn't wanted to find out what it was.

When another car showed, coming the opposite direction, I thought I should talk to them. "Can you keep the baby?" I asked the truck driver.

"You'd better hang on to him," the driver said. "It's a boy, isn't it?"

"Well, I think so," I said.

The man hanging out of the wrecked car was still alive as I passed, and I stopped, grown a little more used to the idea now of how really badly broken he was, and made sure there was nothing I could do. He was snoring loudly and rudely. His blood bubbled out of his mouth with every breath. He wouldn't be taking many more. I knew that, but he didn't, and therefore I looked down into the great pity of a person's life on this earth. I don't mean that we all end up dead, that's not the great pity. I mean that he couldn't tell me what he was dreaming, and I couldn't tell him what was real.

Before too long there were cars backed up for a ways at either end of the bridge, and headlights giving a night-game atmosphere in the steaming rubble, and ambulances and cop cars nudging through so that the air pulsed with color. I didn't talk to anyone. My secret was that in this short while I had gone from being the president of this tragedy to being a faceless onlooker at a gory wreck. At some point an officer learned that I was one of the passengers, and took my statement. I don't remember any of this, except that he told me, "Put out your cigarette." We paused in our conversation to watch the dying man being loaded into the ambulance. He was still alive, still dreaming obscenely. The blood ran off of him in strings. His knees jerked and his head rattled.

There was nothing wrong with me, and I hadn't seen anything, but the policeman had to question me and take me to the hospital anyway. The word came over his car radio that the man was now dead, just as we came under the awning of the emergency room entrance.

I stood in a tiled corridor with my wet sleeping bag bunched against the wall beside me, talking to a man from the local funeral home.

The doctor stopped to tell me I'd better have an x-ray.

"No."

"Now would be the time. If something turns up later . . ."

"There's nothing wrong with me."

Down the hall came the wife. She was glorious, burning. She didn't know yet that her husband was dead. We knew. That's what gave her such power over us. The doctor took her into a room with a desk at the end of the hall, and from under the closed door a slab of brilliance radiated as if, by some stupendous process, diamonds were being incinerated in there. What a pair of lungs! She shrieked as I imagined an eagle would shriek. It felt wonderful to be alive to hear it! I've gone looking for that feeling everywhere.

"There's nothing wrong with me" — I'm surprised I let those words out. But it's always been my tendency to lie to doctors, as if good health consisted only of the ability to fool them.

Some years later, one time when I was admitted to the detox at Seattle General Hospital, I took the same tack.

"Are you hearing unusual sounds or voices?" the doctor asked.

"Help us, oh God, it hurts," the boxes of cotton screamed.

"Not exactly," I said.

"Not exactly," he said. "Now what does that mean?"

"I'm not ready to go into all that," I said. A yellow bird fluttered close to my face, and my muscles grabbed. Now I was flopping like a fish. When I squeezed shut my eyes, hot tears exploded from the sockets. When I opened them, I was on my stomach.

"How did the room get so white?" I asked.

A beautiful nurse was touching my skin. "These are vitamins," she said, and drove the needle in.

It was raining. Gigantic ferns leaned over us. The forest drifted down a hill. I could hear a creek rushing down among rocks. And you, you ridiculous people, you expect me to help you.

DENNIS McFARLAND

Nothing to Ask For

FROM THE NEW YORKER

INSIDE MACK'S APARTMENT, a concentrator — a medical machine that looks like an elaborate stereo speaker on casters — sits behind an orange swivel chair, making its rhythmic, percussive noise like ocean waves, taking in normal filthy air, humidifying it, and filtering out everything but oxygen, which it sends through clear plastic tubing to Mack's nostrils. He sits on the couch, as usual, channel grazing, the remote-control button under his thumb, and he appears to be scrutinizing the short segments of what he sees on the TV screen with Zenlike patience. He has planted one foot on the beveled edge of the long oak coffee table, and he dangles one leg — thinner at the thigh than my wrist — over the other. In the sharp valley of his lap, Eberhardt, his old long-haired dachshund, lies sleeping. The table is covered with two dozen medicine bottles, though Mack has now taken himself off all drugs except cough syrup and something for heartburn. Also, stacks of books and pamphlets — though he has lost the ability to read — on how to heal yourself, on Buddhism, on Hinduism, on dying. In one pamphlet there's a long list that includes most human ailments, the personality traits and character flaws that cause these ailments, and the affirmations that need to be said in order to overcome them. According to this well-intentioned misguidedness, most disease is caused by self-hatred, or rejection of reality, and almost anything can be cured by learning to love yourself — which is accomplished by saying, aloud and often, "I love myself." Next to these books are pamphlets and Xeroxed articles describing more unorthodox remedies — herbal brews, ultrasound, lemon juice, urine, even penicillin. And, in a ceramic dish next to these, a small, waxy envelope that contains "ash" — a very fine, gray-white, spiritually enhancing powder materialized out of thin air by Swami Lahiri Baba.

As I change the plastic liner inside Mack's trash can, into which he throws his millions of Kleenex, I block his view of the TV screen — which he endures serenely, his head perfectly still, eyes unaverted. "Do you remember old Dorothy Hughes?" he asks me. "What do you suppose ever happened to her?"

"I don't know," I say. "I saw her years ago on the nude beach at San Gregorio. With some black guy who was down by the surf doing cartwheels. She pretended she didn't know me."

"I don't blame her," says Mack, making bug-eyes. "I wouldn't like to be seen with any grown-up who does cartwheels, would you?"

"No," I say.

Then he asks, "Was everybody we knew back then crazy?"

What Mack means by "back then" is our college days, in Santa Cruz, when we judged almost everything in terms of how freshly it rejected the status quo: the famous professor who began his twentieth-century-philosophy class by tossing pink rubber dildos in through the classroom window; Antonioni and Luis Buñuel screened each weekend in the dormitory basement; the artichokes in the student garden, left on their stalks and allowed to open and become what they truly were — enormous, purple-hearted flowers. There were no paving-stone quadrangles or venerable colonnades — our campus was the redwood forest, the buildings nestled among the trees, invisible one from the other — and when we emerged from the woods at the end of the school day, what we saw was nothing more or less than the sun setting over the Pacific. We lived with thirteen other students, in a rented Victorian mansion on West Cliff Drive, and at night the yellow beacon from the nearby lighthouse invaded our attic windows; we drifted to sleep listening to the barking of seals. On weekends we had serious softball games in the vacant field next to the house — us against a team of tattooed, long-haired townies — and afterward, keyed up, tired and sweating, Mack and I walked the north shore to a place where we could watch the waves pound into the rocks and send up sun-ignited columns of water twenty-five and thirty feet tall. Though most of what we initiated "back then" now seems to have been faddish and wrongheaded, our friendship was exceptionally sane and has endured for twenty years. It endured the melodramatic confusion of Dorothy Hughes, our beautiful shortstop — I loved her, but she loved Mack. It endured the subsequent revelation that Mack was gay — any tension on that count managed by him with remarks about what a homely bastard I was. It endured his fury and frustration over my low-bottom alcoholism, and my sometimes raging (and *en*-raging) process of getting clean and sober. And it has endured the onlooking fish-eyes of his long string of lovers and my two wives. Neither of us had a biological brother — that could account for something — but at recent moments when I have felt most frightened, now that Mack is so ill, I've thought that we persisted simply because we couldn't let go of the sense of *thoroughness* our friendship gave us; we constantly reported to each other on our separate lives, as if we knew that by doing so we were getting more from life than we would ever have been entitled to individually.

In answer to his question — was everybody crazy back then — I say, "Yes, I think so."

He laughs, then coughs. When he coughs these days — which is often — he goes on coughing until a viscous, bloody fluid comes up, which he catches in a Kleenex and tosses into the trash can. Earlier, his doctors could drain his lungs with a needle through his back — last time they collected an entire liter from one lung — but now that Mack has developed the cancer, there are tumors that break up the fluid into many small isolated pockets, too many to drain. Radiation or chemotherapy would kill him; he's too weak even for a flu shot. Later today, he will go to the hospital for another bronchoscopy; they want to see if there's anything they can do to help him, though they have already told him there isn't. His medical care comes in the form of visiting nurses, physical therapists, and a curious duo at the hospital: one doctor who is young, affectionate, and incompetent but who comforts and consoles, hugs and holds hands; another — old, rude, brash, and expert — who says things like "You might as well face it. You're going to die. Get your papers in order." In fact, they've given Mack two weeks to two months, and it has now been ten weeks.

"Oh, my God," cries Lester, Mack's lover, opening the screen door, entering the room, and looking around. "I don't recognize this hovel. And what's that wonderful smell?"

This morning, while Lester was out, I vacuumed and generally straightened up. Their apartment is on the ground floor of a building like all the buildings in this southern California neighborhood — a two-story motel-like structure of white stucco and steel railings. Outside the door are an X-rated hibiscus (blood red, with its jutting, yellow, powder-tipped stamen), a plastic macaw on a swing, two enormous yuccas; inside, carpet, and plainness. The wonderful smell is the turkey I'm roasting; Mack can't eat anything before the bronchoscopy, but I figure it will be here for them when they return from the hospital, and they can eat off it for the rest of the week.

Lester, a South Carolina boy in his late twenties, is sick, too — twice he has nearly died of pneumonia — but he's in a healthy period now. He's tall, thin, and bearded, a devotee of the writings of Shirley MacLaine — an unlikely guru, if you ask me, but my wife, Marilyn, tells me I'm too judgmental. Probably she is right.

The dog, Eberhardt, has woken up and waddles sleepily over to where Lester stands. Lester extends his arm toward Mack, two envelopes in his hand, and after a moment's pause Mack reaches for them. It's partly this typical hesitation of Mack's — a slowing of the mind, actually — that makes him appear serene, contemplative these days. Occasionally, he really does get confused, which terrifies him. But I can't help thinking that something in there has sharpened as well — maybe a kind of simplification. Now he stares at the top envelope for a full minute, as Lester and I watch him. This is something we do: we watch him. "Oh-h-h," he says, at last. "A letter from my mother."

"And one from Lucy, too," says Lester. "Isn't that nice?"

"I guess," says Mack. Then: "Well, yes. It is."

"You want me to open them?" I ask.

"Would you?" he says, handing them to me. "Read 'em to me, too."

They are only cards, with short notes inside, both from Des Moines. Mack's mother says it just makes her *sick* that he's sick, wants to know if there's anything he needs. Lucy, the sister, is gushy, misremembers a few things from the past, says she's writ-

ing instead of calling because she knows she will cry if she tries
to talk. Lucy, who refused to let Mack enter her house at Christmastime one year — actually left him on the stoop in sub-zero
cold — until he removed the gold earring from his ear. Mack's
mother, who waited until after the funeral last year to let Mack
know that his father had died; Mack's obvious illness at the funeral would have been an embarrassment.

But they've come around, Mack has told me in the face of my
anger.

I said better late than never.

And Mack, all forgiveness, all humility, said that's exactly right:
much better.

"Mrs. Mears is having a craft sale today," Lester says. Mrs.
Mears, an elderly neighbor, lives out back in a cottage with her
husband. "You guys want to go?"

Eberhardt, hearing "go," begins leaping at Lester's shins, but
when we look at Mack, his eyelids are at half-mast — he's half
asleep.

We watch him for a moment, and I say, "Maybe in a little
while, Lester."

Lester sits on the edge of his bed reading the newspaper, which
lies flat on the spread in front of him. He has his own TV in his
room, and a VCR. On the dresser, movies whose cases show men
in studded black leather jockstraps, with gloves to match — dun-
geon masters of startling handsomeness. On the floor, a stack of
gay magazines. Somewhere on the cover of each of these magazines the word "macho" appears; and inside some of them, in
the personal ads, men, meaning to attract others, refer to themselves as pigs. "Don't putz," Lester says to me as I straighten
some things on top of the dresser. "Enough already."

I wonder where he picked up "putz" — surely not in South
Carolina. I say, "You need to get somebody in. To help. You
need to arrange it now. What if you were suddenly to get sick
again?"

"I know," he says. "He's gotten to be quite a handful, hasn't
he? Is he still asleep?"

"Yes," I answer. "Yes and yes."

The phone rings and Lester reaches for it. As soon as he begins to speak I can tell, from his tone, that it's my four-year-old on the line. After a moment Lester says, "Kit," smiling, and hands me the phone, then returns to his newspaper.

I sit on the other side of the bed, and after I say hello, Kit says, "We need some milk."

"O.K.," I say. "Milk. What are you up to this morning?"

"Being angry mostly," she says.

"Oh?" I say. "Why?"

"Mommy and I are not getting along very well."

"That's too bad," I say. "I hope you won't stay angry for long."

"We won't," she says. "We're going to make up in a minute."

"Good," I say.

"When are you coming home?"

"In a little while."

"After my nap?"

"Yes," I say. "Right after your nap."

"Is Mack very sick?"

She already knows the answer, of course. "Yes," I say.

"Is he going to die?"

This one, too. "Most likely," I say. "He's that sick."

"Bye," she says suddenly — her sense of closure always takes me by surprise — and I say, "Don't stay angry for long, O.K.?"

"You already said that," she says, rightly, and I wait for a moment, half expecting Marilyn to come on the line; ordinarily she would, and hearing her voice right now would do me good. After another moment, though, there's the click.

Marilyn is back in school, earning a Ph.D. in religious studies. I teach sixth grade, and because I'm faculty adviser for the little magazine the sixth graders put out each year, I stay late many afternoons. Marilyn wanted me home this Saturday morning. "You're at work all week," she said, "and then you're over there on Saturday. Is that fair?"

I told her I didn't know — which was the honest truth. Then, in a possibly dramatic way, I told her that fairness was not my favorite subject these days, given that my best friend was dying.

We were in our kitchen, and through the window I could see Kit playing with a neighbor's cat in the back yard. Marilyn turned on the hot water in the kitchen sink and stood still while the steam rose into her face. "It's become a question of where you belong," she said at last. "I think you're too involved."

For this I had no answer, except to say, "I agree" — which wasn't really an answer, since I had no intention of staying home, or becoming less involved, or changing anything.

Now Lester and I can hear Mack's scraping cough in the next room. We are silent until he stops. "By the way," Lester says at last, taking the telephone receiver out of my hand, "have you noticed that he *listens* now?"

"I know," I say. "He told me he'd finally entered his listening period."

"Yeah," says Lester, "as if it's the natural progression. You blab your whole life away, ignoring other people, and then right before you die you start to listen."

The slight bitterness in Lester's tone makes me feel shaky inside. It's true that Mack was always a better talker than a listener, but I suddenly feel that I'm walking a thin wire, and that anything like collusion would throw me off balance. All I know for sure is that I don't want to hear any more. Maybe Lester reads this in my face, because what he says next sounds like an explanation: he tells me that his poor old backwoods mother was nearly deaf when he was growing up, that she relied almost entirely on reading lips. "All she had to do when she wanted to turn me off," he says, "was to just turn her back on me. Simple," he says, making a little circle with his finger. "No more Lester."

"That's terrible," I say.

"I was a terrible coward," he says. "Can you imagine Kit letting you get away with something like that? She'd bite your knee-caps."

"Still," I say, "that's terrible."

Lester shrugs his shoulders, and after another moment I say, "I'm going to the K mart. Mack needs a padded toilet seat. You want anything?"

"Yeah," he says. "But they don't sell it at K mart."

"What is it?" I ask.

"It's a *joke,* Dan, for Chrissake," he says. "Honestly, I think you've completely lost your sense of humor."

When I think about this, it seems true.

"Are you coming back?" he asks.

"Right back," I answer. "If you think of it, baste the turkey."

"How could I not think of it?" he says, sniffing the air.

In the living room, Mack is lying with his eyes open now, staring blankly at the TV. At the moment, a shop-at-home show is on, but he changes channels, and an announcer says, "When we return, we'll talk about tree pruning," and Mack changes the channel again. He looks at me, nods thoughtfully, and says, "Tree pruning. Interesting. It's just like the way they put a limit on your credit card, so you don't spend too much."

"I don't understand," I say.

"Oh, you know," he says. "Pruning the trees. Didn't the man just say something about pruning trees?" He sits up and adjusts the plastic tube in one nostril.

"Yes," I say.

"Well, it's like the credit cards. The limit they put on the credit cards is . . ." He stops talking and looks straight into my eyes, frightened. "It doesn't make any sense, does it?" he says. "Jesus Christ. I'm not making sense."

Way out east on University, there is a video arcade every half mile or so. Adult peepshows. Also a McDonald's, and the rest. Taverns — the kind that are open at eight in the morning — with clever names: Tobacco Rhoda's, the Cruz Inn. Bodegas that smell of cat piss and are really fronts for numbers games. Huge discount stores. Lester, who is an expert in these matters, has told me that all these places feed on addicts. "What do you think — those peepshows stay in business on the strength of the occasional customer? No way. It's a steady clientele of people in there every day, for hours at a time, dropping in quarters. That whole strip of road is *made* for addicts. And all the strips like it. That's what America's all about, you know. You got your alcoholics in the bars. Your food addicts sucking it up at Jack-in-the-Box — you ever go in one of those places and count the fat people? You got your sex addicts in the peepshows. Your shopping addicts at the K mart. Your gamblers running numbers in the bodegas and your junkies in the alleyways. We're all nothing but a bunch of addicts. The whole fucking addicted country."

In the arcades, says Lester, the videos show myriad combinations and arrangements of men and women, men and men, women and women. Some show older men being serviced by eager, selfless young women who seem to live for one thing only, who can't get enough. Some of these women have put their hair into pigtails and shaved themselves — they're supposed to look like children. Inside the peepshow booths there's semen on the floor. And in the old days, there were glory holes cut into the wooden walls between some of the booths, so, if it pleased you, you could communicate with your neighbor. Not anymore. Mack and Lester tell me that some things have changed. The holes have been boarded up. In the public men's rooms you no longer read, scribbled in the stalls, "All faggots should die." You read, "All faggots should die of AIDS." Mack rails against the moratorium on fetal-tissue research, the most promising avenue for a cure. "If it was Legionnaires dying, we wouldn't have any moratorium," he says. And he often talks about Africa, where governments impede efforts to teach villagers about condoms: a social worker, attempting to explain their use, isn't allowed to remove the condoms from their foil packets; in another country, with a slightly more liberal government, a field nurse stretches a condom over his hand, to show how it works, and later villagers are found wearing the condoms like mittens, thinking this will protect them from disease. Lester laughs at these stories but shakes his head. In our own country, something called "family values" has emerged with clarity. "*Whose* family?" Mack wants to know, holding out his hands palms upward. "I mean we *all* come from families, don't we? The dizziest queen comes from a family. The ax murderer. Even Dan *Quayle* comes from a family of some kind."

But Mack and Lester are dying, Mack first. As I steer my pickup into the parking lot at the K mart, I almost clip the front fender of a big, deep-throated Chevy that's leaving. I have startled the driver, a young Chicano boy with four kids in the back seat, and he flips me the bird — aggressively, his arm out the window — but I feel protected today by my sense of purpose: I have come to buy a padded toilet seat for my friend.

When he was younger, Mack wanted to be a cultural anthropologist, but he was slow to break in after we were out of graduate school — never landed anything more than a low-paying position assisting someone else, nothing more than a student's job, really. Eventually, he began driving a tour bus in San Diego, which not only provided a steady income but suited him so well that in time he was managing the line and began to refer to the position not as his job but as his calling. He said that San Diego was like a pretty blond boy without too many brains. He knew just how to play up its cultural assets while allowing its beauty to speak for itself. He said he liked being "at the controls." But he had to quit work over a year ago, and now his hands have become so shaky that he can no longer even manage a pen and paper.

When I get back to the apartment from my trip to the K mart, Mack asks me to take down a letter for him to an old high school buddy back in Des Moines, a country-and-western singer who has sent him a couple of her latest recordings. *"Whenever I met a new doctor or nurse,"* he dictates, *"I always asked them whether they believed in miracles."*

Mack sits up a bit straighter and rearranges the pillows behind his back on the couch. "What did I just say?" he asks me.

" 'I always asked them whether they believed in miracles.' "

"Yes," he says, and continues. *"And if they said no, I told them I wanted to see someone else. I didn't want them treating me. Back then, I was hoping for a miracle, which seemed reasonable.* Do you think this is too detailed?" he asks me.

"No," I say. "I think it's fine."

"I don't want to depress her."

"Go on," I say.

"But now I have lung cancer," he continues. *"So now I need not one but two miracles. That doesn't seem as possible somehow.* Wait. Did you write 'possible' yet?"

"No," I say. " 'That doesn't seem as . . .' "

"Reasonable," he says. "Didn't I say 'reasonable' before?"

"Yes," I say. " 'That doesn't seem as reasonable somehow.' "

"Yes," he says. "How does that sound?"

"It sounds fine, Mack. It's not for publication, you know."

"It's not?" he says, feigning astonishment. "I thought it was: 'Letters of an AIDS Victim.' " He says this in a spooky voice and makes his bug-eyes. Since his head is a perfect skull, the whole effect really is a little spooky.

"What else?" I say.

"Thank you for your nice letter," he continues, *"and for the tapes."* He begins coughing — a horrible, rasping seizure. Mack has told

me that he has lost all fear; he said he realized this a few weeks
ago, on the skyride at the zoo. But when the coughing sets in,
when it seems that it may never stop, I think I see terror in his
eyes: he begins tapping his breastbone with the fingers of one
hand, as if he's trying to wake up his lungs, prod them to do
their appointed work. Finally he does stop, and he sits for a moment in silence, in thought. Then he dictates: "*It makes me very
happy that you are so successful.*"

At Mrs. Mears's craft sale, in the alley behind her cottage, she
has set up several card tables: Scores of plastic dolls with hand-
knitted dresses, shoes, and hats. Handmade doll furniture.
Christmas ornaments. A whole box of knitted bonnets and scarves
for dolls. Also, some baked goods. Now, while Lester holds Eberhardt, Mrs. Mears, wearing a large straw hat and sunglasses, outfits the dachshund in one of the bonnets and scarves. "There
now," she says. "Have you ever seen anything so *precious?* I'm
going to get my camera."

Mack sits in a folding chair by one of the tables; next to him
sits Mr. Mears, also in a folding chair. The two men look very
much alike, though Mr. Mears is not nearly as emaciated as Mack.
And of course Mr. Mears is eighty-seven. Mack, on the calendar,
is not quite forty. I notice that Mack's shoelaces are untied, and
I kneel to tie them. "The thing about reincarnation," he's saying
to Mr. Mears, "is that you can't remember anything and you
don't recognize anybody."

"Consciously," says Lester, butting in. "*Sub*consciously you do."

"Subconsciously," says Mack. "What's the point? I'm not the
least bit interested."

Mr. Mears removes his houndstooth-check cap and scratches
his bald, freckled head. "I'm not, either," he says with great res-
ignation.

As Mrs. Mears returns with the camera, she says, "Put him
over there, in Mack's lap."

"It doesn't matter whether you're interested or not," says Lester, dropping Eberhardt into Mack's lap.

"Give me good old-fashioned heaven and hell," says Mr. Mears.

"I should think you would've had enough of that already,"
says Lester.

Mr. Mears gives Lester a suspicious look, then gazes down at his own knees. "Then give me nothing," he says finally.

I stand up and step aside just in time for Mrs. Mears to snap the picture. "Did you ever *see* anything?" she says, all sunshades and yellow teeth, but as she heads back toward the cottage door, her face is immediately serious. She takes me by the arm and pulls me along, reaching for something from one of the tables — a doll's bed, white with a red strawberry painted on the headboard. "For your little girl," she says aloud. Then she whispers, "You better get him out of the sun, don't you think? He doesn't look so good."

But when I turn again, I see that Lester is already helping Mack out of his chair. "Here — let me," says Mrs. Mears, reaching an arm toward them, and she escorts Mack up the narrow, shaded sidewalk, back toward the apartment building. Lester moves alongside me and says, "Dan, do you think you could give Mack his bath this afternoon? I'd like to take Eberhardt for a walk."

"Of course," I say, quickly.

But a while later — after I have drawn the bath, after I've taken a large beach towel out of the linen closet, refolded it into a thick square, and put it into the water to serve as a cushion for Mack to sit on in the tub; when I'm holding the towel under, against some resistance, waiting for the bubbles to stop surfacing, and there's something horrible about it, like drowning a small animal — I think Lester has tricked me into this task of bathing Mack, and the saliva in my mouth suddenly seems to taste of Scotch, which I have not actually tasted in nine years.

There is no time to consider any of this, however, for in a moment Mack enters the bathroom, trailing his tubes behind him, and says, "Are you ready for my Auschwitz look?"

"I've seen it before," I say.

And it's true. I have, a few times, helping him with his shirt and pants after Lester has bathed him and gotten him into his underwear. But that doesn't feel like preparation. The sight of him naked is like a powerful, scary drug: you forget between trips, remember only when you start to come on to it again. I help him off with his clothes now and guide him into the tub and gently onto the underwater towel. "That's nice," he says, and I begin soaping the hollows of his shoulders, the hard wash-board of his back. This is not human skin as we know it but something already dead — so dry, dense, and pleasantly brown as to appear manufactured. I soap the cage of his chest, his stomach — the hard, depressed abdomen of a greyhound — the steep vaults of his armpits, his legs, his feet. Oddly, his hands and feet appear almost normal, even a bit swollen. At last I give him the slippery bar of soap. "Your turn," I say.

"My poor cock," he says as he begins to wash himself.

When he's done, I rinse him all over with the hand spray at-tached to the faucet. I lather the feathery white wisps of his hair — we have to remove the plastic oxygen tubes for this — then rinse again. "You know," he says, "I know it's irrational, but I feel kind of turned off to sex."

The apparent understatement of this almost takes my breath away. "There are more important things," I say.

"Oh, I know," he says. "I just hope Lester's not too unhappy." Then, after a moment, he says, "You know, Dan, it's only logical that they've all given up on me. And I've accepted it mostly. But I still have days when I think I should at least be given a chance."

"You can ask them for anything you want, Mack," I say.

"I know," he says. "That's the problem — there's nothing to ask for."

"Mack," I say. "I think I understand what you meant this morning about the tree pruning and the credit cards."

"You do?"

"Well, I think your mind just shifted into metaphor. Because I can see that pruning trees is like imposing a limit — just like the limit on the credit cards."

Mack is silent, pondering this. "Maybe," he says at last, hesi-tantly — a moment of disappointment for us both.

I get him out and hooked up to the oxygen again, dry him off, and begin dressing him. Somehow I get the oxygen tubes trapped between his legs and the elastic waistband of his sweatpants — no big deal, but I suddenly feel panicky — and I have to take them off his face again to set them to rights. After he's safely back on the living room couch and I've returned to the bath-room, I hear him: low, painful-sounding groans. "Are you all right?" I call from the hallway.

"Oh, yes," he says, "I'm just moaning. It's one of the few pleasures I have left."

The bathtub is coated with a crust of dead skin, which I wash away with the sprayer. Then I find a screwdriver and go to work on the toilet seat. After I get the old one off, I need to scrub around the area where the plastic screws were. I've sprinkled Ajax all around the rim of the bowl and found the scrub brush when Lester appears at the bathroom door, back with Eberhardt from their walk. "Oh, Dan, really," he says. "You go too far. Down on your knees now, scrubbing our toilet."

"Lester, leave me alone," I say.

"Well, it's true," he says. "You really do."

"Maybe I'm working out my survivor's guilt," I say, "if you don't mind."

"You mean because your best buddy's dying and you're not?"

"Yes," I say. "It's very common."

He parks one hip on the edge of the sink, and after a moment he says this: "Danny boy, if you feel guilty about surviving . . . that's not irreversible, you know. I could fix that."

We are both stunned. He looks at me. In another moment, there are tears in his eyes. He quickly closes the bathroom door, moves to the tub and turns on the water, sits on the side, and bursts into sobs. "I'm sorry," he says. "I'm so sorry."

"Forget it," I say.

He begins to compose himself almost at once. "This is what Jane Alexander did when she played Eleanor Roosevelt," he says. "Do you remember? When she needed to cry she'd go in the bathroom and turn on the water, so nobody could hear her. Remember?"

In the pickup, on the way to the hospital, Lester — in the middle, between Mack and me — says, "Maybe after they're down there you could doze off, but on the *way* down, they want you awake." He's explaining the bronchoscopy to me — the insertion of the tube down the windpipe — with which he is personally familiar: "They reach certain points on the way down where they have to ask you to swallow."

"*He's* not having the test, is he?" Mack says, looking confused.

"No, of course not," says Lester.

"Didn't you just say to him that he had to swallow?"

"I meant *anyone*, Mac," says Lester.

"Oh," says Mack. "Oh, yeah."

"The general 'you,' " Lester says to me. "He keeps forgetting little things like that."

Mack shakes his head, then points at his temple with one finger. "My mind," he says.

Mack is on tank oxygen now, which comes with a small caddy. I push the caddy, behind him, and Lester assists him along the short walk from the curb to the hospital's front door and the elevators. Nine years ago, it was Mack who drove *me* to a different wing of this same hospital — against my drunken, slobbery will — to dry out. And as I watch him struggle up the low inclined ramp toward the glass and steel doors, I recall the single irrefutable thing he said to me in the car on the way. "You stink," he said. "You've puked and probably pissed your pants and you *stink*," he said — my loyal, articulate, and best friend, saving my life, and causing me to cry like a baby.

Inside the clinic upstairs, the nurse, a sour young blond woman in a sky-blue uniform who looks terribly overworked, says to Mack, "You know better than to be late."

We are five minutes late to the second. Mack looks at her incredulously. He stands with one hand on the handle of the oxygen-tank caddy. He straightens up, perfectly erect — the indignant, shockingly skeletal posture of a man fasting to the death for some holy principle. He gives the nurse the bug-eyes, and says, "And you know better than to keep me waiting every time I come over here for some goddamn procedure. But get over yourself: shit happens."

He turns and winks at me.

Though I've offered to return for them afterward, Lester has insisted on taking a taxi, so I will leave them here and drive back home, where again I'll try — successfully, this time — to explain to my wife how all this feels to me, and where, a few minutes later, I'll stand outside the door to my daughter's room, comforted by the music of her small high voice as she consoles her dolls.

Now the nurse gets Mack into a wheelchair and leaves us in the middle of the reception area; then, from the proper position

at her desk, she calls Mack's name, and says he may proceed to
the laboratory.

"Dan," Mack says, stretching his spotted, broomstick arms
toward me. "Old pal. Do you remember the Christmas we drove
out to Des Moines on the motorcycle?"

We did go to Des Moines together, one very snowy Christmas — but of course we didn't go on any motorcycle, not in December.

"We had fun," I say and put my arms around him, awkwardly,
since he is sitting.

"Help me up," he whispers — confidentially — and I begin to
lift him.

STEVEN MILLHAUSER

Eisenheim the Illusionist

FROM ESQUIRE

IN THE LAST YEARS of the nineteenth century, when the empire
of the Hapsburgs was nearing the end of its long dissolution, the
art of magic flourished as never before. In obscure villages of
Moravia and Galicia, from the Istrian Peninsula to the mists of
Bukovina, bearded and black-caped magicians in market squares
astonished townspeople by drawing streams of dazzling silk
handkerchiefs from empty paper cones, removing billiard balls
from children's ears, and throwing into the air decks of cards
that assumed the shapes of fountains, snakes, and angels before
returning to the hand. In cities and larger towns, from Zagreb
to Lvov, from Budapest to Vienna, on the stages of opera houses,
town halls, and magic theaters, traveling conjurers equipped with
the latest apparatus enchanted sophisticated audiences with
elaborate stage illusions. It was the age of levitations and decap-
itations, of ghostly apparitions and sudden vanishings, as if the
tottering empire were revealing through the medium of its magicians its secret desire for annihilation. Among the remarkable
conjurers of that time, none achieved the heights of illusion at-
tained by Eisenheim, whose enigmatic final performance was
viewed by some as a triumph of the magician's art, by others as
a fateful sign.

Eisenheim, né Eduard Abramowitz, was born in Bratislava in
1859 or 1860. Little is known of his early years, or indeed of his
entire life outside the realm of illusion. For the scant facts we
are obliged to rely on the dubious memoirs of magicians, on
comments in contemporary newspaper stories and trade peri-

odicals, on promotional material and brochures for magic acts; here and there the diary entry of a countess or ambassador records attendance at a performance in Paris, Cracow, Vienna. Eisenheim's father was a highly respected cabinetmaker, whose ornamental gilt cupboards and skillfully carved lowboys with lion-paw feet and brass handles shaped like snarling lions graced the halls of the gentry of Bratislava. The boy was the eldest of four children; like many Bratislavan Jews, the family spoke German and called their city Pressburg, although they understood as much Slovak and Magyar as was necessary for the proper conduct of business. Eduard went to work early in his father's shop. For the rest of his life he would retain a fondness for smooth pieces of wood joined seamlessly by mortise and tenon. By the age of seventeen he was himself a skilled cabinetmaker, a fact noted more than once by fellow magicians who admired Eisenheim's skill in constructing trick cabinets of breathtaking ingenuity. The young craftsman was already a passionate amateur magician, who is said to have entertained family and friends with card sleights and a disappearing-ring trick that required a small beechwood box of his own construction. He would place a borrowed ring inside, fasten the box tightly with twine, and quietly remove the ring as he handed the box to a spectator. The beechwood box, with its secret panel, was able to withstand the most minute examination.

A chance encounter with a traveling magician is said to have been the cause of Eisenheim's lifelong passion for magic. The story goes that one day, returning from school, the boy saw a man in black sitting under a plane tree. The man called him over and lazily, indifferently removed from the boy's ear first one coin and then another, and then a third, coin after coin, a whole handful of coins, which suddenly turned into a bunch of red roses. From the roses the man in black drew out a white billiard ball, which turned into a wooden flute that suddenly vanished. One version of the story adds that the man himself then vanished, along with the plane tree.

Eduard had once seen a magic shop, without much interest; he now returned with passion. On dark winter mornings on the way to school he would remove his gloves to practice manipulating balls and coins, with chilled fingers, in the pockets of his coat. He enchanted his three sisters with intricate shadowgraphs representing Rumpelstiltskin and Rapunzel, American buffaloes and Indians, the golem of Prague. Later a local conjurer called Ignazc Molnar taught him juggling for the sake of coordinating movements of the eye and hand. Once, on a dare, the thirteen-year-old boy carried an egg on a soda straw all the way to Bratislava Castle and back. Much later, when all this was far behind him, the Master would be sitting gloomily in the corner of a Viennese apartment where a party was being held in his honor, and reaching up wearily he would startle his hostess by producing from the air five billiard balls that he proceeded to juggle flawlessly.

But who can unravel the mystery of the passion that infects an entire life, bending it away from its former course in one irrevocable swerve? Abramowitz seems to have accepted his fate slowly. It was as if he kept trying to evade the disturbing knowledge of his difference. At the age of twenty-four he was still an expert cabinetmaker who did occasional parlor tricks.

As if suddenly, Eisenheim appeared at a theater in Vienna and began his exhilarating and fatal career. The brilliant newcomer was twenty-eight years old. In fact, contemporary records show that the cabinetmaker from Bratislava had appeared in private performances for at least a year before moving to the Austrian capital. Although the years preceding the first private performances remain mysterious, it is clear that Abramowitz gradually shifted his attention more and more to magic, by way of the trick chests and cabinets that he had begun to supply to local magicians. Eisenheim's nature was like that: he proceeded slowly and cautiously, step by step, and then, as if he had earned the right to be daring, he would take a sudden leap.

The first public performances were noted less for their daring than for their subtle mastery of the stage illusions of the day, although even then there were artful twists and variations. One of Eisenheim's early successes was The Mysterious Orange Tree, a feat made famous by Robert-Houdin. A borrowed handkerchief was placed in a small box and handed to a member of the audience. An assistant strode onto the stage, bearing in his arms a small green orange tree in a box. He placed the box on the magician's table and stepped away. At a word from Eisenheim, accompanied by a pass of his wand, blossoms began to appear on the tree. A moment later, oranges began to emerge; Eisenheim plucked several and handed them to members of the audience. Suddenly two butterflies rose from the leaves, carrying a handkerchief. The spectator, opening his box, discovered that his handkerchief had disappeared; somehow the butterflies had found it in the tree. The illusion depended on two separate deceptions: the mechanical tree itself, which produced real flowers, real fruit, and mechanical butterflies by means of concealed mechanisms; and the removal of the handkerchief from the trick box as it was handed to the spectator. Eisenheim quickly developed a variation that proved popular; the tree grew larger each time he covered it with a red silk cloth, the branches produced oranges, apples, pears, and plums, at the end a whole flock of colorful, real butterflies rose up and fluttered over the audience, where children screamed with delight as they reached up to snatch the delicate silken shapes, and at last, under a black velvet cloth that was suddenly lifted, the tree was transformed into a birdcage containing the missing handkerchief.

At this period, Eisenheim wore the traditional silk hat, frock coat, and cape, and performed with an ebony wand tipped with ivory. The one distinctive note was his pair of black gloves. He began each performance by stepping swiftly through the closed curtains onto the stage apron, removing the gloves, and tossing them into the air, where they turned into a pair of sleek ravens.

Early critics were quick to note the young magician's interest in uncanny effects, as in his popular Phantom Portrait. On a darkened stage, a large black canvas was illuminated by limelight. As Eisenheim made passes with his right hand, the white canvas gradually and mysteriously gave birth to a brighter and brighter painting. Now, it is well known among magicians and mediums that a canvas of unbleached muslin may be painted with chemical solutions that appear invisible when dry; if sulphate of iron is used for blue, nitrate of bismuth for yellow, and copper sulphate for brown, the picture will appear if sprayed with a weak solution of prussiate of potash. An atomizer, concealed in the conjurer's sleeve, gradually brings out the invisible portrait. Eisenheim increased the mysterious effect by producing full-length portraits that began to exhibit lifelike movements of the eyes and lips. The fiendish portrait of an archduke, or a devil, or Eisenheim himself, would then read the contents of sealed envelopes, before vanishing at a pass of the magician's wand.

However skillful, a conjurer cannot earn and sustain a major reputation without producing original feats of his own devising. It was clear that the restless young magician would not be content with producing clever variations of familiar tricks, and by 1890 his performances regularly concluded with an illusion of striking originality. A large mirror in a carved frame stood on the stage, facing the audience. A spectator was invited onto the stage, where he was asked to walk around the mirror and examine it to his satisfaction. Eisenheim then asked the spectator to don a hooded red robe and positioned him some ten feet from the mirror, where the vivid red reflection was clearly visible to the audience; the theater was darkened, except for a brightening light that came from within the mirror itself. As the spectator waved his robed arms about, and bowed to his bowing reflection, and leaned from side to side, his reflection began to show signs of disobedience — it crossed its arms over its chest instead of waving them about, it refused to bow. Suddenly the reflection grimaced, removed a knife, and stabbed itself in the chest. The reflection collapsed onto the reflected floor. Now a ghostlike white form rose from the dead reflection and hovered in the mirror. All at once the ghost emerged from the glass, floated toward the startled and sometimes terrified spectator, and at the bidding of Eisenheim rose into the dark and vanished. This masterly illusion mystified even professional magicians, who agreed only that the mirror was a trick cabinet with black-lined doors at the rear and a hidden assistant. The lights were probably concealed in the frame between the glass and the lightly silvered back; as the lights grew brighter the mirror became transparent and a red-robed assistant showed himself in the glass. The ghost was more difficult to explain, despite a long tradition of stage ghosts; it was said that concealed magic lanterns produced the phantom, but no other magician was able to imitate the effect. Even in these early years, before Eisenheim achieved disturbing effects unheard of in the history of stage magic, there was a touch of the uncanny about his illusions; and some said even then that Eisenheim was not a showman at all, but a wizard who had sold his soul to the Devil in return for unholy powers.

Eisenheim was a man of medium height, with broad shoulders and large, long-fingered hands. His most striking feature was his powerful head: the black, intense eyes in the strikingly pale face, the broad black beard, the thrusting forehead with its receding hairline, all lent an appearance of unusual mental force. The newspaper accounts mention a minor trait that must have been highly effective: when he leaned his head forward, in intense concentration, there appeared over his right eyebrow a large vein shaped like an inverted *Y*.

As the last decade of the old century wore on, Eisenheim gradually came to be acknowledged as the foremost magician of his day. These were the years of the great European tours, which brought him to Egyptian Hall in London and the Théâtre Robert-Houdin in Paris, to royal courts and ducal palaces, to halls in Berlin and Milan, Zurich and Salamanca. Although his repertoire continued to include perfected variations of popular illusions like The Vanishing Lady, The Blue Room, The Flying Watch, The Spirit Cabinet (or Specters of the Inner Sanctum), The Enchanted House, The Magic Kettle, and The Arabian Sack Mystery, he appeared to grow increasingly impatient with known effects and began rapidly replacing them with striking inventions of his own. Among the most notable illusions of those years were The Tower of Babel, in which a small black cone mysteriously grew until it filled the entire stage; The Satanic Crystal Ball, in which a ghostly form summoned from hell smashed through the glass globe and rushed out onto the stage with unearthly cries; and The Book of Demons, in which black smoke rose from an ancient book which suddenly burst into flames that released hideous dwarfs in hairy jerkins who ran howling across the stage. In 1898 he opened his own theater in Vienna, called simply Eisenheimhaus, or The House of Eisenheim, as if that were his real home and all other dwellings illusory. It was here that he presented The Pied Piper of Hamelin. Holding his wand like a flute, Eisenheim led children from the audience into a misty hill with a cavelike opening and then, with a pass of his wand, caused the entire hill to vanish into thin air. Moments later a black chest materialized, from which the children emerged and looked around in bewilderment before running back to their parents. The children told their parents that they had been in a wondrous mountain, with golden tables and chairs and white angels flying in the air; they had no idea how they had gotten into the box, or what had happened to them. A few complaints were made; and when, in another performance, a frightened child told his mother that he had been in hell and seen the Devil, who was green and breathed fire, the chief of the Viennese police, one Walther Uhl, paid Eisenheim a visit. The Pied Piper of Hamelin never appeared again, but two results had emerged: a certain disturbing quality in Eisenheim's art was now officially acknowledged, and it was rumored that the stern Master was being closely watched by Franz Josef's secret police. This last was unlikely, for the emperor, unlike his notorious grandfather, took little interest in police espionage; but the rumor surrounded Eisenheim like a mist, blurring his sharp outline, darkening his features, and enhancing his formidable reputation.

Eisenheim was not without rivals, whose challenges he invariably met with a decisiveness, some would say ferocity, that left no doubt of his self-esteem. Two incidents of the last years of the century left a deep impression among contemporaries. In Vienna in 1898 a magician called Benedetti had appeared. Benedetti, whose real name was Paul Henri Cortot, of Lyon, was a master illusionist of extraordinary smoothness and skill; his mistake was to challenge Eisenheim by presenting imitations of original Eisenheim illusions, with clever variations, much as Eisenheim had once alluded to his predecessors in order to outdo them. Eisenheim learned of his rival's presumption and let it be known through the speaking portrait of a devil that ruin awaits the proud. The very next night, on Benedetti's stage, a speaking portrait of Eisenheim intoned in comic accents that ruin awaits the proud. Eisenheim, a proud and brooding man, did not allude to the insult during his Sunday-night performance. On Monday night, Benedetti's act went awry: the wand leaped from his fingers and rolled across the stage; two fishbowls with watertight lids came crashing to the floor from beneath Benedetti's cloak; the speaking portrait remained mute; the levitating lady was seen to be resting on black wires. The excitable Benedetti, vowing revenge, accused Eisenheim of criminal tampering; two

nights later, before a packed house, Benedetti stepped into a
black cabinet, drew a curtain, and was never seen again. The
investigation by Herr Uhl failed to produce a trace of foul play.
Some said the unfortunate Benedetti had simply chosen the most
convenient way of escaping to another city, under a new name,
far from the scene of his notorious debacle; others were convinced that Eisenheim had somehow spirited him off, perhaps
to hell. Viennese society was enchanted by the scandal, which
made the rounds of the cafés; and Herr Uhl was seen more than
once in a stall of the theater, nodding his head appreciatively at
some particularly striking effect.

If Benedetti proved too easy a rival, a far more formidable
challenge was posed by the mysterious Passauer. Ernst Passauer
was said to be a Bavarian; his first Viennese performance was
watched closely by the Austrians, who were forced to admit that
the German was a master of striking originality. Passauer took
the city by storm; and for the first time there was talk that Eisenheim had met his match, perhaps even — was it possible? — his
master. Unlike the impetuous and foolhardy Benedetti, Passauer made no allusion to the Viennese wizard; some saw in this
less a sign of professional decorum than an assertion of arrogant
indifference, as if the German refused to acknowledge the possibility of a rival. But the pattern of their performances, that
autumn, was the very rhythm of rivalry: Eisenheim played on
Sunday, Wednesday, and Friday nights, and Passauer on Tuesday, Thursday, and Saturday nights. It was noted that as his
rival presented illusions of bold originality, Eisenheim's own illusions became more daring and dangerous; it was as if the two
of them had outsoared the confines of the magician's art and
existed in some new realm of dexterous wonder, of sinister beauty.
In this high but by no means innocent realm, the two masters
vied for supremacy before audiences that were increasingly the
same. Some said that Eisenheim appeared to be struggling or
straining against the relentless pressure of his brilliant rival; others argued that Eisenheim had never displayed such mastery;
and as the heavy century lumbered to its close, all awaited the
decisive event that would release them from the tension of an
unresolved battle.

And it came: one night in mid-December, after a particularly daring illusion, in which Passauer caused first his right arm to vanish, then his left arm, then his feet, until nothing was left of him but his disembodied head floating before a black velvet curtain, the head permitted itself to wonder whether Herr "Eisenzeit," or Iron Age, had ever seen a trick of that kind. The mocking allusion caused the audience to gasp. The limelight went out; when it came on, the stage contained nothing but a heap of black cloth, which began to flutter and billow until it gradually assumed the shape of Passauer, who bowed coolly to tumultuous applause; but the ring of a quiet challenge was not lost in the general uproar. The following night Eisenheim played to a packed, expectant house. He ignored the challenge while performing a series of new illusions that in no way resembled Passauer's act. As he took his final bow, he remarked casually that Passauer's hour had passed. The fate of the unfortunate Benedetti had not been forgotten, and it was said that if the demand for Passauer's next performance had been met, the entire city of Vienna would have become a magic theater.

Passauer's final performance was one of frightening brilliance; it was well attended by professional magicians, who agreed later that as a single performance it outshone the greatest of Eisenheim's evenings. Passauer began by flinging into the air a handful of coins that assumed the shape of a bird and flew out over the heads of the audience, flapping its jingling wings of coins; from a silver thimble held in the flat of his hand he removed a tablecloth, a small mahogany table, and a silver salver on which sat a steaming roast duck. At the climax of the evening, he caused the properties of the stage to vanish one by one: the magician's table, the beautiful assistant, the far wall, the curtain. Standing alone in a vanished world, he looked at the audience with an expression that grew more and more fierce. Suddenly he burst into a demonic laugh, and reaching up to his face he tore off a rubber mask and revealed himself to be Eisenheim. The collective gasp sounded like a great furnace igniting; someone burst into hysterical sobs. The audience, understanding at last, rose to its feet and cheered the great master of illusion, who himself had been his own greatest rival and had at the end unmasked himself. In his box, Herr Uhl rose to his feet and joined in the applause. He had enjoyed the performance immensely.

Perhaps it was the strain of that sustained deception, perhaps it was the sense of being alone, utterly alone, in any case Eisenheim did not give another performance in the last weeks of the fading century. As the new century came in with a fireworks display in the Prater and a one-hundred-gun salute from the grounds of the Imperial Palace, Eisenheim remained in his Vienna apartment, with its distant view of the same river that flowed through his childhood city. The unexplained period of rest continued, developing into a temporary withdrawal from performance, some said a retirement; Eisenheim himself said nothing. In late January he returned to Bratislava to attend to details of his father's business; a week later he was in Linz; within a month he had purchased a three-story villa in the famous wooded hills on the outskirts of Vienna. He was forty or forty-one, an age when a man takes a hard look at his life. He had never married, although romantic rumors occasionally united him with one or another of his assistants; he was handsome in a stern way, wealthy, and said to be so strong that he could do thirty knee bends on a single leg. Not long after his move to the Wienerwald he began to court Sophie Ritter, the twenty-six-year-old daughter of a local landowner who disapproved of Eisenheim's profession and was a staunch supporter of Lueger's anti-Semitic Christian Social Party; the girl appears to have been in love with Eisenheim, but at the last moment something went wrong, she withdrew abruptly, and a month later married a grain merchant from Graz. For a year Eisenheim lived like a reclusive country squire. He took riding lessons in the mornings, in the afternoons practiced with pistols at his private shooting range, planted a spring garden, stocked his ponds, designed a new orchard. In a meadow at the back of his house he supervised the building of a long low shedlike structure that became known as the Teufelsfabrik, or Devil's Factory, for it housed his collection of trick cabinets, deceptive mirrors, haunted portraits, and magic caskets. The walls were lined with cupboards that had sliding glass doors and held Eisenheim's formidable collection of magical apparatus: vanishing birdcages, inexhaustible punch bowls, Devil's targets, Schiller's bells, watch-spring flowers, trick bouquets, and an array of secret devices used in sleight-of-hand feats: ball shells, coin droppers, elastic handkerchief-pulls for making handkerchiefs vanish, dummy cigars, color-changing tubes for handkerchief tricks, hollow thumb-tips, miniature spirit lamps for the magical lighting of candles, false fingers, black silk ball-tubes. In the basement of the factory was a large room in which he conducted chemical and electrical experiments, and a curtained darkroom; Eisenheim was a close student of photography and the new art of cinematography. Often he was seen working late at night, and some said that ghostly forms appeared in the dim-lit windows.

On the first of January, 1901, Eisenheim suddenly returned to his city apartment, with its view of the Danube and the Vienna hills. Three days later he reappeared onstage. A local wit remarked that the master of illusion had simply omitted the year 1900, which with its two zeros no doubt struck him as illusory. The yearlong absence of the Master had sharpened expectations, and the standing-room-only crowd was tensely quiet as the curtains parted on a stage strikingly bare except for a plain wooden chair behind a small glass table. For some in that audience, the table already signaled a revolution; others were puzzled or disappointed. From the right wing Eisenheim strode onto the stage. A flurry of whispers was quickly hushed. The Master wore a plain dark suit and had shaved off his beard. Without a word he sat down on the wooden chair behind the table and faced the audience. He placed his hands lightly on the tabletop, where they remained during the entire performance. He stared directly before him, leaning forward slightly and appearing to concentrate with terrific force.

In the middle of the eighteenth century the magician's table was a large table draped to the floor; beneath the cloth an assistant reached through a hole in the tabletop to remove objects concealed by a large cone. The modern table of Eisenheim's day had a short cloth that exposed the table legs, but the disappearance of the hidden assistant and the general simplification of design in no sense changed the nature of the table, which remained an ingenious machine equipped with innumerable contrivances to aid the magician in the art of deception: hidden receptacles, or *servantes,* into which disappearing objects secretly dropped, invisible wells and traps, concealed pistons, built-in spring pulls for effecting the disappearance of silk handkerchiefs. Eisenheim's transparent glass table announced the end of the magician's table as it had been known throughout the history of stage magic. This radical simplification was not only aesthetic: it meant the refusal of certain kinds of mechanical aid, the elimination of certain effects.

And the audience grew restless: nothing much appeared to be happening. A balding man in a business suit sat at a table, frowning. After fifteen minutes a slight disturbance or darkening in the air was noticeable near the surface of the table. Eisenheim concentrated fiercely; over his right eyebrow the famous vein, shaped like an inverted *Y*, pressed through the skin of his forehead. The air seemed to tremble and thicken — and before him, on the glass table, a dark shape slowly formed. It appeared to be a small box, about the size of a jewel box. For a while its edges quivered slightly, as if it were made of black smoke. Suddenly Eisenheim raised his eyes, which one witness described as black mirrors that reflected nothing; he looked drained and weary. A moment later he pushed back his chair, stood up, and bowed. The applause was uncertain; people did not know what they had seen.

Eisenheim next invited spectators to come onto the stage and examine the box on the table. One woman, reaching for the box and feeling nothing, nothing at all, stepped back and raised a hand to her throat. A girl of sixteen, sweeping her hand through the black box, cried out as if in pain.

The rest of the performance consisted of two more "materializations": a sphere and a wand. After members of the audience had satisfied themselves of the immaterial nature of the objects, Eisenheim picked up the wand and waved it over the box. He next lifted the lid of the box, placed the sphere inside, and closed the lid. When he invited spectators onto the stage, their hands passed through empty air. Eisenheim opened the box, removed the sphere, and laid it on the table between the box and the wand. He bowed, and the curtain closed.

Despite a hesitant, perplexed, and somewhat disappointed response from that first audience, the reviews were enthusiastic; one critic called it a major event in the history of stage illusions. He connected Eisenheim's phantom objects with the larger tradition of stage ghosts, which he traced back to Robertson's Phantasmagoria at the end of the eighteenth century. From concealed magic lanterns Robertson had projected images onto smoke rising from braziers to create eerie effects. By the middle of the nineteenth century magicians were terrifying spectators with a far more striking technique: a hidden assistant, dressed like a ghost and standing in a pit between the stage and the auditorium, was reflected onto the stage through a tilted sheet of glass invisible to the audience. Modern ghosts were based on the technique of the black velvet backdrop: overhead lights were directed toward the front of the stage, and black-covered white objects appeared to materialize when the covers were pulled away by invisible black-hooded assistants dressed in black. But Eisenheim's phantoms, those immaterial materializations, made use of no machinery at all — they appeared to emerge from the mind of the magician. The effect was startling, the unknown device ingenious. The writer considered and rejected the possibility of hidden magic lanterns and mirrors; discussed the properties of the cinematograph recently developed by the Lumière brothers and used by contemporary magicians to produce unusual effects of a different kind; and speculated on possible scientific techniques whereby Eisenheim might have caused the air literally to thicken and darken. Was it possible that one of the Lumière machines, directed onto slightly misted air above the table, might have produced the phantom objects? But no one had detected any mist, no one had seen the necessary beam of light. However Eisenheim had accomplished the illusion, the effect was incomparable; it appeared that he was summoning objects into existence by the sheer effort of his mind. In this the master illusionist was rejecting the modern conjurer's increasing reliance on machinery and returning the spectator to the troubled heart of magic, which yearned beyond the constricting world of ingenuity and artifice toward the dark realm of transgression.

The long review, heavy with fin-de-siècle portentousness and shot through with a secret restlessness or longing, was the first of several that placed Eisenheim beyond the world of conjuring and saw in him an expression of spiritual striving, as if his art could no longer be talked about in the old way.

During the next performance Eisenheim sat for thirty-five minutes at his glass table in front of a respectful but increasingly restless audience before the darkening was observed. When he sat back, evidently spent from his exertions, there stood on the table the head and shoulders of a young woman. The details of witnesses differ, but all reports agree that the head was of a young woman of perhaps eighteen or twenty, with short dark hair and heavy-lidded eyes. She faced the audience calmly, a little dreamily, as if she had just wakened from sleep, and spoke her name: Greta. Fräulein Greta answered questions from the audience. She said she came from Brünn; she was seventeen years old; her father was a lens grinder; she did not know how she had come here. Behind her, Eisenheim sat slumped in his seat, his broad face pale as marble, his eyes staring as if sightlessly. After a while Fräulein Greta appeared to grow tired. Eisenheim gathered himself up and fixed her with his stare; gradually she wavered and grew dim, and slowly vanished.

With Fräulein Greta, Eisenheim triumphed over the doubters. As word of the new illusion spread, and audiences waited with a kind of fearful patience for the darkening of the air above the glass table, it became clear that Eisenheim had touched a nerve. Greta fever was in the air. It was said that Fräulein Greta was really Marie Vetsera, who had died with Crown Prince Rudolf in the bedroom of his hunting lodge at Mayerling; it was said that Fräulein Greta, with her dark, sad eyes, was the girlhood spirit of Empress Elizabeth, who at the age of sixty had been stabbed to death in Geneva by an Italian anarchist. It was said that Fräulein Greta knew things, all sorts of things, and could tell secrets about the other world. For a while Eisenheim was taken up by the spiritualists, who claimed him as one of their own: here at last was absolute proof of the materialization of spirit forms. A society of disaffected Blavatskyites called the Daughters of Dawn elected Eisenheim to an honorary membership, and three bearded members of a Salzburg Institute for Psychic Research began attending performances with black notebooks in hand. Magicians heaped scorn on the mediumistic confraternity but could not explain or duplicate the illusion; a shrewd group of mediums, realizing they could not reproduce the Eisenheim phenomena, accused him of fraud while defending themselves against the magicians' charges. Eisenheim's rigorous silence was taken by all sides as a sign of approval. The "manifestations," as they began to be called, soon included the

head of a dark-haired man of about thirty, who called himself
Frankel and demonstrated conventional tricks of mind reading
and telepathy before fading away. What puzzled the profession-
als was not the mind reading but the production of Frankel himself. The possibility of exerting a physical influence on air was
repeatedly argued; it was suggested in some quarters that Eisenheim had prepared the air in advance with a thickening agent
and treated it with invisible chemical solutions, but this allusion
to the timeworn trick of the muslin canvas convinced no one.

In late March Eisenheim left Vienna on an imperial tour that
included bookings in Ljubljana, Prague, Teplitz, Budapest, Ko-
lozsvar, Czernowitz, Tarnopol, Uzghorod. In Vienna, the return
of the Master was awaited with an impatience bordering on frenzy.
A much-publicized case was that of Anna Scherer, the dark-eyed
sixteen-year-old daughter of a Vienna banker, who declared that
she felt a deep spiritual bond with Greta and could not bear life
without her. The troubled girl ran away from home and was
discovered by the police two days later wandering disheveled in
the wooded hills northeast of the city; when she returned home
she shut herself in her room and wept violently and uncontrol-
lably for six hours a day. An eighteen-year-old youth was arrested at night on the grounds of Eisenheim's villa and later con-
fessed that he had planned to break into the Devil's Factory and
learn the secret of raising the dead. Devotees of Greta and Frankel met in small groups to discuss the Master, and it was rumored that in a remote village in Carinthia he had demonstrated
magical powers of a still more thrilling and disturbing kind.

And the Master returned, and the curtains opened, and fingers tightened on the blue velvet chair arms. On a bare stage
stood nothing but a simple chair. Eisenheim, looking pale and
tired, with shadowy hollows in his temples, walked to the chair
and sat down with his large, long hands resting on his knees. He
fixed his stare at the air and sat rigidly for forty minutes, while
rivulets of sweat trickled along his high-boned cheeks and a thick
vein pressed through the skin of his forehead. Gradually a darkening of the air was discernible and a shape slowly emerged. At
first it seemed a wavering and indistinct form, like shimmers
above a radiator on a wintry day, but soon there was a thickening, and before the slumped form of Eisenheim stood a beauti-

ful boy. His large brown eyes, fringed with dark lashes, looked out trustingly, if a little dreamily; he had a profusion of thick hay-colored curls and wore a school uniform with dark green shorts and gray socks. He seemed surprised and shy, uncomfortable before the audience, but as he began to walk about he became more animated and told his name: Elis. Many commented on the striking contrast between the angelic boy and the dark, brooding magician. The sweetness of the creature cast a spell over the audience, broken only when a woman was invited onto the stage. As she bent over to run her fingers through Elis's hair, her hand passed through empty air. She gave a cry that sounded like a moan and hurried from the stage in confusion. Later she said that the air had felt cold, very cold.

Greta and Frankel were forgotten in an outbreak of Elis fever. The immaterial boy was said to be the most enchanting illusion ever created by a magician; the spiritualist camp maintained that Elis was the spirit of a boy who had died in Helgoland in 1787. Elis fever grew to such a pitch that often sobs and screams would erupt from tense, constricted throats as the air before Eisenheim slowly began to darken and the beautiful boy took shape. Elis did not engage in the conventions of magic, but simply walked about on the stage, answering questions put to him by the audience or asking questions of his own. He said that his parents were dead; he seemed uncertain of many things and grew confused when asked how he had come to be there. Sometimes he left the stage and walked slowly along the aisle, while hands reached out and grasped empty air. After half an hour Eisenheim would cause him to waver and grow dim, and Elis would vanish away. Screams often accompanied the disappearance of the beautiful boy; and after a particularly troubling episode, in which a young woman leaped onto the stage and began clawing the vanishing form, Herr Uhl was once again seen in attendance at the theater, watching with an expression of keen interest.

He was in attendance when Eisenheim stunned the house by producing a companion for Elis, a girl who called herself Rosa. She had long dark hair and black, dreamy eyes and Slavic cheekbones; she spoke slowly and seriously, often pausing to think of the exact word. Elis seemed shy of her and at first refused to speak in her presence. Rosa said she was twelve years old; she said she knew the secrets of the past and future, and offered to predict the death of anyone present. A young man with thin cheeks, evidently a student, raised his hand. Rosa stepped to the edge of the stage and stared at him for a long while with her earnest eyes; when she turned away she said that he would cough up blood in November and would die of tuberculosis before the end of the following summer. Pale, visibly shaken, the young man began to protest angrily, then sat down suddenly and covered his face with his hands.

Rosa and Elis were soon fast friends. It was touching to observe Elis's gradual overcoming of shyness and the growth of his intense attachment to her. Immediately after his appearance he would begin to look around sweetly, with his large, anxious eyes, as if searching for his Rosa. As Eisenheim stared with rigid intensity, Elis would play by himself but steal secret glances at the air in front of the magician. The boy would grow more and more agitated as the air began to darken; and a look of almost painful rapture would glow on his face as Rosa appeared with her high cheekbones and her black, dreamy eyes.

Often the children would play by themselves onstage, as if oblivious of an audience. They would hold hands and walk along imaginary paths, swinging their arms back and forth, or they would water invisible flowers with an invisible watering can; and the exquisite charm of their gestures was noted by more than one witness. During these games Rosa would sing songs of haunting, melancholy beauty in an unfamiliar Low German dialect.

It remains unclear precisely when the rumors arose that Eisenheim would be arrested and his theater closed. Some said that Uhl had intended it from the beginning and had simply been waiting for the opportune moment; others pointed to particular incidents. One such incident occurred in late summer, when a disturbance took place in the audience not long after the appearance of Elis and Rosa. At first there were sharp whispers, and angry shushes, and suddenly a woman began to rise and then leaned violently away as a child rose from the aisle seat beside her. The child, a boy of about six, walked down the aisle and climbed the stairs to the stage, where he stood smiling at the audience, who immediately recognized that he was of the race of Elis and Rosa. Although the mysterious child never appeared again, spectators now began to look nervously at their neighbors; and it was in this charged atmosphere that the rumor of impending arrest sprang up and would not go away. The mere sight of Herr Uhl in his box each night caused tense whispers. It began to seem as if the policeman and the magician were engaged in a secret battle: it was said that Herr Uhl was planning a dramatic arrest, and Eisenheim a brilliant escape. Eisenheim, for his part, ignored the whispers and did nothing to modify the disturbing effects that Elis and Rosa had on his audience; and as if to defy the forces gathering against him, one evening he brought forth another figure, an ugly old woman in a black dress who frightened Elis and Rosa and caused fearful cries from the audience before she melted away.

The official reason given for the arrest of the Master, and the seizure of his theater, was the disturbance of public order; the police reports, in preparation for more than a year, listed more than one hundred incidents. But Herr Uhl's private papers reveal a deeper cause. The chief of police was an intelligent and well-read man who was himself an amateur conjurer, and he was not unduly troubled by the occasional extreme public responses to Eisenheim's illusions, although he recorded each instance scrupulously and asked himself whether such effects were consonant with public safety and decorum. No, what disturbed Herr Uhl was something else, something for which he had difficulty finding a name. The phrase "crossing of boundaries" occurs pejoratively more than once in his notebooks; by it he appears to mean that certain distinctions must be strictly maintained. Art and life constituted one such distinction; illusion and reality, another. Eisenheim deliberately crossed boundaries and therefore disturbed the essence of things. In effect, Herr Uhl was accusing Eisenheim of shaking the foundations of the universe, of undermining reality, and in consequence, of doing something far worse: subverting the empire. For where would the empire be, once the idea of boundaries became blurred and uncertain?

On the night of February 14, 1902 — a cold, clear night, when horseshoes rang sharply on the avenues, and fashionable women in chin-high black boas plunged their forearms into heavy, furry muffs — twelve uniformed policemen took their seats in the audience of Eisenheimhaus. The decision to arrest the Master during a performance was later disputed; the public arrest was apparently intended to send a warning to devotees of Eisenheim, and perhaps to other magicians as well. Immediately after the appearance of Rosa, Herr Uhl left his box. Moments later he strode through a side door onto the stage and announced the arrest of Eisenheim in the name of His Imperial Majesty and the City of Vienna. Twelve officers stepped into the aisles and stood at attention. Eisenheim turned his head wearily toward the intruding figure and did not move. Elis and Rosa, who had been standing at the edge of the stage, began to look about fearfully: the lovely boy shook his head and murmured "No" in his angelic voice, while Rosa hugged herself tightly and began to hum a low melody that sounded like a drawn-out moan or keen. Herr Uhl, who had paused some ten feet from Eisenheim in order to permit the grave Master to rise unaided, saw at once that things were getting out of hand — someone in the audience began murmuring "No" and the chant was taken up. Swiftly Uhl strode to the seated magician and placed a hand on his shoulder. That was when it happened: his hand fell through Eisenheim's shoulder, he appeared to stumble, and in a fury he began striking at the magician, who remained seated calmly through the paroxysm of meaningless blows. At last the officer drew his sword and sliced through Eisenheim, who at this point rose with great dignity and turned to Elis and Rosa. They looked at him imploringly as they wavered and grew dim. The Master then turned to the audience; and slowly, gravely, he bowed. The applause began in scattered sections and grew louder and wilder until the curtains were seen to tremble. Six officers leaped onto the stage and attempted to seize Eisenheim, who looked at them with an expression of such melancholy that one policeman felt a shadow pass over his heart. And now a nervousness rippled through the crowd as the Master seemed to gather himself for some final effort: his face became rigid with concentration, the famous vein pressed through his forehead, the unseeing eyes were dark autumn nights when the wind picks up and branches creak. A shudder was seen to pass along his arms. It spread to his legs, and from the crowd rose the sound of a great inrush of breath as Eisenheim began his unthinkable final act: bending the black flame of his gaze inward, locked in savage concentration, he began to unknit the threads of his being. Wavering, slowly fading, he stood dark and unmoving there. In the Master's face some claimed to see, as he dissolved before their eyes, a look of fearful exaltation. Others said that at the end he raised his face and uttered a cry of icy desolation. When it was over the audience rose to its feet. Herr Uhl promptly arrested a young man in the front row, and a precarious order was maintained. On a drab stage, empty except for a single wooden chair, policemen in uniform looked tensely about.

Later that night the police ransacked the apartment with a distant view of the Danube, but Eisenheim was not there. The failed arrest was in one respect highly successful: the Master was never seen again. In the Devil's Factory trick mirrors were found, exquisite cabinets with secret panels, ingenious chests and boxes representing high instances of the art of deception, but not a clue about the famous illusions, not one, nothing. Some said that Eisenheim had created an illusory Eisenheim from the first day of the new century; others said that the Master had gradually grown illusory from trafficking with illusions. Someone suggested that Herr Uhl was himself an illusion, a carefully staged part of the final performance. Arguments arose over whether it was all done with lenses and mirrors, or whether the Jew from Bratislava had sold his soul to the Devil for the dark gift of magic. All agreed that it was a sign of the times; and as precise memories faded, and the everyday world of coffee cups, doctors' visits, and war rumors returned, a secret relief penetrated the souls of the faithful, who knew that the Master had passed safely out of the crumbling order of history into the indestructible realm of mystery and dream.

LORRIE MOORE

You're Ugly, Too

FROM THE NEW YORKER

YOU HAD TO get out of them occasionally, those Illinois towns with the funny names: Paris, Oblong, Normal. Once, when the Dow Jones dipped two hundred points, a local paper boasted the banner headline "NORMAL MAN MARRIES OBLONG WOMAN." They knew what was important. They did! But you had to get out once in a while, even if it was just across the border to Terre Haute for a movie.

Outside of Paris, in the middle of a large field, was a scatter of brick buildings, a small liberal-arts college by the improbable name of Hilldale-Versailles. Zoë Hendricks had been teaching American history there for three years. She taught "The Revolution and Beyond" to freshmen and sophomores, and every third semester she had the senior seminar for majors, and although her student evaluations had been slipping in the last year and a half — *Professor Hendricks is often late for class and usually arrives with a cup of hot chocolate, which she offers the class sips of* — generally the department of nine men was pleased to have her. They felt she added some needed feminine touch to the corridors — that faint trace of Obsession and sweat, the light, fast clicking of heels. Plus they had had a sex-discrimination suit, and the dean had said, well, it was time.

The situation was not easy for her, they knew. Once, at the start of last semester, she had skipped into her lecture hall singing "Getting to Know You" — all of it. At the request of the dean, the chairman had called her into his office, but did not ask her for an explanation, not really. He asked her how she was and

then smiled in an avuncular way. She said, "Fine," and he studied the way she said it, her front teeth catching on the inside of
her lower lip. She was almost pretty, but her face showed the
strain and ambition of always having been close but not quite.
There was too much effort with the eyeliner, and her earrings,
worn, no doubt, for the drama her features lacked, were a little
frightening, jutting out the sides of her head like antennae.

"I'm going out of my mind," said Zoë to her younger sister,
Evan, in Manhattan. *Professor Hendricks seems to know the entire
soundtrack to "The King and I." Is this history?* Zoë phoned her every
Tuesday.

"You always say that," said Evan, "but then you go on your
trips and vacations and then you settle back into things and then
you're quiet for a while and then you say you're fine, you're busy,
and then after a while you say you're going crazy again, and you
start all over." Evan was a part-time food designer for photo
shoots. She cooked vegetables in green dye. She propped up
beef stew with a bed of marbles and shopped for new kinds of
silicone sprays and plastic ice cubes. She thought her life was
O.K. She was living with her boyfriend of many years, who was
independently wealthy and had an amusing little job in book
publishing. They were five years out of college, and they lived
in a luxury midtown high rise with a balcony and access to a
pool. "It's not the same as having your own pool," Evan was always sighing, as if to let Zoë know that, as with Zoë, there were
still things she, Evan, had to do without.

"Illinois. It makes me sarcastic to be here," said Zoë on the
phone. She used to insist it was irony, something gently layered
and sophisticated, something alien to the Midwest, but her students kept calling it sarcasm, something they felt qualified to
recognize, and now she had to agree. It wasn't irony. "What is
your perfume?" a student once asked her. "Room freshener,"
she said. She smiled, but he looked at her, unnerved.

Her students were by and large good midwesterners, spacey
with estrogen from large quantities of meat and eggs. They shared
their parents' suburban values; their parents had given them
things, things, things. They were complacent. They had been
purchased. They were armed with a healthy vagueness about
anything historical or geographic. They seemed actually to know

very little about anything, but they were good-natured about it. "All those states in the East are so tiny and jagged and bunched up," complained one of her undergraduates the week she was lecturing on "The Turning Point of Independence: The Battle at Saratoga." "Professor Hendricks, you're from Delaware originally, right?" the student asked her.

"Maryland," corrected Zoë.

"Aw," he said, waving his hand dismissively. "New England."

Her articles — chapters toward a book called *Hearing the One About: Uses of Humor in the American Presidency* — were generally well received, though they came slowly for her. She liked her pieces to have something from every time of day in them — she didn't trust things written in the morning only — so she reread and rewrote painstakingly. No part of a day — its moods, its light — was allowed to dominate. She hung on to a piece for a year sometimes, revising at all hours, until the entirety of a day had registered there.

The job she'd had before the one at Hilldale-Versailles had been at a small college in New Geneva, Minnesota, Land of the Dying Shopping Mall. Everyone was so blond there that brunettes were often presumed to be from foreign countries. *Just because Professor Hendricks is from Spain doesn't give her the right to be so negative about our country.* There was a general emphasis on cheerfulness. In New Geneva you weren't supposed to be critical or complain. You weren't supposed to notice that the town had overextended and that its shopping malls were raggedy and going under. You were never to say you weren't "fine, thank you — and yourself?" You were supposed to be Heidi. You were supposed to lug goat milk up the hills and not think twice. Heidi did not complain. Heidi did not do things like stand in front of the new IBM photocopier saying, "If this fucking Xerox machine breaks on me one more time, I'm going to slit my wrists."

But now in her second job, in her fourth year of teaching in the Midwest, Zoë was discovering something she never suspected she had: a crusty edge, brittle and pointed. Once she had pampered her students, singing them songs, letting them call her at home even, and ask personal questions, but now she was losing sympathy. They were beginning to seem different. They were beginning to seem demanding and spoiled.

"You act," said one of her senior-seminar students at a scheduled conference, "like your opinion is worth more than everyone else's in the class."

Zoë's eyes widened. "I *am* the teacher," she said. "I do get paid to act like that." She narrowed her gaze at the student, who was wearing a big leather bow in her hair like a cowgirl in a TV ranch show. "I mean, otherwise *everybody* in the class would have little offices and office hours." *Sometimes Professor Hendricks will take up the class's time just talking about movies she's seen.* She stared at the student some more, then added, "I bet you'd like that."

"Maybe I sound whiny to you," said the girl, "but I simply want my history major to mean something."

"Well, there's your problem," said Zoë, and, with a smile, she showed the student to the door. "I like your bow," she said.

Zoë lived for the mail, for the postman — that handsome blue jay — and when she got a real letter with a real full-price stamp from someplace else, she took it to bed with her and read it over and over. She also watched television until all hours and had her set in the bedroom — a bad sign. *Professor Hendricks has said critical things about Fawn Hall, the Catholic religion, and the whole state of Illinois. It is unbelievable.* At Christmastime she gave twenty-dollar tips to the mailman and to Jerry, the only cabbie in town, whom she had gotten to know from all her rides to and from the Terre Haute airport, and who, since he realized such rides were an extravagance, often gave her cut rates.

"I'm flying in to visit you this weekend," announced Zoë.

"I was hoping you would," said Evan. "Charlie and I are having a party for Halloween. It'll be fun."

"I have a costume already. It's a bonehead. It's this thing that looks like a giant bone going through your head."

"Great," said Evan.

"It is, it's great."

"All I have is my moon mask from last year and the year before. I'll probably end up getting married in it."

"Are you and Charlie getting *married?*" Zoë felt slightly alarmed.

"Hmmmmmmnnno, not immediately."

"Don't get married."

"Why?"

"Just not yet. You're too young."

"You're only saying that because you're five years older than I am and *you're* not married."

"*I'm* not married? Oh, my God," said Zoë, "I forgot to get married."

Zoë had been out with three men since she'd come to Hilldale-Versailles. One of them was a man in the municipal bureaucracy who had fixed a parking ticket she'd brought in to protest and then asked her out for coffee. At first, she thought he was amazing — at last, someone who did not want Heidi! But soon she came to realize that all men, deep down, wanted Heidi. Heidi with cleavage. Heidi with outfits. The parking-ticket bureaucrat soon became tired and intermittent. One cool fall day, in his snazzy, impractical convertible, when she asked him what was wrong he said, "You would not be ill served by new clothes, you know." She wore a lot of gray-green corduroy. She had been under the impression that it brought out her eyes, those shy stars. She flicked an ant from her sleeve.

"Did you have to brush that off in the car?" he said, driving. He glanced down at his own pectorals, giving first the left, then the right, a quick survey. He was wearing a tight shirt.

"Excuse me?"

He slowed down at an amber light and frowned. "Couldn't you have picked it up and thrown it outside?"

"The ant? It might have bitten me. I mean, what difference does it make?"

"It might have bitten you! Ha! How ridiculous! Now it's going to lay eggs in my car!"

The second guy was sweeter, lunkier, though not insensitive to certain paintings and songs, but too often, too, things he'd do or say would startle her. Once, in a restaurant, he stole the garnishes off her dinner plate and waited for her to notice. When she didn't, he finally thrust his fist across the table and said, "Look," and when he opened it, there was her parsley sprig and her orange slice crumpled to a wad. Another time, he described to her his recent trip to the Louvre. "And there I was in front of Delacroix's *The Barque of Dante*, and everyone else had wandered off, so I had my own private audience with it, all those agonized shades splayed in every direction, and there's this motion in that painting that starts at the bottom, swirling and building up into the red fabric of Dante's hood, swirling out into the distance, where you see these orange flames —" He was breathless in the telling. She found this touching, and smiled in encouragement. "A painting like that," he said, shaking his head. "It just makes you shit."

"I have to ask you something," said Evan. "I know every woman complains about not meeting men, but really, on my shoots I meet a lot of men. And they're not all gay, either." She paused. "Not anymore."

"What are you asking?"

The third guy was a political-science professor named Murray Peterson, who liked to go out on double dates with colleagues whose wives he was attracted to. Usually, the wives would consent to flirt with him. Under the table sometimes there was footsie, and once there was even kneesie. Zoë and the husband would be left to their food, staring into their water glasses, chewing like goats. "Oh, Murray," said one wife, who had never finished her master's in physical therapy and wore great clothes. "You know, I know everything about you: your birthday, your license-plate number. I have everything memorized. But then that's the kind of mind I have. Once, at a dinner party, I amazed the host by getting up and saying goodbye to every single person there, first *and* last names."

"I knew a dog who could do that," said Zoë with her mouth full. Murray and the wife looked at her with vexed and rebuking expressions, but the husband seemed suddenly twinkling and amused. Zoë swallowed. "It was a talking Lab, and after about ten minutes of listening to the dinner conversation this dog knew everyone's name. You could say, 'Take this knife to Murray Peterson,' and it would."

"Really," said the wife, frowning, and Murray Peterson never called again.

"Are you seeing anyone?" said Evan. "I'm asking for a particular reason. I'm not just being like Mom."

"I'm seeing my house. I'm tending to it when it wets, when it cries, when it throws up." Zoë had bought a mint-green ranch house near campus, though now she was thinking that maybe she shouldn't have. It was hard to live in a house. She kept wandering in and out of the rooms, wondering where she had put things. She went downstairs into the basement for no reason at all except that it amused her to own a basement. It also amused her to own a tree.

Her parents, in Maryland, had been very pleased that one of their children had at last been able to afford real estate, and when she closed on the house they sent her flowers with a congratulations card. Her mother had even UPS'd a box of old decorating magazines saved over the years — photographs of beautiful rooms her mother used to moon over, since there never had been any money to redecorate. It was like getting her mother's pornography, that box, inheriting her drooled-upon fantasies, the endless wish and tease that had been her life. But to her mother it was a rite of passage that pleased her. "Maybe you will get some ideas from these," she had written. And when Zoë looked at the photographs, at the bold and beautiful living rooms, she was filled with longing. Ideas and ideas of longing.

Right now Zoë's house was rather empty. The previous owner had wallpapered around the furniture, leaving strange gaps and silhouettes on the walls, and Zoë hadn't done much about that yet. She had bought furniture, then taken it back, furnishing and unfurnishing, preparing and shedding, like a womb. She had bought several plain pine chests to use as love seats or boot boxes, but they came to look to her more and more like children's coffins, so she returned them. And she had recently bought an Oriental rug for the living room, with Chinese symbols on it she didn't understand. The salesgirl had kept saying she was sure they meant "Peace" and "Eternal Life," but when Zoë got the rug home she worried. What if they didn't mean "Peace" and "Eternal Life"? What if they meant, say, "Bruce Springsteen"? And the more she thought about it, the more she became convinced she had a rug that said "Bruce Springsteen," and so she returned that, too.

She had also bought a little baroque mirror for the front entryway, which, she had been told by Murray Peterson, would keep away evil spirits. The mirror, however, tended to frighten *her,* startling her with an image of a woman she never recognized. Sometimes she looked puffier and plainer than she remembered. Sometimes shifty and dark. Most times she just looked vague. "You look like someone I know," she had been told twice in the last year by strangers in restaurants in Terre Haute. In fact, sometimes she seemed not to have a look of her own, or any look whatsoever, and it began to amuse her that her students and colleagues were able to recognize her at all. How did they know? When she walked into a room, how did she look so that they knew it was she? Like this? Did she look like this? And so she returned the mirror.

"The reason I'm asking is that I know a man I think you should meet," said Evan. "He's fun. He's straight. He's single. That's all I'm going to say."

"I think I'm too old for fun," said Zoë. She had a dark bristly hair in her chin, and she could feel it now with her finger. Perhaps when you had been without the opposite sex for too long, you began to resemble them. In an act of desperate invention, you began to grow your own. "I just want to come, wear my bonehead, visit with Charlie's tropical fish, ask you about your food shoots."

She thought about all the papers on "Our Constitution: How It Affects Us" she was going to have to correct. She thought about how she was going in for ultrasound tests on Friday, because, according to her doctor and her doctor's assistant, she had a large, mysterious growth in her abdomen. Gallbladder, they kept saying. Or ovaries or colon. "You guys practice medicine?" asked Zoë, aloud, after they had left the room. Once, as a girl, she brought her dog to a vet, who had told her, "Well, either your dog has worms or cancer or else it was hit by a car."

She was looking forward to New York.

"Well, whatever. We'll just play it cool. I can't wait to see you, hon. Don't forget your bonehead," said Evan.

"A bonehead you don't forget," said Zoë.

"I suppose," said Evan.

The ultrasound Zoë was keeping a secret, even from Evan. I feel like I'm dying," Zoë had hinted just once on the phone.

"You're not dying," said Evan, "you're just annoyed."

"Ultrasound," Zoë now said jokingly to the technician who put the cold jelly on her bare stomach. "Does that sound like a really great stereo system or what?"

She had not had anyone make this much fuss over her bare

stomach since her boyfriend in graduate school, who had hovered over her whenever she felt ill, waved his arms, pressed his hands upon her navel, and drawled evangelically, "Heal! Heal for thy Baby Jesus' sake!" Zoë would laugh and they would make love, both secretly hoping she would get pregnant. Later they would worry together, and he would sink a cheek to her belly and ask whether she was late, was she late, was she sure, she might be late, and when after two years she had not gotten pregnant they took to quarreling and drifted apart.

"O.K.," said the technician absently.

The monitor was in place, and Zoë's insides came on the screen in all their gray and ribbony hollowness. They were marbled in the finest gradations of black and white, like stone in an old church or a picture of the moon. "Do you suppose," she babbled at the technician, "that the rise in infertility among so many couples in this country is due to completely different species trying to reproduce?" The technician moved the scanner around and took more pictures. On one view in particular, on Zoë's right side, the technician became suddenly alert, the machine he was operating clicking away.

Zoë stared at the screen. "That must be the growth you found there," suggested Zoë.

"I can't tell you anything," said the technician rigidly. "Your doctor will get the radiologist's report this afternoon and will phone you then."

"I'll be out of town," said Zoë.

"I'm sorry," said the technician.

Driving home, Zoë looked in the rearview mirror and decided she looked — well, how would one describe it? A little wan. She thought of the joke about the guy who visits his doctor and the doctor says, "Well, I'm sorry to say, you've got six weeks to live."

"I want a second opinion," says the guy. *You act like your opinion is worth more than everyone else's in the class.*

"You want a second opinion? O.K.," says the doctor. "You're ugly, too." She liked that joke. She thought it was terribly, terribly funny.

She took a cab to the airport. Jerry the cabbie was happy to see her.

"Have fun in New York," he said, getting her bag out of the

trunk. He liked her, or at least he always acted as if he did. She called him Jare.

"Thanks, Jare."

"You know, I'll tell you a secret: I've never been to New York. I'll tell you two secrets: I've never been on a plane." And he waved at her sadly as she pushed her way in through the terminal door. "Or an escalator!" he shouted.

The trick to flying safely, Zoë always said, was to never buy a discount ticket and to tell yourself you had nothing to live for anyway, so that when the plane crashed it was no big deal. Then, when it didn't crash, when you had succeeded in keeping it aloft with your own worthlessness, all you had to do was stagger off, locate your luggage, and, by the time a cab arrived, come up with a persuasive reason to go on living.

"You're here!" shrieked Evan over the doorbell, before she even opened the door. Then she opened it wide. Zoë set her bags on the hall floor and hugged Evan hard. When she was little, Evan had always been affectionate and devoted. Zoë had always taken care of her — advising, reassuring — until recently, when it seemed Evan had started advising and reassuring *her*. It startled Zoë. She suspected it had something to do with her being alone. It made people uncomfortable.

"How *are* you?"

"I threw up on the plane. Besides that, I'm O.K."

"Can I get you something? Here, let me take your suitcase. Sick on the plane. *Eeeyew.*"

"It was into one of those sickness bags," said Zoë, just in case Evan thought she'd lost it in the aisle. "I was very quiet."

The apartment was spacious and bright, with a view all the way downtown along the East Side. There was a balcony, and sliding glass doors. "I keep forgetting how nice this apartment is. Twenty-first floor, doorman . . ." Zoë could work her whole life and never have an apartment like this. So could Evan. It was Charlie's apartment. He and Evan lived in it like two kids in a dorm, beer cans and clothes strewn around. Evan put Zoë's bag away from the mess, over by the fish tanks. "I'm so glad you're here," she said. "Now what can I get you?"

Evan made them lunch — soup from a can and saltines.

"I don't know about Charlie," she said after they had finished. "I feel like we've gone all sexless and middle-aged already."

"Hmm," said Zoë. She leaned back into Evan's sofa and stared out the window at the dark tops of the buildings. It seemed a little unnatural to live up in the sky like this, like birds that out of some wrongheaded derring-do had nested too high. She nodded toward the lighted fish tanks and giggled. "I feel like a bird," she said, "with my own personal supply of fish."

Evan sighed. "He comes home and just sacks out on the sofa, watching fuzzy football. He's wearing the psychic cold cream and curlers, if you know what I mean."

Zoë sat up, readjusted the sofa cushions. "What's fuzzy football?"

"We haven't gotten cable yet. Everything comes in fuzzy. Charlie just watches it that way."

"Hmm, yeah, that's a little depressing," Zoë said. She looked at her hands. "Especially the part about not having cable."

"This is how he gets into bed at night." Evan stood up to demonstrate. "He whips all his clothes off, and when he gets to his underwear he lets it drop to one ankle. Then he kicks up his leg and flips the underwear in the air and catches it. I, of course, watch from the bed. There's nothing else. There's just that."

"Maybe you should just get it over with and get married."

"Really?"

"Yeah. I mean, you guys probably think living together like this is the best of both worlds, but —" Zoë tried to sound like an older sister; an older sister was supposed to be the parent you could never have, the hip, cool mom. "But I've always found that as soon as you think you've got the best of both worlds" — she thought now of herself, alone in her house, of the toad-faced cicadas that flew around like little men at night and landed on her screens, staring; of the size-fourteen shoes she placed at the doorstep, to scare off intruders; of the ridiculous, inflatable blowup doll someone had told her to keep propped up at the breakfast table — "it can suddenly twist and become the worst of both worlds."

"Really?" Evan was beaming. "Oh, Zoë. I have something to tell you. Charlie and I *are* getting married."

"Really." Zoë felt confused.

"I didn't know how to tell you."

"Yeah, I guess the part about fuzzy football misled me a little."

"I was hoping you'd be my maid of honor," said Evan, waiting. "Aren't you happy for me?"

"Yes," said Zoë, and she began to tell Evan a story about an award-winning violinist at Hilldale-Versailles — how the violinist had come home from a competition in Europe and taken up with a local man who made her go to all his summer softball games, made her cheer for him from the stands, with the wives, until she later killed herself. But when Zoë got halfway through, to the part about cheering at the softball games, she stopped.

"What?" said Evan. "So what happened?"

"Actually, nothing," said Zoë lightly. "She just really got into softball. You should have seen her."

Zoë decided to go to a late afternoon movie, leaving Evan to chores she needed to do before the party — "I have to do them alone, really," she'd said, a little tense after the violinist story. Zoë thought about going to an art museum, but women alone in art museums had to look good. They always did. Chic and serious, moving languidly, with a great handbag. Instead, she walked down through Kips Bay, past an earring boutique called Stick It in Your Ear, past a hair salon called Dorian Gray. That was the funny thing about "beauty," thought Zoë. Look it up in the yellow pages and you found a hundred entries, hostile with wit, cutesy with warning. But look up "truth" — Ha! There was nothing at all.

Zoë thought about Evan getting married. Would Evan turn into Peter Pumpkin Eater's wife? Mrs. Eater? At the wedding, would she make Zoë wear some flouncy lavender dress, identical with the other maids'? Zoë hated uniforms, had even in the first grade refused to join Elf Girls because she didn't want to wear the same dress as everyone else. Now she might have to. But maybe she could distinguish it. Hitch it up on one side with a clothespin. Wear surgical gauze at the waist. Clip to her bodice one of those pins that say in loud letters "Shit Happens."

At the movie — *Death by Number* — she bought strands of red licorice to tug and chew. She took a seat off to one side in the theater. She felt strangely self-conscious sitting alone, and hoped for the place to darken fast. When it did, and the coming attractions came on, she reached inside her purse for her glasses. They were in a Baggie. Her Kleenex was also in a Baggie. So were her pen and her aspirin and her mints. Everything was in Baggies. This was what she'd become: *a woman alone at the movies with everything in a Baggie.*

At the Halloween party, there were about two dozen people. There were people with ape heads and large hairy hands. There was someone dressed as a leprechaun. There was someone dressed as a frozen dinner. Some man had brought his two small daughters: a ballerina and a ballerina's sister, also dressed as a ballerina. There was a gaggle of sexy witches — women dressed entirely in black, beautifully made up and jeweled. "I hate those sexy witches. It's not in the spirit of Halloween," said Evan. Evan had abandoned the moon mask and dolled herself up as hausfrau, in curlers and an apron, a decision she now regretted. Charlie, because he liked fish, because he owned fish and collected fish, had decided to go as a fish. He had fins, and eyes on the sides of his head. "Zoë! How are you! I'm sorry I wasn't here when you first arrived!" He spent the rest of his time chatting up the sexy witches.

"Isn't there something I can help you with here?" Zoë asked her sister. "You've been running yourself ragged." She rubbed her sister's arm, gently, as if she wished they were alone.

"Oh, God, not at all," said Evan, arranging stuffed mushrooms on a plate. The timer went off, and she pulled another sheetful out of the oven. "Actually, you know what you can do?"

"What?" Zoë put on her bonehead.

"Meet Earl. He's the guy I had in mind for you. When he gets here, just talk to him a little. He's nice. He's fun. He's going through a divorce."

"I'll try," Zoë groaned. "O.K.? I'll try." She looked at her watch.

When Earl arrived, he was dressed as a naked woman, steel wool glued strategically to a body stocking, and large rubber breasts protruding like hams.

"Zoë, this is Earl," said Evan.

"Good to meet you," said Earl, circling Evan to shake Zoë's hand. He stared at the top of Zoë's head. "Great bone."

Zoë nodded. "Great tits," she said. She looked past him, out

the window at the city thrown glittering up against the sky; people were saying the usual things: how it looked like jewels, like
bracelets and necklaces unstrung. You could see the clock of the
Con Ed building, the orange-and-gold-capped Empire State, the
Chrysler like a rocket ship dreamed up in a depression. Far west
you could glimpse Astor Plaza, with its flying white roof like a
nun's habit. "There's beer out on the balcony, Earl. Can I get
you one?" Zoë asked.

"Sure, uh, I'll come along. Hey, Charlie, how's it going?"

Charlie grinned and whistled. People turned to look. "Hey,
Earl," someone called from across the room. "Va-va-va-voom."

They squeezed their way past the other guests, past the apes
and the sexy witches. The suction of the sliding door gave way
in a whoosh, and Zoë and Earl stepped out onto the balcony, a
bonehead and a naked woman, the night air roaring and smoky
cool. Another couple were out there, too, murmuring privately.
They were not wearing costumes. They smiled at Zoë and Earl.
"Hi," said Zoë. She found the plastic-foam cooler, dug in and
retrieved two beers.

"Thanks," said Earl. His rubber breasts folded inward, dim-
pled and dented, as he twisted open the bottle.

"Well," sighed Zoë anxiously. She had to learn not to be afraid
of a man, the way, in your childhood, you learned not to be
afraid of an earthworm or a bug. Often, when she spoke to men
at parties, she rushed things in her mind. As the man politely
blathered on, she would fall in love, marry, then find herself in
a bitter custody battle with him for the kids and hoping for a
reconciliation, so that despite all his betrayals she might no longer
despise him, and, in the few minutes remaining, learn, perhaps,
what his last name was and what he did for a living, though
probably there was already too much history between them. She
would nod, blush, turn away.

"Evan tells me you're a history professor. Where do you teach?"

"Just over the Indiana border into Illinois."

He looked a little shocked. "I guess Evan didn't tell me that
part."

"She didn't?"

"No."

"Well, that's Evan for you. When we were kids we both had
speech impediments."

"That can be tough," said Earl. One of his breasts was hidden behind his drinking arm, but the other shone low and pink, full as a strawberry moon.

"Yes, well, it wasn't a total loss. We use to go to what we called peach pearapy. For about ten years of my life, I had to map out every sentence in my mind, way ahead, before I said it. That was the only way I could get a coherent sentence out."

Earl drank from his beer. "How did you do that? I mean, how did you get through?"

"I told a lot of jokes. Jokes you know the lines to already. You can just say them. I love jokes. Jokes and songs."

Earl smiled. He had on lipstick, a deep shade of red, but it was wearing off from the beer. "What's your favorite joke?"

"Uh, my favorite joke is probably — O.K., all right. This guy goes into a doctor's office, and —"

"I think I know this one," interrupted Earl, eagerly. He wanted to tell it himself. "A guy goes into a doctor's office, and the doctor tells him he's got some good news and some bad news — that one, right?"

"I'm not sure," said Zoë. "This might be a different version."

"So the guy says, 'Give me the bad news first,' and the doctor says, 'O.K. You've got three weeks to live.' And the guy cries, 'Three weeks to live! Doctor, what is the good news?' And the doctor says, 'Did you see that secretary out front? I finally fucked her.'"

Zoë frowned.

"That's not the one you were thinking of?"

"No." There was accusation in her voice. "Mine was different."

"Oh," said Earl. He looked away and then back again. "What kind of history do you teach?"

"I teach American, mostly — eighteenth- and nineteenth-century." In graduate school, at bars the pickup line was always "So what's your century?"

"Occasionally, I teach a special theme course," she added. "Say, 'Humor and Personality in the White House.' That's what my book's on." She thought of something someone once told her about bowerbirds, how they build elaborate structures before mating.

"Your book's on *humor*?"

"Yeah, and, well, when I teach a theme course like that I do all the centuries." *So what's your century?*

"All three of them."

"Pardon?" The breeze glistened her eyes. Traffic revved beneath them. She felt high and puny, like someone lifted into heaven by mistake and then spurned.

"Three. There's only three."

"Well, four, really." She was thinking of Jamestown, and of the Pilgrims coming here with buckles and witch hats to say their prayers.

"I'm a photographer," said Earl. His face was starting to gleam, his rouge smearing in a sunset beneath his eyes.

"Do you like that?"

"Well, actually, I'm starting to feel it's a little dangerous."

"Really?"

"Spending all your time in a dark room with that red light and all those chemicals. There's links with Parkinson's, you know."

"No, I didn't."

"I suppose I should wear rubber gloves, but I don't like to. Unless I'm touching it directly, I don't think of it as real."

"Hmm," said Zoë. Alarm buzzed mildly through her.

"Sometimes, when I have a cut or something, I feel the sting and think, *Shit.* I wash constantly and just hope. I don't like rubber over the skin like that."

"Really."

"I mean, the physical contact. That's what you want, or why bother?"

"I guess," said Zoë. She wished she could think of a joke, something slow and deliberate with the end in sight. She thought of gorillas, how when they had been kept too long alone in cages they would smack each other in the head instead of mating.

"Are you — in a relationship?" Earl suddenly blurted.

"Now? As we speak?"

"Well, I mean, I'm sure you have a relationship to your *work.*" A smile, a little one, nestled in his mouth like an egg. She thought of zoos in parks, how when cities were under siege, during world wars, people ate the animals. "But I mean, with a *man.*"

"No, I'm not in a relationship with a *man.*" She rubbed her chin with her hand and could feel the one bristly hair there.

"But my last relationship was with a very sweet man," she said. She made something up. "From Switzerland. He was a botanist — a weed expert. His name was Jerry. I called him Jare. He was so funny. You'd go to the movies with him and all he would notice was the plants. He would never pay attention to the plot. Once, in a jungle movie, he started rattling off all these Latin names, out loud. It was very exciting for him." She paused, caught her breath. "Eventually, he went back to Europe to, uh, study the edelweiss." She looked at Earl. "Are you involved in a relationship? With a *woman?*"

Earl shifted his weight and the creases in his body stocking changed, splintering outward like something broken. His pubic hair slid over to one hip, like a corsage on a saloon girl. "No," he said, clearing his throat. The steel wool in his underarms was inching down toward his biceps. "I've just gotten out of a marriage that was full of bad dialogue like 'You want more *space?* I'll give you more space!' *Clonk.* Your basic Three Stooges."

Zoë looked at him sympathetically. "I suppose it's hard for love to recover after that."

His eyes lit up. He wanted to talk about love. "But I keep thinking love should be like a tree. You look at trees and they've got bumps and scars from tumors, infestations, what have you, but they're still growing. Despite the bumps and bruises, they're — straight."

"Yeah, well," said Zoë, "where I'm from they're all married or gay. Did you see that movie *Death by Number?*"

Earl looked at her, a little lost. She was getting away from him. "No," he said.

One of his breasts had slipped under his arm, tucked there like a baguette. She kept thinking of trees, of parks, of people in wartime eating the zebras. She felt a stabbing pain in her abdomen.

"Want some hors d'oeuvres?" Evan came pushing through the sliding door. She was smiling, though her curlers were coming out, hanging bedraggled at the ends of her hair like Christmas decorations, like food put out for the birds. She thrust forward a plate of stuffed mushrooms.

"Are you asking for donations or giving them away?" said Earl wittily. He liked Evan, and he put his arm around her.

"You know, I'll be right back," said Zoë.

"Oh," said Evan, looking concerned.

"Right back. I promise."

Zoë hurried inside, across the living room into the bedroom, to the adjoining bath. It was empty; most of the guests were using the half-bath near the kitchen. She flicked on the light and closed the door. The pain had stopped, and she didn't really have to go to the bathroom, but she stayed there anyway, resting. In the mirror above the sink, she looked haggard beneath her bonehead, violet-grays showing under the skin like a plucked and pocky bird's. She leaned closer, raising her chin a little to find the bristly hair. It was there, at the end of the jaw, sharp and dark as a wire. She opened the medicine cabinet, pawed through it until she found some tweezers. She lifted her head again and poked at her face with the metal tips, grasping and pinching and missing. Outside the door, she could hear two people talking low. They had come into the bedroom and were discussing something. They were sitting on the bed. One of them giggled in a false way. Zoë stabbed again at her chin, and it started to bleed a little. She pulled the skin tight along the jawbone, gripped the tweezers hard around what she hoped was the hair, and tugged. A tiny square of skin came away, but the hair remained, blood bright at the root of it. Zoë clenched her teeth. "Come on," she whispered. The couple outside in the bedroom were now telling stories, softly, and laughing. There was a bounce and squeak of mattress, and the sound of a chair being moved out of the way. Zoë aimed the tweezers carefully, pinched, then pulled gently, and this time the hair came, too, with a slight twinge of pain, and then a great flood of relief. "Yeah!" breathed Zoë. She grabbed some toilet paper and dabbed at her chin. It came away spotted with blood, and so she tore off some more and pressed hard until it stopped. Then she turned off the light, opened the door, and rejoined the party. "Excuse me," she said to the couple in the bedroom. They were the couple from the balcony, and they looked at her, a bit surprised. They had their arms around each other, and they were eating candy bars.

Earl was still out on the balcony, alone, and Zoë rejoined him there. "Hi," she said.

He turned around and smiled. He had straightened his costume out a bit, though all the secondary sex characteristics seemed
slightly doomed, destined to shift and flip and zip around again
any moment. "Are you O.K.?" he asked. He had opened another
beer and was chugging.

"Oh, yeah. I just had to go to the bathroom." She paused.
"Actually, I have been going to a lot of doctors recently."

"What's wrong?" asked Earl.

"Oh, probably nothing. But they're putting me through tests."
She sighed. "I've had sonograms. I've had mammograms. Next
week I'm going in for a candygram." He looked at her, concerned. "I've had too many gram words," she said.

"Here, I saved you these." He held out a napkin with two stuffed
mushroom caps. They were cold and leaving oil marks on the
napkin.

"Thanks," said Zoë, and pushed them both in her mouth.
"Watch," she said with her mouth full. "With my luck it'll be a
gallbladder operation."

Earl made a face. "So your sister's getting married," he said,
changing the subject. "Tell me, really, what you think about love."

"*Love?*" Hadn't they done this already? "I don't know." She
chewed thoughtfully and swallowed. "All right. I'll tell you what
I think about love. Here is a love story. This friend of mine —"

"You've got something on your chin," said Earl, and he reached
over to touch it.

"What?" said Zoë, stepping back. She turned her face away
and grabbed at her chin. A piece of toilet paper peeled off it,
like tape. "It's nothing," she said. "It's just — it's nothing."

Earl stared at her.

"At any rate," she continued, "this friend of mine was this
award-winning violinist. She traveled all over Europe and won
competitions; she made records, she gave concerts, she got famous. But she had no social life. So one day she threw herself at
the feet of this conductor she had a terrible crush on. He picked
her up, scolded her gently, and sent her back to her hotel room.
After that, she came home from Europe. She went back to her
old hometown, stopped playing the violin, and took up with a
local boy. This was in Illinois. He took her to some Big Ten bar
every night to drink with his buddies from the team. He used to

say things like 'Katrina here likes to play the violin,' and then he'd pinch her cheek. When she once suggested that they go home, he said, 'What, you think you're too famous for a place like this? Well, let me tell you something. You may think you're famous, but you're not *famous* famous.' Two famouses. 'No one here's ever heard of you.' Then he went up and bought a round of drinks for everyone but her. She got her coat, went home, and shot a bullet through her head."

Earl was silent.

"That's the end of my love story," said Zoë.

"You're not at all like your sister," said Earl.

"Oh, really," said Zoë. The air had gotten colder, the wind singing minor and thick as a dirge.

"No." He didn't want to talk about love anymore. "You know, you should wear a lot of blue — blue and white — around your face. It would bring out your coloring." He reached an arm out to show her how the blue bracelet he was wearing might look against her skin, but she swatted it away.

"Tell me, Earl. Does the word 'fag' mean anything to you?"

He stepped back, away from her. He shook his head in disbelief. "You know, I just shouldn't try to go out with career women. You're all stricken. A guy can really tell what life has done to you. I do better with women who have part-time jobs."

"Oh, yes?" said Zoë. She had once read an article entitled "Professional Women and the Demographics of Grief." Or, no, it was a poem. *If there were a lake, the moonlight would dance across it in conniptions.* She remembered that line. But perhaps the title was "The Empty House: Aesthetics of Barrenness." Or maybe "Space Gypsies: Girls in Academe." She had forgotten.

Earl turned and leaned on the railing of the balcony. It was getting late. Inside, the party guests were beginning to leave. The sexy witches were already gone. "Live and learn," Earl murmured.

"Live and get dumb," replied Zoë. Beneath them on Lexington there were no cars, just the gold rush of an occasional cab. He leaned hard on his elbows, brooding.

"Look at those few people down there," he said. "They look like bugs. You know how bugs are kept under control? They're sprayed with bug hormones — female bug hormones. The male bugs get so crazy in the presence of this hormone they're screwing everything in sight — trees, rocks, everything but female bugs. Population control. That's what's happening in this country," he said drunkenly. "Hormones sprayed around, and now men are screwing rocks. Rocks!"

In the back, the Magic Marker line on his buttocks spread wide, a sketchy black on pink, like a funnies page. Zoë came up, slow, from behind, and gave him a shove. His arms slipped forward, off the railing, out over the street. Beer spilled out of his bottle, raining twenty stories down to the street.

"Hey, what are you doing!" he said, whipping around. He stood straight and readied, and moved away from the railing, sidestepping Zoë. "What the *hell* are you doing?"

"Just kidding," she said. "I was just kidding." But he gazed at her, appalled and frightened, his Magic Marker buttocks turned away now toward all of downtown, a naked pseudo-woman with a blue bracelet at the wrist, trapped out on a balcony with — with *what?* "Really, I was just kidding!" Zoë shouted. The wind lifted the hair up off her head, skyward in spines behind the bone. If there were a lake, the moonlight would dance across it in conniptions. She smiled at him and wondered how she looked.

ALICE MUNRO

Differently

FROM THE NEW YORKER

GEORGIA ONCE TOOK a creative-writing course, and what the instructor told her was: Too many things. Too many things going on at the same time; also too many people. Think, he told her. What is the important thing? What do you want us to pay attention to? Think.

Eventually she wrote a story that was about her grandfather killing chickens, and the instructor seemed to be pleased with it. Georgia herself thought that it was a fake. She made a long list of all the things that had been left out and handed it in as an appendix to the story. The instructor said that she expected too much, of herself and of the process, and that she was wearing him out.

The course was not a total loss, because Georgia and the instructor ended up living together. They still live together, in Ontario, on a farm. They sell raspberries, and run a small publishing business. When Georgia can get the money together, she goes to Vancouver, to visit her sons. This fall Saturday she has taken the ferry across to Victoria, where she used to live. She did this on an impulse that she doesn't really trust, and by midafternoon, when she walks up the driveway of the splendid stone house where she used to visit Maya, she had already been taken over some fairly shaky ground.

When she phoned Raymond, she wasn't sure that he would ask her to the house. She wasn't sure that she even wanted to go there. She had no notion of how welcome she would be. But Raymond opens the door before she can touch the bell, and he hugs her around the shoulders and kisses her twice (surely he didn't use to do this?) and introduces his wife, Anne. He says he has told her what great friends they were, Georgia and Ben and he and Maya. Great friends.

Maya is dead. Georgia and Ben are long divorced.

They go to sit in what Maya used to call, with a certain flat cheerfulness, "the family room."

(One evening Raymond had said to Ben and Georgia that it looked as if Maya wasn't going to be able to have any children. "We try our best," he said. "We use pillows and everything. But no luck."

"Listen, old man, you don't do it with pillows," Ben said boisterously. They were all a little drunk. "I thought you were the expert on all the apparatus, but I can see that you and I are going to have to have a little talk."

Raymond was an obstetrician and gynecologist.

By that time Georgia knew all about the abortion in Seattle, which had been set up by Maya's lover, Harvey. Harvey was also a doctor, a surgeon. The bleak apartment in the run-down building, the bad-tempered old woman who was knitting a sweater, the doctor arriving in his shirtsleeves, carrying a brown paper bag that Maya hysterically believed must contain the tools of his trade. In fact it contained his lunch — an egg-and-onion sandwich. Maya had the smell of that in her face all the time he and Mme. Defarge were working her over.

Maya and Georgia smiled at each other primly while their husbands continued their playful conversation.)

Raymond's curly caramel-brown hair has turned into a silvery fluff, and his face is lined. But nothing dreadful has happened to him — no pouches or jowls or alcoholic flush or sardonic droop of defeat. He is still thin, and straight, and sharp-shouldered, still fresh smelling, spotless, appropriately, expensively dressed. He'll make a brittle, elegant old man, with an obliging boy's smile. There's that sort of shine on both of them, Maya once said glumly. She was speaking of Raymond and Ben. Maybe we should soak them in vinegar, she said.

The room has changed more than Raymond has. An ivory leather sofa has replaced Maya's tapestry-covered couch, and of course all the old opium-den clutter, Maya's cushions and pam-

pas grass and the gorgeous multicolored elephant with the tiny
sewn-on mirrors — that's all gone. The room is beige and ivory,
smooth and comfortable as the new blond wife, who sits on the
arm of Raymond's chair and maneuvers his arm around her,
placing his hand on her thigh. She wears slick-looking white pants
and a cream-on-white appliquéd sweater, with gold jewelry. Raymond gives her a couple of hearty and defiant pats.

"Are you going someplace?" he says. "Possibly shopping?"

"Righto," says the wife. "Old times." She smiles at Georgia.
"It's O.K.," she says. "I really do have to go shopping."

When she has gone, Raymond pours drinks for Georgia and
himself. "Anne is a worrywart about the booze," he says. "She
won't put salt on the table. She threw out all the curtains in the
house to get rid of the smell of Maya's cigarettes. I know what
you may be thinking. *Friend Raymond has got hold of a luscious
blonde.* But this is actually a very serious girl, and a very steady
girl. I had her in my office, you know, quite a while before Maya
died. I mean, I had her *working* in my office. I don't mean that
the way it sounds! She isn't as young as she looks, either. She's
thirty-six."

Georgia had thought forty. She is tired of the visit already, but
she has to tell about herself. No, she is not married. Yes, she
works. She and the friend she lives with have a farm and a publishing business. Touch and go, not much money. Interesting. A
male friend, yes.

"I've lost all track of Ben somehow," Raymond says. "The last
I heard, he was living on a boat."

"He and his wife sail around the West Coast every summer,"
Georgia says. "In the winter they go to Hawaii. The navy lets
you retire early."

"Marvelous," says Raymond.

Seeing Raymond has made Georgia think that she has no idea
what Ben looks like now. Has he gone white-haired, has he
thickened around the middle? Both of these things have happened to her — she has turned into a chunky woman with a
healthy olive skin, a crest of white hair, wearing loose and rather
splashy clothes. When she thinks of Ben she sees him still as a
handsome navy officer, with a perfect navy look — keen and serious and self-effacing. The look of someone who longed, bravely,
to be given orders. Her sons must have pictures of him around —

they both see him, they spend holidays on his boat. Perhaps they put the pictures away when she comes to visit. Perhaps they think of protecting these images of him from one who did him hurt.

On the way to Maya's house — Raymond's house — Georgia walked past another house, which she could easily have avoided. A house in Oak Bay, which in fact she had to go out of her way to see.

It was still the house that she and Ben had read about, in the real estate columns of the *Victoria Colonist*. Roomy bungalow under picturesque oak trees. Arbutus, dogwood, window seats, fireplace, diamond-paned windows, character. Georgia stood outside the gate and felt a most predictable pain. Here Ben had cut the grass, here the children had made their paths and hideaways in the bushes, and laid out a graveyard for the birds and snakes killed by the black cat, Domino. She could recall the inside of the house perfectly — the oak floors she and Ben had laboriously sanded, the walls they had painted, the room where she had lain in drugged misery after having her wisdom teeth out. Ben had read aloud to her, from *Dubliners*. She couldn't remember the title of the story. It was about a timid poetic sort of young man, with a mean pretty wife. Poor bugger, said Ben when he'd finished it.

Ben liked fiction, which was surprising in a man who also liked sports, and had been popular at school.

She ought to have stayed away from this neighborhood. Everywhere she walked here, under the chestnut trees with their flat gold leaves, and the red-limbed arbutus, and the tall Garry oaks, which suggested fairy stories, European forests, woodcutters, witches — everywhere her footsteps reproached her, saying what-for, what-for, what-for. This reproach was just what she had expected — it was what she courted — and there was something cheap about doing such a thing. Something cheap and useless. She knew it. But what-for, what-for, what-for, wrong-and-waste, wrong-and-waste went her silly, censorious feet.

Raymond wants Georgia to look at the garden, which he says was made for Maya during the last months of her life. Maya designed it; then she lay on the tapestry couch (setting fire to it twice, Raymond says, by dozing off with a cigarette lit), and she was able to see it all take shape.

Georgia sees a pond, a stone-rimmed pond with an island in

the middle. The head of a wicked-looking stone beast — a mountain goat? — rears up on the island, spouting water. Around the pond a jungle of Shasta daisies, pink and purple cosmos, dwarf pines and cypresses, some other miniature tree with glossy red leaves. On the island, now that she looks more closely, are mossy stone walls — the ruins of a tiny tower.

"She hired a young chap to do the work," Raymond says. "She lay there and watched him. It took all summer. She just lay all day and watched him making her garden. Then he'd come in and they'd have tea, and talk about it. You know, Maya didn't just design that garden. She imagined it. She'd tell him what she'd been imagining about it, and he'd take off from there. I mean, this to them was not just a garden. The pond was a lake in this country they had some name for, and all around the lake were forests and territories where different tribes and factions lived. Do you get the picture?"

"Yes," says Georgia.

"Maya had a dazzling imagination. She could have written fantasy or science fiction. Whatever. She was a creative person, without any doubt about it. But you could not get her to seriously use her creativity. That goat was one of the gods of that country, and the island was like a sacred place with a former temple on it. You can see the ruins. They had the religion all worked out. Oh, and the literature, the poems and the legends and the history — everything. They had a song that the queen would sing. Of course it was supposed to be a translation, from that language. They had some of that figured out, too. There had been a queen that was shut up in that ruin. That temple. I forget why. She was getting sacrificed, probably. Getting her heart torn out or some gruesome thing. It was all complicated and melodramatic. But think of the effort that went into it. The creativity. The young chap was an artist by profession. I believe he thought of himself as an artist. I don't know how she got hold of him, actually. She knew people. He supported himself doing this kind of thing, I imagine. He did a good job. He laid the pipes, everything. He showed up every day. Every day he came in when he was finished and had tea and talked to her. Well, in my opinion, they didn't have just tea. To my knowledge, not just tea. He would bring a little substance, they would have a little smoke. I told Maya she should write it all down.

"But you know, the instant he was finished, off he went. Off he went. I don't know. Maybe he got another job. It didn't seem to me that it was my place to ask. But I did think that even if he had got a job he could have come back and visited her now and then. Or if he'd gone off on a trip somewhere he could have written letters. I thought he could have. I expected that much of him. It wouldn't have been any skin off his back. Not as I see it. It would have been nice of him to make her think that it hadn't been just a case of — of hired friendship, you know, all along."

Raymond is smiling. He cannot repress, or perhaps is not aware of, this smile.

"For that was the conclusion she must have come to," he says. "After all that nice time and imagining together and egging each other on. She must have been disappointed. She must have been. Even at that stage, such a thing would matter a lot to her. You and I know it, Georgia. It would have mattered. He could have treated her a little more kindly. It wouldn't have had to be for very long."

Maya died a year ago, in the fall, but Georgia did not hear about it until Christmas. She got the news in Hilda's Christmas letter. Hilda, who used to be married to Harvey, is now married to another doctor, in a town in the interior of British Columbia. A few years ago she and Georgia, both visitors, met by chance on a Vancouver street, and they have written occasional letters since.

"Of course you knew Maya so much better than I did," Hilda wrote. "But I've been surprised how often I've thought about her. I've been thinking of all of us, really, how we were, fifteen or so years ago, and I think we were just as vulnerable in some ways as the kids with their acid trips and so on, that were supposed to be marked for life. Weren't we marked — all of us smashing up our marriages and going out looking for adventure? Of course, Maya didn't smash up her marriage, she of all people stayed where she was, so I suppose it doesn't make much sense what I'm saying. But Maya seemed the most vulnerable person of all to me, so gifted and brittle. I remember I could hardly bear to look at that vein in her temple where she parted her hair."

What an odd letter for Hilda to write, thought Georgia. She remembered Hilda's expensive pastel plaid shirtdresses, her neat, short, fair hair, her good manners. Did Hilda really think she had smashed up her marriage and gone out looking for adventure under the influence of dope and rock music and revolutionary costumes? Georgia's impression was that Hilda had left Harvey, once she found out what he was up to — or some of what he was up to — and gone to the town in the interior where she sensibly took up her old profession of nursing and in due time married another, presumably more trustworthy doctor. Maya and Georgia had never thought of Hilda as a woman like themselves. And Hilda and Maya had not been close — they had particular reason not to be. But Hilda had kept track; she knew of Maya's death, she wrote these generous words. Without Hilda, Georgia would not have known. She would still have been thinking that someday she might write to Maya, there might come a time when their friendship could be mended.

The first time that Ben and Georgia went to Maya's house, Harvey and Hilda were there. Maya was having a dinner party for just the six of them. Georgia and Ben had recently moved to Victoria, and Ben had phoned Raymond, who had been a friend of his at school. Ben had never met Maya, but he told Georgia that he had heard that she was very clever, and weird. People said that she was weird. But she was rich — an heiress — so she could get away with it.

Georgia groaned at the news that Maya was rich, and she groaned again at the sight of the house — the great stone-block house with its terraced lawns and clipped bushes and circular drive.

Georgia and Ben came from the same small town in Ontario, and had the same sort of families. It was a fluke that Ben had been sent to a good private school — the money had come from a great-aunt. Even in her teens, when she was proud of being Ben's girl and prouder than she liked to let on about being asked to the dances at that school, Georgia had a low opinion of the girls she met there. She thought rich girls were spoiled and brainless. She called them twits. She thought of herself as a girl — and then a woman — who didn't much like other girls and women. She called the other navy wives "the navy *ladies.*" Ben was sometimes entertained by her opinions of people and at other times asked if it was really necessary to be so critical.

He had an inkling, he said, that she was going to like Maya. This didn't predispose Georgia in Maya's favor. But Ben turned out to be right. He was very happy then, to have come up with somebody like Maya as an offering to Georgia, to have found a couple with whom he and Georgia could willingly link up as friends. "It'll be good for us to have some non-navy friends," he was to say. "Some wife for you to knock around with who isn't so conventional. You can't say Maya's conventional."

Georgia couldn't. The house was more or less what she had expected — soon she learned that Maya called it "your friendly neighborhood fortress" — but Maya was a surprise. She opened the door herself, barefoot, wearing a long shapeless robe of coarse brown cloth that looked like burlap. Her hair was long and straight, parted high at one temple. It was almost the same dull brown color as the robe. She did not wear lipstick, and her skin was rough and pale, with marks like faint bird tracks in the hollows of her cheeks. This lack of color, this roughness of texture about her, seemed a splendid assertion of quality. How indifferent she looked, how arrogant and indifferent, with her bare feet, her unpainted toenails, her queer robe. The only thing that she had done to her face was to paint her eyebrows blue — to pluck out all the hairs of her eyebrows, in fact, and paint the skin blue. Not an arched line — just a daub of blue over each eye, like a swollen vein.

Georgia, whose dark hair was teased, whose eyes were painted in the style of the time, whose breasts were stylishly proffered, found all this disconcerting, and wonderful.

Harvey was the other person there whose looks Georgia found impressive. He was a short man with heavy shoulders, a slight potbelly, puffy blue eyes, and a pugnacious expression. He came from Lancashire. His gray hair was thin on top but worn long at the sides — combed over his ears in a way that made him look more like an artist than a surgeon. "He doesn't even look to me exactly clean enough to be a surgeon," Georgia said to Ben afterward. "Wouldn't you think he'd be something like a sculptor? With gritty fingernails? I expect he treats women badly." She was recalling how he had looked at her breasts. "Not like Raymond," she said. "Raymond worships Maya. And he is extremely clean."

(Raymond has the kind of looks everybody's mother is crazy

about, Maya was to say to Georgia, with slashing accuracy, a few weeks after this.)

The food that Maya served was no better than you would expect at a family dinner, and the heavy silver forks were slightly tarnished. But Raymond poured good wine that he would have liked to talk about. He did not manage to interrupt Harvey, who told scandalous and indiscreet hospital stories, and was blandly outrageous about necrophilia and masturbation. Later, in the living room, the coffee was made and served with some ceremony. Raymond got everybody's attention as he ground the beans in a Turkish cylinder. He talked about the importance of the aromatic oils. Harvey, halted in midanecdote, watched with an unkindly smirk, Hilda with patient polite attention. It was Maya who gave her husband radiant encouragement, hung about him like an acolyte, meekly and gracefully assisting. She served the coffee in beautiful little Turkish cups, which she and Raymond had bought in a shop in San Francisco, along with the coffee grinder. She listened demurely to Raymond talking about the shop, as if she recalled other holiday pleasures.

Harvey and Hilda were the first to leave. Maya hung on Raymond's shoulder, saying goodbye. But she detached herself once they were gone, her slithery grace and wifely demeanor discarded. She stretched out casually and awkwardly on the sofa and said, "Now, don't you go yet. Nobody gets half a chance to talk while Harvey is around — you have to talk after."

And Georgia saw how it was. She saw that Maya was hoping not to be left alone with the husband whom she had aroused — for whatever purposes — by her showy attentions. She saw that Maya was mournful and filled with a familiar dread at the end of her dinner party. Raymond was happy. He sat down on the end of the sofa, lifting Maya's reluctant feet to do so. He rubbed one of her feet between his hands.

"What a savage," Raymond said. "This is a woman who won't wear shoes."

"Brandy!" said Maya, springing up. "I knew there was something else you did at dinner parties. You drink brandy!"

"He loves her but she doesn't love him," said Georgia to Ben, just after she had remarked on Raymond's worshiping Maya and being very clean. But Ben, perhaps not listening carefully, thought she was talking about Harvey and Hilda.

"No, no, no. There I think it's the other way round. It's hard to tell with English people. Maya was putting on an act for them. I have an idea about why."

"You have an idea about everything," said Ben.

Georgia and Maya became friends on two levels. On the first level, they were friends as wives, on the second as themselves. On the first level, they had dinner at each other's houses. They listened to their husbands talk about their school days. The jokes and fights, the conspiracies and disasters, the bullies and the victims. Terrifying or pitiable schoolfellows and teachers, treats and humiliations. Maya asked if they were sure they hadn't read all that in a book. "It sounds just like a story," she said. "A boys' story about school."

They said that their experiences were what the books were all about. When they had talked enough about school, they talked about movies, politics, public personalities, places they had traveled to or wanted to travel to. Maya and Georgia could join in then. Ben and Raymond did not believe in leaving women out of the conversation. They believed that women were every bit as intelligent as men.

On the second level, Georgia and Maya talked in each other's kitchens, over coffee. Or they had lunch downtown. There were two places, and only two, where Maya liked to have lunch. One was the Moghul's Court — a seedy, grandiose bar in a large, grim railway hotel. The Moghul's Court had curtains of moth-eaten pumpkin-colored velvet, and desiccated ferns, and waiters who wore turbans. Maya always dressed up to go there, in droopy, silky dresses and not very clean white gloves and amazing hats that she found in secondhand stores. She pretended to be a widow who had served with her husband in various outposts of the Empire. She spoke in fluty tones to the sullen young waiters, asking them, "Could you be so good as to . . ." and then telling them they had been terribly, terribly kind.

She and Georgia worked out the history of the Empire widow, and Georgia was added to the story as a grumpy, secretly socialistic hired companion named Miss Amy Jukes. The widow's name was Mrs. Allegra Forbes-Bellyea. Her husband had been Nigel Forbes-Bellyea. Sometimes Sir Nigel. Most of one rainy afternoon in the Moghul's Court was spent in devising the horrors of the Forbes-Bellyea honeymoon, in a damp hotel in Wales.

The other place that Maya liked was a hippie restaurant on Blanshard Street, where you sat on dirty plush cushions tied to the tops of stumps and ate brown rice with slimy vegetables and drank cloudy cider. (At the Moghul's Court, Maya and Georgia drank only gin.) When they lunched at the hippie restaurant they wore long, cheap, pretty Indian cotton dresses and pretended to be refugees from a commune, where they had both been the attendants or concubines of a folksinger named Bill Bones. They made up several songs for Bill Bones, all mild and tender blue-eyed songs that contrasted appallingly with his greedy and licentious ways. Bill Bones had very curious personal habits.

When they weren't playing these games, they talked in a headlong fashion about their lives, childhoods, problems, husbands.

"That was a horrible place," Maya said. "That school."

Georgia agreed.

"They were poor boys at a rich kids' school," Maya said. "So they had to try hard. They had to be a credit to their families."

Georgia would not have thought Ben's family poor, but she knew that there were different ways of looking at such things.

Maya said that whenever they had people in for dinner or the evening, Raymond would pick out beforehand all the records he thought suitable and put them in a suitable order. "I think sometime he'll hand out conversational topics at the door," Maya said.

Georgia revealed that Ben wrote a letter every week to the great-aunt who had sent him to school.

"Is it a nice letter?" said Maya.

"Yes. Oh, yes. It's very nice."

They looked at each other bleakly, and laughed. Then they announced — they admitted — what weighed on them. It was the innocence of these husbands — the hearty, decent, firm, contented innocence. That is a wearying and finally discouraging thing. It makes intimacy a chore.

"But do you feel badly," Georgia said, "talking like this?"

"Of course," said Maya, grinning and showing her large perfect teeth — the product of expensive dental work from the days before she had charge of her own looks. "I have another reason to feel badly," she said. "But I don't know whether I do. I do and I don't."

"I know," said Georgia, who up until that moment hadn't known, for sure.

"You're very smart," Maya said. "Or I'm very obvious. What do you think of him?"

"A lot of trouble," Georgia said judiciously. She was pleased with that answer, which didn't show how flattered she felt by the disclosure, or how heady she found this conversation.

"You aren't just a-whistlin' 'Dixie,'" Maya said, and she told the story about the abortion. "I am going to break up with him," she said. "Any day now."

But she kept on seeing Harvey. She would relate, at lunch, some very disillusioning facts about him, then announce that she had to go, she was meeting him at a motel out on the Gorge Road, or at the cabin he had on Prospect Lake.

"Must scrub," she said.

She had left Raymond once. Not for Harvey. She had run away with, or to, a musician. A pianist — Nordic and sleepy looking but bad-tempered — from her society-lady, symphony-benefit days. She traveled with him for five weeks, and he deserted her in a hotel in Cincinnati. She then developed frightful chest pains, appropriate to a breaking heart. What she really had was a gallbladder attack. Raymond was sent for, and he came and got her out of the hospital. They had a little holiday in Mexico before they came home.

"That was it, for me," Maya said. "That was your true and desperate love. Nevermore."

What, then, was Harvey?

"Exercise," said Maya.

Georgia got a part-time job in a bookstore, working several evenings a week. Ben went away on his yearly cruise. The summer turned out to be unusually hot and sunny for the West Coast. Georgia combed her hair out and stopped using most of her make-up and bought a couple of short halter dresses. Sitting on her stool at the front of the store, showing her bare brown shoulders and sturdy brown legs, she looked like a college girl — clever but full of energy and bold opinions. The people who came into the store liked the look of a girl — a woman — like Georgia. They liked to talk to her. Most of them came in alone. They were not exactly lonely people, but they were lonely for somebody to talk to about books. Georgia plugged in the kettle behind the desk and made mugs of raspberry tea. Some favored customers brought in their own mugs. Maya came to visit and lurked about in the background, amused and envious.

"You know what you've got?" she said to Georgia. "You've got a salon! Oh, I'd like to have a job like that! I'd even like an ordinary job in an ordinary store, where you fold things up and find things for people and make change and say thank you very much, and colder out today, will it rain?"

"You could get a job like that," said Georgia.

"No, I couldn't. I don't have the discipline. I was too badly brought up. I can't even keep house without Mrs. Hanna and Mrs. Cheng and Sadie."

It was true. Maya had a lot of servants, for a modern woman, though they came at different times and did separate things and were nothing like an old-fashioned household staff. Even the food at her dinner parties, which seemed to show her own indifferent touch, had been prepared by someone else.

Usually, Maya was busy in the evenings. Georgia was just as glad, because she didn't really want Maya coming into the store, asking for crazy titles that she had made up, making Georgia's employment there a kind of joke. Georgia took the store seriously. She had a serious, secret liking for it which she could not explain. It was a long, narrow store with an old-fashioned funneled entryway between two angled display windows. From her stool behind the desk Georgia was able to see the reflections in one window reflected in the other. This street was not one of those decked out to receive tourists. It was a wide east-west street filled in the early evening with a faintly yellow light, a light reflected off pale stucco buildings that were not very high, plain storefronts, nearly empty sidewalks. Georgia found this plainness liberating after the winding shady streets, flowery yards, and vine-framed windows of Oak Bay. Here the books could come into their own, as they never could in a more artful and enticing suburban bookshop. Straight long rows of paperbacks.

(Most of the Penguins then still had their orange and white or blue and white covers, with no designs or pictures, just the un-adorned, unexplained titles.) The store was a straight avenue of bounty, of plausible promises. Certain books that Georgia had never read, and probably never would read, were important to her, because of the stateliness or mystery of their titles. In Praise of Folly. The Roots of Coincidence. The Flowering of New England. Ideas and Integrities.

Sometimes she got up and put the books in stricter order. The fiction was shelved alphabetically, by author, which was sensible but not very interesting. The history books, however, and the philosophy and psychology and other science books were ar-ranged according to certain intricate and delightful rules — having to do with chronology and content — that Georgia grasped immediately and even elaborated on. She did not need to read much of a book to know about it. She got a sense of it easily, almost at once, as if by smell.

At times the store was empty, and she felt an abundant calm. It was not even the books that mattered then. She sat on the stool and watched the street — patient, expectant, by herself, in a finely balanced and suspended state.

She saw Miles's reflection — his helmeted ghost parking his motorcycle at the curb — before she saw him. She believed that she had noted his valiant profile, his pallor, his dusty red hair (he took off his helmet and shook out his hair before coming into the store), and his quick, slouching, insolent, invading way of moving even in the glass.

It was no surprise that he soon began to talk to her, as others did. He told her that he was a diver. He looked for wrecks, and lost airplanes, and dead bodies. He had been hired by a rich couple in Victoria who were planning a treasure-hunting cruise, getting it together at the moment. Their names, the destination, were all secrets. Treasure hunting was a lunatic business. He had done it before. His home was in Seattle, where he had a wife and a little daughter.

Everything he told her could easily have been a lie.

He showed her pictures in books — photographs and draw-ings, of mollusks, jellyfish, the Portuguese man-of-war, sargasso weed, the Caribbean flying fish, the girdle of Venus. He pointed out which pictures were accurate, which were fakes. Then he went away and paid no more attention to her, even slipping out of the store while she was busy with a customer. Not a hint of a goodbye. But he came in another evening, and told her about a drowned man wedged into the cabin of a boat, looking out the watery window in an interested way. By attention and avoidance, impersonal conversations in close proximity, by his oblivious prowling, and unsmiling, lengthy, gray-eyed looks, he soon had Georgia in a disturbed and not disagreeable state. He stayed away two nights in a row, then came in and asked her, abruptly, if she would like a ride home on his motorcycle.

Georgia said yes. She had never ridden on a motorcycle in her life. Her car was in the parking lot; she knew what was bound to happen.

She told him where she lived. "Just a few blocks up from the beach," she said.

"We'll go to the beach, then. We'll go and sit on the logs."

That was what they did. They sat for a while on the logs. Then, though the beach was not quite dark or completely deserted, they made love in the imperfect shelter of some broombushes. Georgia walked home, a strengthened and lightened woman, not in the least in love, favored by the universe.

"My car wouldn't start," she told the babysitter, a grandmother from down the street. "I walked all the way home. It was lovely, walking. Lovely. I enjoyed it so much."

Her hair was wild, her lips were swollen, her clothes were full of sand.

Her life filled up with such lies. Her car would be parked beside outlying beaches, on the logging roads so conveniently close to the city, on the wandering back roads of the Saanich Peninsula. The map of the city that she had held in her mind up till now, with its routes to shops and work and friends' houses, was overlaid with another map, of circuitous routes followed in fear (not shame) and excitement, of flimsy shelters, temporary hiding places, where she and Miles made love, often within hearing distance of passing traffic or a hiking party or a family picnic. And Georgia herself, watching her children on the roundabout, or feeling the excellent shape of a lemon in her hand at the super-

market, contained another woman, who only a few hours before
had been whimpering and tussling on the ferns, on the sand, on
the bare ground, or, during a rainstorm, in her own car — who
had been driven hard and gloriously out of her mind and drifted
loose and gathered her wits and made her way home again. Was
this a common story? Georgia cast an eye over the other women
at the supermarket. She looked for signs — of dreaminess or
flaunting, a sense of drama in a woman's way of dressing, a special rhythm in her movements.

How many? she asked Maya.

"God knows," said Maya. "Do a survey."

Trouble began, perhaps, as soon as they said that they loved
each other. Why did they do that — defining, inflating, obscur-
ing whatever it was they did feel? It seemed to be demanded,
that was all — just the way changes, variations, elaborations in
the lovemaking itself might be demanded. It was a way of going
further. So they said it, and that night Georgia couldn't sleep.
She did not regret what had been said or think that it was a lie,
though she knew that it was absurd. She thought of the way
Miles sought to have her look into his eyes during lovemaking —
something Ben expressly did not do — and she thought of how
his eyes, at first bright and challenging, became cloudy and calm
and somber. That way she trusted him — it was the only way.
She thought of being launched out on a gray, deep, baleful,
magnificent sea. Love.

"I didn't know this was going to happen," she said in Maya's
kitchen the next day, drinking her coffee. The day was warm,
but she had put on a sweater to huddle in. She felt shaken, and
submissive.

"No. And you don't know," said Maya rather sharply. "Did he
say it, too? Did he say he loved you, too?"

Yes, said Georgia, yes, of course.

"Look out, then. Look out for next time. Next time is always
pretty tricky when they've said that."

And so it was. Next time a rift opened. At first they simply
tested it, to see if it was there. It was almost like a new diversion
to them. But it widened, it widened. Before any words were said
to confirm that it was there, Georgia felt it widen, she coldly felt
it widen, though she was desperate for it to close. Did he feel the

same thing? She didn't know. He, too, seemed cold — pale, deliberate, glittering with some new malicious intent.

They were sitting recklessly, late at night, in Georgia's car among the other lovers at Clover Point.

"Everybody here in these cars doing the same thing we're doing," Miles had said. "Doesn't that idea turn you on?"

He had said that at the very moment in their ritual when they had been moved, last time, to speak brokenly and solemnly of love.

"You ever think of that?" he said. "I mean, we could start with Ben and Laura. You ever imagine how it would be with you and me and Ben and Laura?"

Laura was his wife, at home in Seattle. He had not spoken of her before, except to tell Georgia her name. He had spoken of Ben, in a way that Georgia didn't like but passed over.

"What does Ben think you do for fun," he'd said, "while he is off cruising the ocean blue?"

"Do you and Ben usually have a big time when he gets back?"

"Does Ben like that outfit as much as I do?"

He spoke as if he and Ben were friends in some way, or at least partners, co-proprietors.

"You and me and Ben and Laura," he said, in a tone that seemed to Georgia insistently and artificially lecherous, sly, derisive. "Spread the joy around."

He tried to fondle her, pretending not to notice how offended she was, how bitterly stricken. He described the generous exchanges that would take place among the four of them abed. He asked whether she was getting excited. She said no, disgusted. Ah, you are but you won't give in to it, he said. His voice, his caresses, grew more bullying. What is so special about you, he asked softly, despisingly, with a hard squeeze at her breasts. Georgia, why do you think you're such a queen?

"You are being cruel and you know you're being cruel," said Georgia, pulling at his hands. "Why are you being like this?"

"Honey, I'm not being cruel," said Miles, in a slippery mock-tender voice. "I'm being horny. I'm horny again is all." He began to pull Georgia around, to arrange her for his use. She told him to get out of the car.

"Squeamish," he said, in that same artificially and hatefully tender voice, as if he were licking fanatically at something loath-some. "You're a squeamish little slut."

Georgia told him that she would lean on the horn if he didn't stop. She would lean on the horn if he didn't get out of the car. She would yell for somebody to call the police. She did lean against the horn as they struggled. He pushed her away, with a whim-pering curse such as she'd heard from him at other times, when it meant something different. He got out.

She could not believe that such ill will had erupted, that things had so stunningly turned around. When she thought of this afterward — a good long time afterward — she thought that perhaps he had acted for conscience's sake, to mark her off from Laura. Or to blot out what he had said to her last time. To hu-miliate her because he was frightened. Perhaps. Or perhaps all this seemed to him simply a further, and genuinely interesting, development in lovemaking.

She would have liked to talk it over with Maya. But the possi-bility of talking anything over with Maya had disappeared. Their friendship had come suddenly to an end.

The night after the incident at Clover Point, Georgia was sitting on the living room floor playing a bedtime card game with her sons. The phone rang, and she was sure that it was Miles. She had been thinking all day that he would call, he would have to call to explain himself, to beg her pardon, to say that he had been testing her, in a way, or had been temporarily deranged by circumstances that she knew nothing about. She would not for-give him immediately. But she would not hang up.

It was Maya.

"Guess what weird thing happened," Maya said. "Miles phoned me. Your Miles. It's O.K., Raymond isn't here. How did he even know my name?"

"I don't know," said Georgia.

She had told him it, of course. She had offered wild Maya up for his entertainment, or to point out what a novice at this game she herself was — a relatively chaste prize.

"He says he wants to come and talk to me," Maya said. "What do you think? What's the matter with him? Did you have a fight? . . . Yes? Oh, well, he probably wants me to persuade you to make up. I must say he picked the right night. Raymond's at the hospital. He's got this balky woman in labor; he may have to stay and do a section on her. I'll phone and tell you how it goes. Shall I?"

After a couple of hours, with the children long asleep, Georgia began to expect Maya's call. She watched the television news, to take her mind off expecting it. She picked up the phone, to make sure there was a dial tone. She turned off the television after the news, then turned it on again. She started to watch a movie; she watched it through three commercial breaks without going to the kitchen to look at the clock.

At half past midnight she went out and got into her car and drove to Maya's house. She had no idea what she would do there. And she did not do much of anything. She drove around the circular drive with the lights off. The house was dark. She could see that the garage was open and Raymond's car was not there. The motorcycle was nowhere in sight.

She had left her children alone, the doors unlocked. Nothing happened to them. They didn't wake up and discover her defection. No burglar, or prowler, or murderer surprised her on her return. That was a piece of luck that she did not even appreciate. She had gone out leaving the door open and the lights on, and when she came back she hardly recognized her folly, though she closed the door and turned out some lights and lay down on the living room sofa. She didn't sleep. She lay still, as if the smallest movement would sharpen her suffering, until she saw the day getting light and heard the birds waking. Her limbs were stiff. She got up and went to the phone and listened again for the dial tone. She walked stiffly to the kitchen and put on the kettle and said to herself the words "a paralysis of grief."

A paralysis of grief. What was she thinking of? That was what she would feel, how she might describe the way she would feel, if one of her children had died. Grief is for serious matters, important losses. She knew that. She would not have bartered away an hour of her children's lives to have had the phone ring at ten o'clock last night, to have heard Maya say, "Georgia, he's desperate. He's sorry; he loves you very much."

No. But it seemed that such a phone call would have given her a happiness that no look or word from her children could give her. Than anything could give her.

She phoned Maya before nine o'clock. As she was dialing, she thought that there were still some possibilities to pray for. Maya's phone had been temporarily out of order. Maya had been ill last night. Raymond had been in a car accident on his way home from the hospital.

All these possibilities vanished at the first sound of Maya's voice, which was sleepy (pretending to be sleepy?) and silky with deceit. "Georgia? Is that Georgia? Oh, I thought it was going to be Raymond. He had to stay over at the hospital in case this poor wretched woman needed a C-section. He was going to call me —"

"You told me that last night," said Georgia.

"He was going to call me — Oh, Georgia, I was supposed to call you! Now I remember. Yes. I was supposed to call you, but I thought it was probably too late. I thought the phone might wake up the children. I thought, Oh, better just leave it till morning!"

"How late was it?"

"Not awfully. I just thought."

"What happened?"

"What do you mean, what happened?" Maya laughed, like a lady in a silly play. "Georgia, are you in a state?"

"What happened?"

"Oh, Georgia," said Maya, groaning magnanimously but showing an edge of nerves. "Georgia, I'm sorry. It was nothing. It was just nothing. I've been rotten, but I didn't mean to be. I offered him a beer. Isn't that what you do when somebody rides up to your house on a motorcycle? You offer him a beer. But then he came on very lordly and said he only drank Scotch. And he said he'd only drink Scotch if I would drink with him. I thought he was pretty high-handed. Pretty high-handed pose. But I really was doing this for you, Georgia — I was wanting to find out what was on his mind. So I told him to put the motorcycle behind the garage, and I took him to sit in the back garden. That was so if I heard Raymond's car I could chase him out the back way and he could walk the motorcycle down the lane. I am not about to unload anything *new* onto Raymond at this point. I mean even something innocent, which this started out to be."

Georgia, with her teeth chattering, hung up the phone. She never spoke to Maya again. Maya appeared at her door, of course,

a little while later, and Georgia had to let her in, because the
children were playing in the yard. Maya sat down contritely at
the kitchen table and asked if she could smoke. Georgia did not
answer. Maya said she would smoke anyway and she hoped it
was all right. Georgia pretended that Maya wasn't there. While
Maya smoked, Georgia cleaned the stove, dismantling the elements and putting them back together again. She wiped the
counters and polished the taps and straightened out the cutlery
drawer. She mopped the floor around Maya's feet. She worked
briskly, thoroughly, and never quite looked at Maya. At first she
was not sure whether she could keep this up. But it got easier.
The more earnest Maya became — the further she slipped from
sensible remonstrance, half-amused confession, into true and
fearful regret — the more fixed Georgia was in her resolve, the
more grimly satisfied in her heart. She took care, however, not
to appear grim. She moved about lightly. She was almost humming.

She took a knife to scrape out the grease from between the
counter tiles by the stove. She had let things get into a bad way.

Maya smoked one cigarette after another, stubbing them out
in a saucer that she fetched for herself from the cupboard. She
said, "Georgia, this is so stupid. I can tell you, he's not worth it.
It was nothing. All it was was Scotch and opportunity."

She said, "I am really sorry. Truly sorry. I know you don't
believe me. How can I say it so you will?"

And, "Georgia, listen. You are humiliating me. Fine. Fine.
Maybe I deserve it. I do deserve it. But after you've humiliated
me enough we'll go back to being friends and we'll laugh about
this. When we're old ladies, I swear we'll laugh. We won't be able
to remember his name. We'll call him the motorcycle sheikh. We
will."

Then, "Georgia, what do you want me to do? Do you want me
to throw myself on the floor? I'm about ready to. I'm trying to
keep myself from sniveling, and I can't. I'm sniveling, Georgia.
O.K.?"

She had begun to cry. Georgia put on her rubber gloves and
started to clean the oven.

"You win," said Maya. "I'll pick up my cigarettes and go home."

She phoned a few times. Georgia hung up on her. Miles

phoned, and Georgia hung up on him, too. She thought he sounded cautious but smug. He phoned again and his voice trembled, as if he were striving just for candor and humility, bare love. Georgia hung up at once. She felt violated, shaken.

Maya wrote a letter, which said, in part, "I suppose you know that Miles is going back to Seattle and whatever home fires he keeps burning there. It seems the treasure thing had fallen through. But you must have known he was bound to go sometime and you'd have felt rotten then, so now you've got the rotten feeling over with. So isn't that O.K.? I don't say this to excuse myself. I know I was weak and putrid. But can't we put it behind us now?"

She went on to say that she and Raymond were going on a long-planned holiday to Greece and Turkey, and that she hoped very much that she would get a note from Georgia before she left. But if she didn't get any word she would try to understand what Georgia was telling her, and she would not make a nuisance of herself by writing again.

She kept her word. She didn't write again. She sent, from Turkey, a pretty piece of striped cloth large enough for a tablecloth. Georgia folded it up and put it away. She left it for Ben to find after she moved out, several months later.

"I'm happy," Raymond tells Georgia. "I'm very happy, and the reason is that I'm content to be an ordinary sort of person with an ordinary calm life. I am not looking for any big revelation or any big drama or any messiah of the opposite sex. I don't go around figuring out how to make things more interesting. I can say to you quite frankly I think Maya made a mistake. I don't mean she wasn't very gifted and intelligent and creative and so on, but she was looking for something; maybe she was looking for something that just is not there. And she tended to despise a lot that she had. It's true. She didn't want the privileges she had. We'd travel, for example, and she wouldn't want to stay in a comfortable hotel. No. She had to go on some trek that involved riding on poor, miserable donkeys and drinking sour milk for breakfast. I suppose I sound very square. Well, I suppose I am. I am square. You know, she had such beautiful silver. Magnificent silver. It was passed down through her family. And she couldn't be bothered to polish it or get the cleaning woman to polish it. She wrapped it all up in plastic and hid it away. She hid it away — you'd think it was a disgrace. How do you think she envisaged herself? As some kind of hippie, maybe? Some kind of free spirit? She didn't even realize it was her money that kept her afloat. I'll tell you, some of the free spirits I've seen pass in and out of this house wouldn't have been long around her without it.

"I did all I could," said Raymond. "I didn't scoot off and leave her, like her Prince of Fantasy Land."

Georgia got a vengeful pleasure out of breaking with Maya. She was pleased with the controlled manner in which she did it. The deaf ear. She was surprised to find herself capable of such control, such thoroughgoing punishment. She punished Maya. She punished Miles, through Maya, as much as she could. What she had to do, and she knew it, was to scrape herself raw, to root out all addiction to the gifts of those two pale prodigies. Miles and Maya. Both of them slippery, shimmery — liars, seducers, finaglers. But you would have thought that after such scourging she'd have scuttled back into her marriage and locked its doors, and appreciated what she had there as never before.

That was not what happened. She broke with Ben. Within a year, she was gone. Her way of breaking was strenuous and unkind. She told him about Miles, though she spared her own pride by leaving out the part about Miles and Maya. She took no care — she had hardly any wish — to avoid unkindness. On the night when she waited for Maya to call, some bitter, yeasty spirit entered into her. She saw herself as a person surrounded by, living by, sham. Because she had been so readily unfaithful, her marriage was a sham. Because she had gone so far out of it, so quickly, it was a sham. She dreaded, now, a life like Maya's. She dreaded just as much a life like her own before this happened. She could not but destroy. Such cold energy was building in her she had to blow her own house down.

She had entered, with Ben, when they were both so young, a world of ceremony, of safety, of gestures, concealment. Fond appearances. More than appearances. Fond contrivance. (She thought when she left that she would have no use for contrivance anymore.) She had been happy there, from time to time. She had been sullen, restless, bewildered, and happy. But she said most vehemently, Never, never. I was never happy, she said.

People always say that.

People make momentous shifts but not the changes they imagine.

Just the same, Georgia knows that her remorse about the way she changed her life is dishonest. It is real and dishonest. Listening to Raymond, she knows that whatever she did she would have to do again. She would have to do it again, supposing that she had to be the person she was.

Raymond does not want to let Georgia go. He does not want to part with her. He offers to drive her downtown. When she has gone, he won't be able to talk about Maya. Very likely Anne has told him that she does not want to hear any more on the subject of Maya.

"Thank you for coming," he says on the doorstep. "Are you sure about the ride? Are you sure you can't stay to dinner?"

Georgia reminds him again about the bus, the last ferry. She says no, no, she really wants to walk. It's only a couple of miles. The late afternoon so lovely, Victoria so lovely. I had forgotten, she says.

Raymond says once more, "Thank you for coming."

"Thank you for the drinks," Georgia says. "Thank you, too. I guess we never believe we are going to die."

"Now, now," says Raymond.

"No. I mean we never behave — we never behave as if we believed we were going to die."

Raymond smiles more and more and puts a hand on her shoulder. "How should we behave?" he says.

"Differently," says Georgia. She puts a foolish stress on the word, meaning that her answer is so lame that she can offer it only as a joke.

Raymond hugs her, then involves her in a long chilly kiss. He fastens on to her with an appetite that is grievous but unconvincing. A parody of passion, whose intention neither one of them, surely, will try to figure out.

She doesn't think about that as she walks back to town through the yellow-leafed streets with their autumn smells and silences. Past Clover Point, the cliffs crowned with broombushes, the mountains across the water. The mountains of the Olympic Peninsula, assembled like a blatant backdrop, a cutout of rainbow tissue paper. She doesn't think about Raymond, or Miles, or Maya, or even Ben.

She thinks about sitting in the store in the evenings. The light in the street, the complicated reflections in the windows. The accidental clarity.

ALICE MUNRO

Wigtime

FROM THE NEW YORKER

WHEN HER MOTHER was dying in the Walley hospital, Anita came home to take care of her — though nursing was not what she did anymore. She was stopped one day in the corridor by a short, broad-shouldered, broad-hipped woman with clipped grayish-brown hair.

"I heard you were here, Anita," this woman said, with a laugh that seemed both aggressive and embarrassed. "Don't look so dumbfounded!"

It was Margot, whom Anita had not seen for more than thirty years.

"I want you to come out to the house," Margot said. "Give yourself a break. Come out soon."

Anita took a day off and went to see her. Margot and her husband had built a new house overlooking the harbor, on a spot where there used to be nothing but scrubby bushes and children's secret paths. It was built of gray brick and was long and low. But high enough at that, Anita suggested — high enough to put some noses out of joint across the street, in the handsome hundred-year-old houses with their prize view.

"Bugger them," said Margot. "They took up a petition against us. They went to the Committee."

But Margot's husband already had the Committee sewed up.

Margot's husband had done well. Anita had already heard that. He owned a fleet of buses that took children to school and senior citizens to see the blossoms in Niagara and the fall leaves in Haliburton. Sometimes they carried singles clubs and other holidayers on more adventurous trips — to Nashville or Las Vegas.

Margot showed her around. The kitchen was done in almond — Anita made a mistake, calling it cream — with teal-green and butter-yellow trim. Margot said that all that natural-wood look was passé. They did not enter the living room, with its rose carpet, striped silk chairs, and yards and yards of swooping, pale green figured curtains. They admired it from the doorway — all exquisite, shadowy, inviolate. The master bedroom and its bath were done in white and gold and poppy red. There was a Jacuzzi and a sauna.

"I might have liked something not so bright myself," said Margot. "But you can't ask a man to sleep in pastels."

Anita asked her if she ever thought about getting a job.

Margot flung back her head and snorted with laughter. "Are you kidding? Anyway, I do have a job. Wait till you see the big lunks I have to feed. Plus this place doesn't exactly run itself on magic horsepower."

She took a pitcher of sangria out of the refrigerator and put it on a tray, with two matching glasses. "You like this stuff? Good. We'll sit and drink out on the deck."

Margot was wearing green flowered shorts and a matching top. Her legs were thick and marked with swollen veins, the flesh of her upper arms was dented, her skin was brown, mole-spotted, leathery from lots of sun. "How come you're still thin?" she asked with amusement. She flipped Anita's hair. "How come you're not gray? Any help from the drugstore? You look pretty." She said this without envy, as if speaking to somebody younger than herself, still untried and unseasoned.

It looked as if all her care, all her vanity, went into the house.

Margot and Anita both grew up on farms in Ashfield Township. Anita lived in a drafty shell of a brick house that hadn't had any new wallpaper or linoleum for twenty years, but there was a stove in the parlor which could be lit, and she sat in there in peace and comfort to do her homework. Margot often did her homework sitting up in the bed she had to share with two little sisters. Anita seldom went to Margot's house, because of the crowdedness and confusion, and the terrible temper of Margot's father. Once, she had gone there when they were getting ducks ready for market. Feathers floated everywhere. There were feathers in the milk jug and a horrible smell of feathers burning on the stove. Blood was puddled on the oilclothed table and dripping to the floor.

Margot seldom went to Anita's house, because without exactly saying so Anita's mother disapproved of the friendship. When Anita's mother looked at Margot, she seemed to be totting things up — the blood and feathers, the stovepipe sticking through the kitchen roof, Margot's father yelling that he'd tan somebody's arse.

But they met every morning, struggling head down against the snow that blew off Lake Huron, or walking as fast as they could through a predawn world of white fields, icy swamps, pink sky, and fading stars and murderous cold. Away beyond the ice on the lake they could see a ribbon of open water, ink-blue or robin's-egg, depending upon the light. Pressed against their chests were notebooks, textbooks, homework. They wore the skirts, blouses, and sweaters that had been acquired with difficulty (in Margot's case there had been subterfuge and blows) and were kept decent with great effort. They bore the stamp of Walley High School, where they were bound, and they greeted each other with relief. They had got up in the dark in cold rooms with frost-whitened windows and pulled underwear on under their nightclothes, while stove lids banged in the kitchen, dampers were shut, younger brothers and sisters scurried to dress themselves downstairs. Margot and her mother took turns going out to the barn to milk cows and fork down hay. The father drove them all hard, and Margot said they'd think he was sick if he didn't hit somebody before breakfast. Anita could count herself lucky, having brothers to do the barn work and a father who did not usually hit anybody. But she still felt, these mornings, as if she'd come up through deep dark water.

"Think of the coffee," they told each other, battling on toward the store on the highway, a ramshackle haven. Strong tea, steeped black in the country way, was the drink in both their houses.

Teresa Gault unlocked the store before eight o'clock, to let them in. Pressed against the door, they saw the fluorescent lights come on, blue spurts darting from the ends of the tubes, wavering, almost losing heart, then blazing white. Teresa came smiling like a hostess, edging around the cash register, holding a cherry-red quilted satin dressing gown tight at the throat, as if that could protect her from the freezing air when she opened the door. Her eyebrows were black wings made with a pencil, and she used another pencil — a red one — to outline her mouth. The bow in the upper lip looked as if it had been cut with scissors.

What a relief, what a joy, then, to get inside, into the light, to smell the oil heater and set their books on the counter and take their hands out of their mittens and rub the pain from their fingers. Then they bent over and rubbed their legs — the bare inch or so that was numb and in danger of freezing. They did not wear stockings, because it wasn't the style. They wore ankle socks inside their boots (their saddle shoes were left at school). Their skirts were long — this was the winter of 1948–49 — but there was still a crucial bit of leg left unprotected. Some country girls wore stockings under their socks. Some even wore ski pants pulled up bulkily under their skirts. Margot and Anita would never do that. They would risk freezing rather than risk getting themselves laughed at for such countrified contrivances.

Teresa brought them cups of coffee, hot black coffee, very sweet and strong. She marveled at their courage. She touched a finger to their cheeks or their hands and gave a little shriek and a shudder. "Like ice! Like ice!" To her it was amazing that anybody would go out in the Canadian winter, let alone walk a mile in it. What they did every day to get to school made them heroic and strange in her eyes, and a bit grotesque.

This seemed to be particularly so because they were girls. She wanted to know if such exposure interfered with their periods. "Will it not freeze the eggs?" was what she actually said. Margot and Anita figured this out and made a point, thereafter, of warning each other not to get their eggs frozen. Teresa was not vulgar — she was just foreign. Reuel had met and married her overseas, in Alsace-Lorraine, and after he went home she followed on the boat with all the other war brides. It was Reuel who ran the school bus, this year when Margot and Anita were seventeen and in grade twelve. Its run started here at the store and gas station that the Gaults had bought on the Kincardine highway, within sight of the lake.

Teresa told about her two miscarriages. The first one took

place in Walley, before they moved out here and before they
owned a car. Reuel scooped her up in his arms and carried her
to the hospital. (The thought of being scooped up in Reuel's
arms caused such a pleasant commotion in Anita's body that she
was almost ready to put up with the agony that Teresa said she
had undergone to experience it.) The second time happened
here in the store. Reuel, working in the garage, could not hear
her weak cries as she lay on the floor in her blood. A customer
came in and found her. Thank God, said Teresa, for Reuel's
sake even more than her own. Reuel would not have forgiven
himself. Her eyelids fluttered, her eyes did a devout downward
swoop when she referred to Reuel and their intimate life together.

While Teresa talked, Reuel would be passing in and out of the
store. He went out and got the engine running, then left the bus
to warm up and went back into the living quarters, without ac-
knowledging any of them, or even answering Teresa, who interrupted herself to ask if he had forgotten his cigarettes, or did he
want more coffee, or perhaps he should have warmer gloves.
He stomped the snow from his boots in a way that was more an
announcement of his presence than a sign of any concern for
floors. His tall, striding body brought a fan of cold air behind it,
and the tail of his open parka usually managed to knock something down — Jell-O boxes or tins of corn, arranged in a fancy
way by Teresa. He didn't turn around to look.

Teresa gave her age as twenty-eight — the same age as Reuel's.
Everybody believed she was older — up to ten years older. Margot and Anita examined her close up and decided that she looked
burned. Something about her skin, particularly at the hairline
and around the mouth and eyes, made you think of a pie left
too long in the oven, so that it was not charred but dark brown
around the edges. Her hair was thin, as if affected by the same
drought or fever, and it was too black — they were certain it was
dyed. She was short, and small-boned, with tiny wrists and feet,
but her body seemed puffed out below the waist, as if it had
never recovered from those brief, dire pregnancies. Her smell
was like something sweet cooking — spicy jam.

She would ask anything, just as she would tell anything. She
asked Margot and Anita if they were going out with boys yet.

"Oh, why not? Does your fathers not let you? I was attracting to boys by the time I was fourteen, but my father would not let me. They come and whistle under my window, he chases them away. You should pluck your eyebrows. You both. That would make you look nicer. Boys like a girl when she makes herself all nice. That is something I never forget. When I was on the boat coming across the Atlantic Ocean with all the other wives I spend all my time preparing myself for my husband. Some of those wives, they just sat and played cards. Not me! I was washing my hair and putting on a beautiful oil to soften my skin and I rubbed and rubbed with a stone to get the rough spots off my feet. I forgot what you call them — the rough spots on the feet's skin? And polish my nails and pluck my eyebrows and do myself all up like a prize! For my husband to meet me in Halifax. While all those others do is sit and play cards and gossiping, gossiping with each other."

They had heard a different story about Teresa's second miscarriage. They had heard that it happened because Reuel told her he was sick of her and wanted her to go back to Europe, and in her despair she had thrown herself against a table and dislodged the baby.

At side roads and at farm gates Reuel stopped to pick up students who were waiting, stomping their feet to keep warm or scuffling in the snowbanks. Margot and Anita were the only girls of their age riding the bus that year. Most of the others were boys in grades nine and ten. They could have been hard to handle, but Reuel quelled them even as they came up the steps.

"Cut it out. Hurry up. On board if you're coming on board."

And if there was any start of a fracas on the bus, any hooting or grabbing or punching, or even any moving from seat to seat or too much laughing and loud talk, Reuel would call out, "Smarten up if you don't want to walk! Yes, you there — I mean you!" Once he had put a boy out for smoking, miles from Walley. Reuel himself smoked all the time. He had the lid of a mayonnaise jar sitting on the dashboard for an ashtray. Nobody challenged him, ever, about anything he did. His temper was well known. It was thought to go naturally with his red hair.

People said he had red hair, but Margot and Anita remarked that only his mustache and the hair right above his ears were red. The rest of it, the hair receding from the temples but thick and wavy elsewhere, especially in the back, which was the part they most often got to see — the rest was a tawny color like the pelt of a fox they had seen one morning crossing the white road. And the hair of his heavy eyebrows, the hair along his arms and on the backs of his hands was still more faded, though it glinted in any light. How had his mustache kept its fire? They spoke of this. They discussed in detail, coolly, everything about him. Was he good looking or was he not? He had a redhead's flushed and spotty skin, a high, shining forehead, light-colored eyes that seemed ferocious but indifferent. Not good looking, they decided. Queer looking, actually.

But when Anita was anywhere near him she had a feeling of controlled desperation along the surface of her skin. It was something like the far-off beginning of a sneeze. This feeling was at its worst when she had to get off the bus and he was standing beside the step. The tension flitted from her front to her back as she went past him. She never spoke of this to Margot, whose contempt for men seemed to her firmer than her own. Margot's mother dreaded Margot's father's lovemaking as much as the children dreaded his cuffs and kicks, and had once slept all night in the granary, with the door bolted, to avoid it. Margot called lovemaking "carrying on." She spoke disparagingly of Teresa's "carrying on" with Reuel. But it had occurred to Anita that this very scorn of Margot's, her sullenness and disdain, might be a thing that men could find attractive. Margot might be attractive in a way that she herself was not. It had nothing to do with prettiness. Anita thought that she was prettier, though it was plain that Teresa wouldn't give high marks to either of them. It had to do with a bold lassitude that Margot showed sometimes in movement, with the serious breadth of her hips and the already womanly curve of her stomach, and a look that would come over her large brown eyes — a look both defiant and helpless, not matching up with anything Anita had ever heard her say.

By the time they reached Walley, the day had started. Not a star to be seen anymore, nor a hint of pink in the sky. The town, with its buildings, streets, and interposing routines, was set up like a barricade against the stormy or frozen-still world they'd woken up in. Of course their houses were barricades, too, and so was the store, but those were nothing compared to town. A block inside town, it was as if the countryside didn't exist. The great drifts of snow on the roads and the wind tearing and howling through the trees — that didn't exist. In town, you had to behave as if you'd always been in town. Town students, now thronging the streets around the high school, led lives of privilege and ease. They got up at eight o'clock in houses with heated bedrooms and bathrooms. (This was not always the case, but Margot and Anita believed it was.) They were apt not to know your name. They expected you to know theirs, and you did.

The high school was like a fortress, with its narrow windows and decorative ramparts of dark red brick, its long flight of steps and daunting doors, and the Latin words cut in stone: *Scientia Atque Probitas*. When they got inside those doors, at about a quarter to nine, they had come all the way from home, and home, and all stages of the journey, seemed improbable. The effects of the coffee had worn off. Nervous yawns overtook them under the harsh lights of the assembly hall. Ranged ahead were the demands of the day: Latin, English, geometry, chemistry, history, French, geography, physical training. Bells rang at ten to the hour, briefly releasing them. Upstairs, downstairs, clutching books and ink bottles, they made their anxious way, under the hanging lights and the pictures of royalty and dead educators. The wainscoting, varnished every summer, had the same merciless gleam as the principal's glasses. Humiliation was imminent. Their stomachs ached and threatened to growl as the morning wore on. They feared sweat under their arms and blood on their skirts. They shivered going into English or geometry classes, not because they did badly in those classes (the fact was that they did quite well in almost everything) but because of the danger of being asked to get up and read something, say a poem off by heart, or write the solution to a problem on the blackboard in front of the class. *In front of the class* — those were dreadful words to them.

Then, three times a week, came physical training — a special problem for Margot, who had not been able to get the money out of her father to buy a gym suit. She had to say that she had left her suit at home, or borrow one from some girl who was

being excused. But once she did get a suit on she was able to
loosen up and run around the gym, enjoying herself, yelling for
the basketball to be thrown to her, while Anita went into such
rigors of self-consciousness that she allowed the ball to hit her
on the head.

Better moments intervened. At noon hour they walked downtown and looked in the windows of a beautiful carpeted store
that sold only wedding and evening clothes. Anita planned a
springtime wedding, with bridesmaids in pink and green silk and
overskirts of white organza. Margot's wedding was to take place
in the fall, with the bridesmaids wearing apricot velvet. In Wool-
worth's they looked at lipsticks and earrings. They dashed into
the drugstore and sprayed themselves with sample cologne. If
they had any money to buy some necessity for their mothers,
they spent some of the change on cherry Cokes or sponge toffee.
They could never be deeply unhappy, because they believed that
something remarkable was bound to happen to them. They could
become heroines, love and power of some sort were surely waiting.

Teresa welcomed them, when they got back, with coffee, or hot
chocolate with cream. She dug into a package of store cookies
and gave them Fig Newtons or marshmallow puffs dusted with
colored coconut. She took a look at their books and asked what
homework they had. Whatever they mentioned, she, too, had
studied. In every class, she had been a star.

"English — perfect marks in my English! But I never knew
then that I would fall in love and come to Canada. Canada! I
think it is only polar bears living in Canada!"

Reuel wouldn't have come in. He'd be fooling around with the
bus or with something in the garage. His mood was usually fairly
good as they got on the bus. "All aboard that's coming aboard!"
he would call. "Fasten your seat belts! Adjust your oxygen masks!
Say your prayers! We're takin' to the highway!" Then he'd sing
to himself, just under the racket of the bus, as they got clear of
town. Nearer home his mood of the morning took over, with its
aloofness and unspecific contempt. He might say, "Here you are,
ladies — end of a perfect day," as they got off. Or he might say
nothing. But indoors Teresa was full of chat. Those school days

she talked about led into wartime adventures: a German soldier hiding in the garden, to whom she had taken a little cabbage soup, then the first Americans she saw — black Americans — arriving on tanks and creating a foolish and wonderful impression that the tanks and the men were all somehow joined together. Then her little wartime wedding dress being made out of her mother's lace tablecloth. Pink roses pinned in her hair. Unfortunately, the dress had been torn up for rags to use in the garage. How could Reuel know?

Sometimes Teresa was deep in conversation with a customer. No treats or hot drinks then — all they got was a flutter of her hand, as if she were being borne past in a ceremonial carriage. They heard bits of the same stories. The German soldier, the black Americans, another German blown to pieces, his leg, in its boot, ending up at the church door, where it remained, everybody walking by to look at it. The brides on the boat. Teresa's amazement at the length of time it took to get from Halifax to here on the train. The miscarriages.

They heard her say that Reuel was afraid for her to have another baby.

"So now he always uses protections."

There were people who said they never went into that store anymore because you never knew what you'd have to listen to, or when you'd get out.

In all but the worst weather Margot and Anita lingered at the spot where they had to separate. They spun the day out a little longer, talking. Any subject would do. Did the geography teacher look better with or without his mustache? Did Teresa and Reuel still actually carry on, as Teresa implied? They talked so easily and endlessly that it seemed they talked about everything. But there were things they held back.

Anita held back two ambitions of hers which she did not reveal to anybody. One of them — to be an archeologist — was too odd, and the other — to be a fashion model — was too conceited. Margot told her ambition, which was to be a nurse. You didn't need any money to get into it — not like university — and once you graduated you could go anywhere and get a job. New York City, Hawaii — you could get as far away as you liked.

The thing that Margot kept back, Anita thought, was how it

must really be at home, with her father. According to her, it was all like some movie comedy. Her father beside himself, a hapless comedian, racing around in vain pursuit (of fleet, mocking Margot) and rattling locked doors (the granary) and shouting monstrous threats and waving over his head whatever weapon he could get hold of — a chair or a hatchet or a stick of firewood. He tripped over his own feet and got mixed up in his own accusations. And no matter what he did, Margot laughed. She laughed, she despised him, she forestalled him. Never, never did she shed a tear or cry out in terror. Not like her mother. So she said.

After Anita graduated as a nurse, she went to work in the Yukon. There she met and married a doctor. This should have been the end of her story, and a good end, too, as things were reckoned in Walley. But she got a divorce, she moved on. She worked again and saved money and went to the University of British Columbia, where she studied anthropology. When she came home to look after her mother, she had just completed her Ph.D. She did not have any children.

"So what will you do, now you're through?" said Margot.

People who approved of the course Anita had taken in life usually told her so. Often an older woman would say, "Good for you!" or, "I wish I'd had the nerve to do that, when I was still young enough for it to make any difference." Approval came sometimes from unlikely quarters. It was not to be found everywhere, of course. Anita's mother did not feel it, and that was why, for many years, Anita had not come home. Even in her present sunken, hallucinatory state her mother had recognized her, and gathered her strength to mutter, "Down the drain."

Anita bent closer.

"*Life*," her mother said. "Down the *drain*."

But another time, after Anita had dressed her sores, she said, "So glad. So glad to have — a *daughter*."

Margot didn't seem to approve or disapprove. She seemed puzzled, in an indolent way. Anita began talking to her about some things she might do, but they kept being interrupted. Margot's sons had come in, bringing friends. The sons were tall, with hair of varying redness. Two of them were in high school and

one was home from college. There was one even older, who was
married and living in the west. Margot was a grandmother. Her
sons carried on shouted conversations with her about the whereabouts of their clothes, and what supplies of food, beer, and soft
drinks there were in the house, also which cars would be going
where at what times. Then they all went out to swim in the pool
beside the house, and Margot called, "Don't anybody dare go in
that pool that's got suntan lotion on!"

One of the sons called back, "Nobody's *got* it on," with a great
show of weariness and patience.

"Well, somebody had it on yesterday, and they went in the
pool, all right," replied Margot. "So I guess it was just somebody
that snuck up from the beach, eh?"

Her daughter, Debbie, arrived home from dancing class and
showed them the costume she was going to wear when her dancing school put on a program at the shopping mall. She was to
impersonate a dragonfly. She was ten years old, brown-haired,
and stocky, like Margot.

"Pretty hefty dragonfly," said Margot, lolling back in the deck
chair. Her daughter did not arouse in her the warring energy
that her sons did. Debbie tried for a sip of the sangria, and Margot batted her away lazily.

"Go get yourself a drink out of the fridge," she said. "Listen.
This is our visit. O.K.? Why don't you go phone up Rosalie?"

Debbie left, trailing an automatic complaint. "I wish it wasn't
pink lemonade. Why do you always make pink lemonade?"

Margot got up and shut the sliding doors to the kitchen. "Peace,"
she said. "Drink up. After a while I'll get us some sandwiches."

Spring in that part of Ontario comes in a rush. The ice breaks
up into grinding, jostling chunks on the rivers and along the
lake shore, it slides underwater in the pond and turns the water
green. The snow melts and the creeks flood and in no time comes
a day when you open your coat and stuff your scarf and mittens
in your pockets. There is still snow in the woods when the black
flies are out and the spring wheat showing.

Teresa didn't like spring any better than winter. The lake was
too big and the fields too wide and the traffic went by too fast on
the highway. Now that the mornings had turned balmy, Margot

and Anita didn't need the store's shelter. They were tired of Teresa. Anita read in a magazine that coffee discolored your skin. They talked about whether miscarriages could cause chemical changes in your brain. They stood outside the store, wondering whether they should go in, just to be polite. Teresa came to the door and waved at them, peekaboo. They waved back with a little flap of their hands the way Reuel waved back every morning — just lifting a hand from the steering wheel at the last moment before he turned onto the highway.

Reuel was singing in the bus one afternoon when he had dropped off all the other passengers. "He knew the world was round-o," he sang. "And uh-uhm could be found-o."

He was singing a word in the second line so softly they couldn't catch it. He was doing it on purpose, teasing. Then he sang it again, loud and clear so that there was no mistake.

> He knew the world was round-o,
> And tail-o could be found-o.

They didn't look at each other or say anything till they were walking down the highway. Then Margot said, "Big fat nerve he's got, singing that song in front of us. Big fat *nerve*," she said, spitting the word out like the worm in an apple.

But only the next day, shortly before the bus reached the end of its run, Margot started humming. She invited Anita to join, poking her in the side and rolling her eyes. They hummed the tune of Reuel's song, then they started working words into the humming, muffling one word, then clearly singing the next, until they finally got their courage up and sang the whole two lines, bland and sweet as "Jesus Loves Me."

> He knew the world was round-o,
> And tail-o could be found-o.

Reuel did not say a word. He didn't look at them. He got off the bus ahead of them and didn't wait by the door. Yet less than an hour before, in the school driveway, he had been most genial. One of the other drivers looked at Margot and Anita and said, "Nice load you got there," and Reuel said, "Eyes front, buster," moving so that the other driver could not watch them stepping onto the bus.

Next morning before he pulled away from the store, he delivered a lecture. "I hope I'm going to have a couple of ladies on my bus today and not like yesterday. A girl saying certain things is not like a man saying them. Same thing as a woman getting drunk. A girl gets drunk or talks dirty, first thing you know she's in trouble. Give that some thought."

Anita wondered if they had been stupid. Had they gone too far? They had displeased Reuel and perhaps disgusted him, made him sick of the sight of them, just as he was sick of Teresa. She was ashamed and regretful and at the same time she thought Reuel wasn't fair. She made a face at Margot to indicate this, turning down the corners of her mouth. But Margot took no notice. She was tapping her fingertips together, looking demurely and cynically at the back of Reuel's head.

Anita woke up in the night with an amazing pain. She thought at first she'd been wakened by some calamity, such as a tree falling on the house or flames shooting up through the floorboards. This was shortly before the end of the school year. She had felt sick the evening before, but everybody in the family was complaining of feeling sick, and blaming it on the smell of paint and turpentine. Anita's mother was painting the linoleum, as she did every year at this time.

Anita had cried out with pain before she was fully awake, so that everybody was roused. Her father did not think it proper to phone the doctor before daybreak, but her mother phoned him anyway. The doctor said to bring Anita in to Walley, to the hospital. There he operated on her and removed a burst appendix, which in a few hours might have killed her. She was very sick for several days after the operation, and had to stay nearly three weeks in the hospital. Until the last few days, she could not have any visitors but her mother.

This was a drama for the family. Anita's father did not have the money to pay for the operation and the stay in hospital — he was going to have to sell a stand of hard-maple trees. Her mother took the credit, rightly, for saving Anita's life, and as long as she lived she would mention this, often adding that she had gone against her husband's orders. (It was really only against his advice.) In a flurry of independence and self-esteem she began to drive the car, a thing she had not done for years. She

visited Anita every afternoon and brought news from home. She
had finished painting the linoleum, in a design of white and yellow done with a sponge on a dark green ground. It gave the
impression of a distant meadow sprinkled with tiny flowers. The
milk inspector had complimented her on it when he stayed for
dinner. A late calf had been born across the creek and nobody
could figure out how the cow had got there. The honeysuckle
was in bloom in the hedge, and she brought a bouquet and com-
mandeered a vase from the nurses. Anita had never seen her
sociability turned on like this before for anybody in the family.

Anita was happy, in spite of weakness and lingering pain. Such
a fuss had been made to prevent her dying. Even the sale of the
maple trees pleased her, made her feel unique and treasured.
People were kind and asked nothing of her, and she took up
that kindness and extended it to everything around her. She
forgave everyone she could think of — the principal with his
glittery glasses, the smelly boys on the bus, unfair Reuel and
chattering Teresa and rich girls with lamb's-wool sweaters and
her own family and Margot's father, who must suffer in his ram-
pages. She didn't tire all day of looking at the thin yellowish
curtains at the window and the limb and trunk of a tree visible
to her. It was an ash tree, with strict-looking corduroy lines of
bark and thin petal leaves that were losing their fragility and
sharp spring green, toughening and darkening as they took on
summer maturity. Everything made or growing in the world
seemed to her to deserve congratulations.

She thought later that this mood of hers might have come
from the pills they gave her for the pain. But perhaps not entirely.

She had been put in a single room because she was so sick.
(Her father had told her mother to ask how much extra this was
costing, but her mother didn't think they would be charged, since
they hadn't asked for it.) The nurses brought her magazines,
which she looked at but could not read, being too dazzled and
comfortably distracted. She couldn't tell whether time passed
quickly or slowly, and she didn't care. Sometimes she dreamed
or imagined that Reuel visited her. He showed a somber tenderness, a muted passion. He loved but relinquished her, caressing
her hair.

A couple of days before she was due to go home, her mother

came in shiny-faced from the heat of summer, which was now upon them, and from some other disruption. She stood at the end of Anita's bed and said, "I always knew you thought it wasn't fair of me."

By this time Anita had felt a few holes punched in her happiness. She had been visited by her brothers, who banged against the bed, and her father, who seemed surprised that she expected to kiss him, and by her aunt, who said that after an operation like this a person always got fat. Now her mother's face, her mother's voice, came pushing at her like a fist through gauze.

Her mother was talking about Margot. Anita knew by a twitch of her mouth.

"You always thought I wasn't fair to your friend Margot. I was never fussy about that girl and you thought I wasn't fair. I know you did. So now it turns out. It turns out I wasn't so wrong after all. I could see it in her from an early age. I could see what you couldn't. That she had a sneaky streak and she was oversexed."

Her mother delivered each sentence separately, in a reckless loud voice. Anita did not look at her eyes. She looked at the little brown mole beneath one nostril. It seemed increasingly loathsome.

Her mother calmed down a little, and said that Reuel had taken Margot to Kincardine on the school bus at the end of the day's run on the very last day of school. Of course they had been alone in the bus at the beginning and the end of the run, ever since Anita got sick. All they did in Kincardine, they said, was eat French-fried potatoes. What nerve! Using a school bus for their jaunts and misbehaving. They drove back that evening, but Margot did not go home. She had not gone home yet. Her father had come to the store and beat on the gas pumps and broken them, scattering glass as far as the highway. He phoned the police about Margot, and Reuel phoned them about the pumps. The police were friends of Reuel's, and now Margot's father was bound over to keep the peace. Margot stayed on at the store, supposedly to escape a beating.

"That's all it is, then," Anita said. "Stupid goddamned gossip."

But no. But no. And don't swear at me, young lady.

Her mother said that she had kept Anita in ignorance. All this had happened and she had said nothing. She had given Margot the benefit of the doubt. But now there was no doubt. The news was that Teresa had tried to poison herself. She had recovered. The store was closed. Teresa was still living there, but Reuel had taken Margot with him and they were living here, in Walley. In a back room somewhere, in the house of friends of his. They were living together. Reuel was going out to work at the garage every day, so you could say that he was living with them both. Would he be allowed to drive the school bus in future? Not likely. Everybody was saying Margot must be pregnant. Javex, was what Teresa took.

"And Margot never confided in you," Anita's mother said. "She never sent you a note or one thing all the time you've been in here. Supposed to be your friend."

Anita had a feeling that her mother was angry at her not only because she'd been friends with Margot, a girl who had disgraced herself, but for another reason as well. She had the feeling that her mother was seeing the same thing that she herself could see — Anita unfit, passed over, disregarded, not just by Margot but by life. Didn't her mother feel an angry disappointment that Anita was not the one chosen, the one enfolded by drama and turned into a woman and swept out on such a surge of life? She would never admit that. And Anita could not admit that she felt a great failure. She was a child, a know-nothing, betrayed by Margot, who had turned out to know a lot. She said sulkily, "I'm tired talking." She pretended to fall asleep, so that her mother would have to leave.

Then she lay awake. She lay awake all night. The nurse who came in the next morning said, "Well, don't you look like the last show on earth! Is it that incision bothering you? Should I see if I can get you back on the pills?"

"I hate it here," Anita said.

"Do you? Well, you only have one more day till you can go home."

"I don't mean the hospital," Anita said. "I mean *here*. I want to go and live somewhere else."

The nurse did not seem to be surprised. "You got your grade twelve?" she said. "O.K. You can go in training. Be a nurse. All it costs is to buy your stuff. Because they can work you for nothing while you're training. Then you can go and get a job anyplace. You can go all over the world."

That was what Margot had said. And now Anita was the one

who would become a nurse, not Margot. She made up her mind that day. But she felt that it was second best. She would rather have been chosen. She would rather have been pinned down by a man and his desire and the destiny that he arranged for her. She would rather have been the subject of a scandal.

"Do you want to know?" said Margot. "Do you want to know really how I got this house? I mean, I didn't go after it till we could afford it. But you know with men — something else can always come first? I put in my time living in dumps. We lived one place, there was just that stuff, you know that under-carpeting stuff, on the floor? That brown hairy stuff looks like the skin off some beast? Just look at it and you can feel things crawling on you. I was sick all the time anyway. I was pregnant with Joe. This was in behind the Toyota place, only it wasn't the Toyota then. Reuel knew the landlord. Of course. We got it cheap."

But there came a day, Margot said. There came a day about five years ago. Debbie wasn't going to school yet. It was in June. Reuel was going away for the weekend, on a fishing trip up to northern Ontario. Up to the French River, in northern Ontario. Margot had got a phone call that she didn't tell anybody about.

"Is that Mrs. Gault?"

Margot said yes.

"Is it Mrs. Reuel Gault?"

Yes, said Margot, and the voice — it was a woman's or maybe a young girl's voice, muffled and giggling — asked her if she wanted to know where her husband might be found next weekend.

"You tell me," said Margot.

"Why don't you check out the Georgian Pines?"

"Fine," said Margot. "Where is that?"

"Oh, it's a campground," the voice said. "It's a real nice place. Don't you know it? It's up on Wasaga Beach. You just check it out."

That was about ninety miles to drive. Margot made arrangements for Sunday. She had to get a sitter for Debbie. She couldn't get her regular sitter, Lana, because Lana was going to Toronto on a weekend jaunt with members of the high school band. She was able to get a friend of Lana's who wasn't in the band. She was just as glad that it turned out that way, because it was Lana's mother, Dorothy Slote, that she was afraid she might find with Reuel. Dorothy Slote did Reuel's bookkeeping. She was divorced, and so well known in Walley for her numerous affairs that high school boys would call to her from their cars on the street, "Dorothy Slot, she's hot to trot!" Sometimes she was referred to as Dorothy Slut. Margot felt sorry for Lana — that was why she had started hiring her to take care of Debbie. Lana was not going to be as good looking as her mother, and she was shy and not too bright. Margot always got her a little present at Christmastime.

On Saturday afternoon Margot drove to Kincardine. She was gone only a couple of hours, so she let Joe and his girlfriend take Debbie to the beach. In Kincardine she rented another car — a van, as it happened, an old blue crockpot of a thing like what the hippies drove. She also bought a few cheap clothes and a rather expensive, real-looking wig. She left them in the van, parked in a lot behind a supermarket. On Sunday morning she drove her car that far, parked it in the lot, got into the van and changed her clothes and donned the wig, as well as some extra make-up. Then she continued driving north.

The wig was a nice light brown color, ruffled up on top and long and straight in the back. The clothes were tight pink denim pants and a pink-and-white-striped top. Margot was thinner then, though not *thin*. Also, buffalo sandals, dangly earrings, big pink sunglasses. The works.

"I didn't miss a trick," said Margot. "I did my eyes up kind of Cleopatraish. I don't believe my own kids could've recognized me. The mistake I made was those pants — they were too tight and too hot. Them and the wig just about killed me. Because it was a blazing hot day. And I was kind of awkward at parking the van, because I'd never driven one before. Otherwise, no problems."

She drove up Highway 21, the Bluewater, with the window down to get a breeze off the lake, and her long hair blowing and the van radio tuned to a rock station, just to get her in the mood. In the mood for what? She had no idea. She smoked one cigarette after another, trying to steady her nerves. Men driving along kept honking at her. Of course the highway was busy, of course

Wasaga Beach was jammed, a bright, hot Sunday like this, in June. Around the beach the traffic was just crawling, and the smell of French fries and noon-hour barbecues pressed down like a blanket. It took her a while just to find the campground, but she did, and paid her day fee, and drove in. Round and round the parking lot she drove, trying to spot Reuel's car. She didn't see it. Then it occurred to her that the lot would be just for day visitors. She found a parking place.

Now she had to reconnoiter the entire grounds, on foot. She walked first all through the campground part. Trailer hookups, tents, people sitting out beside the trailers and tents drinking beer and playing cards and barbecuing lunch — more or less just what they would have been doing at home. There was a central playground, with swings and slides kept busy, and kids throwing Frisbees, and babies in the sandbox. A refreshment stand, where Margot got a Coke. She was too nervous to eat anything. It was strange to her to be in a family place yet not part of any family.

Nobody whistled or made remarks to her. There were lots of long-haired girls around showing off more than she did. And you had to admit that what they had was in better condition to be shown.

She walked the sandy paths under the pines, away from the trailers. She came to a part of the grounds that looked like an old resort, probably there long before anybody ever thought of trailer hookups. The shade of the big pines was a relief to her. The ground underneath was brown with their needles — hard dirt had turned to a soft and furry dust. There were double cabins and single cabins, painted dark green. Picnic tables beside them. Stone fireplaces. Tubs of flowers in bloom. It was nice.

There were cars parked by some of the cabins, but Reuel's wasn't there. She didn't see anybody around — maybe the people who stayed in cabins were the sort who went down to the beach. Across the road was a place with a bench and a drinking fountain and a trash can. She sat down on the bench to rest.

And out he came. Reuel. He came out of the cabin right across from where she was sitting. Right in front of her nose. He was wearing his bathing trunks and he had a couple of towels slung over his shoulders. He walked in a lazy, slouching way. A roll of white fat sloped over the waistband of his trunks. "Straighten up at least!" Margot wanted to yell at him. Was he slouching like that because he felt sneaky and ashamed? Or just worn out with happy exercise? Or had he been slouching for a long time and she hadn't noticed? His big strong body turning into something like custard.

He reached into the car parked beside the cabin, and she knew he was reaching for his cigarettes. She knew, because at the same moment she was fumbling in her bag for hers. If this was a movie, she thought — if this was only a movie, he'd come springing across the road with a light, keen to assist the stray pretty girl. Never recognizing her, while the audience held its breath. Then recognition dawning, and horror — incredulity and horror. While she the wife sat there cool and satisfied, drawing deep on her cigarette. But none of this happened, of course none of it happened, he didn't even look across the road. She sat sweating in her denim pants, and her hands shook so that she had to put her cigarette away.

The car wasn't his. What kind of car did Dorothy Slut drive?

Maybe he was with somebody else, somebody totally unknown to Margot, a stranger. Some stranger who figured she knew him as well as his wife.

No. No. Not unknown. Not a stranger. Not in the least a stranger. The door of the cabin opened again, and there was Lana Slote. Lana, who was supposed to be in Toronto with the band. Couldn't baby-sit Debbie. Lana, whom Margot had always felt sorry for and been kind to because she thought the girl was slightly lonesome or unlucky. Because she thought it showed that Lana was brought up mostly by old grandparents. Lana seemed old-fashioned, prematurely serious without being clever, and not very healthy, as if she were allowed to live on soft drinks and sugared cereal and whatever mush of canned corn and fried potatoes and macaroni-and-cheese loaf those old people dished up for supper. She got bad colds with asthmatic complications, her complexion was dull and pale. But she did have a chunky, appealing little figure, well developed front and back, and chipmunk cheeks when she smiled, and silky, flat, naturally blond hair. She was so meek that even Debbie could boss her around, and the boys thought she was a joke.

Lana was wearing a bathing suit that her grandmother might have chosen for her. A shirred top over her bunchy little breasts and a flowered skirt. Her legs were stumpy, untanned. She stood there on the step as if she was afraid to come out — afraid to appear in a bathing suit or afraid to appear at all. Reuel had to go over and give her a loving little spank, to get her moving. With numerous lingering pats he arranged one of the towels around her shoulders. He touched his cheek to her flat blond head, then rubbed his nose in her hair, no doubt to inhale its baby fragrance. Margot watched it all.

They walked away, down the road to the beach, respectably keeping their distance. Father and child.

Margot observed now that the car was a rented one. From a place in Walkerton. How funny, she thought, if it had been rented in Kincardine, at the same place where she rented the van. She wanted to put a note under the windshield wiper, but she didn't have anything to write on. She had a pen but no paper. But on the grass beside the trash can she spied a Kentucky Fried Chicken bag. Hardly a grease spot on it. She tore it into pieces, and on the pieces she wrote — or printed, actually, in capital letters — these messages:

> YOU BETTER WATCH YOURSELF,
> YOU COULD END UP IN JAIL.
>
> THE VICE SQUAD WILL GET YOU
> IF YOU DON'T WATCH OUT.
>
> PERVERTS NEVER PROSPER.
>
> LIKE MOTHER LIKE DAUGHTER.
>
> BETTER THROW THAT ONE BACK IN THE
> FRENCH RIVER, IT'S NOT FULL GROWN.
>
> SHAME.
>
> SHAME.

She wrote another that said "BIG FAT SLOB WITH YOUR BABY-FACED MORON," but she tore that up — she didn't like the tone of it. Hysterical. She stuck the notes where she was sure they would be found — under the windshield wiper, in the crack of the door, weighed down by stones on the picnic table. Then she hurried away with her heart racing. She drove so badly, at first, that she almost killed a dog before she got out of the parking lot. She did not trust herself on the highway, so she drove on back roads, gravel roads, and kept reminding herself to keep her speed down. She wanted to go fast. She wanted to take off. She felt right on the edge of blowing up, blowing to smithereens. Was it good or was it terrible, the way she felt? She couldn't say. She felt that she had been cut loose, nothing mattered to her, she was as light as a blade of grass.

But she ended up in Kincardine. She changed her clothes and took off the wig and rubbed the make-up off her eyes. She put the clothes and the wig in the supermarket trash bin — not without thinking what a pity — and she turned in the van. She wanted to go into the hotel bar and have a drink, but she was afraid of what it might do to her driving. And she was afraid of what she might do if any man saw her drinking alone and came up with the least remark to her. Even if he just said, "Hot day," she might yelp at him, she might try to claw his face off.

Home. The children. Pay the sitter. A friend of Lana's. Could she be the one who had phoned? Get takeout for supper. Pizza — not Kentucky Fried, which she would never be able to think of again without being reminded. Then she sat up late, waiting. She had some drinks. Certain notions kept banging about in her head. Lawyer, Divorce, Punishment. These notions hit her like gongs, then died away without giving her any idea about how to proceed. What should she do first, what should she do next, how should her life go on? The children all had appointments of one kind or another, the boys had summer jobs, Debbie was about to have a minor operation on her ear. She couldn't take them away, she'd have to do it all herself, right in the middle of everybody's gossip — which she'd had enough of once before. Also, she and Reuel were invited to a big anniversary party next weekend, she had to get the present. A man was coming to look at the drains.

Reuel was so late getting home that she was afraid he'd had an accident. He'd had to go around by Orangeville, to deliver Lana to the home of her aunt. He'd pretended to be a high school teacher transporting a member of the band. (The real teacher had been told, meanwhile, that Lana's aunt was sick and Lana was in Orangeville looking after her.) Reuel's stomach was upset, naturally, after those notes. He sat at the kitchen table chewing tablets and drinking milk. Margot made coffee, to sober herself for the fray.

Reuel said it was all innocent. An outing for the girl. As with Margot, he'd felt sorry for her. Innocent.

Margot laughed at that. She laughed, telling about it.

"I said to him, 'Innocent! I know your innocent! Who do you think you're talking to,' I said, 'Teresa?' And he said, '*Who?*' No, really. Just for a minute he looked blank, before he remembered. He said, '*Who?*' "

Margot thought then, What punishment? Who for? She thought he'd probably marry that girl and there'd be babies for sure and pretty soon not enough money to go around.

Before they went to bed at some awful hour in the morning, she had the promise of her house.

"Because there comes a time with men, they really don't want the hassle. They'd rather weasel out. I bargained him down to the wire, and I got pretty near everything I wanted. If he got balky about something later on, all I'd have to say was 'Wigtime!' I'd told him the whole thing — the wig and the van and where I sat and everything. I'd say that in front of the kids or anybody, and none of them would know what I was talking about. But he'd know. Reuel would know. *Wigtime!* I still say it once in a while, whenever I think it's appropriate."

She fished a slice of orange out of her glass and sucked, then chewed on it. "I put a little something else in this besides the wine," she said. "I put a little vodka, too. Notice?"

She stretched her arms and legs out in the sun.

"Whenever I think it's — appropriate."

Anita thought that Margot might have given up on vanity but she probably hadn't given up on sex. Margot might be able to contemplate sex without fine-looking bodies or kindly sentiments. A healthy battering.

And what about Reuel — what had he given up on? Whatever he did, it wouldn't be till he was ready. That was what all Margot's hard bargaining would really be coming up against — whether Reuel was ready or not. That was something he'd never feel obliged to tell her. So a woman like Margot can still be fooled — this was what Anita thought, with a momentary pleasure, a completely comfortable treachery — by a man like Reuel.

"Now you," said Margot, with an ample satisfaction. "I told you something. Time for you to tell me. Tell me how you decided to leave your husband."

Anita told her what had happened in a restaurant in British Columbia. Anita and her husband, on a holiday, went into a roadside restaurant, and Anita saw there a man who reminded her of a man she had been in love with — no, perhaps she had better say infatuated with — years and years ago. The man in the restaurant had a pale-skinned, heavy face, with a scornful and evasive expression, which could have been a dull copy of the face of the man she loved, and his long-legged body could have been a copy of that man's body if it had been struck by lethargy. Anita could hardly tear herself away when it came time to leave the restaurant. She understood that expression — she felt that she was tearing herself away, she got loose in strips and tatters. All the way up the Island Highway, between the dark enclosing rows of tall fir and spruce trees, and on the ferry to Prince Rupert, she felt an absurd pain of separation. She decided that if she could feel such a pain, if she could feel more for a phantom than she could ever feel in her marriage, she had better go.

So she told Margot. It was more difficult than that, of course, and it was not so clear.

"Then did you go and find that other man?" said Margot.

"No. It was one-sided. I couldn't."

"Somebody else, then?"

"And somebody else, and somebody else," said Anita, smiling. The other night when she had been sitting beside her mother's bed, waiting to give her mother an injection, she had thought about men, putting names one upon another as if to pass the time, just as you'd name great rivers of the world, or capital cities, or the children of Queen Victoria. She felt regret about some of them but no repentance. Warmth, in fact, spread from the tidy buildup. An accumulating satisfaction.

"Well, that's one way," said Margot staunchly. "But it seems weird to me. It does. I mean — I can't see the use of it, if you don't marry them." She paused. "Do you know what I do, some-

times?" She got up quickly and went to the sliding doors. She
listened, then opened the door and stuck her head inside. She
came back and sat down.

"Just checking to see Debbie's not getting an earful," she said.
"Boys, you can tell any horrific personal stuff in front of them
and you might as well be speaking Hindu, for all they ever listen.
But girls listen. Debbie listens . . .

"I'll tell you what I do," she said. "I go out and see Teresa."

"Is she still there?" said Anita. "Is Teresa still out at the store?"

"What store?" said Margot. "Oh, no! No, no. The store's gone.
The gas station's gone. Torn down years ago. Teresa's in the
County Home. They have this what they call the Psychiatric Wing
out there now. The weird thing is, she worked out there for
years and years, just handing round trays and tidying up and
doing this and that for them. Then she started having funny
spells herself. So now she's sometimes sort of working there and
she's sometimes just *there*, if you see what I mean. When she goes
off she's never any trouble. She's just pretty mixed up. Talk-talk-
talk-talk-talk. The way she always did, only more so. All she has
any idea of doing is talk-talk-talk, and fix herself up. If you come
and see her she always wants you to bring her some bath oil or
perfume or make-up. Last time I went out I took her some of
that highlight stuff for her hair. I thought that was taking a
chance, it was kind of complicated for her to use. But she read
the directions, she made out fine. She didn't make a mess. What
I mean by mixed up is, she figures she's on the boat. The boat
with the war brides. Bringing them all out to Canada."

"War brides," Anita said. Such a long time since she'd heard
of them.

"You know what just flashed on my mind?" said Margot. "Just
how the store used to look in the morning. And us coming in
half froze."

Then she said in a flattened, disbelieving voice, "She used to
come and beat on the door. Out there. Out there, when Reuel
was with me in the room. It was awful. I don't know. I don't
know — do you think it was love?"

From up here on the deck the two long arms of the breakwa-
ter look like floating matchsticks. The towers and pyramids and
conveyor belts of the salt mine look like large solid toys. The lake

is glinting like foil. Everything seems bright and distinct and harmless. Spellbound.

"We're all on the boat," says Margot. "She thinks we're all on the boat. But she's the one Reuel's going to meet in Halifax, lucky her."

Margot and Anita have got this far. They are not ready, yet, to stop talking. They are fairly happy.

Typical

FROM GRAND STREET

YESTERDAY a few things happened. Every day a few do. My dog beat up another dog. He does this when he can. It's his living, more or less, though I've never let him make money doing it. He could. Beating up other dogs is his thing. He means no harm by it, expects other dogs to beat him up — no anxiety about it. If anything makes him nervous, it's that he won't get a chance to beat up or be beaten up. He's healthy. I don't think I am.

For one thing, after some dog-beating-up, I think I feel better than even the dog. It's an occasion calls for drinking. I have gotten a pain in the liver zone, which it is supposed to be impossible to feel. My doctor won't say I can't feel anything, outright, but he does say *he* can't feel anything. He figures I'll feel myself into quitting if he doesn't say I'm nuts. Not that I see any reason he'd particularly cry if I drank myself into the laundry bag.

I drank so much once, came home, announced to my wife it was high time I went out, got me a black woman. A friend of mine, well before this, got in the laundry bag and suddenly screamed at his wife to keep away from him because she had *turned* black, but I don't think there's a connection. I just told mine I was heading for some black women pronto, and I knew where the best ones were, they were clearly in Beaumont. The next day she was not speaking, little rough on pots and pans, so I had to begin the drunk detective game and open the box of bad breath no drunk ever wants to open. That let out the black women of Beaumont, who were not so attractive in the shaky

light of day with your wife standing there pink-eyed holding her
lips still with little inside bites. I sympathized fully with her, fully.

I'm not nice, not too smart, don't see too much point in pretending to be either. Why I am telling anyone this trash is a good
question, and it's stuff it obviously doesn't need me to tell myself.
Hell, I know it, it's mine. It would be like the retired justice of
the peace that married me and my wife.

We took a witness which it turned out we didn't need him, all
a retired JP needs to marry is a twenty-dollar tip, and he'd gotten two thousand of those tips in his twenty years retired, cash.
Anyway, he came to the part asks did anyone present object to
our holy union please speak up now or forever shut up, looked
up at the useless witness, said, "Well, hell, he's the only one here,
and y'all brought him, so let's get on with it." Which we did.

This was in Sealy, Texas. We crossed the town square, my wife
feeling very married, proper and weepy, not knowing yet I was
the kind to talk of shagging black whores, and we went into a
nice bar with a marble bartop and good stools and geezers at
dominoes in the back, and we drank all afternoon on one ten-
dollar bill from large frozen goblet-steins of some lousy Texas
beer we're supposed to be so proud of and this once it wasn't
actually terribly bad beer. There was our bouquet of flowers on
the bar and my wife was in a dressy dress and looked younger
and more innocent than she really was. The flowers were yellow,
as I recall, the marble white with a blue vein, and her dress a
light, flowery blue. Light was coming into the bar from high
transomlike windows making glary edges and silhouettes — the
pool players were on fire, but the table was a black hole. All the
stuff in the air was visible, smoke and dust and tiny webs. The
brass nails in the old floor looked like stars. And the beer was
fifty cents. What else? It was pretty.

She's not so innocent as it looked that day because she had a
husband for about ten years who basically wouldn't sleep with
her. That tends to reduce innocence about marriage. So she was
game for a higher stepper like me, but maybe thinks about the
cold frying pan she quit when I volunteer to liberate the dark
women of the world.

I probably mean no harm, to her or to black women, probably
am like my dog, nervous I won't get *the chance*. I might fold up

at the first shot. I regret knowing I'll never have a date with Candice Bergen, this is in the same line of thought. Candice Bergen is my pick for the most good to look at and probably kiss and maybe all-you-could-do woman in the world. All fools have their whims. Should an ordinary, daily kind of regular person carry around desire like this? Why do people do this? Of course a lot of money is made on fools with pinups in the back of their heads, but why do we continue to buy? We'd be better off with movie stars what look like the girls from high school that had to have sex to get any attention at all. You put Juicy Lucy Spoonts on the silver screen and everybody'd be happy to go home to his faithful, hopeful wife. I don't know what they do in Russia, on film, but if the street women are any clue, they're on to a way of reducing foolish desire. They look like good soup makers, and no head problems, but they look like potatoes, I'm sorry. They've done something over there that prevents a common man from wanting the women of Beaumont.

There are many mysteries in this world. I should be a better person, I know I should, but I don't see that finally being up to choice. If it were, I would not stop at being a better person. Who would? The girls what could not get dates in high school, for example, are my kind of people now, but *then* they weren't. I was like everybody else.

I thought I was the first piece of sliced bread to come wrapped in plastic, then. Who didn't. To me it is really comical, how people come to realize they are really a piece of shit. More or less. Not everybody's the Candy Man or a dog poisoner. I don't mean that. But a whole lot of folk who once thought otherwise of themself come to see they're just not that hot. That is something to think on, if you ask me, but you don't, and you shouldn't, which it proves my point. I'm a fellow discovers he's nearly worth disappearing without a difference to anyone or anything, no one to be listened to, trying to say that not being worth being listened to is the discovery we make in our life that then immediately, sort of, ends the life and its feedbag of self-serious and importance.

I used to think niggers were the worst. First they were loud as Zulus at bus stations and their own bars and then they started walking around with radio stations with jive jamming up the entire air. Then I realized you get the same who-the-hell-asked-for-it noise off half, more than half, the white fools everywhere you are. Go to the ice house: noise. Rodeo: Jesus. Had to quit football games. There's a million hotshots in this world wearing shorts and loud socks won't take no for an answer.

And un*like* high school, you can't make them go home, quit coming. You can't make them quit playing life. I'd like to put up a cut-list on the locker room door to the world itself. Don't suit up today, the following:

And I'm saying I'd be in the cut myself. Check your pads in, sell your shoes if you haven't fucked them up. I did get cut once, and a nigger who was going to play for UT down the road wouldn't buy my shoes because he said they stank — a nigger now. He was goddamned right about the toe jam which a pint of foo foo water had made worse, but the hair on his ass to say something like that to me. I must say he was nice about it, and I'm kind of proud to tell it was Earl Campbell wouldn't wear a stink shoe off me.

Hell, just take what I'm saying right here in that deal. *I'm* better than a nigger who breaks all the rushing records they had at UT twice and then pro records and on bad teams, when I get *cut* from a bad team that names itself after a tree. Or something, I've forgotten. We might have been the Tyler Rosebuds. That's the lunacy I'm saying. People have to *wake up*. Some do. Some don't. I have: I'm nobody. A many hasn't. Go to the ice house and hold your ears.

This is not that important. It just surprised me when I came to it, is all. You're a boob, a boob for life, I realized one day. Oh, I got Stetsons, a Silverado doolie, ten years at ARMCO, played poker with Mickey Gilley, shit, and my girlfriends I don't keep in a little black book but on candy wrappers flying around loose in the truck. One flies out, so what? More candy, more wrappers at the store. But one day, for no reason, or no reason I know it or can remember anything happening which it meant anything, I stopped at what I was doing and said, John Payne, you are a piece of crud. You are a common, long-term drut. *Look* at it.

It's not like this upset me or anything, why would it? It's part of the truth to what I'm saying. You can't disturb a nobody with evidence he's a nobody. A nobody is not disturbed by anything significant. It's like trying to disturb a bum by yelling "Poor fuck" at him. What's new? he says. So when I said, John Payne, you final asshole, I just kept on riding. But the moment stuck. I began watching myself. I watched and proved I was an asshole.

This does not give you a really good feeling, unless you are drunk, which is when you do a good part of the proving.

I've been seeing things out of the corners of my eyes and feeling like I have worms since this piece-of-crud thing. It works like this. I'm in a ice house out Almeda, about to Alvin in fact, and I see this pretty cowboy type must work for Nolan Ryan's ranch or something start to come up to me to ask for a light. That's what I *would* have seen, before. But now it works like this: before he gets to me, before he even starts coming over, see, because I'm legged up in a strange bar thinking I'm a piece of shit and a out-of-work beer at three in the afternoon in a dump in Alvin it proves it, I see out the corner of my eye this guy put his hand in his pants and give a little wink to his buddies as he starts to come over. That's enough, whatever it means, he may think I'm a fag, or he may be one himself, but he thinks you're enough a piece of shit he can touch his dick and wink about you, only he don't know that he is winking about a known piece of shit, and winking about a known piece of shit is a dangerous thing to do.

Using the mirror over the bar about like Annie Oakley shooting backwards, I spot his head and turn and slap him in the temple hard enough to get the paint to fall off a fender. He goes down. His buddies start to push back their chairs and I step one step up and they stop.

"What's all the dick and grinning about, boys?"

On the floor says, "I cain't *see*."

"He cain't see," I tell the boys.

I walk out.

Outside it's some kind of dream. There's ten Hell's Angel things running around a pickup in the highway like a Chinese fire drill, whatever that is. In the middle by the truck is a by-God muscle man out of Charles Atlas swinging chains. He's *whipping* the bikers with their own motorcycle chains. He's got all of the leather hogs bent over and whining where he's stung them. He picks up a bike and drops it head first on the rakes. Standing there with a hot Bud, the only guy other than Tarzan not bent over and crying, I get the feeling we're some kind of tag team. I drive off.

That's how it works. Start out a piece of shit, slap some queer-bait blind, watch a wrestling match in the middle of Almeda Road, drive home a piece of shit, spill the hot beer I forgot about all over the seat and my leg.

I didn't always feel this way, who could afford to? When I was fifteen, my uncle, who was always kind of my real dad, gave me brand-new Stetson boots and a hundred-dollar bill on a street corner in Galveston and said spend it all and spend it all on whores. It was my birthday. I remember being afraid of the black whores and the ones with big tits, black or white, otherwise I was a ace. In those days a hundred dollars went a long way with ladies in Galveston. I got home very tired, a fifteen-year-old *king* with new boots and a wet dick.

That's what you do with the world before you doubt yourself. You buy it, dress up in it, fuck it. Then, somehow, it starts fucking back. A Galveston whore you'd touch now costs the whole hundred dollars, for example, in other words. I don't know. Today I would rather just *talk* to a girl on the street than fuck one, and I damn sure don't want to talk to one. There's no point. I need some kind of pills or something. There must be ways which it will get you out of feeling like this.

For a while I thought about having a baby. But Brillo Tucker thought this up about fifteen years ago, and two years ago his boy whips his ass. When I heard about that I refigured. I don't need a boy whipping my ass, mine or anybody else's. That would just about bind the tit. And they'll do that, you know, because like I say they come out *kings* for a while. Then the crown slips and pretty soon the king can't get a opera ticket, or something, I don't know anything about kings.

This reminds me of playing poker with Mickey Gilley, stud. First he brings ten times as much money as anyone, sits down in new boots, creaking, and hums all his hit songs so nobody can think. He wins a hand, which it is rare, and makes this touch-down kind of move and comes down slowly and rakes the pot to his little pile. During the touchdown, we all look at this dry-cleaning tag stapled to the armpit of his vest. That's the Pasadena crooner.

*

I was at ARMCO Steel for ten years, the largest integrated steel mill west of the Mississippi, a word we use having nothing to do with niggers for once. It means we could take ore and make it all the way to steel. Good steel. However, I admit that with everybody standing around eating candy bars in their new Levi's, it cost more than Jap steel. I have never seen a Japanese eating a candy bar or dipping Skoal showing off his clothes. They wear lab coats, like they're all dentists. We weren't dentists.

We were, by 1980, out of a job, is what we were. It goes without saying it, that is life. They were some old-timers that just moped about it, and some middle-lifer types that had new jobs in seconds, and then us young turks that moped *mad*. We'd filler up and drive around all day bitching about the capitalist system, whatever that is, and counting ice houses. We discovered new things, like Foosball. Foosball was one of the big discoveries. Pool we knew about, shuffleboard we knew about, Star Wars pinball we knew about, but Foosball was a kick.

For a while we bitched as a club. We were on the ice-house frontier, tent-city bums with trucks. Then a truckload of us — not me, but come to think of it, Brillo Tucker was with them, which is perfect — get in it on the Southwest Freeway with a truckload of niggers and they all pull over outside the *Post* building and the niggers whip their *ass*. They're masons or something, plumbers. A photographer at the *Post* sees it all and takes pictures. The next day a thousand ARMCO steel workers out of a job read about themselves whipped by employed niggers on the freeway. This lowered our sail. We got to be less of a club, quick. I don't know what any of my buddies are doing now and I don't care. ARMCO was ARMCO. It was along about in here I told my wife I was off to Beaumont for black chicks, and there could be a connection, but I doubt it.

As far as I can really tell, I'm still scared of them in the plain light of day. At a red light on Jensen Drive one day, a big one in a fur coat says to me, "Come here, Sugar, I got something for you," and opens her coat on a pair of purple hot pants and a yellow bra.

I say, "I know you do," and step on it. Why in hell I'd go home and pick on a perfectly innocent wife about it is the kind of evidence it convinces you you're not a prince in life.

Another guy I knew in the ARMCO club had a brother who *was* a dentist, and this guy tells him not to worry about losing his job, to come out with him golfing on Thursdays and *relax*. Our guy starts going — can't remember his name — and he can't hit the ball for shit. It's out of bounds or it's still on the tee. And the dentist who wants him to relax starts ribbing him until our guy says if you don't shut the fuck up I'm going to put this ball down and aim it at *you*. The dentist laughs. So Warren — that's his name — puts the ball down and aims at the dentist who's standing there like William Tell giggling and swings and hits his brother, the laughing dentist who wants him to relax, square in the forehead. End of relaxing golf.

Another guy's brother, a yacht broker, whatever that is, became a flat *hero* when we got laid off because he found his brother the steel worker in the shower with his shotgun and took it away from him. Which it wasn't hard to do, because he'd been drinking four days and it wasn't loaded.

Come to look at it, *we* all sort of disappeared and all these Samaritans *with* jobs creamed to the top and took the headlines, except for the freeway. The whole world loves a job holder.

One day I drove out to the Highway 90 bridge over the San Jacinto and visited Tent City, which was a bunch of pure bums pretending to be unfortunate. There were honest-to-God river rats down there, never lived anywhere but on a river in a tent, claiming to be victims of the economy. They had elected themselves a mayor, who it turns out the day I got there was up for re-election. But he wasn't going to run again because God had called him to a higher cause, preaching. He announced this with shaking hands and wearing white shoes and a white belt and a maroon leisure suit. Out the back of his tent was a pyramid of beer cans all the way to the river, looked like a mud slide in Colombia. People took me around because they thought I was out there to *hire* someone.

I met the new mayor-to-be, who was a Yankee down here on some scam that busted, had left a lifelong position in dry cleaning, had a wife who swept their little camp to where it was smoother and cleaner than concrete. I told him to call Mickey Gilley. He was a nice guy, they both were, makes you think a little more softly about the joint. How a white woman from

Michigan, I think, knew how to sweep dirt like a Indian I'll never know. Maybe it's natural. I don't think it's typical though.

This one dude, older dude, they called Mr. C, was walking around asking everybody if this stick of wood he was carrying belonged to them. He had this giant blue and orange thing coming off his nose, about *like* an orange, which it is why they called him Mr. C, I guess. A kid who was very pretty, built well — could of made a fortune in Montrose — ran to him with a bigger log and took him by the arm all the way back to his spot, some hanging builder's plastic and a chair, and set a fire for him. It's corny as hell, but I started liking the place. It was like a pilgrim place for pieces of shit, pieces of crud.

Then a couple gets me, tells me their life story if I'll drink instant coffee with them. The guy rescued the girl from some kind of mess in Arkansas that makes Tent City look like Paradise. He's about six eight with mostly black teeth and sideburns growing into his mouth, and she's about four foot flat with a nice ass and all I can think of is how can they fuck and why would she let him. For some reason I asked him if he played basketball, and the *girl* pipes up, "*I* played basketball."

"Where?"

"In high school."

"Then what did you do?" I meant by this, how is it Yardog here has you and I don't.

"Nothing," she says.

"What do you mean, nothing?"

"I ain't done *nuttin.*" That's the way she said it, too.

It was O.K. by me, but if she had fucked somebody other than the buzzard, it would have been *something.*

I was just kind of cruising there at this point, about like leg-up in Alvin, ready to buy them all a case of beer and talk about hard luck the way they wanted to, when something happened. This gleaming, purring, fully restored, *immaculate,* as Brillo Tucker would say, '57 Chevy two-door pulls in and eases around Tent City and up to us, and out from behind the mirrored windshield, wearing sunglasses to match it, steps this nigger who was a kind of shiny, shoe-polish brown, and *exact* color and finish of the car. The next thing you saw was that his hair was black and oily and so were the sidewalls of his car. Everything had dressing on it.

The nigger comes up all smiles and takes cards out of a special little pocket in his same brown suit as the car and himself. The card says something about community development.

"I am prepared to offer all of you, if we have enough, a seminar in job-skills acquisition and full-employment methodology." This comes out of the gleaming nigger beside his purring '57 Chevy.

The girl with the nice butt who's done nothing but fuck a turkey vulture says, "Do what?"

Then the nigger starts on a roll about the seminar, about the only thing which in it people can catch is it will take six hours. That is longer than most of these people want to *hold* a job, including me at this point. I want to steal his car.

"Six hours?" the girl repeats. "For *what?*"

"Well, there are a lot of tricks to getting a job."

I say, "Like what?"

"Well, like shaking hands."

"Shaking hands." I remember Earl Campbell not buying my stinky shoes. That was O.K. This is too far.

"Do you know how to shake hands?" the gleaming nigger asks. Out of the corner of my eye I see the turkey buzzard looking at his girl with a look that is like they're in high school and in love.

"Let's find out," I say. I grab him and crush him one, he winces.

"You know how to shake hands."

"I thought I did."

Who the fuck taught *him* how? Maybe Lyndon Johnson.

He purrs off to find a hall for the seminar and the group at Tent City proposes putting a gas cylinder in the river and shooting it with a .22.

I've got my own brother to contend with, but we got over it a long time ago. He was long gone when ARMCO troubles let everybody else's brother loose on him. He, *my* brother, goes off to college, which I don't, which it pissed me off at the time, but no so much now. Anyway, he goes off and comes back with half-ass long hair talking *Russian*. Saying, *Goveryou po rooskie* in my face. It's about the time Earl Campbell has told me he won't wear my cleats because they stink, so I take all my brother's college crap laying down.

Then he says, "I study Russian with an old woman who escaped the revolution with nothing. There's only one person in the class, so we meet at her house. Actually, we meet in her back yard, in a hole."

"You what?"

"We sit in a hole she dug and study Russian. All I lack being Dostoevsky's underground man is more time." He laughed.

"All I lack being a gigolo," I said, "is having a twelve-inch dick." And hit him, which is why he doesn't talk to me today, and I don't care. If he found out I was in the shower with my shotgun he'd pass in a box of shells. Underground man. What a piece of shit.

That's about it. Thinking of my brother, now, I don't feel so hot about running at the mouth. I'm not feeling so hot about living, so what? What call is it to drill people in their ear? I'm typical.

LORE SEGAL

The Reverse Bug

FROM THE NEW YORKER

"LET'S GET the announcements out of the way," said Ilka, the teacher, to her foreigners in Conversational English for Adults. "Tomorrow evening the institute is holding a symposium. Ahmed," she asked the Turkish student with the magnificently drooping mustache, who also wore the institute's janitorial keys hooked to his belt, "where are they holding the symposium?"

"In the New Theater," said Ahmed.

"The theme," said the teacher, "is 'Should there be a statute of limitations on genocide?' with a wine and cheese reception —"

"In the lounge," said Ahmed.

"To which you are all invited. Now," Ilka said in the bright voice of a hostess trying to make a sluggish dinner party go, "what shall we talk about? Doesn't do me a bit of good, I know, to ask you all to come forward and sit in a nice cozy clump. Who would like to start us off? Tell us a story, somebody. We love stories. Tell the class how you came to America."

The teacher looked determinedly past the hand, the arm, with which Gerti Gruner stirred the air — death, taxes, and Thursdays, Gerti Gruner in the front row center. Ilka's eye passed over Paulino, who sat in the last row with his back to the wall. Matsue, a pleasant, older Japanese from the university's engineering department, smiled at Ilka and shook his head, meaning "Please, not me!" Matsue was sitting in his usual place by the window, but Ilka had to orient herself as to the whereabouts of Izmira, the Cypriot doctor, who always left two empty rows between herself and Ahmed, the Turk. Today it was Juan, the Basque, who sat in the rightmost corner, and Eduardo, the Spaniard from Madrid, in the leftmost.

Ilka looked around for someone too shy to self-start who might enjoy talking if called upon, but Gerti's hand stabbed the air immediately underneath Ilka's chin, so she said, "Gerti wants to start. Go, Gerti. When did you come to the United States?"

"In last June," said Gerti.

Ilka corrected her, and said, "Tell the class where you came from, and, everybody, please speak in whole sentences."

Gerti said, "I have lived before in Uruguay."

"We would say, '*Before that I lived,*' " said Ilka, and Gerti said, "And *before that* in Vienna."

Gerti's story bore a family likeness to the teacher's own superannuated, indigestible history of being sent out of Hitler's Europe as a little girl.

Gerti said, "In the Vienna train station has my father told to me . . ."

"*Told me.*"

"*Told me* that so soon as I am coming to Montevideo . . ."

Ilka said, "*As* soon as I *come,* or more colloquially, *get* to Montevideo . . ."

Gerti said, "*Get* to Montevideo, I should tell to all the people . . ."

Ilka corrected her. Gerti said, "*Tell* all the people to bring my father out from Vienna before come the Nazis and put him in concentration camp."

Ilka said, "In *the* or *a* concentration camp."

"Also my mother," said Gerti, "and my Opa, and my Oma, and my Onkel Peter, and the twins, Hedi and Albert. My father has told, 'Tell to the foster mother, "Go, please, with me, to the American Consulate." ' "

"*My* father went to the American Consulate," said Paulino, and everybody turned and looked at him. Paulino's voice had not been heard in class since the first Thursday, when Ilka had got her students to go around the room and introduce themselves to one another. Paulino had said that his name was Paulino Patillo and that he was born in Bolivia. Ilka was charmed to realize it was Danny Kaye of whom Paulino reminded her — fair, curly, middle-aged, smiling. He came punctually every Thursday. Was he a very sweet or a very simple man?

Ilka said, "Paulino will tell us his story after Gerti has finished. How old were you when you left Europe?" Ilka asked, to reactivate Gerti, who said, "Eight years," but she and the rest of the class, and the teacher herself, were watching Paulino put his right hand inside the left breast pocket of his jacket, withdraw an envelope, turn it upside down, and shake out onto the desk before him a pile of news clippings. Some looked sharp and new, some frayed and yellow; some seemed to be single paragraphs, others the length of several columns.

"You got to Montevideo . . ." Ilka prompted Gerti.

"And my foster mother has fetched me from the ship. I said, 'Hello, and will you please bring out from Vienna my father before come the Nazis and put him in — *a* concentration camp!' " Gerti said triumphantly.

Paulino had brought the envelope close to his eyes and was looking inside. He inserted a forefinger, loosened something that was stuck, and shook out a last clipping. It broke at the fold when Paulino flattened it onto the desk top. Paulino brushed away the several paper crumbs before beginning to read: "La Paz, September 19."

"Paulino," said Ilka, "you must wait till Gerti is finished."

But Paulino read, "Señora Pilar Patillo has reported the disappearance of her husband, Claudio Patillo, after a visit to the American Consulate in La Paz on September 15."

"Gerti, go on," said Ilka.

"The foster mother has said, 'When comes home the Uncle from the office, we will ask.' I said, 'And bring out, please, also my mother, my Opa, my Oma, my Onkel Peter . . .' "

Paulino read, "A spokesman for the American Consulate contacted in La Paz states categorically that no record exists of a visit from Señor Patillo within the last two months . . ."

"Paulino, you really *have* to wait your turn," Ilka said.

Gerti said, " 'Also the twins.' The foster mother has made such a desperate face with her lips."

Paulino read, "Nor does the consular calendar for September show any appointment made with Señor Patillo. Inquiries are said to be under way with the Consulate at Sucre." And Paulino folded his column of newsprint and returned it to the envelope.

"O.K., thank you, Paulino," Ilka said.

Gerti said, "When the foster father has come home, he said, 'We will see, tomorrow,' and I said, 'And will you go, please, with me, to the American Consulate?' and the foster father has made a face."

Paulino was flattening the second column of newsprint on his desk. He read, "New York, December 12 . . ."

"Paulino," said Ilka, and caught Matsue's eye. He was looking expressly at her. He shook his head ever so slightly and with his right hand, palm down, he patted the air three times. In the intelligible language of charade with which humankind frustrated God at Babel, Matsue was saying, "Calm down, Ilka. Let Paulino finish. Nothing you can do will stop him." Ilka was grateful to Matsue.

"A spokesman for the Israeli Mission to the United Nations," read Paulino, "denies a report that Claudio Patillo, missing after a visit to the American Consulate in La Paz since September 15, is en route to Israel . . ." Paulino finished reading this column also, folded it into the envelope, and unfolded the next column. "UPI, January 30. The car of Pilar Patillo, wife of Claudio Patillo, who was reported missing from La Paz last September, has been found at the bottom of a ravine in the eastern Andes. It is not known whether any bodies were found inside the wreck," Paulino read with the blind forward motion of a tank that receives no messages from any sound or movement in the world outside. The students had stopped looking at Paulino; they were not looking at the teacher. They were looking into their laps. Paulino read one column after the other, returning each to his envelope before he took the next, and when he had read and returned the last, and returned the envelope to his breast pocket, he leaned his back against the wall and turned to the teacher his sweet, habitual smile of expectant participation.

Gerti said, "In that same night have I woken up . . ."

"That night I *woke* up," the teacher helplessly said.

"Woke up," Gerti Gruner said, "and I have thought, What if it is even now, this exact minute, that one Nazi is knocking at the door, and I am here lying not telling to anybody anything, and

I have stood up and gone into the bedroom where were sleeping the foster mother and father. Next morning has the foster mother gone with me to the refugee committee, and they found for me a different foster family."

"Your turn, Matsue," Ilka said. "How, when, and why did you come to the States? We're all here to help you!" Matsue's written English was flawless, but he spoke with an accent that was almost impenetrable. His contribution to class conversation always involved a communal interpretative act.

"Aisutudieddu attoza unibashite innu munhen," Matsue said.

A couple of stabs and Eduardo, the madrileño, got it: "You studied at the university in Munich!"

"You studied acoustics?" ventured Izmira, the Cypriot doctor.

"The war trapped you in Germany?" proposed Ahmed, the Turk.

"You have been working in the ovens," suggested Gerti, the Viennese.

"Acoustic ovens?" marveled Ilka. "Do you mean stoves? Ranges?"

No, what Matsue meant was that he had got his first job with a Munich firm employed in soundproofing the Dachau ovens so that what went on inside could not be heard on the outside. "I made the tapes," said Matsue. "Tapes?" they asked him. They figured out that Matsue had returned to Japan in 1946. He had collected Hiroshima "tapes." He had been brought to Washington as an acoustical consultant to the Kennedy Center, and had come to Connecticut to design the sound system of the New Theater at Concordance University, where he subsequently accepted a research appointment in the department of engineering. He was now returning home, having finished his work — Ilka thought he said — on the reverse bug.

Ilka said, "I thought, ha ha, you said 'the reverse bug'!"

"The reverse bug" was what everybody understood Matsue to say that he had said. With his right hand he performed a row of air loops, and, pointing at the wall behind the teacher's desk, asked for, and received, her O.K. to explain himself in writing on the blackboard.

Chalk in hand, he was eloquent on the subject of the regular bug, which can be introduced into a room to relay to those outside what those inside want them not to hear. A sophisticated modern bug, explained Matsue, was impossible to locate and deactivate. Buildings had had to be taken apart in order to rid them of alien listening devices. The reverse bug, equally impossible to locate and deactivate, was a device whereby those outside were able to relay *into* a room what those inside would prefer not to have to hear.

"And how would such a device be used?" Ilka asked him.

Matsue was understood to say that it could be useful in certain situations to certain consulates, and Paulino said, "My father went to the American Consulate," and put his hand into his breast pocket. Here Ilka stood up, and, though there was still a good fifteen minutes of class time, said, "So! I will see you all next Thursday. Everybody — be thinking of subjects you would like to talk about. Don't forget the symposium tomorrow evening!" She walked quickly out the door.

Ilka entered the New Theater late and was glad to see Matsue sitting on the aisle in the second row from the back with an empty seat beside him. The platform people were already settling into their places. On the right, an exquisite golden-skinned Latin man was talking, in a way people talk to people they have known a long time, with a heavy, rumpled man, whom Ilka pegged as Israeli. "Look at the thin man on the left," Ilka said to Matsue. "He has to be from Washington. Only a Washingtonian's hair gets to be that particular white color." Matsue laughed. Ilka asked him if he knew who the woman with the oversized glasses and the white hair straight to the shoulders might be, and Matsue said something that Ilka did not understand. The rest of the panelists were institute people, Ilka's colleagues — little Joe Bernstine from philosophy, Yvette Gordot, a mathematician, and Leslie Shakespere, an Englishman, the institute's new director, who sat in the moderator's chair.

Leslie Shakespere had the soft weight of a man who likes to eat and the fine head of a man who thinks. It had not as yet occurred to Ilka that she was in love with Leslie. She watched him fussing with the microphone. "Why do we need this?" she could read Leslie's lips saying. "Since when do we use microphones in the New Theater?" Now he quieted the hall with a grateful welcome for this fine attendance at a discussion of one of our generation's unmanageable questions — the application of justice in an era of genocides.

Here Rabbi Shlomo Grossman rose from the floor and wished to take exception to the plural formulation: "All killings are not murders; all murders are not 'genocides.' "

Leslie said, "Shlomo, could you hold your remarks until question time?"

Rabbi Grossman said, "Remarks? Is that what I'm making? Remarks! The death of six million — is it in the realm of a question?"

Leslie said, "I give you my word that there will be room for the full expression of what you want to say when we open the discussion to the floor." Rabbi Grossman acceded to the evident desire of the friends sitting near him that he should sit down.

Director Leslie Shakespere gave the briefest accounts of the combined federal and private funding that had enabled the Concordance Institute to invite these very distinguished panelists to take part in the institute's Genocide Project. "The institute, as you know, has a long-standing tradition of 'debriefings,' in which the participants in a project that is winding down sum up their thinking for the members of the institute, the university, and the public. But this evening's panel has agreed, by way of an experiment, to talk in an informal way of our notions, of the history of the interest each of us brings to this question — problem — at the point of entry. I want us to interest ourselves in the *nature of inquiry:* Will we come out of this project with our original notions reinforced? Modified? Made over?

"I imagine that his inquiry will range somewhere between the legal concept of a statute of limitations that specifies the time within which human law must respond to a specific crime, and the biblical concept of the visitation of punishment of the sins of the fathers upon the children. One famous version plays itself out in the *Oresteia,* where a crime is punished by an act that is itself a crime and punishable, and so on, down the generations. Enough. Let me introduce our panel, whom it will be our very great pleasure to have among us in the coming months."

The white-haired man turned out to be the West German ex-mayor of Obernpest, Dieter Dobelmann. Ilka felt the prompt conviction that she had known all along — that one could tell from a mile — that that mouth, that jaw, had to be German. Leslie dwelled on Dobelmann's persuasive anti-Nazi credentials. The woman with the glasses was on loan to the institute from Georgetown University. ("The white hair! You see!" Ilka whispered to Matsue, who laughed.) She was Jerusalem-born Shulamit Gershon, professor of international law and long-time adviser to Israel's ongoing project to identify Nazi war criminals and bring them to trial. The rumpled man was the English theologian William B. Thayer. The Latin really was a Latin — Sebastian Maderiaga, who was taking time off from his consulate in New York. Leslie squeezed his eyes to see past the stage lights into the well of the New Theater. There was a rustle of people turning to locate the voice that had said, "My father went to the American Consulate," but it said nothing further and the audience settled back. Leslie introduced Yvette and Joe, the institute's own fellows assigned to Genocide.

Ilka and Matsue leaned forward, watching Paulino across the aisle. Paulino was withdrawing the envelope from his breast pocket. "Without a desk?" whispered Ilka anxiously. Paulino upturned the envelope onto the slope of his lap. The young student sitting beside him got on his knees to retrieve the sliding batch of newsprint and held on to it while Paulino arranged his coat across his thighs to create a surface.

"My own puzzle," said Leslie, "with which I would like to puzzle our panel, is this: Where do I, where do we all, get these feelings of moral malaise when wrong goes unpunished and right goes unrewarded?"

Paulino had brought his first newspaper column up to his eyes and read, "La Paz, September 19. Señora Pilar Patillo has reported the disappearance of her husband, Claudio Patillo . . ."

"Where," Leslie was saying, "does the human mind derive its expectation of a set of consequences for which it finds no evidence whatsoever in nature or in history, or in looking around its own autobiography? . . . Could I *please* ask for quiet from the floor until we open the discussion?" Leslie was once again peering out into the hall.

The audience turned and looked at Paulino reading, "Nor does the consular calendar for September show any appointment . . ."

Shulamit Gershon leaned toward Leslie and spoke to him for several moments while Paulino read, "A spokesman for the Israeli Mission to the United Nations denies a report . . ."

It was after several attempts to persuade him to stop that Leslie said, "Ahmed? Is Ahmed in the hall? Ahmed, would you be good enough to remove the unquiet gentleman as gently as necessary force will allow. Take him to my office, please, and I will meet with him after the symposium."

Everybody watched Ahmed walk up the aisle with a large and sheepish-looking student. The two lifted the unresisting Paulino out of his seat by the armpits. They carried him reading, "The car of Pilar Patillo, wife of Claudio Patillo . . ." — backward, out the door.

The action had something about it of the classic comedy routine. There was a cackling, then the relief of general laughter. Leslie relaxed and sat back, understanding that it would require some moments to get the evening back on track, but the cackling did not stop. Leslie said, "Please." He waited. He cocked his head and listened: it was more like a hiccupping that straightened and elongated into a sound drawn on a single breath. Leslie looked at the panel. The panel looked. The audience looked all around. Leslie bent his ear down to the microphone. It did him no good to turn the button off and on, to put his hand over the mouthpiece, to bend down as if to look it in the eye. "Anybody know — is the sound here centrally controlled?" he asked. The noise was growing incrementally. Members of the audience drew their heads back and down into their shoulders. It came to them — it became impossible to not know — that it was not laughter to which they were listening but somebody yelling. Somewhere there was a person, and the person was screaming.

Ilka looked at Matsue, whose eyes were closed. He looked an old man.

The screaming stopped. The relief was spectacular, but lasted only for that same unnaturally long moment in which a howling child, having finally exhausted its strength, is fetching up new breath from some deepest source for a new onslaught. The howl resumed at a volume that was too great for the small theater; the human ear could not accommodate it. People experienced a physical distress. They put their hands over their ears.

Leslie had risen. He said, "I'm going to suggest an alteration in the order of this evening's proceedings. Why don't we clear the hall — everybody, please, move into the lounge, have some wine, have some cheese while we locate the source of the trouble."

Quickly, while people were moving along their rows, Ilka popped out into the aisle and collected the trail of Paulino's news clippings. The young student who had sat next to Paulino found and handed her the envelope.

Ilka walked down the hall in the direction of Leslie Shakespere's office, diagnosing in herself an inappropriate excitement at having it in her power to throw light.

Ilka looked into Leslie's office. Paulino sat on a hard chair with his back to the door, shaking his head violently from side to side. Leslie stood facing him. He and Ahmed and all the panelists, who had disposed themselves about Leslie's office, were screwing their eyes up as if wanting very badly to close every bodily opening through which unwanted information is able to enter. The intervening wall had somewhat modified the volume, but not the variety — length, pitch, and pattern — of the sounds that continually altered as in response to a new and continually changing cause.

Leslie said, "We know this stuff goes on whether we are hearing it or not, but this . . ." He saw Ilka at the door and said, "Mr. Patillo is your student, no? He refuses to tell us how to locate the screaming unless they release his father."

Ilka said, "*Paulino*? Does Paulino *say* he 'refuses'?"

Leslie said to Paulino, "Will you please tell us how to find the source of this noise so we can shut it off?"

Paulino shook his head and said, "It is my father screaming."

Ilka followed the direction of Leslie's eye. Maderiaga was perched with a helpless elegance on the corner of Leslie's desk, speaking Spanish into the telephone. Through the open door that led into a little outer office, Ilka saw Shulamit Gershon hang up the phone. She came back in and said, "Patillo is the name this young man's father adopted from his Bolivian wife. He's Klaus Herrmann, who headed the German Census Bureau. After the Anschluss they sent him to Vienna to put together the registry of Jewish names and addresses. Then on to Budapest, and so on. After the war we traced him to La Paz. I think he got into trouble with some mines or weapons deals. We put him on the back burner when it turned out the Bolivians were after him as well."

Now Maderiaga hung up and said, "Hasn't he been the busy little man! My office is going to check if it's the Gonzales people who got him for expropriating somebody's tin mine, or the RRN. If they suspect Patillo of connection with the helicopter crash that killed President Barrientos, they'll have more or less killed him."

"It is my father screaming," said Paulino.

"It's got nothing to do with his father," said Ilka. While Matsue was explaining the reverse bug on the blackboard the previous evening, Ilka had grasped the principle. It disintegrated as she was explaining it to Leslie. She was distracted, moreover, by a retrospective image: Last night, hurrying down the corridor, Ilka had turned her head and must have seen, since she was now able to recollect, young Ahmed and Matsue moving away together down the hall. If Ilka had thought them a curious couple, the thought, having nothing to feed on, had died before her lively wish to maneuver Gerti and Paulino into one elevator just as the doors were closing, so she could come down in the other.

Now Ilka asked Ahmed, "Where did you and Matsue go after class last night?"

Ahmed said, "He wanted to come into the New Theater."

Leslie said, "Ahmed, forgive me for ordering you around all evening, but will you go and find me Matsue and bring him here to my office?"

"He has gone," said Ahmed. "I saw him leave by the front door with a suitcase on wheels."

"He is going home," said Ilka. "Matsue has finished his job."

Paulino said, "It is my father screaming."

"No, it's not, Paulino," said Ilka. "Those screams are from Dachau and they are from Hiroshima."

"It is my father," said Paulino, "and my mother."

Leslie asked Ilka to come with him to the airport. They caught up with Matsue queuing, with only five passengers ahead of him, to enter the gangway to his plane.

Ilka said, "Matsue, you're not going away without telling us
how to shut the thing off!"

Matsue said, "Itto dozunotto shattoffu."

Ilka and Leslie said, "Excuse me?"

With the hand that was not holding his boarding pass, Matsue
performed a charade of turning a faucet and he shook his head.
Ilka and Leslie understood him to be saying, "It does not shut
off." Matsue stepped out of the line, kissed Ilka on the cheek,
stepped back, and passed through the door.

When Concordance Institute takes hold of a situation, it deals
humanely with it. Leslie found funds to pay a private sanitarium
to evaluate Paulino. Back at the New Theater, the police, a bomb
squad, and a private acoustics company from Washington set
themselves to locate the source of the screaming.

Leslie looked haggard. His colleagues worried when their director, a sensible man, continued to blame the microphone after
the microphone had been removed and the screaming continued. The sound seemed not to be going to loop back to any
familiar beginning, so that the hearers might have become familiar — might, in a manner of speaking, have made friends —
with one particular roar or screech, but to be going on to per-
petually new and fresh howls of pain.

Neither the Japanese Embassy in Washington nor the American Embassy in Tokyo had got anywhere with the tracers sent
out to locate Matsue. Leslie called in a technician. "Look into
the wiring!" he said, and saw in the man's eyes that look experts wear when they have explained something and the layman
says what he said in the beginning all over again. The expert
had another go. He talked to Leslie about the nature of the
sound wave; he talked about cross-Atlantic phone calls and about
the electric guitar. Leslie said, "Could you look *inside* the wiring?"

Leslie fired the first team of acoustical experts, found another
company, and asked them to check inside the wiring. The new
man reported back to Leslie: He thought they might start by
taking down the stage portion of the theater. If the sound people worked closely with the demolition people, they might be
able to avoid having to mess with the body of the hall.

*

The phone call that Maderiaga had made on the night of the symposium had, in the meantime, set in motion a series of official acts that were bringing to America — to Concordance — Paulino Patillo's father, Claudio/Klaus Patillo/Herrmann. The old man was eighty-nine, missing an eye by an act of man and a lung by an act of God. On the plane he suffered a collapse and was rushed from the airport straight to Concordance University's Medical Center.

Rabbi Grossman walked into Leslie's office and said, "Am I hearing things? You've approved a house, on this campus, for the accomplice of the genocide of Austrian and Hungarian Jewry?"

"And a private nurse!" said Leslie.

"Are you out of your mind?" asked Rabbi Grossman.

"Practically. Yes," said Leslie.

"You look terrible," said Shlomo Grossman, and sat down.

"What," Leslie said, "am I the hell to do with an old Nazi who is postoperative, whose son is in the sanitarium, who doesn't know a soul, doesn't have a dime, doesn't have a roof over his head?"

"Send him home to Germany," shouted Shlomo.

"I tried. Dobelmann says they won't recognize Claudio Patillo as one of their nationals."

"So send him to his comeuppance in Israel!"

"Shulamit says they're no longer interested, Shlomo! They have other things on hand!"

"Put him back on the plane and turn it around."

"For another round of screaming? Shlomo!" cried Leslie, and put his hands over his ears against the noise that, issuing out of the dismembered building materials piled in back of the institute, blanketed the countryside for miles around, made its way down every street of the small university town, into every back yard, and filtered in through Leslie's closed and shuttered windows. "Shlomo," Leslie said, "come over tonight. I promise Eliza will cook you something you can eat. I want you, and I want Ilka — and we'll see who all else — to help me think this thing through."

"We . . . I," said Leslie that night, "need to understand how the scream of Dachau is the same, and how it is a different scream from the scream of Hiroshima. And after that I need to learn how to listen to the selfsame sound that rises out of the hell in which the torturer is getting what he's got coming . . ."

His wife called, "Leslie, can you come and talk to Ahmed?"

Leslie went out and came back in carrying his coat. A couple of young punks with an agenda of their own had broken into Patillo/Herrmann's new American house. They had gagged the nurse and tied her and Klaus up in the new American bathroom. Here Ilka began to laugh. Leslie buttoned his coat and said, "I'm sorry, but I have to go on over. Ilka, Shlomo, please, I leave for Washington tomorrow, early, to talk to the Superfund people. While I'm there I want to get a Scream Project funded. Ilka? Ilka, what is it?" But Ilka was helplessly giggling and could not answer him. Leslie said, "What I need is for you two to please sit down, here and now, and come up with a formulation I can take with me to present to Arts and Humanities."

The Superfund granted Concordance an allowance, for scream disposal, and the dismembered stage of the New Theater was loaded onto a flatbed truck and driven west. The population along Route 90 and all the way down to Arizona came out into the street, eyes squeezed together, heads pulled back and down into shoulders. They buried the thing fifteen feet under, well away from the highway, and let the desert howl.

ELIZABETH TALLENT

Prowler

FROM THE NEW YORKER

A NEW DEVELOPMENT, and more than he can bear: his ex-wife is abruptly back from Europe, her boyfriend of the last two years nowhere in sight. The tortoiseshell glasses alert him that Christie, confronting him across his own living room, has reinvented herself yet again. She has never before worn glasses, and it is plain to Dennis only because he knows her so well that they still excite her as a novelty, a kind of prop. She has a new gesture — index finger laid against the bridge of her nose to give the specs a tiny upward shove, brown eyes widening — that manages to get across the impression that she is taking life more seriously, yet her account of the last year smells of evasiveness. Déjà vu, because his old sense, with Christie, was often that she was skipping details that might not reflect well on her, editing and enlarging as she went, and that he was essentially helpless to pin her to the truth. Christie is all in baggy black, her legs crossed, one black, doltish boot swinging. She wants their son for the summer.

"George has stayed behind," she says with a faint, enigmatic tone of apology. Not even that is clear. Not "I've left him" or "It was all a mistake" but "George has stayed behind." In Paris, where she lived with him for the last year.

By a coincidence, Dennis and Christie both began second families last year, she with George, Dennis with his young wife, Francesca. Christie's baby girl has been left in Santa Fe with a sitter. His twins are asleep upstairs with their mother, all of them exhausted by the cold they have been sharing back and forth.

Kenny, his and Christie's thirteen-year-old, is away overnight with
his best friend; when Dennis heard a car grind to a halt in the
rocky drive, he had a scared flash that Kenny and Leo had got
into trouble and somebody had been sent to tell him so. For next
to no reason, Dennis distrusts Leo, a good-looking, slightly hy-
per kid, self-assured around adults in a way Kenny never will be,
not until he's one himself — maybe not even then. Leo's girlfriend works in a record shop where Kenny and Leo are always
hanging out. Kenny can't drive yet, of course, and neither can
Leo. It's real proof of Leo's fast-talking charm that he has a sixteen-year-old girlfriend. Leo's mother, who doesn't approve of
the girlfriend, drives the boys to the mall, because otherwise, she
says, they'd hitchhike. Maybe it's Leo's mother Dennis dislikes.
She gives in to the boys too easily. She was Christie's lawyer, trim
and venomous, during the divorce.

What kind of trouble does he imagine his son getting into?
Dennis has no very stable or obsessive idea, just occasional glints,
in which Kenny pockets a Baggie of white powder, or, with faked
knowingness, hoovers a furled five-dollar bill over a mirror, talked
into these idiot risks by Leo. None of those fears come true;
instead an altogether different problem materializes. The car
that startled him belongs to Kenny's mother.

Christie's never been in the house before, and one of his re-
actions at letting her in strikes Dennis as inappropriate, disturb-
ingly so, and he hides it: he'd like to know what she thinks. He's
an architect, and when he first came across this house it was a
warren of low-ceilinged rooms whose windows were, in the old-
fashioned way, quite small. Cottonwoods grew right up to the
walls. Such a shaded, wood-fragrant, down-at-heels little place:
he wanted it. In renovating, he's changed it very little.

"Nice," Christie says of the room, sitting, crossing her black
legs, beginning to pick at the cuticle of her thumb, and he asks
himself why he wanted more from her. Glancing up, she reads
his disappointment, and makes a face. *What do you expect?* the
face says. *This is where you live your new life.* The face implies that
she knew such a muted reaction would hurt. More than anything, he wants her to stop picking away at her cuticle. If she can
get at him so fast, so nonchalantly, he'd better watch out.

"Can we turn on another light?" she says.

When he does, he has to admire the kinked mass of her dark hair, backlit. Even with the glasses, she looks good. She's already lost whatever weight she gained with the baby.

"Coffee?" he says, for a chance to leave the room. He pokes through a drawer for Melitta filters, then stares around the kitchen, catching his emotional breath, reorienting himself. "Tea," Christie calls. Her tone's not rude, and he's no longer annoyed with her, but it troubles him that, this long divorced, it's taken them all of five minutes to fall back into marital shorthand. O.K. Tea. He carries their two cups back with him, feeling both more guarded and surer about where to begin.

"Christie, weeks went by when you didn't call him. Once you let it go a month. February, right?"

She has too much at stake to lose her temper with him. That would have been her familiar next move, but she holds it fast, though her black thug's boot kicks air. "It costs a fortune."

"Do you think he understood being abandoned for a year? Then you show up here and you'd like to pick up" — Dennis snaps his fingers — "right where we left off."

"Did he tell you he felt abandoned by me? Are those his words?"

"The agreement that you get him summers depended on your trustworthiness."

"You're saying I have to be as predictable as you are, Dennis. You're saying I should never have had George in my life. I don't think that was the agreement."

A sort of ongoing record of their exchange — the conversation as he will replay it for Francesca — runs through his mind. Francesca listening, taking everything in, sometimes shaking her head or marveling aloud, is his sanity. Francesca illustrates children's books. Christie's mercurial excess, which prevents her carrying anything through to the end, and Francesca's serene attention to detail — to root, trunk, twig, and every small, slanting leaf in the forest — could not be farther apart.

What fairy tale is it, where someone comes back at last for the beloved child? Because she's never seen well in the dark, he walks Christie out to her car. When a rock trips her, he catches her arm, and in the darkness she twists to face him before shaking off his hand. She would rather have fallen. They could be any bitter couple walking in the woods, tired of each other, tired of the way nothing is ever resolved between them. He had thought he was protected from such vivid involuntary remembrance of her past lives: her zazen phase, with its hours of formidable silence; the year during which she was convinced she was an actress; the macrobiotic diet she starved herself on; the novel she finished half of. There is an infant's car seat in the back of her Volvo, and she has wedged a bag of groceries in it, upright. So this visit really was on the spur of the moment.

Leaning into her window as she starts the Volvo, wanting to end on a slightly friendlier note, he asks whether she's found a place to live. She has. A week ago. In one of those apartment complexes where there's always something empty; he knows it.

Then she can't resist circling back to their quarrel. "So you're saying no for the summer?"

"I think too much has changed."

"What's changed is that you're even more judgmental than before."

"You hurt him," he says.

"Dennis, we need to talk about this again." She takes a hand from the wheel, raking her hair from her face, the dark-rimmed glasses picking up tiny spots of light from somewhere. "I'll call you," she says, and he can't tell her not to.

Tonk plunk: something goes in upstream, where dark boulders take the moonlight full force. A head black and broad as a Labrador's, and as purposefully at home, shaves across the glassy, swelling smoothness that is the deepest part of the river. A beaver, a big one, and upwind, or it would have known Dennis was there. The spring wind, balmy and humid, blows across the river, and as it stirs Dennis's hair there is that slight, single instant in which he feels himself blameless.

His divorce seems a tight black tunnel he once forced himself and Kenny through, fearing each forward move, fearing still more getting stuck and suffocating. A blindly crawling exit from pain, his shy kid shoved along before him. So Kenny loves motorcycles, which do not creep, which proclaim in every line speed and certainty. Christie didn't ask, or didn't think she could ask, to see Kenny's room. Dennis believes it tells everything about Kenny: photo-realist motorcycles, chrome and highly evolved threat, grace the walls, along with a frail Kafka razor-bladed from a library book, a sin so small and so unprecedented that Dennis uncharacteristically forgot to mention it to him. If Kenny's motorcycle paintings are depressing, surely jug-eared Kafka promises complexity, contradiction, hope? When he was a little boy, Kenny painted houses with peaked roofs, surreal cats and dogs and birds, petroglyph parents — Dennis and Christie — with their hands linked over the head of a smaller, round-eyed creature, Kenny himself. Orange sun, blue house, green grass, all's well. The garish houses dwindled; the figures grew dwarfish and highly detailed and began carrying machine guns; Dennis and Christie were replaced by superbly muscled superheroes trouncing bad guys and aliens, and Kenny was seven. Ten was the year of the divorce. Thirteen is this plague of motorcycles, Leo's flawless smile, and hanging out at the mall. Oddly — at least Dennis wouldn't have predicted it — Kenny wrote regularly to his mother in France. Because Kenny didn't seem to consider them particularly private, and he was curious, Dennis sometimes read the letters. The light of the computer screen glowed on his son's clear forehead. He wanted her to know that he liked having a little sister. He wanted her to know that he thought about her. He really worked on the letters. None of the obvious things (When was she coming home? Ever?) were in the letters. His son knew by thirteen not to ask Christie certain questions.

At the kitchen table Dennis eats slices of bologna folded into cold tortillas and drinks a beer, then scrapes and washes the day's dishes while the twins' bottles come bobbingly to a boil on the back of the stove. When Gavin wails, Dennis climbs the cantilevered stairs. Tim howls, coming to consciousness alongside his brother. Dennis lights a candle, his habit so that the overhead light won't dazzle Francesca, blinking awake. Dennis lays Gavin and Tim side by side on the bed. Francesca sits up. Theirs is a four-handed assembly line, the twins' bottoms bared, wiped, and diapered, neither boy crying, both staring from their giant calm father to their giant calm mother, who are talking softly together. Francesca takes Gavin; he can't lunge at the breast fast enough, and she laughs down at him. Though they're almost over the cold, the twins' breathing remains raspy. The wings of

Francesca's nose are coarsely red, and her chest has the tonic stink of Vicks Vaporub, which neither boy seems to mind. Dennis cradles Tim, leaning back in an old chair whose upholstery is a kind of friendly maroon moss worn away, on the arms, in matching bald spots his elbows rest in as he angles the bottle up. Tim's warm head rests in a hand large enough to cup it completely. What weight was ever this good? A baseball fresh from the sporting goods store, or his high school girlfriend's breasts released from chilly white bra cups in a dark Chevrolet. Maybe. Francesca is uneasy, Dennis can tell. She isn't sure she understands exactly what is wrong, though he's told her everything that was said.

He says, "She can't have him this summer."

"Kenny has a father *and* a mother."

That lightly stressed *"and"* is criticism, and, subtle as it is, it stirs him to argue. "You wouldn't know that by the last year."

"She was far away."

"That's no excuse," he says, knowing she knows it's not, having advanced it only so that they could both examine its weakness — could see, through the excuse's transparency, Christie's habitual irresponsibility. For a time they sit quietly, each with an urgently sucking baby, until, in Dennis's arm, Tim yawns, a thumb gliding into his mouth, his body's weight going sated and more vague, so that it's only a matter of settling him into the crib. Then Dennis leans to take Gavin. This is tense, because Gavin's crying, if he starts, will rouse his brother, but Gavin sleeps. Ah, silence. "We're good," Dennis says, and the answer is an amused, complicitous, "Good? Great." He sits on the bed, not ready yet to climb under the covers, some chord in him still vibrating at a tense, post-Christie pitch. Francesca stretches, then narrows her attention until it includes only him. To do this, she very deliberately excludes sleep. The intense, the velvety deep desirability of unbroken sleep is what Dennis senses most strongly whenever he enters this room. In any competition he wages for her against sleep, sleep's going to win. It has only to lap inward from the dark corners of the room to close over her head, and she has only to let herself slide luxuriously under, while what he wants, in wanting to make love, would ask effort of her, and an energy she doesn't have.

"Showing up here with no warning," Francesca says.

"It was weird."

"No wonder you resent it, but what convinced you she can't have Kenny?"

"She's lost the French boyfriend."

Francesca says, "What has that got to do with it, really?"

"How many guys does Kenny get to see come and go?"

"In three years there's been George. Not exactly promiscuous."

"Now Kenny has a sister he knows only from pictures."

"The sister was born in Paris," she says reasonably. "Kenny can get to know her here."

He wants Francesca on his side, not mediating between him and Christie. "She kept talking in non sequiturs." He places his hands, palms facing, in the air before her, implying the gaps between what Christie said and what she said next, but Francesca leans forward until his hands slide into a caress of her face, until, with two fingers, he tucks hair behind an ear, and then idly revolves the pearl resting against that ear's lobe, as if he were turning a tiny screw, tightening some connection that had, minutely, loosened.

"What's her baby's name?"

"Emma." He feels strange, saying it.

"I'd hate to see you be so unforgiving toward me," she says.

After a time he tells her thoughtfully, "I couldn't be," but she's asleep, her mouth slightly open, an arm flung out before her, her fingers lightly touching the wall, her entire body relaxed, loose, as lost as if she floated overhead in a Chagall, her nightgown trailing, leaving him and the sleeping babies below, stars around her.

The next afternoon Kenny comes in, home from somewhere, on his way somewhere else, and is struck enough by his father's expression to say, "You look weird." Dennis, lying back on his son's unmade bed under the portrait of a glitteringly malign Harley-Davidson, squeezing a racquetball in his left hand, answers, "Your mom's back."

Two squeezes of the ball before Kenny risks, "Yeah?" He is careful not to let slip how pleased he is, but in a lilting involuntary movement, younger than he is, he goes up on his toes, his long legs braced, and bounces, one arm holding the other arm at the elbow.

Dennis says, "Yes. Just last week. She was here last night."

"Is that what's wrong with you?"

"What's wrong with me is no sleep and I didn't shave and that makes me feel old." He dents the blue raquetball with his thumb and it oozes back into its sphere as he remembers that when his own father used to say he felt old it was a threat that Dennis suffered with an obscure and embarrassed guilt.

He reads in his son the same stiffening, the same resentment, as Kenny, at his dresser, fidgets a drawer open and shut, and Dennis says to his back, appealing to the cocky set of the shoulders and the vulnerability of the nape exposed by the Leolike haircut, "Look, I wanted you to know, but I was thinking you could spend the summer here. With us."

"You hate her," Kenny says intensely, talking down into the drawer, and Dennis starts to say, "Kenny, no, that's not right," when Kenny strips off his T-shirt, tearing it over his dark head, its shapely unknowable stubbornness so much like his mother's, and Dennis sees the violent bruise marbling his son's arm. The bruise resolves into a tattoo of a skeleton on a motorcycle, leaning forward as if into wind, black eye sockets, spiked helmet. Death, grinning on the freckled curve of adolescent biceps. Dennis slams the racquetball at the wall. It caroms past Kenny's shoulder. "Dad!" Kenny cries, like a child, and Dennis is up, taking two fast steps, grabbing the arm. Kenny twists away to stand against the wall, cornered.

"My God, it's ugly." Dennis hears the hoarseness of his own voice, the sound of a father's barely controlled anger. "I didn't want to believe it was real. Was this Leo's idea?"

"No, it was mine. Dad, it didn't hurt. The needles were really clean. I watched the guy sterilize them. That's the first thing you see when you walk into his place, this big sterilizer. Dad, it's my body. You would have said no. You know you would have said no."

It's my body. Dennis can't believe that. He can't conceive of having no say in what happens to this body, in no longer being needed to protect it. Kenny is five, shuddering in his arms; he has fallen into a doorjamb, slitting open his lower lip, and for some reason Dennis is catching the blood in his hand. Kenny is two, shrieking down at his own bare legs as the needle eases in. The nurse has told Dennis, who wanted to hold Kenny in his lap, facing his chest, that it's better if Kenny sees that it's the nurse who's hurting him. That way Kenny won't come to distrust his own father.

"What does it mean?" Dennis asks.

"It doesn't mean anything. It's just cool."

"You're thirteen years old," Dennis says, "and you'll be living with this the rest of your life."

"I want to live with it." Kenny pulls on a black T-shirt from his drawer, and the tattoo disappears under a sleeve. What he's defensive about, it hits Dennis, is that he does not regret the grinning little leather-jacketed death on its motorcycle. Part of him would like to drum up regret if that's the clue to his father's forgiveness, but the truth is he's now too old to summon emotion on demand, and too honest to fake it, without being insulated enough to fight his father without a fair amount of pain. Dennis catches himself making an abrupt accommodating shift, with this insight, in the direction of understanding his son as someone strictly separate from him. Perhaps the tattoo has accomplished what it was meant to. Perhaps it was meant to be something that couldn't be undone and something he couldn't possibly like about his child. That's it. His adoration has been unconditional. He's made Kenny have to wrestle it off. Something has changed between them, and here Kenny is, watching him covertly for signs that this is over. Over, so that he can go.

"You were so perfect when you were born," Dennis says, and is blindsided by the idea that the only other person who will truly mourn that perfection as he does is Christie. "You're grounded," Dennis says. "You can't leave this house."

When the phone rings that night, Francesca answers and mouths, "It's her." Dennis shakes his head. Holding Gavin against her shoulder, Francesca mouths, "Come on." He holds his left hand flat in the air, his right vertically below it, a *T*. Time out. Francesca, exasperated, has just enough grace to smile at him. She says, "Christie, he must have gone out. I didn't hear him leave. Kenny?" Dennis is shaking his head furiously. "Kenny's out with Leo. Sorry. I'll tell them both you called."

Two nights later, and this time Francesca's side of the conversation is: "He never called you? I gave him your message. I am sorry. His partner's away, so, you know. I'm sure he'll get back to you as soon as he can." Francesca listens a moment before adding, "I *agree* with you this can't go on much longer." When she hangs up, Francesca says, "Did you hear that last part?"

"I need time," he says.

Francesca shakes her head, marveling at his hard anger, his evasiveness, troubled by how far he's willing to take this. "She's not helpless," Francesca says. "She can always call her lawyer. I think you are in the wrong."

Without her on his side, it begins to strike him as stale, small-minded, increasingly indefensible, and a day later it comes to him that it's time he talked to Christie. Francesca looks up from drawing to kiss him goodbye, relieved at his decision. He leaves his office early to go to Christie's apartment. It's in a stucco complex of separate four-story buildings spaced around culs-de-sac and traffic islands spiked with dying yucca. He knew he should have called her first, but somehow he never got around to it. "You look terrible," people kept telling him all day, and he got tired of his own small joke, "I feel much worse than I look." Well, she surprised him, showing up without warning. Surely she can't be too put off if he does the same. When his knocks go unanswered, he feels around in the dirt under a flourishing white geranium. Christie's houseplants always thrived. She always left a key under one of her plants by the front door, though he'd asked her not to a thousand times. He lets himself in, telling himself he's going to call out to see if she's there after all, but once inside he makes no sound. Stealth, it strikes him, is no light thing, but very physical. He's breathing faster than he likes, as if he'd run two miles along the river road, his heart banging. Her baby's toys lie all around. The bright clutter, for some reason, makes him panicky. In his own house, he would begin picking things up; he'd know how to go about setting things straight. Here he can't. He's stymied by the very fact that he's an intruder. An intruder is an unreasonable thing to be. *You are in the wrong;* maybe more deeply than ever before. Leo's mother could make a capital case out of this. As if with foresight, he dressed for the part. His Levi's have a tear over one knee, and his shabby sneakers, gray with age, let him move lightly, brimming with guilt and yet slightly high on it, through the mess, which seems to him evidence of happiness, her happiness, which he long ago divorced himself from, which he has no right to know anything of. All this, everything he sees, is contraband. A jack-in-the-box has been left as it was, sprung open, the vacantly grinning head hanging upside down from the long caterpillarlike sleeve of the body, and here is a naked doll seated in a chair, and on the couch *Vanity Fair* open to a picture of Kevin Costner, leaning back, shirt loose, glass in hand. Dennis feels scathingly appraised by Kevin Costner.

On the far side of a narrow counter is the kitchen, furnished in paint-splattered furniture she must have got at the Salvation Army. Four straight-backed chairs are dashed with brilliant blue, while the small table is a scarred palette of yellow, turquoise, hot pink, and silver. It looks as if an abstract expressionist went insane here. There are crumbs of burned toast in the high chair's tray and a smear of apricot jam. The floor is fifties linoleum, tan tiles with faint white cirrus drifting across them, and on one tile Christie — or someone — has painted a tiny airplane. She has been using *The Frugal Gourmet*, which is propped open by her mother's (he remembers) tin recipe box. In the refrigerator, nothing much — milk, bread, juice, the usual, and a half-empty bottle of Beaujolais with the cork floating in the wine. She never handled corkscrews well. Peanut butter. Garlic, fat cloves in mauve-white paper. He takes the garlic out — garlic's not supposed to go in the refrigerator — but, holding the crisp little weight, he doesn't know what to do with it. If he leaves it out, she's going to know someone was here. There's nothing to do but put it back. He does.

Emma's room, sunny and disheveled, the crib against a wall on which hangs a small Amish quilt, its corners frayed, a powdery-pleasant baby smell and folded clothes in wire drawers under a changing table. A basket of teething rings. A kazoo. A child's rocker. Balled up in the crib, a pair of baby tights and a striped sock. A second small bedroom, darker, shades down, must be meant for Kenny. There's something wonderful in being in this room, and he's still high on his amazed apprehension of his own wrongdoing, floating on it, willing to stay with it a little longer now that he's come this far. His hearing feels hyperacute, but there's nothing, no sound, and his sense of what he's seeing seems magnificently, magically clear. He would never have known any of this. She could never have told him. If she'd wanted to tell him, he wouldn't have listened. Here are things she thinks Kenny will like: a cowboy bedspread, a glaring African mask, an aquarium filled with water, oxygen percolating through it, no fish yet but some kind of seaweed hypnotically weaving, and, clinging to the glass, small snails black as capers. A desk fashioned from a sheet of melanite laid over sawhorses. A bright blue dresser. The drawers, when he opens them, are empty, except that the last drawer contains a Hershey's Kiss.

As he sits heavily on the bed, his exhilaration dies. It doesn't so much desert him in a rush as evaporate, and a befuddling gray fatigue fogs over the vacuum it leaves in him. This stupid midafternoon sleepiness feels entirely ordinary. He lies back on the bed and puts an arm over his face, breathing in the smell of himself — slightly sweaty, salty guilt. Still no sound; it feels good. He even feels he's in the right place.

He dreams a dream he thinks of later as intended for Kenny. Kenny should have dreamed it; by accidentally falling asleep in this bed, Dennis got it. In it, Christie is younger, Kenny barely old enough to work a scissors, the two of them sitting on the floor with their dark heads together, cutting animals from brilliant paper, the air between them charged with great, disinterested tenderness, not talking. The animals they cut out come alive. A monkey jumps to his knee, and Kenny giggles. Christie sets a blue giraffe down on the floor and it canters stiffly away. Waking, Dennis's first thought is that he's dreamed a dream he wasn't in. He can't remember ever having had such a dream before. In some subtle shift in the room's shadows, he reads a new degree of lateness, of sheer wrongness in being here, and his body responds with a rising rush of adrenaline, but he still doesn't move. He wonders if what he really wants is to get caught. In another minute he's able to tell himself, *That would really be the height of stupidity,* and sit up. His body hates his refusal to get moving. He shakes his head to clear the last of the sleep from it, but the mysterious peacefulness of the dream still has a hold on him. What he's seen won't let go so easily.

Back through the apartment, each thing in its place, everything exactly as he found it, it begins to appear to him that he's
getting away with this. He lets himself out and finds it is later
than he thought, probably six-thirty or so. When he checks the
parking lot two stories down, she's not there: her dark-rimmed
glasses aren't aimed upward in stunned accusation, and though
he fumbles, locking the door, her Volvo does not materialize.
He twitches geranium leaves out of the way, sliding the key back
where she likes it.

This is not happiness, just a gaudy physiological response to
not getting caught — light head, hands shaking, legs he has to
will steady to get himself down the stairs, world that looks entirely strange.

"I thought I couldn't leave the house until I was thirty-two," Kenny
says, his feet on the dash, looking around the maze of stucco
buildings he's never seen before.

"You can't," Dennis says. "The one place you can come is here.
I want you to call me for your ride home. No taking off. No
improvising."

"But I can stay the weekend."

"You can stay the weekend if you want."

"Why?"

"I was wrong before," Dennis says. "I was just wrong."

"But how did you see you were wrong?"

"You don't get to know all the details."

"Does Mom?"

"I haven't talked to her."

"You mean she doesn't know I'm coming?"

"She's home. There's her car, right?"

"I don't like surprising her," Kenny says quietly.

"O.K. You really don't like it, we turn around, we drive home,
we get on the phone, we arrange this for some other time. Is
that how you want to do this?"

He hesitates, and then says, as quietly, "I guess so." Dennis
starts the car; maybe this was a bad idea, but he'd liked the feel
of it. He'd wanted to change things all at once. He'd wanted the
suddenness of the reversal on his side in convincing Christie that
things were going to be different from now on, and he hadn't

guessed that it might be Kenny who didn't like the idea, who seemed unprepared for it.

"Stop," Kenny says, removing his feet from the dash, sitting up. "I'm going. O.K.?"

"Whatever you want to do."

"I'll call you."

"Call."

He's gone. He's on the stairs, bag on his shoulder, lighter-footed than his father can remember ever being, taking the two flights of stairs as if they were nothing. Then Christie is at the door in black jeans, a man's T-shirt huge on her, her son taller than she is. That she's amazed is clear in every line of her body. She and Kenny don't step nearer or embrace. They just stand talking, and then Dennis sees Christie move to her porch rail, looking down at him bewildered, and he waves at her, a wave that means *I can't explain it.*

CHRISTOPHER TILGHMAN

In a Father's Place

FROM PLOUGHSHARES

DAN HAD FALLEN asleep waiting for Nick and this Patty Keith,
fallen deep into the lapping rhythm of a muggy Chesapeake
evening, and when he heard the slam of car doors the sound
came first from a dream. In the hushed amber light of the foyer
Dan offered Nick a dazed and disoriented father's hug. Crickets
seemed to have come in with them out of the silken night, the
trill of crickets and honeysuckle pollen sharp as ammonia. Dan
finally asked about the trip down, and Nick answered that the
heat in New York had forced whole families onto mattresses in
the streets. It looked like New Delhi, he said. Then they turned
to meet Patty. She stood there in her Bermuda shorts and shirt,
her brown hair in a bun, smelling of sweat and powder and looking impatient. She fixed Dan in her eyes as she shook his hand,
and she said, I'm so glad to meet *you.* Maybe she was just talking
about the father of her boyfriend, and maybe no new lover ever
walked into fair ground in this house, but Dan could not help
thinking Patty meant the steward of this family's ground, the
signer of the will.

"Nick has told me so much about this place," she said. Her
look ran up the winding Georgian staircase, counted off the low,
wide doorways, took note of a single ball-and-claw leg visible in
the dining room, and rested on the highboy.

"Yes," said Dan. "It's marvelous." He could claim no personal
credit for what Patty saw, no collector's eye, not even a decora-
tor's hand.

Rachel had arrived from Wilmington earlier in the evening,

and she appeared on the landing in her nightgown. She looked especially large up there after Dan had taken in Patty's compact, tight features; Rachel was a big girl, once a lacrosse defenseman. "Hey, honey," she yelled. There had been no other greeting for her younger brother since they were teenagers. Nick returned a rather subdued hello. Tired, thought Dan, he's tired from the trip and he's got this girl to think about. Rachel came down the stairs; Patty took her hand with the awkwardness young women often show when shaking hands with other young women, or was it, Dan wondered as he watched these children meet in the breathless hall, a kind of guardedness?

Dan said, "You'll be on the third floor." He remembered his own father standing in this very place, saying these same words to polite tired girls; he remembered the underarms and collar of his father's starched shirt, yellowed and brushed with salt. But it was different now: when Dan offered the third floor — and he had done so for some years now — he meant that Rachel or Nick could arrange themselves and their dates in the three bedrooms however they wished.

"The third floor?" said Patty. "Isn't your room on the second floor looking out on the water?" She appealed to Nick with her eyes.

"Actually, Dad . . ." he said.

Dan was still not alert enough to handle conversation, especially with this response that came from a place outside family tradition. "Of course," he said after a long pause. "Wherever you feel comfortable." She wants a room with a view, that's all, he cautioned himself. They had moved deeper into the hall, into a mildewed stillness that smelled of English linen and straw mats. They listened to the grandfather clock on the landing sounding eleven in an unhurried bass.

Dan turned to Patty. "It just means you'll have to share a bathroom with Ray, and she'll fight you to the last drop on earth."

But Patty did not respond to this attempt at charm, and fortunately did not notice Rachel's skeptical look. It was an old joke, or, at least, old for them. Dan remained standing in the hall, slowly recovering from his dense, inflamed sleep as Nick and Patty took their things to the room. Patty seemed pleased, in the end, with the arrangements, and after Dan had said good night and retired to his room, he heard them touring the house, stopping at the portrait of Edward, the reputed family ghost, and admiring the letters from General Washington in gratitude for service to the cause. Theirs wasn't a family of influence anymore, not even of social standing to those few who cared, but the artifacts in the house bracketed whole epochs in American history, with plenty of years and generations left over. He heard Patty saying "Wow" in her low but quite clear-timbred voice. Then he heard the door openings and closings, the run of toilets, a brief, muffled conversation in the hall, and then a calm that returned the house to its creaks and groans, to sounds either real or imagined, a cry across the fields, the thud of a plastic trash can outside being knocked over by raccoons, the pulse of the tree toads, the hollow splash of rockfish and rays still feeding in the sleepless waters of the bay.

A few years ago Dan had taken to saying that Rachel and Nick were his best friends, and even if he saw Nick rarely these days, he hoped it was largely the truth. He'd married young enough never to learn the art of adult friendship, and then Helen had died young enough for it to seem fate, though it was just a hit-and-run on the main street of Easton. Lucille Jackson had raised the kids. Since Helen died there had been three or four women in his life, depending on whether he counted the first, women he'd known all his life who had become free again one by one, girls he'd grown up with and had then discovered as he masturbated in his teens, or who had appeared with their young husbands at lawn parties in sheer cotton sundresses that heedlessly brushed those young thighs, or who now sat alone and distracted on bleachers in a biting fall wind and watched their sons play football. At some point Dan realized if you stayed in a small town all your life, you could end up making love with every woman you had ever known and truly desired. Sheila Frederick had been there year after year in his dreams, at the lawn parties, and at football games, almost, it seemed to Dan later, as if she were stalking him through time. When they actually came together Dan stepped freely into the fulfillment of his teenage fantasies, and then stood by helplessly as she ripped a jagged hole eight years wide out of the heart of his life. There had been one more woman since then, but it was almost as if he had lost his will, if not his lust; the first time he brought her to the house she asked him where he kept the soup bowls, and in that moment he could barely withstand the fatigue, the unbearable temptation to throw it all in, that this innocent question caused him.

He undressed in the heat and turned the fan to hit him squarely on the bed. The air it brought into the room was damp but no cooler, the fecund heat of greenhouses. He felt soft and pasty, flesh that had lost its tone, more spent than tired. He tried to remember if he had put a fan in Nick's room, knowing that Nick would not look for one but would blame him in the morning for the oversight; Rachel, in a similar place, would simply barge in and steal his. Dan knew better than to compare the two of them, and during adolescence boys and girls were incomparable anyway. But they were adults now, three years apart in their mid-twenties, and noticing their differences was something he did all the time. Rachel welcomed being judged among men; and her lovers, like the current Henry, were invariably cheerful, willing bores. This tough, assertive Patty Keith with those distrustful sharp eyes, there was something of Nick's other girls there, spiky, nursing some kind of damage, expecting fear. Patty would do better in the morning. They always did. As he fell asleep finally, he was drifting back into history and memory, and it was not Patty Keith, and not even Helen meeting his father, but generations of young Eastern Shore women he saw, coming to this house to meet and be married, the ones who were pretty and eager for sex, the ones who were silent, the ones the parents loved much too soon, and the ones who broke their children's hearts.

In the morning Dan and Rachel ate breakfast together in the dining room, under the scrutiny of cousin Oswald, who had last threatened his sinful parishioners in 1681. The portraitist had caught a thoroughly unpleasant scowl, a look the family had often compared to Lucille on off days. She had prepared a full meal with eggs, fried green tomatoes, and grits, a service reserved as a reward when they were all in the house. When Nick and the new girl did not come down, Lucille cleared their places so roughly that Dan was afraid she would chip the china.

"I'm done with mothering," she said, when Dan asked if she wasn't curious to meet Patty.

Dan and Rachel looked at each other and held their breath.

"I got six of my own to think about," she said. And then, as she had done for years, a kind of rebuke when Nick and Rachel were fighting or generally disobeying her iron commands, she listed their names in a single word. "LonFredMaryHenny-TykeDerek."

"And you'd have six more if you could, besides Nick and me," said Rachel.

"And you better get started, *Miss* Rachel," she said.

"How about a walk," said Dan quickly.

August weather had settled in like a member of the family, part of the week's plans. The thick haze lowered a scorching dust onto the trees and fields, a blanched air that made the open pastures pitiless for the Holsteins, each of them solitary in the heat except for the white specks of cowbirds perched on their withers. Dan was following Rachel down a narrow alley of brittle, dried-out box bushes. She was wearing a short Mexican shift and her legs looked just as solid now as they did when she cut upfield in her Princeton tunic. He would not imagine calling her manly, because hers was a big female form in the most classic sense, but he could understand that colleagues and clients, predominantly men, would find her unthreatening. She gave off no impression that she was prone to periodic weaknesses; they could count on her stamina, which, the older he got, Dan recognized as the single key to business. Nick was slight and not very athletic, just like Helen.

"So what do you think?" she asked over her shoulder.

"If you're talking about Patty I'm not going to answer, I don't think anything."

She gave him an uncompromising shrug.

They came out of the box bush on the lower lawn at the edge of the water and fanned out to stand side by side. "The truth is," said Dan, "what I'm thinking about these days is Nick. I think I've made a hash of Nick."

"That's ridiculous." She stooped to pick a four-leaf clover out of an expanse of grass; she could do the same with arrowheads on the beach. They stood silently for a moment looking at the sailboat resting slack on its mooring. It was a heavy boat, a nineteen-foot fiberglass sloop with a high bow, which Dan had bought after a winter's deliberation, balancing safety and speed the way a father must. When it arrived Nick hadn't even bothered to be polite. He wanted a "racing machine," something slender and unforgiving and not another "beamy scow." He was maybe ten at the time, old enough to know he could charm or hurt anytime he chose. Rachel didn't care much one way or the other — life was all horses for her — and Dan was so disappointed and angry with them both that he went behind the toolshed and wept.

"It's not. I really don't communicate with him at all. I don't even know what his book is about. Do you?"

"Well, I guess what it's really about is you. Not really you, but a father, and this place."

"Just what I was afraid of," said Dan.

"I don't think any of it will hurt your feelings, at least not the pieces I've read."

"Stop being so reassuring. A kiss-and-tell is not my idea of family fun." But Dan was already primed to be hurt. He'd been to a cocktail party recently where a woman he hardly knew forced him to read a letter from her daughter. It was a kind of retold family history, shaped by contempt, a letter filled with the word "never." This woman was not alone. It seemed so many of the people he knew were just now learning that their children would never forgive things, momentary failures of affection and pride, mistakes made in the barren ground between trying to keep hands off and the sin of intruding too much, things that seemed so trivial compared to a parent's embracing love. And even at the time Dan had never been sure what kind of father Nick wanted, what kind of man Nick needed in his life. Instead, Dan remembered confusion, such as the telephone calls he made when he still traveled, before Helen died. Rachel came to the phone terse and quick — she really was a kind of disagreeable girl, but so easy to read. Nick never had the gift of summarizing; his earnest tales of friends and school went on and on, until Dan, tired, sitting in a hotel room in Chicago, could not help but drop his coaxing, nurturing tone and urge him to wrap it up. Too often, in those few short years, calls with Nick ended with the agreement that they'd talk about it more when he got home, which they rarely did.

"But that's really my point," said Dan after Rachel found

nothing truly reassuring to say. "This has been going on for quite a while. I'm losing him. Maybe since your mother died, for all I know."

"Oh, give him time."

"He's changed. You can't deny that. He's lost the joy."

"No one wants to go through life grinning for everyone. It's like being a greeter in Atlantic City."

"I don't think he would have come at all this week if you weren't here." It felt good to say these things, even if he knew Rachel was about to tell him to stop feeling sorry for himself.

But Rachel cleared her throat, just the way her mother did when she had something important to say. "See," she said, "that's the thing. I've been waiting to tell you. I've got a job offer from a firm in Seattle, and I think I'm going to take it."

Dan stopped dead; the locusts were buzzing overhead like taut wires through the treetops. "What?"

"It's really a better job for me. It's general corporate practice, not just contracts."

"But you'll have to start all over again," he whined. "I'd really hate to see you go so far away."

"Well, that's the tough part."

Dan nodded, still standing in his footsteps. "I keep thinking, 'She can't do this, she's a girl.' I'm sorry."

He forced himself to resume walking, and then to continue the conversation with the right kinds of questions — the new firm, how many attorneys, prospects for making partner — the questions of a father who has taught his children to live their own lives. They didn't touch on why she wanted to go to Seattle; three thousand miles seemed its own reason for the move, to be taken well or badly, just like Nick's novel. Dan pictured Seattle as a wholesome and athletic place, as if the business community all left work on Fridays in canoes across Puget Sound. It sounded right for Rachel. They kept walking up toward the stable, and Dan hung back while Rachel went in for a peek at a loved, but now empty, place. When she came back she stood before him and gave him a long hug.

"I'm sorry, but you'll have to humor the old guy," he said.

She did her best; Dan and Lucille had raised a kind woman. But there was nothing further to say and they continued the wide arc along the hayfield fences heavy with honeysuckle, and back out onto the white road paved with oyster shells. They approached the house from the land side, past the old toolsheds and outbuildings, and Dan suddenly remembered the time, Rachel was ten, when they were taking down storm windows and she had insisted on carrying them around for storage in the chicken coop. He was up on the ladder and heard a shattering of glass, and jumped from too high to find her covered in blood. Dr. Stout pulled the shards from her head without permanent damage or visible scar before turning to Dan's ankle, which was broken. Helen was furious. But the next time Dan saw Dr. Stout was in the emergency room at Easton Hospital, and they were both covered with Helen's blood, and she was dead.

Patty and Nick had come down while they were gone, and Dan found her alone on the screened porch that had been once, and was still called, the summer kitchen. It was open on three sides, separated from the old smokehouse on the far end by a small open space, where Raymond, Lucille's old uncle, used to slaughter chickens and ducks. The yellow brick floor was hollowed by cooks' feet where the chimney and hearth had been; Dan could imagine the heat even in this broad, airy place. Patty was sitting on a wicker chair with her legs curled under her, wearing a men's strap undershirt and blue jogging shorts. She was reading a book, held so high that he could not fail to notice that it was by Jacques Derrida, a writer of some sort whose name Dan had begun to notice in the Sunday *New York Times*. Perhaps she had really not heard his approach, because she put the book down sharply when he called a good morning.

"Actually we've been up for hours," she said.

"Ah. Where's Nick?"

"He's working," she said with a protective edge on it.

Again, all Dan could find to say was "Ah." She smiled obscurely — her smiles, he observed, seemed to be directed inward — and he stood for a few more seconds before asking her if she would like anything from the kitchen. There was no question in his mind now: he was going to have to work with this one.

Rachel had just broken her news to Lucille, and the wiry, brusque lady who was "done mothering" at breakfast was crying soundlessly into a paper towel.

"I don't know what it is about you children, moving so far away," she said finally. Dan knew at least one of her sons had moved to Salisbury, and she had daughters who had married and were gone even farther.

"We've gotten by, by ourselves," said Dan.

"But that was just for schooling, for training," she answered; training, if Dan understood her right, for coming back and assuming their proper places in the family tethers. She was leaning against the sink, a vantage point on her terrain, like Dan's desk chair in his Queensville office, the places where both of them were putting in their allotted time. Rachel was sitting at the kitchen table and she stayed there, much as she might have liked to come closer to Lucille and reach out to her.

Dan went back to the summer kitchen and sat beside the girl. "You'll have to excuse us. Rachel's just dropped a bit of a bombshell and we're all a little shaky."

"You mean about her moving to Seattle."

"Well, yes. That's right." He waited for her to offer some kind of vague sympathies, but she did not; it was asking too much of a young person to understand how much this news hurt.

"So," he said finally, "I hope you're comfortable here."

At this she brightened noticeably and put her book face-down on the table. "It's a museum! Nick was going to set up his computer on that pie crust table. Can you imagine?"

Dan could picture it well and he supposed it would be no worse than the time Nick had ascended the highboy, climbing from pull to pull, leaving deep sneaker scuffs on the mahogany burl as he struggled for purchase. But she was right, of course, and she had known enough to notice and identify a pie crust table. "You know antiques, then?"

Yes, she said, her mother was a corporate art consultant and her father, as long as Dan had asked, was a doctor who lived on the West Coast. She mentioned a few more pieces of furniture that caught her eye.

"My mother thinks Chippendales and Queen Anne have peaked, maybe for a long time."

"I wouldn't know," said Dan.

"But the graveyard!" she exclaimed at the end.

Dan was relieved that she had finally listed something of no monetary value, peak or valley, something that couldn't be sold by her mother to Exxon. "As they say in town," he answered, "when most people die they go to heaven; if you're a Williams you just walk across the lawn."

"That's funny."

"I guess," he said. It was all of it crap, he reflected, if he became the generation that lost its children. He'd be just as dead now as later.

"They're the essential past."

Essential past? Whatever could she mean, with her Derrida at her side, her antiques? "I'm not sure I understand what you mean, but to tell you the truth," he said, "I often think the greatest gift I could bestow on the kids is to bulldoze the place and relieve them of the burden."

"I think that's something for the two of them to decide."

"I suppose coming to terms with all this is what Nick is up to in his novel." The girl had begun to annoy him terribly and he could not resist this statement, even as he regretted opening himself to her answer.

"Oh," she said coyly, "I wouldn't say 'coming to terms.' No, I think just looking at it more reflexively. He's trying to deconstruct this family."

"Deconstruct? You mean destroy?" he said quickly, trying not to sound genuinely alarmed.

Patty gave him a patronizing look. "No. It's a critical term. It's very complicated."

Fortunately Nick walked in on this last line. It was Dan's first chance to get a look at him and he saw the full enthusiasm — and the smug satisfaction — of one who has worked a long morning while others took aimless walks. Nick was gangly, he would always be even if he gained weight, but surprisingly quick. As unathletic as he was, he had been the kind of kid who could master inconsequential games of dexterity; he once hit a pong paddle ball a thousand times without missing, and could balance on a teeter-totter until he quit out of boredom. All his gestures, even his expressions, came on like compressed air. And while Dan had to work not to speculate on what part of himself had been "deconstructed" today, this tall, pacing, energetic man was the boy he treasured in his heart.

"The Squire has been surveying the grounds?" said Nick.

"Someone has to work for a living," said Dan, quickly worrying that Nick might miss the irony.

"I was wondering what you called it," he answered.

Patty watched this exchange with a confused look. Any kind of humor, even very bad humor, seemed utterly to escape her. "Did you finish the chapter?" she asked.

"No, but I broke through. I'm just a scene away. Maybe two."

"Well," she said with a deliberate pause, "wasn't that what you said yesterday?"

Good God, thought Dan, the girl wants to marry a published novelist, a novelist with antiques. He said quickly, "But it seems you had a great" — too much accent on the great — "a really very productive morning of work."

Nick's face darkened slightly, as fine a change as a razor cut. "It's kind of a crucial chapter. It has to be right."

"Were you tired?" she asked.

"No. It's just slow, that's all."

During this conversation Rachel had shouted down that lunch was ready, and Dan hung back for the kids to go first, and he repeated this short conversation to himself. It was not such a large moment, he reflected, but nervous-making just the same, and during lunch Nick sat quietly while Patty filled the air with questions, questions about the family, about Lord Baltimore and the Calverts. They took turns answering her questions, but finally it fell back to Nick to unlace the strands of the family, to place ancestors prominently at the Battle of Yorktown. He looked now and again to Dan for confirmation, and Dan knew how he felt reciting these facts that, even if true, could only sound like family puffery. Dan wanted to do better by his son and did try to engage himself back into the conversation, but by the time Lucille had cleared the plates he felt full of despair, gummy with some kind of sadness for all of them, for himself, for Rachel now off to Seattle in a place where maybe no one would marry her, for Nick with this girl, for Lucille so much older than she looked, and hiding, Dan knew it, her husband's bad health from everyone.

Patty ended the meal by offering flatteries all around the table, including compliments to Lucille that sent her back to the kitchen angrily — but loud enough only for Dan's practiced ear — mimicking the girl's awkward phrase, "So pleasant to have eaten such a good lunch." As they left the table finally, Dan announced he had to spend the afternoon in his office. At this point, he wasn't sure what he would less rather do. He changed quickly and left for town with the three of them discussing the afternoon in the summer kitchen, and he could hear Rachel laboring for every word.

He was so distracted as he drove to town that he nearly ran the single stoplight. Driving mistakes, of any kind, went right to his living memory; once he slightly rear-ended a car on Route 301, and he bolted to the bushes and threw up in front of the kids, in front of a very startled carload of hunters. He crawled to Lawyers' Row and came in the door pale enough for Mrs. McCready — it had always been *Mrs.* McCready — to comment on the heat and ask him if his car air conditioner was working properly. His client was waiting for him, Bobbie Perlee, one of those heavy, fleshy teenagers in Gimme caps and net football jerseys, with greasy long hair. The smell of frying oil and cigarettes filled his office. Whenever he had thought of Rachel joining his practice, he had reminded himself that she would spend her time with clients like this one, court-appointed, Bobbie Perlee in trouble with the law again, assaulting his friend Aldene McSwain with a broken fishing pole. McSwain could lose the eye yet. But Dan couldn't blame a thousand Perlees on anyone but himself; he had made the choice to practice in Queensville when it became clear that the kids needed him closer to home and not working late night after night across the bay in Washington. If she had lived, Helen would have insisted anyway.

"What do you have to say this time, Bobbie?"

Bobbie responded with the round twangy *O*'s of the Eastern Shore, a sound that for so long had spelled ignorance to Dan, living here on a parallel track. He said nothing in response to Bobbie's description of the events; he didn't really hear them. Bobbie Perlee pawed his fat feet into Dan's worn-out Persian rug. For a moment it all seemed so accidental to Dan; sitting in this office with the likes of Bobbie Perlee seemed both frighteningly new and endlessly rehearsed. He could only barely remember the time when escape from the Eastern Shore gave meaning and guided everything he did. It was there when he refused to play with the Baileys and the Pacas, children of family and history like himself. It was there when he refused to go to "the University," which, in the case of Maryland gentry, meant the University of Pennsylvania. It was there even the night he first made love, because it was with his childhood playmate, Molly Tobin. They had escaped north side by side for college, and came together out of loneliness, and went to bed as if breaking her hymen would shatter the last ring that circled them both on these monotonous farmlands and tepid waters.

But he'd come back anyway when his father was dying, and brought Helen with him, a Jew and a midwesterner who came with a sense of discovery, a fresh eye on the landscape. Helen had given the land back to Dan, and Sheila Frederick had chained him to it, coming back out of his youth like a lost bookend, with a phone call saying *I don't look the same, you know,* and because none of them did — it had been thirty years — it meant she was still pretty. She lived in a bright new river-shore condo in Chestertown. She was still pretty, but now when she relaxed, her mouth settled into a tight line of bitterness. Their last night, two years ago, after a year of fighting, she told Dan she worried about his aloneness, not his loneliness which was, she said, her problem and a female one at that, but his aloneness as he rattled around that huge house day after day, with no company but that harsh and unforgiving Lucille. From her, this talk and prediction of a solitary life was a threat; to Dan, at that moment, anyway, being alone was perfect freedom.

Dan finally waved Perlee out of his office without anything further said. These lugs, he could move them around like furniture and they'd never ask why. Dan looked out his office window onto the Queen Anne's County courthouse park, a crosshatching of herringbone brick pathways shaded under the broad leaves of the tulip trees. At the center gathering of the walks was a statue of Queen Anne that had been rededicated by Princess Anne herself. She was only a girl at the time but could have told that wildly enthusiastic crowd a thing or two about history, if they'd chosen to listen. Dan had done well by his children, if today was any indication. They were free not because they had to be, but because they wanted to be. Rachel won a job offer from three thousand miles away because she was that good. My God, how would he bear it when she was gone? And Nick was reaching adulthood with a passion, on the wings of some crazy notion about literary deconstruction that, who knew? could well be what they all needed to hear and understand. So, in many ways, his thoughts ended with this sad girl, this Patty Keith, who seemed the single part of his life that didn't have to be, yet it was she who had been tugging him into depression and ruminations on the bondages of family and place all afternoon.

On the way home he stopped at Mitchell Brothers Liquors, a large windowless block building with a sign on the side made of a giant *S* that formed the first letter of "Spirits, Subs, and Shells." The shells, of course, were the kind you put into shotguns and deer rifles. The Mitchells were clients of his and were very possibly the richest family in town. He bought a large bottle of Soave and at the last minute added a jug of Beefeaters, which was unusual enough for Doris Mitchell to ask if he was having a party. He answered that Nick was home with a girlfriend that looked like trouble, and he was planning to drink the gin himself.

The summer kitchen was empty when he stepped out, gin and tonic in hand. A shower and a first drink had helped. He might have hoped for the three of them, now fully relaxed, to be there trading stories, but instead they came out one by one, and everyone was carrying something to read. He supposed Patty was judging him for staring out at the trees and water, no obscure Eastern European novel in his hand. Nick was uncommunicative, sullen really, this sullenness in the place of the sparkling joy he used to bring into the house. Dinner passed quickly. Afterwards, Patty insisted that Nick take her to the dock and show her the stars and the lights of Kent Island the way, she said firmly, he *promised* he would. Rachel and Dan turned in before they got back, and Dan read *Newsweek* absently until the last of the doors had closed, and he slipped out of his room for one of his house checks, the changing of the guard from the mortals of evening and the ghosts of the midwatch. He was coming back to his room when he heard a cry from Nick's room. In shame and panic he realized that they were making love, but before he could flee he heard her say. "No. No." It wasn't that she was being forced, he could tell that immediately; instead, there was a harshness to it that, even as a father is repelled at the idea of listening to his son have sex, forced Dan to remain there. He had not taken a breath, had not shifted his weight off the ball of his left foot; if anyone had come to the door he would not have been able to move. There was more shuffling from inside, a creak as they repositioned in the old sleigh bed. "*That's* right," said Patty finally. "Like *that*. Like that." Her voice, at least, was softer now, clouded by the dreaminess of approaching orgasm. "Like that," she breathed one last time, and came with a thrust. But from Nick, this whole time, there had not been a word, not a grunt or a sound, so silent he was that he might not have been there at all.

"I think she's a witch," said Rachel. They were on their post-breakfast walk again, this time both of them digging in their heels in purposeful strides.

Dan let out a disgusted and fearful sigh.

"No. I mean it. I think she's using witchcraft on him."

"If you'll forgive the statement, it's cuntcraft if it's anything."

"That's pretty, Dad," she said. They had already reached the water and were turning into the mowed field. "But I'm telling you, it's spooky."

All night Dan had pictured Patty coming, her legs tight around Nick's body, her thin lips clenched pale, and her white teeth dripping blood.

"She controls him. She tells him what to do," said Rachel. "If this were Salem she'd be hanging as we speak."

They had now walked along the hayfield fence line through the brown grass, and said nothing more as they turned for the house, its lime-brushed brick soft and golden in the early morning sun.

"It won't last. He'll get over her," he said.

"Yes, but the older you are the longer it takes to grow out of things, wouldn't you say?"

Dan nodded; Rachel, as usual, was quite right about that. It had taken him six months to figure out that Sheila Frederick was one of the worst mistakes of his life, and another seven years to do something about it. It would not have been so bad if it weren't for the kids. He could admit and confess almost everything in his life except for the fact that he had known, for years, how much they hated her. They hated her so much that when it was over, Nick didn't even bother to comment except to tell Dan he'd seen her twice slipping family teaspoons into her purse.

They skirted the graveyard and without further discussion bypassed the house for another tour. As they went by, Dan glanced over his shoulder, and there she was, Derrida in hand, a small voracious lump that had taken over a corner of the summer kitchen. He looked up at the open window where Nick was working.

"I think I'd better marry Henry," said Rachel.

"He's a very nice guy. You know how fond of him I am," said Dan.

"Nice, but not very interesting. Is that what you mean?"

"Not at all. But as long as you put it this way, I think this Patty Keith is interesting."

"So what are we going to do about Miss Patty?" asked Rachel.

"Well, nothing. What can we do? Nick's already mad at me; I'm not going to give him reason to hate me by butting into his relationships."

"But someday Nick's going to wake up, maybe not for a year, or ten years, and he'll realize he's just given over years of his life to that witch, and then isn't he going to wonder where his sister and father were all that time?"

"It doesn't work that way. Believe me. You don't blame your mistakes in love on others."

Rachel turned to look at him fully with just the slightest narrowing of focus. It was an expression any lawyer, from the first client meeting to the last summary to the jury, had to possess. "Are you talking about Mrs. Frederick?" she said finally.

"I suppose I am. I'm not saying others don't blame you for the mistakes you make in love." Without any trouble, without even a search of his memory, Dan could list several things Sheila had made him do that the kids should never, ever forgive. What leads us to live our lives with people like that?

"No one blames you for her. The cunt."

Dan was certain that Rachel had never before in her whole life used that word. He laughed, and so did Rachel, and he put his arm on her shoulder for a few steps.

She said finally, with an air of summary, "I really think you're making a mistake. I believe she's programming him. I mean it. I think she's dangerous to him and to us. It happens to people a lot more resilient and less sensitive than Nick."

"We'll see." They walked for a few more minutes, in air that was so still the motion of their steps felt like relief. Again Rachel was right; he was a less sensitive man than his son but he had been equally powerless to resist the eight years he had spent with Sheila. Dan couldn't answer for his own life, much less Nick's, so they completed their dejected morning walk and climbed the brick steps to the back portico. As they reached the landing, he took his daughter in his arms again and said, "God, Rachel, I'm going to miss you."

When they came back Patty was in the kitchen talking to Lucille. From the sound of it she had been probing for details about Nick as a boy, which could have been a lovely scene if it hadn't been Patty, eyes sharp, brain calculating every monosyllabic response, as if, in the middle of it, she might take issue with Lucille and start correcting her memories. It's not the girl's fault, thought Dan; it's just a look, the way her face moves, something physical. There was no way for Patty to succeed with Lucille; no girl of Nick's could have done better. It's not Patty's fault, Dan said to himself; she's trying to be nice but she just doesn't have any manners; her parents haven't given her any grace. He said this to himself again later in the morning when she poked her head into his study and asked if his collection of miniature books was valuable. Mother obviously did not deal in miniatures although, Dan supposed, she would be eager to sell Audubons to IBM. Dan answered back truthfully that he didn't know, some of his books may be valuable, as a complete collection it could be of interest to someone. She took this information back with her to the summer kitchen. Dan watched her walk down the hall, a short sweatshirt that exposed the hollow of her back and a pair of those tight jersey pants that made her young body look solid as a brick.

Dan did not see Nick come down, did not hear whether he had finished his chapter and whether that was enough for Patty. At lunch Rachel noted that the Orioles were playing a day game, and Dan had to remind himself again that except for sailing, the athlete in the family was the girl, that she'd been not only older but much more physical than her brother. He remembered how he and Helen had despaired about Nick, a clinger, quick to burst into tears at the first furrowing of disapproval; how Dan had many times caught a tone from the voices in the school playground right across the street from his office, and how he had often stopped to figure out if it was Nick's wail he heard, or just the high-pitched squeals of the girls, or the screech of tires on some distant street. And how curious it was that with this softness also came irrepressible energy, the force of the family, as if he saved every idea and every flight of joy for Dan and Rachel. Yet it had been years now that Nick had turned it on for him.

For once, Patty seemed content to sit at the sidelines while Rachel and Nick continued with the Orioles. Name the four twenty-game winners in 1971, said Rachel, and Nick, of course, could manage only the obvious one, Jim Palmer. Rachel's manners — they were Lucille's doing as much as his, Dan reminded himself — compelled her to ask Patty if she could do any better; Patty made a disgusted look and went back to her crab salad. At that point Dan saw the chance he had been waiting for, and he turned to Nick and told him he had to go see a client's boat — a Hinckley — that was rammed by a drunk at Chestertown mooring. "Come on along and we'll catch up," he said offhandedly. He looked straight into Nick's eyes and would not allow him to glance toward Patty.

"Hey, great," said Nick after the slightest pause. "How about later in the afternoon?"

"Nope. Got to go at low tide. The boat sank." His tone was jocular, the right tone for cornering his son before Patty could move, before she started to break into the conversation with her "Wait a minute" and her "I don't understand." Rachel moved fast as well and quickly suggested, in a similar tone, that they, in the meantime, would go see the Wye Oak, the natural wonder of the Eastern Shore. "We can buy T-shirts," said Rachel.

"But . . ."

A few minutes later Dan and Nick were on the road in Dan's large Buick. There was considerable distance between them on the seat. "I hope Patty doesn't mind me stealing you like this," Dan said finally.

Nick could not hide his discomfort, but he waved it all off.

"Women," said Dan.

Nick let out a small laugh. He was sitting with his body turned slightly toward the door, gazing out at the familiar sights, the long chicken sheds of McCready's Perdue operation, the rustic buildings of the 4-H park under the cool shade of tall loblolly pines.

"So how's it going? The novel."

Good, he said. He'd finished his chapter.

"You know," said Dan, working to something he'd planned to say, "I'm interested to read it anytime you're ready to show it. I won't mention it again, just so long as you know. I can't wait to see what it's about."

"Oh," said Nick, "it's not really *about* anything, not a plot, anyway. I'm more interested in process. It's kind of part of a critical methodology."

Dan wanted to ask what in the world that meant, but could not. "Patty seems interested. I'm sure that's helpful."

"Patty's energy," Nick said, finally turning straight on the seat, "is behind every word."

"She certainly is a forceful girl." Dan realized his heart was pounding, and that it was breaking as he watched Nick come to life at the mention of her name.

"She tore the English department at Columbia *apart*." He laughed at some private memory that Dan really did not want to hear. "I know she's not for everyone, but I've never known anyone who takes less shit in her life."

And I love her, he was saying. I'm in love with her because she doesn't take shit from anyone. Not like you, Dan heard him think, who is living out his life a prisoner of family history. Not like you who let Mrs. Frederick lock me out the night I ran away from my finals in freshman year. Dan supposed the list was endless.

And at this impasse something could well have ended for him and Nick. It would not come as a break, a quarrel, but it would also not come unexpectedly or undeserved. In the end, thought Dan, being Nick's father didn't mean he and his son couldn't grow apart; didn't mean a biological accident gave him any power over the situation. It meant only that it would hurt more. He could not imagine grieving over friends he once loved with all

his heart and now never saw. The Hellmans, how he had loved
them, and where in the world were they now? But Nick, even if
he never spoke to him again, even if this Patty Keith took him
away to some isolation of spirit, Dan would know where he was
and feel the pain.

"So why so glum, Dad?" said Nick, a voice very far away from
the place where Dan was lost in thought.

"What?"

"I mean, we're going to see a wreck, a Hinckley, for Christ's
sake, and you're acting like you owned it yourself."

They were crossing the long bridge over the Chester, lined, as
always, with market fishermen sitting beside plastic pails of bait
and tending three or four poles apiece. Twenty years ago they'd
all been black, now mostly white, but there had not been too
much other change in this seventeenth-century town; Dan had
never known how to take this place, old families jostling to the
last brick even as they washed and sloshed their way down Washington Street on rivers of gin. But it was a lovely town, rising off
the river on the backsides of gracious houses, brick and slate
with sleeping porches resting out over the tulip trees in a line of
brilliant white slats. Dan looked ahead at this pleasant scene while
Nick craned his neck out to the moorings.

"Oh yes," he said. "There's a mast at a rather peculiar angle."

The boat was a mess, lying on its side on a sandbar in a confused struggle of lines, a tremendous fibrous gash opening an
almost indecent view of the forward berths. Nick rowed them
out in a dinghy no one knew who owned; he was full of cheer,
free, no matter what, on the water. The brown sandbar came up
under them at the edge of the mooring like a slowly breaching
whale. As they came alongside, Nick jumped out and waded over
to the boat, peered his head through the jagged scar, and then
started hooting with laughter.

"What is it?" said Dan.

Nick backed his head out of the hull. "Porn videos. God, there
must be fifty of them scattered over the deck."

Dan quickly flashed a picture of his rather proper Philadelphia client, who could have no idea that his most secret com-
partment had been burst in the crash.

"Jesus," said Nick. "Here's one that is actually called *Nick My
Dick*. It's all-male."

"Stop it. It's none of your business," said Dan, but he could not help beaming widely as he said this, and together they plowed the long way back through the moorings, making loud and obnoxious comments about most of the boats they passed. Dan doubted any of these tasteless, coarse stinkpots, all of the new ones featuring a dreadful palette of purples and plums, contained a secret library to compare with the elegant white Hinckley's. After they returned the boat they strolled up Washington Street to the court square and stopped for an ice cream at one of the several new "quality" establishments that had begun to spring up here. Dan hoped, prayed, only that Sheila Frederick, who lived here, would not choose this moment to walk by, but if she did she would simply ignore him anyway, which would not be a bad thing for Nick to see.

But it was all bound by the return, as if Nick were on furlough. And it was certain to be bad, Dan could sense it by now as they turned through the gates back to the farm. This time, when they re-entered the summer kitchen, the Derrida remained raised. As far as Dan could tell she had made little headway in this book, but she stuck to it through Nick's stray, probing comments about their trip. For the first time she struck Dan as funny, touchingly adolescent, with her tight little frown and this pout that she seemed helpless, like a twelve-year-old, to control. No, she had *not* gone to see the Wye Oak. No, she did not wish for any iced tea.

This is how it went for the rest of the day and into the evening. She's in quite a snit, said Rachel when they passed in the front hall, both of them pretending not to be tiptoeing out of range of the summer kitchen, which had seemed to grow large and overpowering around that hard nub of rage. Nick also circled, spending some of the time reading alongside the girl, some of the time upstairs writing a whole new chapter, perhaps a whole new volume, as penance. It was Lucille's day off, and normally eating at the kitchen table gave the family leave to loosen up, a kind of relief from the strictures of life. Patty sat but did not eat, just made sure that everyone understood, as Nick might have said, that she wouldn't take this shit. Dan could not imagine what she was telling herself, how she had reconstructed the events of the afternoon to give her sufficient reason for all this. In the silence, everything in the kitchen, the pots and pans, the appliances and spices, seemed to close in, all this unnecessary clutter. The pork chops tasted like sand; the back of the chair cut into his spine. He tried to picture how she might describe this to friends, if she had any. He could not guess which one of them had earned the highest place in this madness, but he knew which one of them would pay. He'd seen it in couples all his life, these cycles of offense and punishment, had lived the worst of it himself with Sheila Frederick. When she finally left the table, and Nick followed a few minutes later — he gave a kind of shrug but his face was blank — Rachel tried to make a slight joke of it. "We are displeased," she said.

"No. This is tragic," said Dan. "She's mad."

They cleaned the dishes, and after Rachel kissed him good night he went out into the darkness of the summer kitchen. The air, so motionless all week, was still calm but was beginning to come alive; he could hear the muffled clang of the bell buoy a mile into the river. A break in the heat was coming; the wildlife that never stopped encroaching on this Chesapeake life always knew about the weather in advance, and the voices became shortened and sharp. The squirrels' movements through the trees or across the lawns became quick dashes from cover to cover; the beasts and beings were ready, even to a lone firefly, whose brief flashes gave only a staccato edginess to a darkening night. Dan felt old; he was tired. For a moment or two his unspoken words addressed the spirits of the house — they too never stopped encroaching — but he stopped abruptly because he knew, had known since a boy, that if he let them in he would never again be free of them. He wondered if Helen would be among them. He waited long enough, deep into this skittish night, for everyone to be asleep; he could not stand the thought of hearing a single sound from Nick's room. But when he finally did turn in he could not keep from hesitating for a moment at the door, much as he and Helen used to when the children were infants, and they needed only the sound of a moist breath to know all was well.

Under the door he saw that the light was on, and through it he heard the low mumble of a monotone. It was her, and it was just a steady drone, a break now and again, a slightly higher inflection once or twice. It was a sheet of words, sentences, if they were written, that would swallow whole paragraphs, and though Dan wanted to think this unemotional tone meant her anger was spent, he knew immediately that this girl was abusing his son. She was interrogating him without questions; she was damning him without accusations, just this litany, an endless rosary of rage. It could well have been going on for hours, words from her mad depths replacing Nick's, supplanting his thoughts. He could make out no phrase except, once, for a distinct "What we're discussing here . . ." that was simply a pause in the process as she forced him to accept not only her questions, but her answers as well. He did not know how long he stood there; he was waiting, he realized after a time, for the sound of Nick's voice, because as Dan swayed tired back and forth in the hall, he could imagine anything, even that she had killed him and was now incoherently continuing the battle over his body. When finally the voice of his son did appear, it was just two words. "Christ, Patty." There was only one way to read these two names: he was begging, pleading, praying for her to stop. And then the drone began again.

He closed his bedroom door carefully behind him, and sat by his bay window in an old wingback that had been Helen's sewing chair. Her dark mahogany sewing table was empty now, the orderly rows of needles and spooled threads scattered over the years. The wide windows beckoned him. He could feel no breezes on his sweating forehead and neck, but the air was flavored now with manure, milk, gasoline, and rotting silage, a single essence of the farm that was seeping in from the northwest on the feet of change. He stared out into the dark for a long time before he undressed, and was still half awake when the first blades of moving air began to slice through the humidity. He was nodding off when later, on his pillow, he heard the crustacean leaves of the magnolias and beeches begin to clatter in the wind.

The house was awakened by the steady blow, an extravagance of air and energy after these placid weeks of a hot August. Dan could hear excited yips from the kitchen, as if the children were teenagers once again; he thought, after what he had heard and the hallucinations that plagued him all night long, that he was dreaming an especially cruel vision of a family now lost. But he went down to the kitchen and they were all there: Rachel, as

usual grumpy and slow moving in the morning and today looking matronly and heavy in her long unornamented nightgown;
Patty, standing on the other side by the refrigerator with a curiously unsure look; Lucille at her most abrupt, wry best; and Nick,
wearing nothing but his bathing suit, pacing back and forth, filled
with the joy and energy only a few hours ago Dan had given up
as lost forever.

"A real wind," he said. "A goddamn hurricane."

"Shut your mouth with that," said Lucille happily.

"We're going to sail all the way to the *bridge*," he continued,
and poked Rachel in the side with a long wooden spoon until
she snarled at him.

"I've got to wash my hair," said Rachel.

"Fuck your hair."

Lucille grabbed her own wooden spoon and began to move
toward him, and he backed off toward Patty, who was maybe
tired out from her efforts the night before, or maybe just so
baffled by this unseen Nick that even she could not intrude. Nick
picked her up by the waist and spun her around. She was in her
short nightgown and when Nick grabbed her he hiked it over
her underpants; even as Dan helplessly noticed how sexy her
body was, he recoiled at the thought of Nick touching it. With
mounting enthusiasm, Dan watched this nervy move and wondered whether it would work on her, but she struggled to get
down and was clearly furious as she caught her footing.

"I agree with Rachel," she said. It was probably, Dan realized,
the first time she'd ever used Rachel's name.

Nick persisted. "Wind like this happens once a year. It might
blow out."

"It could be flat calm again by lunch," said Dan.

She turned quickly on Dan as if he hadn't the slightest right
to give an opinion, to speak at all. "I *understand*," she whined. "I
just think this is a good chance for him to get work done."

It was "him," Dan noticed. He waited for Nick's next move
and almost shouted with triumph when it came.

"Fuck work." As he said this, a quite large honey locust branch
cracked off the tree outside the window and fell to a thud through
a rustle of leaves.

Patty screwed her face into a new kind of scowl — she had

more frowns, thought Dan, and scowls and pouts than any person he ever met — and announced, "Well I'm not going. I'm going to get *something* done."

"Derrida?" said Dan. He was still giddy with relief.

She glared.

"Oh, come on, sweetie," Nick coaxed. "You won't believe what sailing in wind like this is like." He tried cajoling in other ways, promises of unbroken hours of work, a chance to see the place from the water; he even made public reference to the fight of the day before when he told her a sail would "clear the air after that awful night." He could be worn down by this, Dan knew; he could still lose. But earlier in the conversation Rachel had slipped out and now, with a crash of the door that was probably calculated and intentional, she came back into the kitchen in her bathing suit — she really should watch her weight, Dan couldn't avoid thinking — and that was all the encouragement Nick needed.

Dan walked down to the water with them and sat on the dock as they rigged the boat. The Dacron sails snapped in slicing folds; the boom clanked on the deck like a road sign flattened to the pavement in a gale. "Is it too much?" he called out. Of course it was; under normal circumstances he would be arguing strenuously that it was dangerous. They all knew it was too much. Nick called back something, but he was downwind and the sound was ripped away as soon as he opened his mouth. They cast off and in a second had been blown a hundred feet up the creek. They struggled quickly to haul in the sails; Rachel was on the tiller and Dan wished she wasn't because she was nowhere near the sailor Nick was; she would have been better on the sheets where her brute strength could count. But she let the boat fall off carefully and surely, and all of a sudden the wind caught the sails with a hollow, dense thud, and as they powered past the dock upwind toward the mouth of the creek, Dan heard Nick yell, full voice and full of joy, "Holy shit!"

When he got back to the house she was in her place in the summer kitchen. How tired he was of her presence, of feeling her out there. All the time — it was maybe nothing more than a family joke, but it was true — she had been sitting in his chair. Nick may have told her, or she may have even sensed it. He walked through the house and was met, as he expected, as he had hoped, with an angry, hostile stare.

"You don't approve of water sports, I gather?" he said, ending curiously on a slightly British high point.

She fixed him in her gimlet eyes; this was the master of the Columbia English department.

"Not interested?" he asked again.

"As a matter of fact, I don't approve of very much around here."

"I'm sorry for that," he said. He still held open the possibility that the conversation could be friendly, but he would not lead it in that direction. "It hasn't seemed to have gone well for you."

"There's nothing wrong with *me*."

"Ah-ha."

"I think you're all in a fantasy."

Dan made a show of looking around at the walls, the cane and wicker furniture, and ended by rapping his knuckles on the solid table. He shrugged. "People from the outside seem to make a lot more of this than we do," he said.

She leaned slightly forward; this was the master of his son. "It's not for me to say, but when you read Nick's novel you'll know where *he* stands."

The words exploded from him. "How dare you bring Nick's novel into this."

"Why do you think he wanted to come here, anyway?"

"Patty," said Dan, almost frightened by the rage that was now fevering his muscles, "when it comes to families, I really think you should let people speak for themselves. I think you should reconsider this conversation."

"You have attacked me. You have been sarcastic to me. I have nothing to apologize for." She made a slight show of returning to her book.

"Tell me something. What are your plans? What are your plans for Nick?"

"Nick makes his own plans."

It was not a statement of fact; it was a threat, a show of her larger power over him. "And you? What are your plans?"

"I'm going to live my own life and I'm not going to pretend that all this family shit comes to anything."

"Whose famil   Yours

"You mean do I plan to marry Nick? So I can get my   ds
on this?" She mimicked his earlier gesture. "I suppose th   hy
from the second, the very second I walked in, you have disapproved of me. Well, don't worry" — she said this with a patronizing tone, addressing a child, a pet — "the only thing I care
about around here is Nick and . . ." She cut herself off.

"And what?"

"And his work. Not that it matters to you."

"Oh, cut the crap about his work. You want his soul, you little
Nazi, you want any soul you can get your hands on."

She pounded the table with her small fist. "What we're talking
about here . . ." she shouted, and Dan's body recoiled with this
phrase, "is the shit you have handed out, and I'll cite chapter
and verse, and —"

"Patty, Patty." He interrupted her with difficulty. "Stop this."

"I have some power, you know."

"Patty, I think it would be better for everyone if you left. Right
now."

"What?"

"You heard me."

"You would throw me out?" She did, finally, seem quite stunned.
"And just what do you think Nick's going to do when he gets
back?"

"I don't know. But I will not tolerate you in my house for
another minute."

She slammed her feet down on the brick floor and jumped up
almost as if she planned to attack him, to take a swing at him.
"O.K., I will. I'm not going to take this shit."

She marched through the kitchen, and a moment or two later
he heard a door slam. He moved from his seat to his own chair;
suddenly the view seemed right again, the pecan lined up with
blue spruce by the water, and the corner of the smokehouse
opened onto a hay land that had, from this vantage, always reminded him of the fields of Flanders. A few minutes later he
heard a heavy suitcase being dragged over the yellow pine staircase, the steel feet striking like golf spikes into the Georgian treads.
He heard a mumble as she came to the kitchen to say something
tactical to Lucille, perhaps to give her a note for Nick or to play

the part of the tearful girl unfairly accused. He heard the trunk of her car open and he pictured her hefting her large bag, packed with dresses and shorty nightgowns and diaphragms and make-up, over the lip of her BMW, and then she was off, coming into view at the last minute in a flash of red.

Dan heard Lucille's light step, and then saw her face peer out onto the summer kitchen. As many times as Dan had tried to make her change, she never liked to come into a room to say something, but would stand in the doorway and make everyone crane their necks to see her.

"Mister Dan?"

"Lucille, *please* come out."

She took two steps. "You're in a mess of trouble now."

He held his arms up. "What could I do?"

"You just gotta make sure you're picking a fight with the right woman."

Dan looked away as she said this, and hung his head slightly, as if he expected her to say plenty more. But when he glanced back up she was smiling, such a rare and precious event.

"I got six of my own to worry about," she said. The wind was singing through the screens in a single, sustained high note. "But I do hope to the good Lord that those babies are O.K. out in this storm."

Dan stayed in the summer kitchen all morning. The winds weren't going to die down this time — he knew that the moment he woke up — it was a storm with some power to it and it would bring rain later in the day. He ate lunch in his study, and around two went down to the dock. The water was black and the wind was slicing the wave tops into fine spray. No one should be out in this, and not his two children. He pictured them, taking turns at the tiller as the boat pounded on the bottoms and broke through the peaks in a shattering of foam. He wasn't worried yet; he'd selected that big boat for days like this. It would swamp before it would capsize and they could run for a sandy shore any time they wanted. The winds would send them back to this side; he'd sailed more than one submerged hulk home as a boy, and he'd left a boat or two on the beach and hiked home through the fields. This was the soul of the Chesapeake country, never far from land on the water, the water always meeting the land, always in flux. You could always run from one to the other. The water was there, in the end, with Sheila, because he had triumphed over her, had fought battles for months in telephone calls that lasted for hours and evenings drowned in her liquors, until one morning he had awakened and listened to the songs from the water and realized that he was free.

He lowered his legs over the dock planking and sat looking out into the bay. From this spot, he had watched the loblolly pines on Carpenter's Island fall one by one across the low bank into the irresistible tides. When the last of the pines had gone the island itself was next, and it sank finally out of sight during the hurricanes of the fifties. Across the creek Mr. McHugh's house stood empty, blindfolded by shutters. What was to become of the place now that the old man's will had scattered it among nieces and nephews? What was to happen to his own family ground if Rachel went to Seattle for good and Nick . . . and Nick left this afternoon, never to come back?

Dan tried to think again of what he would say to Nick, what his expression should be as they closed upon the mooring, what his first words should cover. But the wind that had already brought change brushed him clean of all that and left him na-ked, a man. He could not help the rising tide of joy that was coming to him. He was astonished by what had happened to him. By his life. By the work he had done, the wills, the clients, all of them so distant that he couldn't remember ever knowing them at all. By the wife he had loved and lost on the main street of Easton, and by the women who had since then come in and out of life, leaving marks and changes he'd never even bothered to notice. By the children he fathered and raised, those children looking out from photographs over mounds of Christmas wrap-pings and up from the water's edge, smiles undarkened even by their mother's death. By his mistakes and triumphs, from the slap of a doctor's hand to the last bored spadeful of earth. It was all his, it all accumulated back toward him, toward his body, part of a journey back through the flesh to the seed where it started, and would end.

Commuter Marriage

FROM THE HUDSON REVIEW

ON THE PLATFORM at Penn Station, at 6:30 on a Saturday morning, a young woman in a red sweater stood waiting for the Boston train to pull in. She was small and slim, with short light hair
pulled back into a stubby ponytail. Two shiny pieces had slipped
out to frame her face, which looked quite young, schoolgirlish,
although she was twenty-seven. The childish look was height-
ened by the fact that she was wearing bright red lipstick and
smoking a short smelly cigarette, and doing neither with much
authority. On her bony forearm was an enormous man's watch
on a black rubber strap; every few seconds she shook her arm
until the watch flopped down around her wrist, and she frowned
at it, with a crease down the center of her freckled forehead.

The train came in a little late, and very slowly, as though aware
of its own charisma — a faraway circle of light moving in, growing bigger, pulsing a little in the dark air of the tunnel, and then
behind it a lumbering line of coaches, big, gray, dusty, hooked
together like elephants in the circus. She knew that they were
full of people, but it was still a surprise when the train gave a
sigh and the passengers started coming out: sudden clutter and
commotion all over that still platform. I am a woman meeting
her husband at a train, she thought, and it made her feel important, glamorous, like someone in a forties movie. She looked into
the faces of the men surging across the floor past her. How would
I feel if he were my husband? Or he? And then she saw Jack,
and tried to think for one objective moment: and what about
this one? But he was pressing his arms around her and bringing

his face down against hers. "Ow," she said after a minute. "Your suitcase."

He let go of her instantly and stepped backwards with the suitcase which had been pressing into her legs; then he looked down at it, frowning slightly, as though it were a child he had called into his study to scold, but now he had it there he couldn't remember what it had done wrong or figure out how to punish it.

They checked the suitcase, leaving it in a dented metal locker. "Why can't we just go back to the apartment?" Jack said, his mouth against her ear.

She shrugged; he still seemed a little strange and foreign, his hair a different length from when she had seen him last: someone she had just met at a train. "Ed and Caterina are there."

"Toss 'em out," suggested Jack.

"We can't do that. It's their apartment. I thought we'd spend the day doing New York things, and then go home. They're going out to dinner tonight, Caterina said."

"That's tactful of them."

"Don't be so grouchy."

"How about if we check into a hotel for the day? Does that count as a 'New York thing'?"

She hesitated, then kissed him quickly and bent to lift the suitcase and heave it into the locker.

The sight of Maisie as always, even after five years together, turned him shy. She was so pleasing to look at, so neat. When she got out of bed in the morning, the bed was made. Her small body, naked, was surprisingly voluptuous, yet neat: small brownish nipples centered on round breasts, a golden isosceles triangle suspended between small shining hips. Her clothes, folded in the drawer at home, were deceptively inanimate, like sleeping faces — stacks of black jeans, flat-folded sweaters, and T-shirts in all colors, aqua, fuchsia, lime, black. Then she put them on and they belonged to her, she inhabited them.

Marrying Maisie had surprised him, like having a strange cat come to sleep in his lap: the mystery of being singled out. Dreaming his way through graduate school, he had met her at a party one spring and walked her home, up the stairs, into a bare cool apartment where they sat on the floor and talked until morning. He could not remember leaving; his life with Maisie stretched back to that dawn, a continuum, a filibuster: if one of them stopped talking, the whole thing would be over. Maisie seemed like a detour from the fate that really belonged to him, dull, safe; he felt as though he had mistakenly got on the wrong bus, to a much more thrilling destination; his sense of honor prodded him to tell the driver, but he knew that if he told, he'd be put off.

They had lived together before they were married, but not much after. When they met, Jack was in the middle of a Ph.D. in German literature. They lived in each other's apartments and then consolidated into one place, in a noisy student-filled apartment building on the Fenway in Boston. All night long the building shook with the bass notes of a hundred stereos. They had to put their clothes bureau in the living room; their bed completely filled the tiny bedroom. Maisie worked as a secretary in the Harvard natural history museum; she hadn't figured out yet what she wanted to do. She cooked dinners for friends and dragged Jack dancing every couple of months. On Sundays they went for long walks and drank wine by the river and ended up at a foreign movie. Then Jack's father died and left him a French-fry factory up in Maine. That sobered them both, a bucket of cold water. Jack had to go, for a while at least, to untangle the threads of the business and find someone else to run it or buy it. Of course I'm coming, said Maisie. I'll be the boss's wife, and I'll give gracious dinner parties that will intimidate the hell out of your employees. They got married and moved north, to a little cottage in a wintry deserted beach community. Two rooms upstairs and two rooms downstairs, and a fireplace that didn't work.
  Something was wrong with the heat in that house. No matter how high they turned the thermostat, the rooms were still icy; at night the sheets were stiff and painful. One morning the pipes froze. Jack, swearing, put on his coat and brought in shovelfuls of snow, filling the bathtub with it, so that when it melted they would have water. Three days later the snow was still there, frozen, in the tub. Night after night Maisie sat on the couch wrapped in a blanket, watching television. She watched comedies and westerns and late-night reruns and the news, impassively. Her

mother came to visit from Virginia for a few days and said she
thought the house could be charming, if only Maisie would do
something with it. Why didn't they take the car over to Calico
Corners and pick out some nicer curtain fabric, and maybe make
some cushions for the living room? Maisie shook her head; this
question seemed to her unanswerable. Her mother and Jack
looked at each other, worried; good, thought Maisie, good.

So when she said she wanted to try working in publishing, and
that the only place to do that was New York, Jack was actually
relieved. It was the first time she'd wanted to do anything since
they'd moved to Maine. Caterina and Ed said they'd love to have
her. ("Are you kidding?" said Caterina over the phone. "A built-
in babysitter!") Maisie had read articles about husbands and wives
pursuing careers in separate states, with enormous phone bills,
hopping on and off planes. She saw herself arrive back in New
York after a few days in Maine with Jack: a long tanned leg (they
had spent the weekend sailing) thrusting out of a taxicab, followed by a briefcase bulging with manuscripts, and glowing Maisie
saying "Keep the change" and tossing her hair back and running
up the stairs two at a time to her top-floor brownstone apartment. When Jack came down she would let her answering service take all the calls, while she and Jack lay in bed before an
enormous atelier window. Then she would get up naked and call
in for her messages, impatiently writing them down with a silver
pencil: call this agent and that agent, and this famous writer is
stuck on his book and needs your advice, and can you fly out to
California this week to discuss the movie rights for that horrible
but phenomenally successful potboiler you pulled out of the slush
pile last year?

When they left the station, she took him to her office, which he
had not seen in his two previous visits to her in New York. The
Saturday darkness and emptiness stripped it of its importance.
How could she make him see the bustle of the book-lined reception area, the flashing lights on the telephones, the sheets of paper curling out of typewriters and computer printers? On the
other hand, the desertion of the place gave Maisie new power;
she was free to stroll down the long halls pointing out the offices
of editors, walking around conference tables and letting her hand

trail along their gleaming surfaces. She stopped to show him the
aquarium in her boss's office; he bent obediently to look through
the glass at a tower of slow ascending bubbles, rainbow-skinned
fish hanging still in greenish water. She did not tell him it was
part of her job to feed them. Then on to her cubicle, where she
had left the desk strewn with urgent-looking clutter: memos, three
fat manuscripts, message slips, mailing envelopes stamped
PRIORITY, all put there in excitement the night before, knowing that the next time she saw them Jack would be with her,
impressed. But he only glanced at the desktop. He lifted and
dropped the cover of a thesaurus that lay on top of her filing
cabinet, and looked at the topless walls and said, "It must be kind
of distracting, working in here," and she could tell he was thinking, you left me alone up there to come work in a cubicle?

To get to the factory, you drove north, north, north. You smelled
it before you saw it, an oily fried smell breathing out of the pines
along the road. It was cold where the factory was, always winter,
but the building gave off a feverish yellow sweat, and the snow
in the parking lot was slippery with grease. When you came away,
you smelled of it. Jack's hair was cold and greasy, and his clothes;
the first thing he did when he got home was take a shower. He
went to the factory every day and sat in his father's old office
overlooking a slippery ravine behind the building: graying grass-
cloth walls, cans of old paper clips and pencil ends, manila fold-
ers, their ends softened and frayed, iron tiered trays with IN and
OUT written on masking tape in his father's handwriting, faded
and stuck on too long ago now to come off. A diagram on the
wall proclaiming the respective merits of the Maine and Idaho
potatoes, and adjudging the Maine superior; hidden in the desk
a research report revealing that more consumers preferred Idaho.
Under the rickety swivel chair a plastic T-shaped mat designed
to protect the carpet; it was too late for the carpet, which was
filthy and beaten down, but all day Jack swiveled the chair around
on the mat: his island. He was the king in a parliamentary king-
dom; there was nothing for him to do. The business ran itself:
the potato buyers, truckers, peelers, cutters, oilers, packagers,
shippers, and distributors were all in place, doing their jobs. At
home in the first few months, he and Maisie had talked brightly

about changes that would make the company more profitable and more attractive to a prospective buyer: new cuts, new packaging, new advertising, new incentives to make supermarkets carry the brand. But every day, when he came into the office, the heavy oily air sucked the ideas right out of him; he fell into the chair and swiveled, looking out the window, until it was time to go home. The things on the desk acquired the cachet of heirlooms, things his father had wanted him to have.

They walked around on broad, mica-specked sidewalks. They stopped for brunch at a deli. They went to museums, where Maisie stopped intently in front of everything and Jack circled with his hands in his pockets and his jaw tight, willing the day to move along. They had coffee in a coffee shop, their elbows drooping on the scarred Formica tabletop. Being alone this way, in public, was exhausting; they had things to talk about, and the longer the things went unsaid, the bigger they loomed. The afternoon grew cooler; the sun went behind the buildings; and Fifth Avenue was suddenly, miraculously navigable, cleared of shoppers and people with cameras. "Can we go to the apartment yet?" said Jack, his feet dragging like a little boy's.

"Not yet," said Maisie, looking at her watch.

"It's not as though I don't know Caterina and Ed, or don't like them," said Jack. "I have no objection to sitting around and talking to them for a while."

"I want to be alone with you," Maisie said, and took him to walk around Tudor City.

Finally she let them get on a subway. There were free seats in the car, but someone had thrown up in one of them, and there was Kitty Litter sprinkled on top of it and around it. Maisie and Jack stood at the other end, hanging onto metal loops, with Jack's suitcase wedged between them. The trip took an hour. Jack said, "I can't believe you do this every day." Brooklyn, when they got there, was a dark, misty orange sky hanging over squat buildings packed with lamplit windows. "I guess all those kitchens are full of families having Saturday night supper," Jack said. He imagined kids in pajamas, after their baths, and a grandmother reading to them or playing War with them, while the mother scrambled eggs. But Maisie said no, she thought the apartments were full of people taking showers and putting on make-up and getting dressed for dates.

Caterina and Ed's apartment was in a row of brownstones, some of which had carved wooden doors with beveled glass panes, and chandeliers inside and glimpses of living rooms painted dark green, with white shutters at the windows and track lighting overhead; and some of which had iron doors with metal grilles on them, and bedsheets over the windows instead of curtains. They lived in a bedsheet building, up two flights on a black iron staircase that hung off a shiny brown wall. Maisie turned keys in a series of locks and at the last minute the door was pulled open by Ed, who had wet hair and a faint mentholated shaving cream smell. "Caterina's getting dressed," he said, shaking hands with Jack. "How've you been?"

Maisie kept Jack and his suitcase in the kitchen until after Ed and Caterina left, leaving the phone number of the restaurant where they would be. She wanted him to walk through the apartment not as a guest, but as a possessor. Yet following him through it, down the hall to her bedroom, she felt a bit embarrassed, the way she had when her parents came to visit her at college: two worlds, both loved, but best kept apart.

His suitcase lay in the middle of her immaculate floor, filled with a jumble of clothes he hadn't bothered to fold. She thought of him in the little house in Maine last night, bachelorlike, just throwing things in. And now it was as though the pressure of some pent-up desire had burst the suitcase open; socks and shirts had exploded all over the room. The very messiness of it made her nervous. She had a stately plan for this reunion: some wine, dinner in the kitchen with candles and Caterina's linen napkins, a talk over coffee and cigarettes, and then a procession down the dark hall to bed. The sound of Jack splashing in the bathroom, the implacable hiss of the shower, filled her with dread; she felt as though something irreversible had been set in motion, a clock ticking steadily toward an hour. When he came out, red and shiny and scrubbed, she barely looked at him, ducked past him into the steamy bathroom, where she wiped off the mirror to look at her pale reflection and tried to remember how much she had missed him. His wet towel, crowding Caterina's on the towel rack, made the bathroom look sloppy; she took it and hung it on the back of the door. When she came out, she realized she had stayed in the bathroom too long; there was Jack, lying naked with the shades down. She wished he would not do that, take off his own clothes; it seemed so businesslike. But she could hardly ask him to get dressed again so that she could undress him. She untied her shoes and put them side by side next to the bed, and she lay down beside him.

Afterwards she was relieved: a responsibility discharged, the library books renewed and now you didn't have to worry about them for another two weeks. Relief made her lively; she threw back the covers and kissed him and told him not to move, she'd check on the baby and throw together some dinner. But he came after her anyway, slowly belting himself into his bathrobe. The baby was sleeping on her stomach, her head turned to the side, her mouth sucking softly and her tiny fists curling and uncurling. They stood on either side of her crib, looking down at her and then at each other, but neither of them said anything.

They had the dinner Maisie had planned: linguine with shrimp and vegetables. A salad. Raspberry sherbet. Jack ate and ate, plowing through what Maisie considered delicate food. She lit a cigarette and thought how this enthusiasm which should have gratified her instead irritated her. Didn't he understand how carefully she chose the tomatoes and zucchini at the farmers' market? How her hands itched after deveining the shrimp? How long it took to julienne everything?

"So," said Jack. "What do you think?"

"What do I think?"

"How's this going?"

"What do you mean?" said Maisie, putting her cigarette out in her plate.

"We said we'd try it for a while, and see how it worked."

"It's only been four months."

"So —"

"I can't exactly leave the job now. I mean, I like it, it's going well, and I've really only just started to learn. If I came back to Maine, we'd be right back where we started."

"I guess we could try living halfway in between. Boston —"

"Now that's crazy," said Maisie, pushing her chair back and carrying plates to the sink. "I'm not going to commute from Boston to New York every day."

"A couple of times a week."

"You'd be the first to tell me we can't afford it. Plane fares —"

"And what about Caterina and Ed?" said Jack. He was still sitting at the table, twisting to face her as she moved around, putting the food away.

"What about them?"

"You can't stay here forever, you know."

"Who said anything about forever? It's just temporary. Until I can afford my own apartment."

"Your own apartment? But that's so —"

"So what?"

"Definite."

She sighed, squirting dishwashing soap into the sink. Dennis, she thought, yes Dennis, the murder-and-crime editor at her publishing house, he would know how to handle this. They went out for drinks sometimes after work, to a little bar off First Avenue filled with solitary men and women in leather jackets. The tough look of the place at first thrilled Maisie, but nothing ever happened there. No one talked; they just wanted to drink. She and Dennis sat at a tippy little table in the back, Formica made to look like wood, and he told her about his marriage, made so his wife could get out of Russia. His wife was a painter who slept and drank when she was with him and went away for weeks at a time. It sounded very sophisticated to Maisie, this relationship that swung between politics and passion — after all, the wife didn't have to see him ever, they could have completely separate households, bound legally only until she established residency and could get a divorce. She imagined their home, Dennis's Village apartment, as sunlit and messy, empty glasses and vodka bottles, flattened paint tubes, old photographs of Russians stuck into the dusty mirror frame, a rumpled bed, a half-eaten sandwich. Dennis, she was sure, would not get entangled in the logistics of separate households; he would not go trundling back and forth in a sleeping car; he would not ask her in a timid, little-boy voice how long this might go on. He would accept the arrangement grandly, or reject it grandly. But Jack — in these discussions with him she always knew what he should say, but he never said it; and so, although she knew better, she was forced to proceed on what was explicit between them, like a minister who, knowing perfectly well why two people should not be married but receiving no answer to his "speak now or forever hold your peace" line, has no choice but to go on with the ceremony.

Caterina was sitting in a white wicker rocking chair, holding the baby on her lap. "Trot trot to Boston," she said to it. "Trot trot to Lynn. Be careful, be careful, Ellie doesn't fall" — and here she opened her eyes very wide, and her mouth, and the baby looked blandly back, and Caterina said, "IN!" and opened her knees so that the baby dipped briefly between them and came up again, looking surprised. Maisie stood at the window, pulling apart a begonia leaf along its veins. It came apart very neatly, as though the veins were deliberate perforations, put there by some considerate manufacturer. It had rained twice already that morning, but now the sun had come out, outlining the raindrops on the windowpanes in white. A strange overexcited brightness was in the room. "Doesn't it make you feel weird to know that no matter what you do with the baby today, she won't remember it?" she said.

"I don't think of it that way," said Caterina, hoisting the baby straight up in the air so its baggy yellow pajama-feet dangled. "Because all right, maybe she won't remember this specific moment, but she's got to store up all these good days in her subconscious somewhere. And anyway, you never know when things really start to count."

Maisie dropped the pieces of the leaf she was holding and plucked off another one. "I read in a magazine that kids who are treated badly at an early age remember it."

Caterina gazed into the baby's face. "How could anyone treat that badly?" she said. "Look at those little cheeks. Don't you just want to bite them?"

Maisie looked at the baby. She was its godmother; so far this had produced nothing in her but an uncomfortable sense that she was letting the baby down. She had known Caterina for years; they had lived together in college, and seen each other through exams, lovers, jobs, and weddings; but seeing Caterina with the baby made her want to back away, as though she had come too close to the fire. She wanted to ask Caterina sometimes whether she felt trapped, but she knew what Caterina would say: Of course not. Nobody made me have a baby. It was my choice. Everything always seemed so clear to Caterina. Such a simplified idea of morality: this was right, and that was wrong. You did right even when it was unpleasant, and you shunned wrong even when you suspected it might be very pleasant indeed. The most infuriating thing was that so far it had all worked: here was Caterina sitting in her pristine blue and white living room, so milky, so serene, holding her baby aloft in the sunlight. Much as she loved Caterina, Maisie sometimes longed for the day when the moral system messed up, when Ed had an affair or the baby grew up and did cocaine. Then Caterina would come to her for advice for a change; and Maisie would listen sympathetically and then give the answer which, she was becoming convinced, was the only true compassionate one possible: I don't know. It's not fair. Sometimes you do the best you know how, and things go wrong anyway.

"So how are things with Jack?" Caterina asked, rocking in the chair.

"O.K.," Maisie said. She didn't want to talk about it, and she hoped Jack and Ed would get back soon with the Sunday papers. She was itching to light a cigarette, but Caterina didn't like people to smoke around the baby.

"Oh, well, it'll be easier when you go home for your vacation," said Caterina. "Then you'll have more time, and more privacy."

"The awful thing is I don't really feel like that's my home," said Maisie, and instantly regretted it. This was what always happened when she let herself be seduced into a conversation with Caterina: she would swear in advance to keep things on a light level, to keep herself under control, and somehow the lid always came up off the box and all her troubles came swarming out. I am Caterina's screwed-up friend, she thought; she could imagine Caterina and Ed lying side by side in bed at night, sighing and whispering to each other that they hoped everything worked out all right for Maisie. But the truth was that she did feel at home here, where she had her own room with an unfolded old sleep sofa that had once stood on Caterina's parents' sunporch. Right now the baby was sleeping in a narrow dressing room off Caterina and Ed's room, but Maisie knew that the room she occupied was the apartment's real child room, and eventually she would have to get out so that Ellie could get in. "I could always get my own apartment, I guess," she said aloud.

"And have Jack move down here?" Caterina said, wiping the

baby's face with the diaper she always had slung over her shoulder.

"I don't know," Maisie hedged. "I don't think I can really ask him to do that."

"Why not?" said Caterina briskly, the words coming out in a rush, as though she had wanted to say them for a long time. "Frankly, I've never understood why he and Maine have to be a package deal. Let him get someone else to run the place, and move down here."

"I can't," Maisie said again.

"Why not? If he cares about the marriage, he should put you first."

"Yes," said Maisie, pulling off another leaf, "but what if I ask him to move down here, and it doesn't work out?"

Caterina was silent, rocking with the baby, who had begun to whimper. If she starts nursing now, I'll scream, Maisie thought, but Caterina just kept rocking. After a moment Maisie went ahead and lit a cigarette anyway, because her hands were shaking and she knew that Caterina would not rebuke her now; and she thought again how much she hated Caterina when she was unfolding her problems before her this way, like describing the symptoms of some embarrassing infection to the doctor in detail because you know it is your only chance of proper diagnosis and cure. But Caterina couldn't cure anything; she could only anesthetize. Maisie remembered the day before her wedding, driving all over Boston with Caterina, saying, "I don't want to get married." And Caterina soothing, "It's all right, everybody feels like that right before, I felt like that, don't worry." And she had let those words coax her to the altar, like a cat coaxed down from a tree. Caterina knew something about love and safety that she, Maisie, didn't know; but she would let Caterina's words guide her there.

In the dark, in bed, something was waiting to happen. Come on, come on, it said to Maisie, and she knew she ought to ignore it, but there was this immense silence that needed to be filled with something immense, so childishly she put her small hand into its big one and let it pull her along. "You don't love me," she began in a soft voice, as though testing a microphone.

"What?" said Jack, not so much as if he hadn't heard right but as if he wanted to give her a chance to change her mind: are you sure you want to say this?

"You treat me like a chum."

"Oh, come on."

"Yes," she said, her voice shaking now and gaining volume. "I feel like we're hiking up the mountain single-file, wearing lederhosen and *whistling*."

He had the sense not to laugh, or perhaps he was too alarmed to be amused. He pulled himself up on his elbow. "That's not how you feel when we're in bed together."

"Oh, yes it is. That's how you make me feel."

The words lay in the darkness between them, out there with no way to get them back, like a letter dropped into the mail chute. Maisie wished them unsaid, but there was a strange exhilarating sense of having set something going. She had never known before that making trouble could be a palpable physical sensation, like splashing in a still pond or bicycling downhill. I'm making trouble, she thought, and there was a reckless creative urge to make more. She pushed off the covers and got out of bed. Jack's discarded shirt was the first garment she came to, and she pulled it on and went to stand by the window. This discussion seemed to her historic, but it had not happened yet; she felt that she should speak carefully, for posterity, but there was also an itch to get on with it already, like standing backstage before a play and watching the audience trickle in, so slowly, so casually. She said, "You don't love me in a sexy way."

"Of course I do. All weekend I've wanted —"

"That's not what I mean. Your wants are so *healthy*. It's like wanting to exercise, or wanting to eat. It comes from the same part of you that likes to read, or see friends, or pet the cat."

"Maisie, what do you want?"

"I want it to be *dark*," she said. "I want it to be involuntary, to come out of *need*, not affection. I feel like we're so damned *affectionate* all the time. Why can't you ever get angry at me?"

"Keep talking this way and I'll get there."

"You see? You see? You're so rational all the time. You're so good-humored. Don't you know I'm saying horrible things to you? Don't you know we're in trouble? Why don't you stop me?"

But he stayed propped on his elbow looking at her, as though she were a messenger riding wildly ahead of a cyclone, and he was torn between believing her warnings and looking at the blue sky and the safe, quiet countryside all around them.

Jack did not have to catch a train back until Monday afternoon, but Maisie had to work. She had a meeting at lunchtime, she said, so she could not see him then, and she felt terrible about it. She really did seem to feel terrible; she put her arms around his neck and cried, and said she was sorry that things had not gone well. "It's just that we didn't have enough *time*," she sobbed. Jack said it was all right, they couldn't expect things to be perfect every time they saw each other. "But don't let this one become indelible, O.K.?" said Maisie. "Because we won't see each other for a while, so please just don't think about this too much —" He promised that he wouldn't, and that he would call her the following night after work.

After she left, he went into the kitchen, where Caterina was ironing. She clearly had been taken into Maisie's confidence, and was trying to pretend she didn't know anything was wrong; she blushed, and offered him tea, and questioned him gently about his work, and then, when he complained about the factory, said suddenly, sharply, "So why don't you sell it?"

He went into the bedroom and packed his suitcase, told Caterina he was going to spend the day in New York, and thanked her for having him. "Don't be silly," she said, kissing him on the cheek, "Maisie's part of the family."

The lockers in the station were full, so he left the bag in a checkroom and went out walking. In his head as he walked, he had a conversation with Maisie. I don't own you, he said. I want you to be happy. If it makes you happy to be in New York, then that's what I want.

And she said, If you don't love me enough to do something about it, then why should I give up everything to come live with you in that terrible lonely place?

All right, then, I do miss you. Get back here now.

And she said, You don't own me.

When he was tired he went back to the station to get his suitcase, but rummaging in his pockets he couldn't come up with the claim check. "Sorry," said the clerk. "I can't let you have it without the token."

"But I can see it," said Jack, leaning over the counter and pointing. "It's that green leather one right over there."

"Sorry."

"Wait. What am I supposed to do?"

"After thirty days it goes over to lost and found. You can claim it there."

"That's stupid. Why should I wait thirty days when I'm here, now."

They wouldn't give it back to him. So he sat on a bench fingering his return ticket and waiting for them to call the next train. As he sat there, he began to get an idea. What if he got a taxi and went over to Brooklyn and knocked on the door just like that, and said I'm staying? But he could hear voices on the other side of the door, talking and laughing and interrupting each other, stopped suddenly by his knock; and there he was, standing in the doorway, gazing in on the startled faces of his wife and the people she lived with.

JOY WILLIAMS

The Little Winter

FROM GRANTA

SHE WAS in the airport, waiting for her flight to be called, when a woman came to a phone near her chair. The woman stood there dialing, and after a while began talking in a flat, aggrieved voice. Gloria couldn't hear everything by any means, but she did hear her say, "If anything happens to this plane, I hope you'll be satisfied." The woman spoke monotonously and without mercy. She was tall and disheveled and looked the very picture of someone who recently had ceased to be cherished. Nevertheless, she was still being mollified on the other end of the phone. Gloria heard with astounding clarity the part about the plane being repeated several times. The woman then slammed down the receiver and boarded Gloria's flight, flinging herself down in a first-class seat. Gloria proceeded to the rear of the plane and sat quietly, thinking that every person is on the brink of eternity every moment, that the ways and means of leaving this world are innumerable and often inconceivable. She thought in this manner for a while, then ordered a drink.

The plane pushed through the sky and the drink made her think of the way, as a child, she had enjoyed chewing on the collars of her dresses. The first drink of the day did not always bring this to mind but frequently it did. Then she began thinking of the desert which she was leaving behind and how much she liked it. Once she had liked the sea and felt she could not live without it but now missed it almost not at all.

The plane continued. Gloria ordered another drink, no longer resigned to believing that the woman was going to blow it up.

Now she began thinking of where she was going and what she was going to do. She was going to visit Jean, a friend of hers, who was having a hard time — a third divorce, after all, Jean had a lot of energy — but that was only for a day or two. Jean had a child named Gwendal. Gloria hadn't seen them for over a year, she probably wouldn't even recognize Gwendal, who would be almost ten by now. Then she would just keep moving around until it happened. She was thinking of looking for a dog to get. She'd had a number of dogs but hadn't had very good luck with them. This was the thing about pets, of course, you knew that something dreadful was going to befall them, that it was not going to end well. Two of her dogs had been hit by cars, one had been epileptic and another was diagnosed early on as having hip dysplasia. That one she had bought from the same litter that Kafka's great-niece had bought hers from. Kafka's great-niece! Vets had never done very well by Gloria's dogs, much as doctors weren't doing very well by Gloria now. She thought frequently about doctors, though she wasn't going to see them anymore. Under the circumstances, she probably shouldn't acquire a dog, but she felt she wanted one. Let the dog get stuck for a change, she thought.

At the airport, Gloria rented a car. She decided to drive until just outside Jean's town and check into a motel. Jean was a talker. A day with Jean would be enough. A day and a night would be too much. Just outside Jean's town was a monastery where the monks raised dogs. Maybe she would find her dog there tomorrow. She would go over to the monastery early in the morning and spend the rest of the day with Jean. But that was it, other than that, there wasn't much of a plan.

The day was cloudy and there was a great deal of traffic. The land falling back from the highway was green and still. It seemed to her a slightly morbid landscape, obelisks and cemeteries, thick drooping forests, the evergreens dying from the top down. Of course there was hardly any place to live these days. A winding old road ran parallel to the highway and Gloria turned off and drove along it until she came to a group of cabins. The cabins were white with little porches but the office was in a structure built to resemble a tepee. There was a dilapidated miniature golf course and a wooden tower from the top of which you could see into three states. But the tower leaned and the handrail curving optimistically upward was splintered and warped, and only five steps from the ground a rusted chain prevented further ascension. Gloria liked places like this.

In the tepee, a woman in a housedress stood behind a pink Formica counter. A glass hummingbird coated with greasy dust hung in one window. Gloria could smell meat loaf cooking. The woman had red cheeks and white hair, and she greeted Gloria extravagantly, but as soon as Gloria paid for her cabin she became morose. She gazed at Gloria glumly as though perceiving her as one who had already walked off with the blankets, the lamp, and the painting of the waterfall.

The key Gloria had been given did not work. It fitted into the lock and turned, but did not do the job of opening the door. She walked back to the office and a small dog with short legs and a fluffy tail fell in step beside her. Back in the tepee, Gloria said, "I can't seem to make this key work." The smell of the meat loaf was now clangorous. The woman was old, but she came around the counter fast.

The dog was standing in the middle of the turnaround in front of the cabins.

"Is that your dog?" Gloria asked.

"I've never seen it before," the woman said. "It sure is not," she added. "Go home!" she shrieked at the dog. She turned the key in the lock of Gloria's cabin and then gave the door a sharp kick with her sneaker. The door flew open. She stomped back to the office. "Go home!" she screamed again at the dog.

Gloria made herself an iceless drink in a paper cup and called Jean.

"I can't wait to see you," Jean said. "How are you?"

"I'm all right," Gloria said.

"Tell me."

"Really," Gloria said.

"I can't wait to see you," Jean said. "I've had the most god-awful time. I know it's silly."

"How is Gwendal doing?"

"She never liked Chuckie anyway. She's Luke's, you know. But she's not a bit like Luke. You know Gwendal."

Gloria barely remembered the child. She sipped from the paper cup and looked through the screen at the dog, which was gazing over the ruined golf course to the valley beyond.

"I don't know how I manage to pick them," Jean was saying. She was talking about that last one.

"I'll be there by lunch tomorrow," Gloria said.

"Not until then! Well, we'll bring some lunch over to Bill's and eat with him. You haven't met him, have you? I want you to meet him."

Bill was Jean's first ex-husband. She had just bought a house in town where two of her old ex-husbands and her new ex-husband lived. Gloria knew she had quite a day cut out for herself tomorrow. Jean gave her directions and Gloria hung up and made herself a fresh drink in the paper cup. She stood out on the porch. Dark clouds had massed over the mountains. Traffic thundered invisibly past in the distance, beyond the trees. In the town in the valley below, there were tiny hard lights in the enlarging darkness. The light, which had changed, was disappearing, but there was still a lot of light. That's the way it was with light. If you were out in it while it was going you could still see enough for longer. When it was completely dark, Gloria said, "Well, good night."

She woke midmorning with a terrible headache. She was not supposed to drink but what difference did it make, really. It didn't make any difference. She took her pills. Sometimes she thought it had been useless for her to grow older. She was thirty-five. She lay in the musty cabin. Everything seemed perfectly clear. Then it seemed equivocal again. She dressed and went to the office, where she paid for another night. The woman took the money and looked at Gloria worriedly as though she were already saying goodbye to those towels and that old willow chair with the cushion.

It began to rain. The road to the monastery was gravel and wound up the side of a mountain. There were orchards, fields of young corn . . . the rain fell upon it all in a fury. Gloria drove slowly, barely able to make out the road. She imagined it snowing out there, not rain but snow, filling everything up. She imagined thinking — *it was dark now but still snowing* — a line like that, as in a story. A line like that was lovely, she thought. When she was small they had lived in a place where the little winter came first. That's what everyone called it. There was the little winter, then there were pleasant days, sometimes weeks. Then the big winter came. She felt dreamy and cold, a little disconnected from everything. She was on the monastery's grounds now and there were wooden buildings with turreted roofs and minarets. Someone had planted birches. She parked in front of a sign that said INFORMATION/GIFT SHOP and dashed from the car to the door. She was laughing and shaking the water from her hair as she entered.

The situation was that there were no dogs available, or rather that the brother whose duty was the dogs, who knew about the dogs, was away and would not return until tomorrow. She could come back tomorrow. The monk who told her this had a beard and wore a soiled apron. His interest in her questions did not seem intense. He had appeared from a back room, a room that seemed part smokehouse, part kitchen. This was the monk who smoked chickens, hams, and cheese. There was always cheese in this life. The monastery had a substantial mail-order business; the monks smoked things, the nuns made cheesecakes. The monk seemed slightly impatient with Gloria and she was aware that her questions about the dogs seemed desultory. He had given up a great deal, no doubt, in order to be here. The gift shop was crowded with half-price icons and dog beds. In a corner there was a glass case filled with the nuns' cheesecakes. Gloria looked in there, at the white boxes, stacked.

"The deluxe is a standard favorite," the monk said. "The Kahlúa is encased in a chocolate cookie-crumb crust, the rich liqueur from sunny Mexico blending naturally with the nuns' original recipe." The monk droned on as though at matins. "The chocolate is a must for chocolate fanciers. The chocolate amaretto is considered by the nuns to be their *pièce de résistance*."

Gloria bought the chocolate amaretto and left. How gloomy, she thought. The experience had seemed vaguely familiar, as though she had surrendered passively to it in the past. She supposed it was a belief in appearances. She put the cheesecake in the car and walked around the grounds. It was raining less heavily now, but even so her hair was plastered to her skull. She passed the chapel and then turned back and went inside. She picked up a candlestick and jammed it into her coat pocket. This place made her mad. Then she took the candlestick out and set it on the floor. Outside, she wandered around, hearing nothing but the highway, which was humming like something in her head. She finally found the kennels and opened the door and went in. This is the way she thought it would be, nothing closed to her at all. There were four dogs, all young ones, maybe three months old, German shepherds. She watched them for a while. It would be easy to take one, she thought. She could just do it.

She drove back down the mountain into town, where she pulled into a shopping center that had a liquor store. She bought gin and some wine for Jean, then drove down to Jean's house in the valley. She felt tired. There was something pounding behind her eyes. Jean's house was a dirty peach color with a bush in front. Everything was pounding, the house, even the grass. Then the pounding stopped.

"Oh my God," Jean exclaimed. "You've brought the *pièce de résistance!*" Apparently everyone was familiar with the nuns' cheesecakes. They didn't know about the dogs except that there were dogs up there, they knew that. Jean and Gloria hugged each other. "You look good," Jean said. "They got it all, thank God, right? The things that happen . . . There aren't even names for half of what happens, I swear. You know my second husband, Andy, the one who died? He went in and he never came out again and he just submitted to it, but no one could ever figure out what it was. It was something complicated and obscure and the only thing they knew was that he was dying from it. It might have been some insect that bit him. But the worst thing — well, not the worst thing, but the thing I remember because it had to do with me, which is bad of me, I suppose, but that's just human nature. The worst thing was what happened just before he died. He was very fussy. Everything had to be just so."

"This is Andy," Gloria said.

"Andy," Jean agreed. "He had an excellent vocabulary and was very precise. How I got involved with him I'll never know. But he was my husband and I was devastated. I *lived* at the hospital, week after week. He liked me to read to him. I was there

that afternoon and I had adjusted the shade and plumped the
pillows and I was reading to him. And there he was, quietly slipping away right then, I guess, looking back on it. I was reading
and I got to this part about someone being the master of a highly
circumscribed universe and he opened his eyes and said, 'Circumscribed.' 'What, darling?' I said. And he said, 'Circumscribed, not circumcised . . . You said circumcised.' And I said,
'I'm sure I didn't, darling,' and he gave me this long look and
then he gave a big sigh and died. Isn't that awful?"

Gloria giggled, then shook her head.

Jean's eyes darted around the room, which was in high disor-
der. Peeling wallpaper, cracked linoleum. Cardboard boxes
everywhere. Shards of glass had been swept into one corner and
a broken croquet mallet propped one window open. "So what
do you think of this place?" Jean said.

"It's some place," Gloria said.

"Everyone says I shouldn't have. It needs some work, I know,
but I found this wonderful man, or he found me. He came up
to the door and looked at all this and I said, 'Can you help me?
Do you do work like this?' And he nodded and said, 'I puttah.'
Isn't that wonderful! 'I puttah . . .' "

Gloria looked at the sagging floor and the windows loose in
their frames. The mantel was blackened by smoke and grooved
with cigarette burns. It was clear that the previous occupants
had led lives of grinding boredom here and that they had not
led them with composure. He'd better start puttahing soon, Gloria thought. "Don't marry him," she said, and laughed.

"Oh, I know you think I marry everybody," Jean said, "but I
don't. There have only been four. The last one, and I mean the
last, was the worst. What a rodent Chuckie was. No, he's more
like a big predator, a crow or a weasel or something. Cruel, lazy,
deceitful." Jean shuddered. "The best thing about him was his
hair." Jean was frequently undone by hair. "He has great hair.
He wears it in a sort of fifties full flattop."

Gloria felt hollow and happy. Nothing mattered much.

"Love is a chimera," Jean said earnestly.

Gloria laughed.

"I'm pronouncing that right, aren't I?" Jean said, laughing.

"You actually bought this place?" Gloria said.

"Oh, it's crazy," Jean said, "but Gwendal and I needed a home. I've heard that *faux* is the new trend. I'm going to do it all *faux* when I get organized. Do you want to see the upstairs? Gwendal's room is upstairs. Hers is the neatest."

They went up the stairs to a room where a fat girl sat on a bed, writing in a book.

"I'm doing my autobiography," Gwendal said, "but I think I'm going to change my approach." She turned to Gloria. "Would you like to be my biographer?"

Jean said, "Say hello to Gloria. You remember Gloria."

Gloria gave the girl a hug. Gwendal smelled good and had small gray eyes. The room wasn't clean at all, but there was very little in it. Gloria supposed it was the neatest. Conversation lagged.

"Let's go out and sit on the lawn," Jean suggested.

"I don't want to," Gwendal said.

The two women went downstairs. Gloria needed to use the bathroom but Jean said she had to go outside, as the plumbing wasn't all it should be. There was a steep brushy bank behind the house and Gloria crouched there. The day was clear and warm now. At the bottom of the bank, a flat stream moved laboriously around vine-covered trees. The mud glistened in the sun. Blackberries grew in the brush. This place has a lot of candor, Gloria thought.

Jean had laid a blanket on the grass and was sitting there, eating a wedge of cheesecake from a plastic plate. Gloria decided on a drink over cake.

"We'll go to Bill's house for lunch," Jean said. "Then we'll go to Fred's house for a swim." Fred was an old husband too. Gwendal's father was the only one who wasn't around. He lived in Las Vegas. Andy wasn't around either, of course.

Gwendal came out of the house into the sloppy yard. She stopped in the middle of a rhubarb patch, exclaiming silently and waving her arms.

Jean sighed. "It's hard being a single mother."

"You haven't been single for long," Gloria said.

Jean laughed loudly at this. "Poor Gwendal," she said, "I love her dearly."

"A lovely child," Gloria murmured.

"I just wish she wouldn't make up so much stuff sometimes."

"She's young," Gloria said, swallowing her drink. Really, she hardly knew what she was saying. "What *is* she doing?" she asked Jean.

Gwendal leaped quietly around in the rhubarb.

"Whatever it is, it needs to be translated," Jean said. "Gwendal needs a good translator."

"She's pretending something or other," Gloria offered, thinking she would very much like another drink.

"I'm going to put on a fresh dress for visiting Bill," Jean said. "Do you want to put on a fresh dress?"

Gloria shook her head. She was watching Gwendal. When Jean went into the house, the girl trotted over to the blanket. "Why don't you kidnap me?" she said.

"Why don't you kidnap *me?*" Gloria said, laughing. What an odd kid, she thought. "I don't want to kidnap you," she said.

"I'd like to see your house," Gwendal said.

"I don't have a house. I lived in an apartment."

"Apartments aren't interesting," Gwendal said. "Dump it. We could get a van. The kind with the ladder that goes up the back. We could get a wheel cover that says MESS WITH THE BEST, LOSE LIKE THE REST."

There was something truly terrifying about girls on the verge of puberty, Gloria thought. She laughed.

"You drink too much," Gwendal said. "You're always drinking something."

This hurt Gloria's feelings. "I'm dying," she said. "I have a brain tumor. I can do what I want."

"If you're dying you can do anything you want?" Gwendal said. "I didn't know that. That's a new one. So there are compensations."

Gloria couldn't believe she'd told Gwendal she was dying. "You're fat," she said glumly

Gwendal ignored this. She wasn't all that fat. Somewhat fat, perhaps, but not grotesquely so.

"Oh, to hell with it," Gloria said. "You want me to stop drinking, I'll stop drinking."

"It doesn't matter to me," Gwendal said.

Gloria's mouth trembled. I'm drunk, she thought.

"Some simple pleasures are just a bit too simple, you know," Gwendal said.

Gloria felt that she had been handling her upcoming death pretty well. Now she wasn't sure, in fact, she felt awful. What was she doing spending what might be one of her last days sitting on a scratchy blanket in a weedy yard while a fat child insulted her? Her problem was that she had never figured out where it was exactly she wanted to go to die. Some people knew and planned accordingly. The desert, say, or Nantucket. Or a good hotel somewhere. But she hadn't figured it out. En route was the closest she'd come.

Gwendal said, "Listen, I have an idea. We could do it the other way around. Instead of you being my biographer, I'll be yours. *Gloria by Gwendal*." She wrote in the air with her finger. She did not have a particularly flourishing hand, Gloria noted. "Your life as told to Gwendal Crawley. I'll write it all down. At least that's something. We can always spice it up."

"I haven't had a very interesting life," Gloria said modestly. But it was true, she thought. When her parents had named her, they must have been happy. They must have thought something was going to happen now.

"I'm sure you must be having some interesting reflections, though," Gwendal said. "And if you're really dying, I bet you'll feel like doing everything once." She was wringing her hands in delight.

Jean walked toward them from the house.

"C'mon," Gwendal hissed. "Let me go with you. You didn't come all this way just to stay here, did you?"

"Gloria and I are going to visit Bill," Jean said. "Let's all go," she said to Gwendal.

"I don't want to," Gwendal said.

"If I don't see you again, goodbye," Gloria said to Gwendal. The kid stared at her.

Jean was driving, turning this way and that, passing the houses of those she had once loved.

"That's Chuckie's house," Jean said. "The one with the hair." They drove slowly by, looking at Chuckie's house. "Charming on the outside but sleazy inside, just like Chuckie. He broke my

heart, literally broke my heart. Well, his foot is going to slide in
due time, as they say, and I want to be around for that. That's
why I've decided to stay." She said a moment later, "It's not really."
They passed Fred's house. Everybody had a house.

"Fred has a pond," Jean said. "We can go for a swim there
later. I always use Fred's pond. He used to own a whole quarry,
can you imagine? This was before our time with him, Gwendal's
and mine, but the kids were always getting in there and drowning. He put up big signs and barbed wire and everything but
they still got in. It got to be too much trouble, so he sold
it."

"Too much trouble!" Gloria said.

Death seemed preposterous. Totally unacceptable. Those silly
kids, Gloria thought. She was elated and knew that she would
feel tired soon and uneasy, but maybe it wouldn't happen this
time. The day was bright, clean after the rain. Leaves lay on the
streets, green and fresh.

"Those were Fred's words, the too much trouble. Can't I pick
them? I can really pick them." Jean shook her head.

They drove to Bill's house. Next to it was a pasture with horses
in it. "Those aren't Bill's horses, but they're pretty, aren't they?"
Jean said. "You're going to love Bill. He's gotten a little strange
but he always was a little strange. We are who we are, aren't we?
He carves ducks."

Bill was obviously not expecting them. He was a big man with
long hair wearing boxer shorts and smoking a cigar. He looked
at Jean warily.

"This used to be the love of my life," Jean said. To Bill, she
said, "This is Gloria, my dearest friend."

Gloria felt she should demur, but smiled instead. Her situation didn't make her any more honest, she had found.

"Beautiful messengers, bad news," Bill said.

"We just thought we'd stop by," Jean said.

"Let me put on my pants," he said.

The two women sat in the living room, surrounded by wooden
ducks. The ducks, exquisite and oppressive, nested on every surface. Buffleheads, canvasback, scaup, blue-winged teal. Gloria
picked one up. It looked heavy but was light. Shoveler, mallard,
merganser. The names kept coming to her.

"I forgot the lunch so we'll just stay a minute," Jean whispered. "I was *mad* about this man. Don't you ever wonder where it all goes?"

Bill returned, wearing trousers and a checked shirt. He had put his cigar somewhere.

"I *love* these ducks," Jean said. "You're getting so good."

"You want a duck," Bill said.

"Oh yes!" Jean said.

"I wasn't offering you one. I just figured that you did." He winked at Gloria.

"Oh you," Jean said.

"Take one, take one," Bill sighed.

Jean picked up the nearest duck and put it in her lap.

"That's a harlequin," Bill said.

"It's bizarre, I love it." Jean gripped the duck tightly.

"You want a duck?" Bill said to Gloria.

"No," Gloria said.

"Oh, take one!" Jean said excitedly.

"Decoys have always been particularly abhorrent to me," Gloria said, "since they are objects designed to lure a living thing to its destruction with the false promise of safety, companionship, and rest."

They both looked at her, startled.

"Oh wow, Gloria," Jean said.

"These aren't decoys," Bill said mildly. "People don't use them for decoys anymore, they use them for decoration. There are hardly any more ducks to hunt. Ducks are on their way out. They're in a free fall."

"Diminishing habitat," Jean said.

"There you go," Bill said.

Black duck, pintail, widgeon. The names kept moving toward Gloria, then past.

"I'm more interested in creating dramas now," Bill said. "I'm getting away from the static stuff. I want to make dramatic moments. They have to be a little less than life-sized, but otherwise it's all there . . . the whole situation." He stood up. "Just a second," he said.

Once he was out of the room, Jean turned to her. "Gloria?" she said.

Bill returned carrying a large object covered by a sheet. He set it down on the floor and took off the sheet.

"I like it so far," Jean said after a moment.

"Interpret away," Bill said.

"Well," Jean said, "I don't think you should make it too busy."

"I said interpret, not criticize," Bill said.

"I just think the temptation would be to make something like that too busy. The temptation would be to put stuff in all those little spaces."

Bill appeared unmoved by this possible judgment, but he replaced the sheet.

In the car, Jean said, "Wasn't that *awful?* He should stick to ducks."

According to Bill, the situation the object represented seemed to be the acceptance of inexorable fate, this acceptance containing within it, however, a heroic gesture of defiance. This was the situation, ideally always the situation, and it had been transformed, more or less abstractly, by Bill, into wood.

"He liked you."

"Jean, why would he like me?"

"He was flirting with you, I think. Wouldn't it be something if you two got together and we were all here in this one place?"

"Oh my God," Gloria said, putting her hands over her face. Jean glanced at her absent-mindedly. "I should be getting back," Gloria said. "I'm a little tired."

"But you just got here, and we have to take a swim at Fred's. The pond is wonderful, you'll love the pond. Actually, listen, do you want to go over to my parents' for lunch? Or it should be dinner, I guess. They have this big television. My mother can make us something nice for dinner."

"Your parents live around here too?" Gloria asked.

Jean looked frightened for a moment. "It's crazy, isn't it? They're so sweet. You'd love my parents. Oh, I wish you'd talk," she exclaimed. "You're my friend. I wish you'd open up some."

They drove past Chuckie's house again. "Whose car is that now?" Jean wondered.

"I remember trying to feed my mother a spoonful of dust once." Gloria said.

"Why!" Jean said. "Tell!"

"I was little, maybe four. She told me that I had grown in her stomach because she'd eaten some dust."

"No!" Jean said. "The things they tell you when they know you don't know."

"I wanted there to be another baby, someone else, a brother or a sister. So I had my little teaspoon. 'Eat this,' I said. 'It's not a bit dirty. Don't be afraid.' "

"How out of control!" Jean cried.

"She looked at it and said she'd been talking about a different kind of dust, the sort of dust there was on flowers."

"She was just getting in deeper and deeper, wasn't she?" Jean said. She waited for Gloria to say more but the story seemed to be over. "That's a nice little story," Jean said.

It was dark when she got back to the cabins. There were no lights on anywhere. She remembered being happy off and on that day, and then looking at things and finding it all unkind. It had gotten harder for her to talk, and harder to listen to, but she was alone now and she felt a little better. Still, she didn't feel right. She knew she would never be steady. It would never seem all of a piece for her. It would come and go until it stopped.

She pushed open the door and turned on the lamp beside the bed. There were three sockets in the lamp but only one bulb. There had been more bulbs in the lamp last night. She also thought there had been more furniture in the room, another chair. Reading would have been difficult, if she had wanted to read, but she was tired of reading, tired of books. After they had told her the first time and even after they had told her the other times in different ways, she had wanted to read, she didn't want to just stand around gaping at everything, but she couldn't pick the habit up again, it wasn't the same.

The screen behind the lamp was a mottled bluish green, a coppery, oceanic color. She thought of herself as a child with the spoonful of dust, but it was just a memory of her telling it now. She stood close to the screen, to its raw, metallic smell.

In the middle of the night she woke, soaked with sweat. Someone was just outside, she thought. Then this feeling vanished. She gathered up her things and put everything in the car. She did this all hurriedly, and then drove quickly to Jean's house.

She parked out front and turned the lights off. After a few moments, Gwendal appeared. She was wearing an ugly dress and carrying a suitcase. There were creases down one side of her face as though she'd been sleeping hard before she woke. "Where to first?" Gwendal said.

What they did first was to drive to the monastery and steal a dog. Gloria suspected that fatality made her more or less invisible and this seemed to be the case. She drove directly to the kennel, went in, and walked out with a dog. She put him in the back seat and they drove off.

"We'll avoid the highway," Gloria said. "We'll stick to the back roads."

"Fine with me," Gwendal said.

Neither of them said anything for miles, then Gwendal asked, "Would you say he had drop-dead good looks?"

"He's a dog," Gloria said. Gwendal was really mixed up. She was worse than her mother, Gloria thought.

They pulled into a diner and had breakfast. Then they went to a store and bought notebook, pencils, dog food, and gin. They bought sunglasses. It was full day now. They kept driving until dusk. They were quite a distance from Jean's house. Gloria felt sorry for Jean. She liked to have everyone around her, even funny little Gwendal, and now she didn't.

Gwendal had been sleeping. Suddenly she woke up. "Do you want to hear my dream?" she asked.

"Absolutely," Gloria said.

"Someone, it wasn't you, told me not to touch this funny-looking animal, it wasn't him," Gwendal said, gesturing toward the dog. "Every time I'd pat it, it would bite off a piece of my arm or a piece of my chest. I just had to keep going, 'It's cute,' and keep petting it."

"Oh," Gloria said. She had no idea what to say.

"Tell me one of your dreams," Gwendal said, yawning.

"I haven't been dreaming lately," Gloria said.

"That's not good," Gwendal said. "That shows a lack of imagination. Readiness, it shows a lack of readiness maybe. Well, I can put the dreams in later. Don't worry about it." She chose a pencil and opened her notebook. "O.K.," she said. "Married?"

"No."

"Any children?"

"No."

"Allergies?"

Gloria looked at her.

"Do you want to start at the beginning or do you want to work backwards from the Big Surprise?" Gwendal asked.

They were on the outskirts of a town, stopped at a traffic light. Gloria looked straight ahead. Beginnings. She couldn't remember any beginnings.

"Hey," someone said. "Hey!"

She looked to her left at a dented yellow car full of young men. One of them threw a can of beer at her. It bounced off the door and they sped off, howling.

"Everyone knows if someone yells 'hey' you don't look at them," Gwendal said.

"Let's stop for the night," Gloria said.

"How are you feeling?" Gwendal asked . . . not all that solicitously, Gloria thought.

They pulled into the first motel they saw. Gloria fed the dog and had a drink while Gwendal bounced on the bed. He seemed a most equable dog. He drank from the toilet bowl and gnawed peaceably on the bed rail. Gloria and Gwendal ate pancakes in a brightly lit restaurant and strolled around a swimming pool, which had a filthy rubber cover rolled across it. Back in the room, Gloria lay down on one bed while Gwendal sat on the other.

"Do you want me to paint your nails or do your hair?" Gwendal asked.

"No," Gloria said. She was recalling a bad thought she'd had once, a very bad thought. It had caused no damage, however, as far as she knew.

"I wouldn't know how to do your hair actually," Gwendal said.

With a little training this kid could be a mortician, Gloria thought.

That night Gloria dreamed. She dreamed she was going to the funeral of some woman who had been indifferent to her. There was no need for her to be there. She was standing with a group of people. She felt like a criminal, undetected, but she felt chosen too, to be here when she shouldn't be. Then she was lying across the opening of a cement pipe. When she woke, she was filled with relief, knowing she would forget the dream immediately. It was morning again. Gwendal was outside by the unpleasant pool, writing in her notebook.

"*This was happiness then,*" she said to Gloria, scribbling away.

"Where's the dog?" Gloria asked. "Isn't he with you?"

"I don't know," Gwendal said. "I let him out and he took off for parts unknown."

"What do you mean!" Gloria said. She ran back to the room, went to the car, ran across the cement parking lot and around the motel. Gloria didn't have any name to call the dog with. It had just disappeared without having ever been hers. She got Gwendal in the car and they drove down the roads around the motel. She squinted, frightened, at black heaps along the shoulder and in the littered grass, but it was tires, rags, tires. Cars sped by them. Along the median strip, dead trees were planted at fifty-foot intervals. The dog wasn't anywhere that she could find. Gloria glared at Gwendal.

"It was an accident," Gwendal said.

"You have your own ideas about how this should be, don't you?"

"He was a distraction in many ways," Gwendal said.

Gloria's head hurt. Back in the desert, just before she had made this trip, she had had her little winter. Her heart had pounded like a fist on a door. But it was false, all false, for she had survived it.

Gwendal had the hateful notebook on her lap. It had a splatter black cover with the word "Composition" on it. "Now we can get started," she said. "Today's the day. Favorite color?" she asked. "Favorite show tune?" A childish blue barrette was stuck haphazardly in her hair, exposing part of a large, pale ear.

Gloria wasn't going to talk to her.

After a while, Gwendal said, "*They were unaware that the fugitive was in their midst.*" She wrote it down. Gwendal scribbled in the book all day long and asked Gloria to buy her another one. She sometimes referred to Gloria's imminent condition as the Great Adventure.

Gloria was distracted. Hours went by and she was driving, though she could barely recall what they passed. "I'm going to pull in early tonight," she said.

The motel they stopped at late that afternoon was much like

the one before. It was called the Motel Lark. Gloria lay on one bed and Gwendal sat on the other. Gloria missed having a dog. A dog wouldn't let the stranger in, she thought, knowing she was being sentimental. Whereas Gwendal would in a minute.

"We should be able to talk," Gwendal said.

"Why should we be able to talk?" Gloria said. "There's no reason we should be able to talk."

"You're not open is your problem. You don't want to share. It's hard to imagine what's real all by yourself, you know."

"It is not!" Gloria said hotly. They were bickering like an old married couple.

"This isn't working out," Gloria said. "This is crazy. We should call your mother."

"I'll give you a few more days, but it's true," Gwendal said. "I thought this would be a more mystical experience. I thought you'd tell me something. You don't even know about make-up. I bet you don't even know how to check the oil in that car. I've never seen you check the oil."

"I know how to check the oil," Gloria said.

"How about an electrical problem? Would you know how to fix an electrical problem?"

"No!" Gloria yelled.

Gwendal was quiet. She stared at her fat knees.

"I'm going to take a bath," Gloria said.

She went into the bathroom and shut the door. The tile was turquoise and the stopper to the tub hung on a chain. This was the Motel Lark, she thought. She dropped the rubber stopper in the drain and ran the water. A few tiles were missing and the wall showed a gray, failed adhesive. She wanted to say something but even that wasn't it. She didn't want to say anything. She wanted to realize something she couldn't say. She heard a voice, it must have been Gwendal's, in the bedroom. Gloria lay down in the tub. The water wasn't as warm as she expected. *Your silence is no deterrent to me, Gloria,* the voice said. She reached for the hot water faucet but it ran in cold. If she let it run, it might get warm, she thought. That's what they say. Or again, that might be it.

Contributors' Notes

*100 Other Distinguished
Stories of 1989*

Editorial Addresses

Contributors' Notes

EDWARD ALLEN's first novel, *Straight Through the Night*, was published by Soho Press in 1989. His fiction has appeared in *The New Yorker* and *Southwest Review*, and his poetry has appeared or is forthcoming in *Prairie Schooner*, *Poetry Northwest*, and *The Black Warrior Review*. He currently teaches literature and creative writing at Rhodes College in Memphis.

▪ I like the idea of place as foreground. At certain periods of my life, I have tried to get by without a car, and have found myself obligated to do a great deal of walking. What has impressed me most during those periods is how much more closely the pedestrian is able to see the world, and I have been interested by the trains of thought I have found myself following in order to pass the time during long and tedious walks through familiar territory.

"River of Toys" has also been influenced in part by my lingering mixed feelings about "In the Heart of the Heart of the Country," by William Gass. I was fascinated by how Gass had succeeded in making the *setting* the main character. But I was also very annoyed with the complaining tone of Gass's story, and I kept wanting to tell his narrator either to cheer up or to move away. So I have tried to bend Gass's place-centered approach into something with more warmth and humor in it.

I like to celebrate the sort of mundane details that contemporary aesthetic values tell us we are supposed to hate. I consider myself very lucky that the sixties were a failure for me, and I am thankful that my attempts to succeed as a hippie and to live close to nature came to nothing. My enjoyment of banal suburban things — supermarket parking lots, roadside trash, bad smells — has given me a spacious and largely private barnyard to root around in.

RICHARD BAUSCH's most recent book is *The Fireman's Wife and Other Stories*. His work has appeared in *The Atlantic Monthly*, *The New Yorker*,

Esquire, and *Wigwag.* He is on the faculty of the writing program at
George Mason University.

▪ "The Fireman's Wife" began in unpleasantness, as of course many
stories do: its first impulse arose out of the fact that I was, through
events too private to describe here, made privy to a moment between
husband and wife, people of my acquaintance, who were at the end of
their marriage and didn't quite realize it yet. The moment was really
little more than a look, an icy, contemptful, dismissive glance from husband to wife, that the husband was quite willing to have me see, almost
as if he were showing off his hatred — it was the kind of hatred that
knows all the secrets, all the scarred places, and uses the knowledge
freely. My sympathy was with the wife, certainly, and as I began to write
the story I had it in mind to skewer the husband for his stupid, public
failure of gentleness, and also for the fact that I knew what unreasonable expectations he entertained concerning her role in the marriage,
expectations that would have been unreasonable in 1952, even if she
weren't holding down a full-time job and paying more than half the
rent. I began wanting to paint a picture of that particular ugliness which
still persists in these postfeminist times, the man who feels himself em-
powered to treat his wife like a servant. I have never begun a story with
such conscious intention, and I soon paid the price for hauling it into
the workroom with me. For I found in the writing that I couldn't paint
the man as he was, not because he was anything but what he was (boring
in the extreme, incredibly narrow, predictably bigoted, and finally, quite
uninterestingly stupid and complacent) but also because, for me anyway, the characters of fiction — if they are not to be the object of jokes
or of irony — must be subjects about which the principal feeling is com-
passion, or at least empathy. As soon as I began to dream of my couple
as wanting better for themselves and each other, and being simply prevented from obtaining it — through faults in character as well as through
events beyond their control — I had the tone and the matter for my
story. And it began to write itself. I remember, too, that during the
writing of it, I came upon the last line somewhere just after the middle.
I circled the line and went on writing, knowing it was the end, and that
I hadn't earned it yet. The whole process of composition took about
five or six days, and I worked straight through, in six- or seven-hour
stints, until it was done.

"A Kind of Simple, Happy Grace" arrived quite differently. In 1982,
while driving each day to Washington to teach in the Georgetown Summer Writers' Conference, I took a route that led me past several churches,
ranged within sight of each other in the lovely hills beyond McLean,
Virginia. I thought then about writing a story concerning two men of
different denominations, and I knew I wanted to bring them to some

pass that would mean a sort of helpless embrace. What I mean is, I saw the embrace, and I didn't, at the time, know what it would mean or be, but I sensed that it would be a moment that transcended the tenets of religion and belief, and I knew I would write to find out what it meant. For a while I entertained the idea that one of the clerics might discover the body of a child on his church grounds and come under suspicion; I thought the story might well be a novel. I even wrote a few pages of an opening, toying with the idea of making my old priest Vincent Shepherd, from the novel *Real Presence,* the first-person speaker. But then I began work on *The Last Good Time,* and for a long while I just carried the story around with me. In the summer of 1988 I resurrected it and began to write it in earnest, this time with a third-person narrator, and the story's elements began to make themselves more clear. I got to about the eleventh page, had it titled ("Russell & Tarmigian, Revs"), and then abandoned it again, because I simply didn't know what was going to happen next, and because the story wasn't about to tell me. Other work was pressing. I was revising a novel, *Mr. Field's Daughter,* and teaching summer school.

Finally in the summer of 1989, because *Wigwag* had called asking for a story and the one I'd sent them was lost in the mail, I pulled the story out again, spent a night finishing it and the following afternoon polishing what I'd done. The new title was "Design." I discovered that I liked it a lot — liked the humor, the sense of increasing sorrow in it, and some of the language, too. The whole thing seemed quite simple to me when I'd finished, and though I'm convinced that if I could have finished the story earlier I would have, I still have no idea why it took seven years from the first impulse to the completion of the thing. "You do not have to be fast," the old gunfighter says in John Wayne's last movie, "you just have to be willing."

MADISON SMARTT BELL is the author of five novels, most recently *Soldier's Joy.* Born and raised in Tennessee, he has lived in New York and London and now lives in Baltimore. He has taught in various creative writing programs, including the Iowa Writers' Workshop, and currently teaches at Goucher College, along with his wife, the poet Elizabeth Spires. His second collection of short stories, *Barking Man,* was published by Ticknor & Fields in 1990, and a sixth novel is forthcoming from Harcourt Brace Jovanovich this fall.

▪ "Finding Natasha" began with a trip to New York I made in the winter of 1987, my first trip there in over a year, during most of which we'd been living in London. I took the train down from Poughkeepsie, where Beth had been doing a residency at Vassar. Going down the Hudson, entering the city, I thought I could feel a lot of my old renounced vices beginning to try to wake up. It was a sort of toxic nostalgia. I bought a notebook and began to write the story out almost immediately, in short vignettes, mostly landscape at first, and then the plottier bits, in no particular order. When I had most of them done I tore the pages out and shuffled them until I found an arrangement which seemed right. I was halfway through two years' work on a long novel and it was a great satisfaction to *finish* something.

From my point of view the story is a sort of regretful love letter to the city, but the plot itself is all made up — except for Stuart's dream, which I had myself a week or so earlier at my family's farm in Tennessee. It was in every way a revelatory dream, but the scrap of it I can remember is no more than a single hint of the revelation, and this story was the best use I could make of it.

C. S. GODSHALK has worked as a free-lance journalist. Her story "Wonderland" appeared in *The Best American Short Stories 1988* and in the 1988–89 *Pushcart Prize* collection. She has lived in Southeast Asia and is now completing a novel about Borneo.
▪ The voices in this story came in a rush with no shutoff valve. The overriding voice said "Listen!" and I knew I could listen or write another story but I couldn't repackage anything. The Wizard's voice was vexing because it was not just black, it was moving up. Some of his words were not yet truly his and so slightly terrifying and he "sent them up," and this melded with the rhythm and grace of his voice and I found myself wishing I could tell it instead of write it.

The true and permanent death of a dream is hard territory. I completely put the story out of my head after it was finished and I could not, even after intense trying, remember the names of any characters. I find I don't want to write about it now and I hope I never see anybody in it again.

PATRICIA HENLEY's first collection of short stories, *Friday Night at Silver Star* (Graywolf Press, 1986), won the Montana First Book Award. She teaches in the Creative Writing Program at Purdue University.
▪ I often write out of obsessive images that take root in my imagination and won't let go. The obsessive image, the seed, of "The Secret of Cartwheels" was the aunt's long green Cadillac, out of place in that country yard, indicating to the children that something was terribly wrong.

The story unfolded chronologically from there. Mike Curtis at *The Atlantic* helped me realize I'd been too harsh with the mother. He wanted something more in the story to show the bond between the mother and the children. I thought about it and decided to add the section on the school bus, wherein Roxie's looking forward to telling her mother about her confirmation name and she's decided to take the same name her mother took, Joan, "a name to carry you into battle."

The title and the advice about cartwheels came from a young friend, Piotr, who can turn magnificent cartwheels, a skill that eludes me to this day.

"The Secret of Cartwheels" is my most autobiographical story, one I'd wanted to write for a long time, ever since the events recorded in the story. I had to wait until I'd confronted hidden facets of the situation. In therapy, I remembered the incident with which the story ends, Roxie turning away from her mother, even though the mother is trying to connect with the girl. Once I had owned my part in the tension and estrangement, I was free to write about the longing and disappointment. With this story I made peace with that time in my life.

PAM HOUSTON's first collection of short stories, *Cowboys Are My Weakness,* will be published by Norton in the spring of 1991. She has recently had short stories published in *Crazyhorse, Cimarron, Puerto del Sol,* and *The Apalachee Quarterly,* and her nonfiction has appeared in *Mirabella.* She lives in Utah, where she is a Ph.D. candidate and a licensed river guide.

▪ The first paragraph of "How to Talk to a Hunter" started out as a poem, which is one of the things that makes it different from all my other stories. I don't write poetry, so I was very surprised when it came out that way, and for half a second I thought maybe I could write poetry after all, but then I came to my senses and turned it into a story.

Another thing that makes "Hunter" different from all my other stories is that it came to me all in a rush, ten straight hours at the computer, and after those first ten hours I never changed a word. I think that's mainly because it came out of my life's first moment of real desperation. I actually wrote the thing on Christmas Day. It is a story so frighteningly close to my own structures of fear and pain and need that I had to write it in the second person, even though (and also because) second person is the most transparent disguise.

Now what I like about the story is the rhythm the second person created, the cadence, the sound. I consider "Hunter" to be my gift from the great writing gods, and I know the whole thing by heart. I probably shouldn't admit this, but sometimes when I'm driving up the canyon late at night I recite it to the empty car.

SIRI HUSTVEDT is the author of *Reading to You,* a collection of poems published by Station Hill Press in 1983. Her work has appeared in *The Paris Review, Pequod, The Ontario Review,* and *Fiction.* She lives in Brooklyn with her husband and two children.

• When I was a graduate student at Columbia University, I was always scrambling for money. During those years, I took on any number of temporary jobs to help pay the rent. I worked as a bartender, a waitress, a floor model of parachute costumes at Bloomingdale's, and a tutor to struggling undergraduates. One source of employment was a bulletin board in Dodge Hall on which were posted small announcements advertising positions for editors, translators, typists, readers, and companions to the elderly, the sick, the blind, the mentally incompetent. Like Iris, I worked for a medical historian, an old man of eighty-five who had me read and summarize articles on rare diseases in a medical library on the Upper East Side. It didn't take me long to realize that the doctor's research was to no purpose and that my labors were merely an excuse for him to keep up appearances and provide himself with youthful company. He particularly enjoyed lecturing me on his talents and accomplishments and pretended to find me woefully undereducated. Once, when he asked me about my languages, and I replied that I knew Norwegian, some German, and less French, he said, "Do you speak Persian?" "No," I answered. The doctor looked appalled. "Not one word?!" he said.

Around the same time I responded to an ad for a research assistant that took me north of the university, to the projects near 125th Street. There, in a cramped and messy apartment, I met a man who offered me a peculiar writing job. Unfortunately, I am unable to tell that story here. The man was not Mr. Morning as I am not Iris, but my encounter with him became the germ of the story. Although my real experience was very different from Iris's, what I felt in the presence of that man was similar to what Iris feels when she meets Herbert Morning. I had an uncanny sense of having stepped over a line into the secret life of another person, of having seen what I shouldn't have seen, and that discomfort has stayed with me for years. Writing the story was a way of exploring my discomfort in fictional terms, a way of trying to articulate feelings that seem to escape the power of words.

DENIS JOHNSON was born in 1949 in Munich, Germany. He was raised in Tokyo, Manila, and Washington, D.C. A graduate of the University of Iowa, he now lives in northern Idaho. His next book, *Resurrection of a Hanged Man*, is forthcoming in January 1991 from Farrar, Straus and Giroux.

• The story started out as a narrative poem, but as it started to sag under an overaccumulation of reported detail I got bored with it. Later I found myself writing a few stories from the point of view of a single narrator — a composite of some people I knew twenty years ago. I wanted to write out each tale in one sitting without changing it later. Some of them I did, a couple of others I had to rework. I took the beginning of the narrative poem and turned it into the jumbled opening of this sad story.

DENNIS MCFARLAND is the author of *The Music Room* (Houghton Mifflin, 1990), a novel. He lives near Boston with his wife and two children.
▪ "Nothing to Ask For" is based on a visit I paid a close friend about two weeks before his death from AIDS. Turning the events and emotions of that farewell visit into a story — examining everything in close detail — was for me a way of grieving. I wrote the first draft very quickly, in about a week, but put it away for several months before attempting to revise. I had some trouble with the narrator — it was hard to let the story be his, while never allowing his concerns to upstage those of the characters who were dying. What I eventually discovered was that it was enough to let Dan's concerns speak through his affection for Mack, and that the horror of the disease spoke for itself.

STEVEN MILLHAUSER is the author of five works of fiction, including *Edwin Mullhouse: The Life and Death of an American Writer, In the Penny Arcade,* and most recently, *The Barnum Museum.* His stories have appeared in *Grand Street, Antaeus, The New Yorker,* and *Esquire.* He lives with his wife and two children in Saratoga Springs, New York, where he teaches one semester a year at Skidmore College.
▪ The birth of a story, at least for me, is a genuine mystery; to speak easily about it strikes me as an obscure crime. Maybe I can say that when the story came to me, I imagined it as taking place in contemporary America. This idea, which at first seemed very attractive, proved quickly boring, and only when I suddenly saw that the story had to be set in the past, at a particular historical moment, in the heart of a crumbling empire, was I allowed to begin writing.

LORRIE MOORE's most recent book is a collection of short stories, *Like Life,* published in May 1990 by Knopf.
▪ This story, like most stories maybe, is written via cobbling and collage — that is, I imagined a woman, invented a Halloween party, borrowed an apartment, added a sonogram and a conversation about photography, filched a Henny Youngman joke, et cetera. It is part of yet another book of fiction about domestic improvisation, particularly that of American women, but what was also of interest to me was the idea of disparate moods keeping pace with one another, neck and neck in the same narrative. I was aiming for that kind of tonal roller derby in this story: the outward, slightly violent humor pitted against the inner longing and sadness. And suddenly there seemed something freeing and

strange running through everything I was including — everything got tinged with its opposite. By the end I felt I'd written Something Very Weird, a thing emotionally inoculated against itself, hermaphroditic, doomed.

ALICE MUNRO'S most recent collection of stories is *Friend of My Youth* (Knopf, 1990). Born in Wingham, Ontario, Ms. Munro now lives in Clinton, Ontario. She has received Canada's Governor General's Literary Award for two of her books.

▪ "Differently" is an attempt to deal with a place and a time in the lives of thirtyish people. Victoria. The period 1968–1974 (?). A peculiar hecticness, destructiveness, happiness, wildness, open play-acting about those years, intensity of friendships and love affairs. Almost a late outbreak of adolescence. Not necessarily to be regretted or deplored or hankered after, just described.

"Wigtime" actually came from an anecdote: the woman going to a trailer park, in disguise, to spy on her husband. I thought about her a lot, this woman I knew only as the subject of an anecdote. What would she do if she caught him? What would happen to her marriage? What was she like as a girl? Her friend Anita appeared and then Teresa and Reuel, and old school days very like my own, and I got to know the story. It became Anita's and Teresa's story as well as Margot's — maybe even Anita's mother's story.

PADGETT POWELL is the author of *Edisto* and *A Woman Named Drown.* Farrar, Straus and Giroux will publish his collection of short stories in 1991.

▪ Allow me to tender the molecular theory of fiction. It seems to serve well in answering at least one frequent kind of question put to writers: Where does the stuff come from? One must rely on the molecular theory of fiction in any attempt to give a fair answer.

The fairest answer, for me, often, but not always, is this: many of the parts are "real," but the sum is entirely not. By our freshman science: two atoms, or a hundred (read: "events in life"), each with distinctly different, unbound characteristics (that is, color, odor, state, physical properties), when bound together into a molecule lose their individual characteristics; it is the assembled molecule (read: "story") that is perceived, and it is unlike any of the discrete atoms that make it up. Any writer can, if he wants to, tell where his "atoms" are and where he got them. What he maybe cannot say, even if he wants to, is how they come together to form the molecule.

The molecule is a mystery of dramatic forces that will, once they choose to, align, orient, distance, and secure the atoms of your personal witness into a substance revealing life *not* as you witnessed it. That's when you have a biography cobbled together of many autobiographical nuggets and gems of the fair and sordid life around you which is nothing like your life or any you know of.

Twelve atoms of "Typical":

1. The Tent City scene is lifted as accurately as possible from True Life.

2. I roofed at ARMCO Steel, where one day an engineer defined "integrated steel mill" and where I witnessed what I judged to be lassitude on the ground from my position of dying of heat on the roof.

3. ARMCO is near Gilley's. I saw a Sunday newspaper magazine photo of Mickey Gilley onstage with one arm held up in an attitude of starlit victorious celebrity, and in the armpit of his sweater vest was a stapled-in dry-cleaning tag.

4. I heard of a dogfighter who delivered the gigolo-equipment line to a man posing as "almost a veterinarian," then hit him, and who got in a fracas on the highway with a bike gang and undid them and their machines.

5. I have never met Earl Campbell or heard of anyone who has, but he was known as the Tyler Rose, and that, slightly twisted, was a good thing for my man to criticize himself with.

6. A man told me of attempting to mask the smell of his shoes by filling them with his mother's face powder. The resulting amalgam stank so badly that everywhere he went *in Chicago* for half a day people suddenly said, "Goddam! What's that *smell?*" "I don't know," he kept responding, "I've been smelling it all day," until he deduced to his horror that it was his own shoes, and walked five miles home in his personal pestilent cloud, refusing rides.

7. I know a man who could propose as a solution to race riots machine-gunning the rioters — this proposed by his miming the action on his lawn with his fly unzipped just below where he holds the kicking, imaginary machine gun. This is a "ghost" atom.

8. A man I know was found in the shower with his shotgun by his brother who was a yacht broker. Another, higher in class, an architect from Virginia, managed to hit his brother in the forehead with a golf ball for laughing at his game.

9. I read a letter to the editor of a bulldog magazine that began, "Dear Editor, I'm typical. I just like these killer dogs."

10. There is a kind of speaker who uses a redundant pronoun in relative clauses — *which is hard to describe but you can imitate it.* He is typically right poetic — Japanese laborers look like dentists — and it might be called the poetry of scorn, and it may include the speaker.

11. A friend of mine did one night consume such an admixture of

intoxicants that he witnessed his girlfriend turn black and refused to let her near him. He was afraid not that she was non-Caucasian but that she was Satanic.

12. I once decided, similarly persuaded by consumption of, in my case, a lot of beer, that Beaumont, Texas, is the epicenter of black womanhood. This was because, I will hazard, I had gone there to breed a dog to a black man's bitch and had had a wonderful time and had found his wife particularly charming. Why I would go home and pick on a perfectly innocent wife of my own, or why any of us would, is anybody's guess, or evidence that we are none of us princes in life.

Certainly I am not. I'm typical, I guess, probably.

LORE SEGAL's recent books include a novel, *Her First American;* a translation from the Bible, *The Book of Adam to Moses;* and a children's book, *The Story of Mrs. Lovewright and Purrless Her Cat.* Mrs. Segal lives in New York and commutes to teach creative writing at the University of Chicago.

▪ Some of the bits and parts and pieces in "The Reverse Bug" have been hanging out in my head for decades, some are recent arrivals: a news item in the *Times* that said the American embassy in Moscow was so thoroughly bugged it might have to be abandoned; a demonstration behind a police barrier outside the Russian consulate in New York where we read the work of the young poet Irina Ratushanskaya, who was ill in a Russian prison. There seemed no reason why those inside the consulate should hear us: my childhood in Hitler's Vienna, when so much of the world was not hearing us, and all the things that are happening in the world today that I am managing not to hear; the mysterious human propensity to hurt, and the many soft human parts capable of feeling a gourmet variety of pain. And something that has nothing to do with anything: I took a course in "creative" writing at the New School in the fifties. One of my fellow students was a smiling fellow as sensible as you and I until someone mentioned flies in diners, a subject about which he carried an envelope full of newsprint that nothing and nobody could stop his reading from the beginning to the end. (There are threads in "The Reverse Bug" that I would leave out if I were writing it today. The radical event, for instance, that makes a father burden a little girl with the duty of saving the family's lives. This is not the place for it.)

Finally, it's been my experience that there comes an unlooked-for and unaccountable moment in which several apparently irrelevant ideas crash into one another. It is the energy created by their conjunction that produces the story.

ELIZABETH TALLENT's most recent book is *Time with Children*, stories. Her work has appeared in *The New Yorker, Grand Street,* and *The Paris Review*.

▪ I began with no very clear idea of where this would go, only a picture of a divorced husband and wife having to sit down, after not having seen each other for a long time, to renegotiate custody of a son. It was important to this picture that the ex-wife be rather disheveled, tired, defensive, and barely able to restrain her impatience at asking for time with her son as a kind of *favor*, and that the ex-husband have achieved, since the divorce, a radical new happiness. I saw that, high on his own domestic good fortune, he was going to seize his ex-wife's unhappiness as a kind of reason for denying her time with their son. I was interested in that — in the way he wanted to blame her for what he perceived as her terrible disarray, in the way trouble made her appear somehow guilty.

The story went through several drafts before the husband prowled the ex-wife's apartment. I was startled when he picked up the key and unlocked her door, and an anxious part of my mind was going *stop stop stop*. I'm glad the story didn't listen.

CHRISTOPHER TILGHMAN lives outside Boston with his wife and two young sons. "In a Father's Place" is the title story of his first collection, published by Farrar, Straus and Giroux in April 1990.

▪ The first few drafts of this story didn't include the girlfriend, Patty, didn't include a single scene of the final version. It was more of an interior monologue, a father brooding upon the details of his life and place . . . kind of deadly. Then one day, in the midst of his endless reveries, the father recalled the time his son "brought a terrible, a really impossible girl home for the weekend." As soon as I wrote that line I pulled the sheet out of the typewriter and began with a new title page. The story went quite quickly from there, proceeding toward a fairly obvious conclusion. Sometimes when you switch a story radically in midstream, all the stuff you labored so hard to create in the first version can become wonderfully dense asides or details in the second. That may be what happened here.

JOAN WICKERSHAM lives in the Boston area and is working on a novel. "Commuter Marriage" was her first published story.

▪ "Commuter Marriage" began with the ending: the image of a man looking at his wife with the people who have become her new family.

I fumbled around with it for a long time — every now and then, cleaning my desk, I'll still come across a fragment that never made it into the story — and then one week it just wrote itself.

I wrote it as a self-contained story, but I found that finishing it didn't get Jack and Maisie out of my system, the way other stories have exorcised other characters. There was another story I'd been struggling with for a while, about a man named Dunnane who drives a talking car. There were two different drafts of it in my files, both of them wrong. The woman in the story never came to life; she seemed to be there only because Dunnane needed an opposite. Then one day, a year after finishing "Commuter Marriage," I started to write about Maisie again, at a different point in her life, taking driving lessons. I made Dunnane her instructor. And now I'm writing a novel.

JOY WILLIAMS's most recent collection of stories, *Escapes*, was published in 1990 by Atlantic Monthly Press. She lives in Florida.
▪ I was spending two weeks of my life in Bennington, Vermont. The landscape there is some of the gloomiest anywhere, I think. That's just my opinion of course. One morning I went with several friends to the monastery in nearby Cambridge, New York. The monks of New Skete there raise dogs. We wanted very much to see the dogs but this pleasure was denied us. The dogs were there, to be sure. We were just not allowed to see them. It was raining and very dark. The rain was like something from another century, frightful, relentless. I began with this. Matter was added — the temporal things of the world — people, conversations, things. I worked on this story for a long time, taking out what I considered to be all the useless words and events, until I couldn't (as Isaac Babel put it) find a speck of mud in the manuscript. By the time I had brushed and cleaned the mud away I had a story concerned with last things, which is what the writer should have left when there's not a speck of mud remaining. It is the unsayable which prompts writing in the first place.

100 Other Distinguished
Stories of 1989

SELECTED BY SHANNON RAVENEL

ANSELL, HELEN
A Visit Home. *Prairie Schooner,*
Winter.
APPLE, MAX
Peace. *Harper's Magazine,* February.
ATWOOD, MARGARET
Death by Landscape. *Saturday Night,*
July.

BAILEY, TOM
Crow Man. *The Greensboro Review,*
Winter.
BAKER, WILL
Field of Fire. *The Georgia Review,*
Summer.
BANKS, RUSSELL
The Travel Writer. *The Antioch Re-
view,* Summer.
BARTHELME, DONALD
Tickets. *The New Yorker,* March 6.
BARTHELME, FREDERICK
With Ray and Judy. *The New Yorker,*
April 24.
BASS, RICK
The History of Rodney. *Ploughshares,*
Vol. 15, Nos. 2 & 3.
BAUSCH, RICHARD
Letter to the Lady of the House. *The
New Yorker,* October 23.
BAXTER, CHARLES
A Fire Story. *Grand Street,* Winter.
Shelter. *The Georgia Review,* Summer.

BEATTIE, ANN
What Was Mine. *Esquire,* November.
BECKER, GEOFFREY
Bluestown. *The North American Review,*
December.
BERNE, SUZANNE
The Affair. *The Quarterly,* Summer.
BERNEY, LOUIS
News of the World. *The New Yorker,*
April 3.
BOOKMAN, MARC
The First Annual Horseshoe Cham-
pionship. *Shenandoah,* Vol. 39,
No. 4.
BOYLE, T. CORAGHESSAN
The Ape Lady in Retirement. *The
Paris Review,* No. 110.
BROUCEK, MARGARET
Alvin Jones's Ignorant Wife. *Tri-
Quarterly,* Winter.
BROUGHTON, T. ALAN
Leaving Home. *The Virginia Quarterly
Review,* Spring.
BROWN, LARRY
Sleep. *Carolina Quarterly,* Fall.

CHABON, MICHAEL
A Model World. *The New Yorker,*
May 8.
CHAON, DAN
Going Out. *TriQuarterly,* Fall.

CHOWDER, KEN
With Pat Boone in the Pentlands. *New England Review and Bread Loaf Quarterly,* Autumn.
CRONE, MOIRA
Just Outside the B.T. *The Southern Review,* Summer.
CUNNINGHAM, MICHAEL
Ghost Night. *The New Yorker,* July 24.
CURLEY, DANIEL
The Spot. *Newsletters,* Spring.

DELBANCO, NICHOLAS
The Writers' Trade. *The Paris Review,* No. 112.
DeMARINIS, RICK
Insulation. *Harper's Magazine,* July.
DILWORTH, SHARON
The Lady on the Plane. *The Crescent Review,* Vol. 6, No. 2.

EDGERTON, CLYDE
Changing Names. *The Southern Review,* Winter.
ELLIAS, DIANE
The Tupperware Party. *The North American Review,* June.
EMSHWILLER, CAROL
Being Mysterious Strangers from Distant Shores. *Voice Literary Supplement,* March.
EPSTEIN, JOSEPH
Kaplan's Big Deal. *Commentary,* June.
Low Anxiety. *Commentary,* January.
ERDRICH, LOUISE
A Wedge of Shade. *The New Yorker,* March 6.
Old Man Potchikoo. *Granta,* Summer.
EUGENIDES, JEFF
Capricious Gardens. *The Gettysburg Review,* Winter.

FLOREY, KITTY BURNS
Running in the Woods. *Crosscurrents,* Vol. 8, No. 3.

GALLANT, MAVIS
In a War. *The New Yorker,* October 30.
GORDON, MARY
Vision. *Antaeus,* Spring.

HALPERN, NICK
How She Kept Us After. *Shenandoah,* Vol. 38, No. 4.
HARRIS, MARK
From the Desk of the Troublesome Editor. *The Virginia Quarterly Review,* Summer.
HEMPEL, AMY
The Day I Had Everything. *Grand Street,* Summer.
HERMAN, ELLEN
Cottages and Frozen River. *The Missouri Review,* Vol. 12, No. 1.
HERSEY, JOHN
The Announcement. *The Atlantic Monthly,* December.
HERZINGER, KIM
The Day I Met Buddy Holly. *Boulevard,* Fall.

JOHNSON, GREG
The Boarder. *The Southern Review,* Summer.
JOHNSON, HILDING
Halsted Street. *Other Voices,* Fall.
JONES, BARBARA
Scholars. *Grand Street,* Autumn.

KINCAID, NANCI
Spittin' Image of a Baptist Boy. *Carolina Quarterly,* Spring.
KIRN, WALTER
My Hard Bargain. *The Quarterly,* Summer.
Yellow Stars of Utah. *Esquire,* July.
KRAWIEC, RICHARD
Learning to Be Human. *Shenandoah,* Vol. 34, No. 4

LANE, PATRICK
Marylou Had Her Teeth Out. *Canadian Fiction Magazine,* No. 66.

LE GUIN, URSULA K.
In and Out. *The New Yorker,* January 16.

LENTRICCHIA, MELISSA
I've Got You Under My Skin. *The Kenyon Review,* Fall.

LISICKY, PAUL
Bad Florida. *Carolina Quarterly,* Spring.

LOMBREGLIA, RALPH
Jungle Video. *The New Yorker,* August 21.

LONG, DAVID
The New World. *Antaeus,* Spring.

McKNIGHT, REGINALD
The Kind of Light That Shines on Texas. *The Kenyon Review,* Summer.

MATTHEWS, WILLIAM
Nessun Dorma. *The Southwest Review,* Autumn.

MATTISON, ALICE
The Library Card. *The Mississippi Review,* Vol. 17, No. 3.

MAYO, ANNA
Dream Trip. *Voice Literary Supplement,* July.

MENAKER, DANIEL
Time and Money. *Grand Street,* Summer.

MIRSKY, MARK JAY
A Dish of Radishes. *The Quarterly,* No. 11.

MUNRO, ALICE
Goodness and Mercy. *The New Yorker,* March 20.

NELSON, ANTONYA
Downstream. *Esquire,* May.
Substitute. *The Indiana Review,* Summer.

NIXON, CORNELIA
Death Angel. *Black Warrior Review,* Spring.

NORDAN, LEWIS
The Cellar of Runt Conroy. *The Southern Review,* Fall.

NOVAK, MARIAN FAYE
A Real Story. *Crazyhorse,* Spring.

O'BRIEN, TIM
The Lives of the Dead. *Esquire,* January.
Sweetheart of the Song Tra Bong. *Esquire,* July.

OLSEN, LANCE
Family. *The Iowa Review,* Winter.

PAINTER, PAMELA
Doing Jane. *The North American Review,* March.

PEARLMAN, EDITH
Swampmaiden. *The Iowa Review,* Winter.

POLLACK, JAMES
The Strange Attraction. *Zyzzyva,* Vol. 5, No. 1.

PRITCHARD, MELISSA
Sweet Feed. *Epoch,* Vol. 38, No. 1.

RICHARD, MARK
Feast of the Earth, Ransom of the Clay. *Antaeus,* Spring.
Plymouth Rock. *Grand Street,* Summer.

ROBINSON, RON
Where We Land. *Phoenix,* Vol. 10.

ROSALER, MAXINE
A Stroke of Luck. *The Southern Review,* Spring.

SANDOR, MARJORIE
Victrola. *Antaeus,* Spring.

SCHUMACHER, JULIE
The Private Life of Robert Schumann. *The Atlantic Monthly,* April.

SEGAL, LORE
Money, Fame, and Beautiful Women. *The New Yorker,* August 28.

SHACOCHIS, BOB
Les Femmes Creoles. *Hayden's Ferry Review,* Spring.

Editorial Addresses of American and Canadian Magazines Publishing Short Stories

When available, the annual subscription rate, the average number of stories published per year, and the name of the editor follow the address.

Agada
2020 Essex Street
Berkeley, CA 94703
$12, 7, Reuven Goldfarb

Agni Review
Creative Writing Department
Boston University
236 Bay State Road
Boston, MA 02115
$12, 15, Askold Melnyczuk

Alabama Literary Review
Smith 264
Troy State University
Troy, AL 36082
$4, Theron E. Montgomery

Alaska Quarterly Review
Department of English
University of Alaska
3221 Providence Drive
Anchorage, AK 99508
$8, 20, Ronald Spatz

Albany Review
4 Central Avenue
Albany, NY 12210
$15, 30, Theodore Bouloukos II

Alfred Hitchcock's Mystery Magazine
Davis Publications
380 Lexington Avenue
New York, NY 10017
$25.97, 130, Cathleen Jordan

Amaryllis
P.O. Box 677
Union Springs, AL 36089
$10, 2, Carl Bear, Lynn Jinks

Ambergris
P.O. Box 29919
Cincinnati, OH 45229
$6, 8, Mark Kissling

Amelia
329 East Street
Bakersfield, CA 93304
$20, 40, Frederick A. Raborg, Jr.

American Book Review
Publications Center
English Department, Box 226
University of Colorado
Boulder, CO 80309

American Voice
332 West Broadway
Louisville, KY 40202
$12, 7, Sallie Bingham, Frederick Smock

Analog Science Fiction/Science Fact
380 Lexington Avenue
New York, NY 10017
$25.97, 70, Stanley Schmidt

Antaeus
26 West 17th Street
New York, NY 10011
$10, 15, Daniel Halpern

Antietam Review
82 West Washington Street
Hagerstown, MD 21740
$5, 6, Suzanne Kass

Antioch Review
P.O. Box 148
Yellow Springs, OH 45387
$18, 20, Robert S. Fogarty

Apalachee Quarterly
P.O. Box 20106
Tallahassee, FL 32316
$12, 10, Barbara Hardy et al.

Arete
715 J Street, Suite 301
San Diego, CA 92101
$18, 5, Alden Mills

Arizona Quarterly
University of Arizona
Tucson, AZ 85721
$5, 12, Albert F. Gegenheimer

Arts Journal
324 Charlotte Street
Asheville, NC 28801
$15, 5, Tom Patterson

Atlantic Monthly
745 Boylston Street
Boston, MA 02116
$9.95, 25, C. Michael Curtis

Aura Literary/Arts Review
P.O. Box University Center
University of Alabama
Birmingham, AL 35294
$6, 10, rotating editorship

Bellowing Ark
P.O. Box 45637
Seattle, WA 98145
$12, 5, Robert R. Ward

Beloit Fiction Journal
P.O. Box 11, Beloit College
Beloit, WI 53511
$9, 15, Clint McCown

Black Ice
P.O. Box 49
Belmont, MA 02178-0001
$6, 20, Dale Shank

Black Warrior Review
P.O. Box 2936
Tuscaloosa, AL 35487-2936
$7.50, 13, Jeff Mock

Boca Chica
The Writers' Group
2 Boxwood Court
Brownsville, TX 78521-3630
$8, 10, rotating editorship

Boston Review
33 Harrison Avenue
Boston, MA 02111
$12, 6, Margaret Ann Roth

Boulevard
4 Washington Square Village, 9R
New York, NY 10012
$12, 13, Richard Burgin

Brooklyn Free Press
268 14th Street
Brooklyn, NY 11215
$1, 10, Raphael Martinez Alequin

California Quarterly
100 Sproul Hall
University of California
Davis, CA 95616
$10, 4, Elliott L. Gilbert

Calyx
P.O. Box B
Corvallis, OR 97339
$18, 10, Margarita Donnelly

Canadian Fiction
Box 946, Station F
Toronto, Ontario
M4Y 2N9 Canada
$40, 16, Geoffrey Hancock

Capilano Review
Capilano College
2055 Purcell Way
North Vancouver
British Columbia
V7J 3H5 Canada
$10, 5, Dorothy Jantzen

Carolina Quarterly
Greenlaw Hall 066A
University of North Carolina
Chapel Hill, NC 27514
$10, 20, rotating editorship

Catalyst
34 Peachtree Street, Suite 2330
Atlanta, GA 30303
$5, 20, Pearl Cleage

Chariton Review
Division of Language & Literature
Northeast Missouri State University
Kirksville, MO 63501
$5, 6, Jim Barnes

Chattahoochee Review
DeKalb Community College
2101 Womack Road
Dunwoody, GA 30338-4497
$15, 20, Lamar York

Chelsea
P.O. Box 5880
Grand Central Station
New York, NY 10163
$11, 6, Sonia Raiziss

Chicago Review
5801 South Kenwood
University of Chicago
Chicago, IL 60637
$18, 20, Elizabeth Arnold

Christopher Street
P.O. Box 1475
Church Street Station
New York, NY 10008
$27, 20, Tom Steele

Cimarron Review
205 Morrill Hall
Oklahoma State University
Stillwater, OK 74078-0135
$12, 15, Gordon Weaver

Clockwatch Review
Department of English
Illinois Wesleyan University
Bloomington, IL 61702
$8, 6, James Plath

Colorado Review
Department of English
360 Eddy Building
Colorado State University
Fort Collins, CO 80523
$9, 10, David Milofsky

Columbia
404 Dodge
Columbia University
New York, NY 10027
$4.50, 6, Jill Bird et al.

Commentary
165 East 56th Street
New York, NY 10022
$39, 5, Norman Podhoretz

Concho River Review
English Department
Angelo State University
San Angelo, TX 76909
$12, 7, Terence A. Dalrymple

Confrontation
English Department
C.W. Post College of Long Island
    University
Greenvale, NY 11548
$8, 25, Martin Tucker

Conjunctions
New Writing Foundation
866 Third Avenue
New York, NY 10022
$16, 6, Bradford Morrow

Cotton Boll/Atlanta Review
P.O. Box 76757, Sandy Springs
Atlanta, GA 30358-0703
$10, 12, Mary Hollingsworth

Crab Creek Review
4462 Whitman Avenue North
Seattle, WA 98103
$8, 3, Linda Clifton

Crazyhorse
Department of English
University of Arkansas
Little Rock, AR 72204
$8, 10, David Jauss

Cream City Review
University of Wisconsin, Milwaukee
P.O. Box 413
Milwaukee, Wisconsin 53201
$10, 30, Ron Tanner

Crescent Review
P.O. Box 15065
Winston-Salem, NC 27113
$10, 17, Dee Shneiderman

Critic
205 West Monroe Street, 6th floor
Chicago, IL 60606-5097
$16, 4, John Sprague

Crosscurrents
2200 Glastonbury Road
Westlake Village, CA 91361
$18, 36, Linda Brown Michelson

CutBank
Department of English
University of Montana
Missoula, MT 59812
$9, 10, rotating editorship

Denver Quarterly
University of Denver
Denver, CO 80208
$15, 27, David Milofsky

descant
Department of English
Texas Christian University
Fort Worth, Texas 76129
*$8, 12, Betsy Colquitt, Stanley Trachten-
berg*

Descant
P.O. Box 314, Station P
Toronto, Ontario
M5S 2S8 Canada
$26, 20, Karen Mulhallen

Epoch
251 Goldwin Smith Hall
Cornell University
Ithaca, NY 14853-3201
$11, 9, C. S. Giscombe

Esquire
1790 Broadway
New York, NY 10019
$17.94, 15, Rust Hills

event
c/o Douglas College
P.O. Box 2503
New Westminster, British Columbia
V3L 5B2 Canada
$9, 15, Maurice Hodgson

Fame
140 West 22nd Street
New York, NY 10011
$12, 10, Gail Love

Fantasy & Science Fiction
P.O. Box 56
Cornwall, CT 06753
$21, 75, Edward L. Ferman

Farmer's Market
P.O. Box 1272
Galesburg, IL 61402
$7, 10, Jean C. Lee

Fiction
Fiction, Inc.
Department of English
The City College of New York
New York, NY 10031
$7, Mark Mirsky

Fiction International
Department of English and
  Comparative Literature
San Diego State University
San Diego, CA 92182
$14, 35, Roger Cunniff, Edwin Gordon

Fiction Network
P.O. Box 5651
San Francisco, CA 94101
$8, 25, Jay Schaefer

Fiction Review
P.O. Box 12268
Seattle, WA 98102
$15, 25, S. P. Miskowski

Fiddlehead
Room 317, Old Arts Building
University of New Brunswick
Fredericton, New Brunswick
E3B 5A3 Canada
$16, 20, Michael Taylor

Fireside Companion
The House of White Birches
306 East Parr Road
Berne, IN 46711
$14.95, 8, Jenine Howard

Florida Review
Department of English
University of Central Florida
P.O. Box 25000
Orlando, FL 32816
$7, 14, Pat Rushin

Folio
Department of Literature
The American University
Washington, D.C. 20016
$9, 12, William O'Sullivan, Anna Watson

Formations
Northwestern University Press
625 Colfax Street
Evanston, IL 60201
$16, 4, Jonathan Brent, Frances Padorr Brent

Forum
Ball State University
Muncie, IN 47306
$15, 40, Bruce W. Hozeski

Four Quarters
LaSalle University
20th and Olney Avenues
Philadelphia, PA 19141
$8, 10, John J. Keenan

Gamut
Room 1216 Rhodes Tower
Cleveland State University
Cleveland OH 44115
$12, 4, Louis T. Milic

Gargoyle
Paycock Press
P.O. Box 30906
Bethesda, MD 20814
$15, 25, Richard Peabody

Georgia Review
University of Georgia
Athens, GA 30602
$12, 15, Stanley W. Lindberg

Gettysburg Review
Gettysburg College
Gettysburg, PA 17325
$12, 20, Peter Stitt

Good Housekeeping
959 Eighth Avenue
New York, NY 10019
$14.97, 24, Naomi Lewis

GQ
350 Madison Avenue
New York, NY 10017
$19.97, 12, Tom Jenks

Grain
Box 3986
Regina, Saskatchewan
S4P 3R9 Canada
$12, 20, Mick Burrs

Grand Street
135 Central Park West
New York, NY 10023
$24, 20, Jean Stein

Granta
250 West 57th Street, Suite 1316
New York, NY 10107
$28, Anne Kinard

Gray's Sporting Journal
20 Oak Street
Beverly Farms, MA 01915
$26.50, 15, Edward E. Gray

Great River Review
211 West 7th
Winona, MN 55987
$9, 6, Orval A. Lund, Jr.

Greensboro Review
Department of English
University of North Carolina
Greensboro, NC 27412
$5, 16, Jim Clark

Groundswell
19 Clinton Avenue
Albany, NY 12207
$11, 12, Kristen Murray

Gulf Coast
Creative Writing Program
University of Houston
4800 Calhoun Road
Houston, TX 77204-5641
$8, 5, Roger Mullins

Harper's Magazine
666 Broadway
New York, NY 10012
$18, 15, Lewis H. Lapham

Hawaii Review
University of Hawaii
Department of English
1733 Donaghho Road
Honolulu, HI 96822
$6, 12, rotating editorship

Hayden's Ferry Review
Matthews Center
Arizona State University
Tempe, Arizona 85287-1502
$10, 8, Salima Keegan

Helicon Nine
P.O. Box 22412
Kansas City, MO 64113
$18, 8, Gloria Vando Hickock

High Plains Literary Review
180 Adams Street, Suite 250
Denver, CO 80206
$20, 4, Clarence Major

Hudson Review
684 Park Avenue
New York, NY 10021
$18, 8, Paula Deitz, Frederick Morgan

Idler
255 Davenport Road
Toronto, Ontario
M5R 1J9 Canada
$20, 3, Paul Wilson

Indiana Review
316 North Jordan Avenue
Bloomington, IN 47405
$10, 9, Kim McKinney

In Earnest
P.O. Box 4177
James Madison University
Harrisonburg, VA 22807
6, Greg Barrett

Iowa Review
Department of English
University of Iowa
308 EPB
Iowa City, IA 52242
$15, 15, David Hamilton

Iowa Woman
P.O. Box 680
Iowa City, IA 52244
$10, 12, Carolyn Hardesty

Isaac Asimov's Science Fiction
Davis Publications, Inc.
380 Lexington Avenue
New York, NY 10017
$25.97, 27, Gardner Dozois

Jewish Currents
22 East 17th Street, Suite 601
New York, NY 10003-3272
$15, 20, editorial board

Jewish Monthly
1640 Rhode Island Avenue NW
Washington, DC 20036
$8, 3, Marc Silver

Journal
Department of English
Ohio State University
164 West 17th Avenue
Columbus, OH 43210
$5, 5, David Citino

Kansas Quarterly
Department of English
Denison Hall
Kansas State University
Manhattan, KS 66506
$20, 20, Harold Schneider

Karamu
English Department
Eastern Illinois University
Charleston, IL 61920
Peggy L. Brayfield

Kenyon Review
Kenyon College
Gambier, OH 43022
$15, 15, T. R. Hummer

Lilith
The Jewish Women's Magazine
250 West 57th Street
New York, NY 10107
$14, 5, Julia Wolf Mazow

Literary Review
Fairleigh Dickinson University
285 Madison Avenue
Madison, NJ 07940
$18, 25, Walter Cummins

Little Magazine
Dragon Press
P.O. Box 78
Pleasantville, NY 10570
$16, 5

McCall's
230 Park Avenue
New York, NY 10169
$13.97, 20, Elizabeth Sloan-Burbrick

Mademoiselle
350 Madison Avenue
New York, NY 10017
$28, 14, Eileen Schnurr

Madison Review
University of Wisconsin
Department of English
H. C. White Hall
600 North Park Street
Madison, WI 53706
$7, 8, Sarah Goldberg

Malahat Review
University of Victoria
P.O. Box 1700
Victoria, British Columbia
V8W 2Y2 Canada
$15, 25, Constance Rooke

Manoa
English Department
University of Hawaii
Honolulu, Hawaii 96822
$12, 10, Robert Shapard

Maryland Review
Department of English and Languages
University of Maryland, Eastern Shore
Princess Ann, MD 21853
$6, 7, Chester M. Hedgepetn, Jr., Cary C. Holladay

Massachusetts Review
Memorial Hall
University of Massachusetts
Amherst, MA 01003
$12, 15, Mary Heath

Matrix
c.p. 100 Ste.-Anne-de-Bellevue
Quebec
H9X 3L4 Canada
$10, 8, Linda Leith

Michigan Quarterly Review
3032 Rackham Building
University of Michigan
Ann Arbor, MI 48109
$13, 10, Laurence Goldstein

Mid-American Review
106 Hanna Hall
Department of English
Bowling Green State University
Bowling Green, OH 43403
$6, 10, Ken Letko

Minnesota Review
Department of English
State University of New York
Stony Brook, NY 11794-5350
$7, 8, Fred Pfeil

Mississippi Review
University of Southern Mississippi
Southern Station, P.O. Box 5144
Hattiesburg, MS 39406-5144
$10, 25, Frederick Barthelme

Missouri Review
Department of English
231 Arts and Sciences
University of Missouri
Columbia, MO 65211
$12, 15, Speer Morgan

MSS
500B Bi-County Boulevard
Farmingdale, NY 11735
$9.95, 30, Larry Steckler

Nebraska Review
Writers' Workshop
ASH 212
University of Nebraska
Omaha, NE 68182-0324
$6, 10, Art Homer, Richard Duggin

Negative Capability
62 Ridgelawn Drive East
Mobile, AL 36605
$12, 15, Sue Walker

New Directions
New Directions Publishing
80 Eighth Avenue
New York, NY 10011
$11.95, 4, James Laughlin

New England Review and Bread
Loaf Quarterly
Middlebury College
Middlebury, VT 05753
$12, 15, Sydney Lea

New Laurel Review
828 Lesseps Street
New Orleans, LA 70117
$8, 2, Lee Meitzer Grue

New Letters
University of Missouri
5216 Rockhill Road
Kansas City, MO 64110
$15, 10, James McKinley

New Mexico Humanities Review
P.O. Box A
New Mexico Tech
Socorro, NM 87801
$8, 15, John Rothfork

New Orleans Review
P.O. Box 195
Loyola University
New Orleans, LA 70118
$25, 4, John Biguenet, John Mosier

New Quarterly
English Language Proficiency Programme
University of Waterloo
Waterloo, Ontario
N2L 3G1 Canada
$14, 15, Peter Hinchcliffe

New Renaissance
9 Heath Road
Arlington, MA 02174
$11.50, 10, Louise T. Reynolds

New Virginia Review
1306 East Cary Street, 2A
Richmond, VA 23219
$13.50, 12, Mary Flinn

New Yorker
25 West 43rd Street
New York, NY 10036
$32, 100

Nimrod
Arts and Humanities Council of
   Tulsa
2210 South Main Street
Tulsa, OK 74114
$10, 10, Francine Ringold

North American Review
University of Northern Iowa
Cedar Falls, IA 50614
$11, 35, Robley Wilson, Jr.

North Atlantic Review
15 Arbutus Lane
Stony Brook, NY 11790-1408
$13, 9, editorial board

North Dakota Quarterly
University of North Dakota
P.O. Box 8237
Grand Forks, ND 58202
$10, 10, Robert W. Lewis

Northwest Review
369 PLC
University of Oregon
Eugene, OR 97403
$11, 10, John Witte

Oak Square
Box 1238
Allston, MA 02134
$10, 20, Anne E. Pluto

Ohio Review
Ellis Hall
Ohio University
Athens, OH 45701-2979
$12, 10, Wayne Dodd

Old Hickory Review
P.O. Box 1178
Jackson, TN 38301
$4, 5, Dorothy Starfill

Omni
1965 Broadway
New York, NY 10023-5965
$24, 20, Bob Guccione

Ontario Review
9 Honey Brook Drive
Princeton, NJ 08540
$11, 8, Raymond J. Smith

Other Voices
820 Ridge Road
Highland Park, IL 60035
$16, 30, Delores Weinberg, Lois Hausel-man

Paris Review
541 East 72nd Street
New York, NY 10021
$20, 15, George Plimpton

Parting Gifts
3006 Stonecutter Terrace
Greensboro, NC 27405
Robert Bixby

Passages North
William Boniface Fine Arts Center
7th Street and 1st Avenue South
Escanaba, MI 49829
$2, 12, Elinor Benedict

Phoebe
4400 University Drive
Fairfax, VA 22030
$13, 20, Stacey Freed

Phoenix
Division of Arts and Letters
Northeastern State University
Tahlequah, OK 74464
$9.50, 10, Joan S. Isom

Plainswoman
P.O. Box 8027
Grand Forks, ND 58202
$10, 10, Emily Johnson

Playboy
Playboy Building
919 North Michigan Avenue
Chicago, IL 60611
$24, 20, Alice K. Turner

Playgirl
801 Second Avenue
New York, NY 10017
$35, 12, Nancy S. Martin

Ploughshares
P.O. Box 529
Cambridge, MA 02139-0529
$15, 25, DeWitt Henry

Potpourri
P.O. Box 8278
Prairie Village, KS 66208
48, Polly W. Swafford

Prairie Schooner
201 Andrews Hall
University of Nebraska
Lincoln, NE 68588-0334
$15, 20, Hilda Raz

Primavera
1212 East 59th Street
Chicago, IL 60637
$5, 10, Ann Gearen

Prism International
Department of Creative Writing
University of British Columbia
Vancouver, British Columbia
V6T 1W5 Canada
$12, 20, Debbie Howlett

Puerto del Sol
P.O. Box 3E
Department of English
New Mexico State University
Las Cruces, NM 88003
$7.75, 12, Kevin McIlvoy

Quarry Magazine
P.O. Box 1061
Kingston, Ontario
K7L 4Y5 Canada
$18, 20, Steven Heighton

The Quarterly
Vintage Books
201 East 50th Street
New York, NY 10022
$32, 81, Gordon Lish

Quarterly West
317 Olpin Union
University of Utah
Salt Lake City, UT 84112
$4.50, 1, rotating editorship

RE:AL
School of Liberal Arts
Stephen F. Austin State University
P.O. Box 13007, SFA Station
Nacogdoches, TX 75962
$6, 5, Lee Schultz

Redbook
959 Eighth Avenue
New York, NY 10017
$11.97, 4, Deborah Dudenhoff Purcell

River City Review
P.O. Box 34275
Louisville, KY 40232
$5, 10, Richard L. Neumayer

River Styx
Big River Association
14 South Euclid
St. Louis, MO 63108
$14, 10, Carol J. Pierman

A Room of One's Own
P.O. Box 46160, Station G
Vancouver, British Columbia
V6R 4G5 Canada
$20, 12, rotating editorship

St. Andrews Review
St. Andrews Presbyterian College
Laurinsburg, NC 28352
$12, 10, Ronald Bayes

Salmagundi
Skidmore College
Saratoga Springs, NY 12866
$12, 2, Robert Boyers

San Jose Studies
c/o English Department
San Jose State University
One Washington Square
San Jose, CA 95192
$12, 5, Fauneil J. Rinn

Santa Monica Review
Center for the Humanities
Santa Monica College
1900 Pico Boulevard
Santa Monica, CA 90405
$10, 16, Jim Krusoe

Saturday Night
511 King Street West, Suite 100
Toronto, Ontario
M5V 2Z4 Canada
Robert Fulford

Seattle Review
Padelford Hall, GN-30
University of Washington
Seattle, WA 98195
$8, 10, Charles Johnson

Sensations
2 Radio Avenue, A5
Secaucus, NJ 07094
$4, 3, rotating editorship

Seventeen
850 Third Avenue
New York, NY 10022
$13.95, 12, Bonni Price

Sewanee Review
University of the South
Sewanee, TN 37375-4009
$18, 10, George Core

Shenandoah
Washington and Lee University
P.O. Box 722
Lexington, VA 24450
$11, 10, Dabney Stuart

Short Story Review
P.O. Box 882108
San Francisco, CA 94188-2108
$9, 8, Dwight Gabbard

Sinister Wisdom
P.O. Box 3252
Berkeley, CA 94703
$17, 25, Elana Dykewoman

Snake Nation Review
2920 North Oak
Valdosta, GA 31602
$12, 16, Roberta George

Sonora Review
Department of English
University of Arizona
Tucson, AZ 85721
$8, 10, rotating editorship

South Carolina Review
Department of English
Clemson University
Clemson, SC 29634-1503
$5, 2, Richard J. Calhoun

South Dakota Review
University of South Dakota
P.O. Box 111 University Exchange
Vermillion, SD 57069
$10, 15, John R. Milton

Southern California Anthology
c/o Master of Professional Writing
    Program, WPH 404
University of Southern California
Los Angeles, CA 90089
$5.95, 6, Suzanne Harper

Southern Humanities Review
9088 Haley Center
Auburn University
Auburn, AL 36849
*$12, 5, Dan R. Latimer, Thomas L.
Wright*

Southern Review
43 Allen Hall
Louisiana State University
Baton Rouge, LA 70803
$12, 20, Fred Hobson, James Olney

Southwest Review
Southern Methodist University
P.O. Box 4374
Dallas, TX 75275
$16, 15, Willard Spiegelman

Sou'wester
School of Humanities
Department of English
Southern Illinois University
Edwardsville, IL 62026-1438
$4, 10, Donald Gilbert

Special Report–Fiction
Whittle Communications L.P.
505 Market Street
Knoxville, TN 37902
$14, 28, Elise Nakhnikian

Stories
14 Beacon Street
Boston, MA 02108
$16, 12, Amy R. Kaufman

Story
1507 Dana Avenue
Cincinnati, OH 45207
$17, 40, Lois Rosenthal

Story Quarterly
P.O. Box 1416
Northbrook, IL 60065
$12, 20, Anne Brashler, Diane Williams

The Sun
107 North Roberson Street
Chapel Hill, NC 27516
$28, 30, Sy Safransky

Tampa Review
P.O. Box 19F
University of Tampa
401 West Kennedy Boulevard
Tampa, FL 33606-1490
$7.50, 2, Andrew Solomon

Threepenny Review
P.O. Box 9131
Berkeley, CA 94709
$10, 10, Wendy Lesser

Tikkun
5100 Leona Street
Oakland, CA 94619
$30, 10, Michael Lerner

Timbuktu
P.O. Box 469
Charlottesville, VA 22902
$6, 6, Molly Turner

Touchstone
Tennessee Humanities Council
P.O. Box 24767
Nashville, TN 37202
Robert Cheatham

TriQuarterly
2020 Ridge Avenue
Northwestern University
Evanston, IL 60208
$18, 15, Reginald Gibbons

Turnstile
175 Fifth Avenue, Suite 2348
New York, NY 10010
$24, 12, Jill Benz

University of Windsor Review
Department of English
University of Windsor
Windsor, Ontario
N9B 3P4 Canada
$10, 6, Joseph A. Quinn

Virginia Quarterly Review
One West Range
Charlottesville, VA 22903
$15, 12, Staige D. Blackford

Voice Literary Supplement
842 Broadway
New York, NY 10003
$12, 8, M. Mark

Wascana Review
English Department
University of Regina
Regina, Saskatchewan
Canada S4S 0A2

Weber Studies
Weber State College
Ogden, UT 84408
$5, 2, Neila Seshachari

Wellspring
770 Tonkawa Road
Long Lake, MN 55356
$6, 10, Vicki Palmquist

West Branch
Department of English
Bucknell University
Lewisburg, PA 17837
$5, 10, Robert Love Taylor

West Wind Review
Stevenson Union, Room 321
Southern Oregon State College
1250 Siskiyou Boulevard
Ashland, OR 97520
$6, 11, Dale Vidmar, Catherine Ordal

Western Humanities Review
University of Utah
Salt Lake City, UT 84112
$18, 10, Barry Weller

Whetstone
Barrington Area Arts Council
P.O. Box 1266
Barrington, IL 60011
Marsha Portnoy

Wigwag
73 Spring Street
New York, NY 10012
$19.95, 20, Alexander Kaplan

William and Mary Review
College of William and Mary
Williamsburg, VA 23185
$4.50, 4, William Clark

Willow Springs
PUB P.O. Box 1063
Eastern Washington University
Cheney, WA 99004
$13, 8, Gillian Conoley

Wind
RFD Route 1
P.O. Box 809K
Pikeville, KY 41501
$7, 20, Quentin R. Howard

Witness
31000 Northwestern Highway, Suite
    200
Farmington Hills, MI 48018
$16, 15, Peter Stine

Worcester Review
6 Chatham Street
Worcester, MA 01609
$10, 8, Rodger Martin

Writ
Innis College
University of Toronto
2 Sussex Avenue
Toronto, Ontario
M5S 1J5 Canada
$12, 7, Roger Greenwald

Writers Forum
University of Colorado
P.O. Box 7150
Colorado Springs, CO 80933-7150
$8.95, 15, Alexander Blackburn

Xavier Review
Xavier University
Box 110C
New Orleans, LA 70125
Rainulf A. Steizmann

Yale Review
1902A Yale Station
New Haven, CT 06520
$16, 12, Mr. Kai Erikson

Yankee
Yankee Publishing, Inc.
Dublin, NH 03444
$19.95, 4, Judson D. Hale, Sr.

Yellow Silk
P.O. Box 6374
Albany, CA 94706
$20, 10, Lily Pond

Z Miscellaneous
P.O. Box 20041, Cherokee Station
New York, NY 10028
$12, 73, Charles Fabrizio

Zyzzyva
41 Sutter Street, Suite 1400
San Francisco, CA 94104
$20, 12, Howard Junker